rbara Wallace ca[...] [...]aming up love storie[...] [...] Mills & Boon is a d[...] t[...] her own Prince Cha[...] [...], with a house full of empty-nest animals. Occasionally h[...] son comes home as well! To stay up to date on [...]rbara's news and releases sign up for her newsletter at [...]barawallace.com.

[...]espite a no-nonsense background as a West Point [...]raduate, army officer and Fortune 100 sales executive, **[...]aro Carson** has always treasured the happily-ever-after [...]f a good romance novel. As a RITA® Award-winning [...]ills & Boon author, Caro is delighted to be living her [...]n happily-ever-after with her husband and two chil-[...]en in Florida, a location that has saved the coaster-[...]ving theme-park fanatic a fortune on plane tickets.

THEIR CHRISTMAS MIRACLE

BARBARA WALLACE

THE MAJORS' HOLIDAY HIDEAWAY

CARO CARSON

MILLS & BOON

First Published in Great Britain 2018
by Mills & Boon, an imprint of HarperCollinsPublishers,
1 London Bridge Street, London, SE1 9GF

Their Christmas Miracle © 2018 Barbara Wallace
The Majors' Holiday Hideaway © 2018 by Caroline Phipps

ISBN: 978-0-263-26541-5

1118

MIX
Paper from
responsible sources
FSC™ C007454

Printed and bound in Spain
by CPI, Barcelona

THEIR CHRISTMAS MIRACLE

BARBARA WALLACE

Life has a way of exploding sometimes, especially when you're on a deadline for a book.

Thank you to all the people who held my hand, gave me pep talks, and put up with my insanity, especially Peter, who didn't see his wife for nights on end, and my ledge buddy, Donna.

down the rabbit hole with him. And mad he had to be, he thought, looking back at the waitress.

How else to explain why he was staring at the face of his dead wife?

CHAPTER TWO

"ROSIE?" THE WORD came out as a hoarse whisper; he could barely speak. Six months. Praying and searching. Mourning.

It couldn't be her.

Who else would have those brown eyes? Dark and rich, like liquid gemstones. Bee-stung lips. And the scar on the bridge of her nose. The one she always hated and that he loved because it connected the smattering of freckles.

How…? When? A million questions swirled in his head, none of which mattered. Not when a miracle was standing in front of him.

"Rosie." Wrapping her in his arms, he buried his face in the crook of her neck. She smelled of lemons and sunshine. "Rosie, Rosie, Rosie." He murmured her name against her skin.

Hands slid up his torso to grip his lapels. He moved to pull her closer, only to have her fists push him away.

He found himself staring into eyes blazing with outrage, confusion and panic. The last one squeezed at his heart.

"Do I know you?" she asked.

Was this some kind of joke? Now he was confused. Why would she pretend? "They told us you were dead. That— that you were swept out to sea." He reached for her again, only to have her take another step back.

"I'm sorry. I don't…" She shook her head, her eyes growing moist with tears. "I don't know…" Pressing a fist to her mouth, she turned and bolted from the room.

"Rosalind!" Thomas started after her, only to have Linus grab his arm. What the hell was his brother doing? He tried to yank his arm free, but Linus had a grip of iron. His brother's fingers were dug in so tightly they were going to leave bruises. "Let me go!" he snarled. "It's Rosalind." If he lost her again…

But Linus held fast, damn him. "Calm down, Thomas. She only looks like Rosalind."

"No." Linus was wrong. It was Rosalind. He knew his wife. Why did she run? Did she hate him that much? "I have to talk with her."

Before he could try and pull free, McKringle barreled his way over. "What's going on here?" he asked, all his earlier friendliness stripped away. "I don't know what you lads do wherever you're from, but here we don't manhandle waitresses and make them cry."

Thomas spun around on him. "And what about hiding someone's wife from him? Are they okay with that here?"

He waited as McKringle's bushy brows pulled together. "Did you say 'your wife'?"

"Rosalind Collier." Where was his phone? Looking around, he found it on the floor by his chair where he snatched it up and quickly began scrolling through its photo collection. "Here," he said, finding the photo they'd used for the missing person poster. He held the phone so McKringle could see. His hand was shaking. "She went missing this summer when her car went off a bridge near Fort William."

Wordlessly, McKringle slipped the phone from his hand and held it closer. Thomas could feel his body tensing with each second of silence. Surely, the man knew what he was talking about. Her disappearance had been all over the news, for crying out loud. They weren't so isolated out here that he couldn't have seen at least one headline.

"She had a car accident?" the man finally said.

"Yes. Her car plunged into the river." Thomas didn't have time for this. His wife was in the other room. He needed to see her. Find out what happened. How she'd ended up out here and why she was pretending he was some kind of stranger. "Please," he said. Desperation cracked his voice. "They told us she was dead. I have to talk to her. Need to know what happened. She… We have a daughter who needs her." His control was starting to slip. Six months of pain rose back to the surface in a groan.

"It's all right, lad. I think you need to sit down."

McKringle tried to lead him back to the table, but again Thomas broke from the contact. "Dammit, why is everyone trying to keep me from seeing my wife?"

"We don't know if it is Rosalind," Linus said. "I think we should hear him out."

"I promise you she's not going anywhere," McKringle said. "But there're a few things I think you ought to know. Please, Mr Collier. Take a seat. I'll get you a drink."

Thomas didn't want a drink. He wanted his wife, but he allowed himself to be led back to his chair. Something in McKringle's eyes said he needed to do as the man said.

"Let me ask you a question," the old man said once they'd all settled in their seats. "Have you ever heard of the term *dissociative fugue*?"

She couldn't stop shaking. Hunched over the bathroom sink, her fingers clutching the vanity edge for support, she could feel her legs trembling beneath her.

Rosie. He'd called her Rosie.

She'd always thought that when she met someone from her past, she would know. Instinct would kick loose whatever it was wrapping her brain in blackness and the memories would be set free. But when this man—this stranger—called her Rosie, she'd felt nothing.

Well, not completely nothing. Her heart had practically beat itself out of her chest when he hugged her. But he could have called her Jane or Susan or Philetta for all the name meant.

Maybe he had her confused with someone else. That must be the answer. What woman could forget a man that devastatingly handsome? Those eyes, blue-gray like the northern sea. If she closed her eyes, she saw them clear as day. Surely, such an indelible couldn't be wiped from her mind.

She looked in the mirror and studied the heart-shaped face that was familiar yet foreign. Dissociative fugue, the doctor at the hospital called it. A type of amnesia brought on by trauma. All she knew was…nothing. Her mind was a void of memories older than a few months.

At first the blankness had terrified her, but lately she'd started to grow comfortable with her empty past. Until the stranger with blue-gray eyes had walked in.

There was knock on the ladies room door. "Lammie?" Chris's gentle voice sounded on the other side. "You doin' all right?"

She warmed at the tender nickname, a term Chris used because he said she was a little lost lamb. "I'm fine," she replied. "A little shaken up, is all."

Hearing his voice made her feel better. Chris would keep her safe; he'd been keeping her safe since the day she'd stumbled into his headlights.

"Do you feel up to stepping outside? We'd like to have a chat."

By "we," she prayed he meant him and his wife, Jessica, not the stranger with the unnervingly warm embrace.

"I'll be right out," she told him.

Ignoring how badly her hands were trembling, she retied her ponytail and wiped the smudges from under her eyes. If she did have to face the stranger again, she was going to look composed, dammit. For some reason it was important he see her pulled together.

When she finally opened the door, she found Chris leaning against the bar. "Better, Lammie?" he asked in a low voice. She nodded, and he gave her an encouraging smile.

She didn't have to look to know who the other half of "we" was. The man's presence hung in the air.

"This is Thomas Collier," Chris said, "and his brother, Linus."

"Like the soap." The comment was automatic. A bottle of Collier's lemon soap sat by the sink in the restaurant's kitchen. Jessica swore by it, and she'd developed an immediate fondness herself.

"That's right. They're up from London."

She looked to her left where both men sat at a nearby table. Both men were far more subdued this time around. The stranger was perched on the edge of his seat, his lanky body resembling a coil fighting not to spring. "Mr Collier's wife, Rosalind, is missing," Chris continued. "She disappeared following a car accident. He's pretty sure she's you."

He'd called her Rosie.

Hoping that if she focused hard enough she might conjure up some spark of recognition, she took a better look at her so-called husband. When she'd first approached their table, before the craziness started, she'd thought both men attractive. Upon second take, she amended her opinion. One was attractive. Thomas Collier was handsome as sin. If they were married, she had fantastic taste. Taller and lankier than his companion, he had the kind of features that separately were nondescript but together formed an arresting picture of angles and slopes. And again, there were those eyes. She could almost imagine white caps dotting their blue-gray depths. A slow whorl of awareness unexpectedly twisted through her midsection.

Attraction aside, however, she might as well have been admiring a stranger. "I told him about your condition," Chris told her.

"And you believe him?" A moot question if ever there was one. Chris wouldn't have asked her to join them if he didn't think Collier's claims had merit.

"Think it's worth you hearing him out," Chris said. "Then you can decide for yourself."

She chewed her lip, unsure what to do. On the one hand, if this man's story turned out to be true, she'd finally have the answers she'd been seeking. On the other hand, everything she did know would be turned upside down, and while she didn't know her past, her present was a good one.

"I promise I'll behave myself," Collier said. "You have my word I won't do anything to frighten you again. Please," he added, gesturing to the seat next to him.

Damn those eyes. How could she say no when they were imploring her?

Chris's whiskers brushed her ear as he leaned close. "No need to worry, Lammie. I'll be right over here at the bar if you need anything," he murmured, before adding in a louder voice, "Mr Collier, might I interest you in something to eat?"

"Don't have to ask me twice. I'll take a giant Scotch, as well." The other man, who she'd already noted was a younger, less arresting version of her "husband," rose to his feet. As he headed past, he stopped to offer a warm smile. "I can't believe it's really you, Rosalind. Thomas is right—it's a miracle."

"Come along, Mr Collier. Let me pour you the best double malt in the Highlands." Taking him by the elbow, Chris led the man to the far end of the bar.

Leaving the two of them alone.

Cautiously, she slipped into the seat to his right, her hands curling over the ends of the chair arms. Jessica was always complaining that the pub tables lacked sufficient leg room underneath, and now she could see why. Her knees and Collier's were close enough that if she shifted in just the right way, their knees would touch. As it was, she could feel the proximity through her jeans. She scooted her chair backward another couple of inches, and waited.

"I'm sorry about before," Collier said. "I didn't mean to frighten you. When I saw you, I couldn't…" He paused and took a deep breath. "We were told you were dead. That you had most likely drowned in the river."

River. She squeezed the chair arms as recollections of her nightmares came to mind. Flashes of pitch-black water and air being sucked from her lungs. She had to take a deep breath herself as a reminder the image wasn't real.

Even so, her voice still came out strangled and hoarse. "Chris told you about my memory?"

"He said you can't remember anything before the past four months."

"That's right. The doctors at the hospital think I suffered a traumatic event that caused my memory to shut itself off." *Traumatic event* being the term they settled on after their battery of tests failed to turn up anything else. "You said your wife was in a car accident."

"There was a bridge collapse and your car—" she noticed he was already using the second person "—was plunged into the River Lochy during a heavy storm."

Plunging into icy waters certainly qualified as traumatic and would explain her nightmares. Then again, drowning in dreams was also a well-established metaphor, or so she was pretty sure. "I had a broken collarbone," she said out loud.

"I'm surprised you didn't break more."

Again with the second person. "You seem awfully positive I'm her. Your wife, I mean."

"Because I'd know you anywhere."

The way Collier looked her in the eye, with both his voice and his expression softening, knocked her off-balance. Here she was groping around in the dark, and he was looking at her with such certainty. Like he'd found a treasure while she was still trying to figure out the map. It left her longing to see what he saw.

"You say you know, but I would be a fool to simply take you at your word." Or be misled by a pair of stormy blue eyes.

"Trust me, Rosie, the last thing I'd ever call you is a fool. I have photos." He pulled out a phone and showed her a photograph.

Of her.

If it wasn't her, it was her perfectly identical twin.

"There are more." He swiped to another photo, this time a more sophisticated version of the same woman, with her hair in a twist and wearing a stunning black gown.

"The museum fund-raiser last May," he said. "You looked beautiful in that dress."

What she looked was unhappy. Her smile didn't reach her eyes.

The next picture must have been taken the same evening, only this time her doppelganger was flanked by a woman with flaming red hair and a handsome older man with shaggy graying hair and spectacles.

"Those are your colleagues from the university. Eve Cunningham and Professor Richard Sinclair."

She couldn't help noticing the firm way the professor held his arm around her waist.

"You're not in these photos." She rubbed her forehead. A throbbing sensation started behind her eye.

"That's because I took them."

And they were on his phone. "Is there one of us to-gether?" Anyone could get random photos from any number of sources. It would be harder, although not impossible, to fake a photo of both of them.

"A few." Seconds later, she was looking at a selfie—and a terrible one at that, with looming faces and the tops of the heads cropped off. No mistaking her face though, right down to the annoying scar across the bridge of her nose.

Unlike the other photographs, their smiles reflected in their eyes.

"We took this two springs ago, when we were in the Lake District," Thomas told her.

"Two springs ago? Nothing more recent?"

"I'm not much of a selfie taker."

That was obvious. She studied the photograph closer. "We look happy."

We. She was starting to believe him. Rosalind Collier. The name sounded strange, but had a comfortable feeling. The way a new outfit felt when it fit properly.

Thomas took back the phone and stared at the photo. "We were," he said. "Happy. You loved being at our place in Cumbria, away from the city."

Then why did his voice suddenly sound sad? Why was he staring at the picture with a pensive expression?

"You were supposed to be in Cumbria when you had your accident," he murmured.

Oh. That was why. A wisp of a thought taunted her, hovering just out of her grasp. Something about ice or rocks, but it slipped back into the blackness before she could be certain.

She was certain of another thought however. "If I was supposed to be in the Lake District, how did I end up here, miles away? Fort William is miles away from Cumbria too. What was I doing there? It doesn't make sense."

"No one knows." He tossed the camera onto the table

where it landed with a *thunk*. "Best theory I can come up with is that you were headed toward Loch Morar. You did some field work there once. You're a geologist," he added when she frowned.

"Geomorphological features." The words popped out of her mouth without her thinking. Thomas's eyes widened in response.

"Exactly," he said. "You did a paper on the glacier marks."

She slipped a step closer to accepting his tale. As it was, the name Rosalind was already taking hold in her brain.

"What we don't understand," he said, "is how you got here. We searched for weeks and everyone was certain you'd been washed into the Atlantic. How did you end up here in the northeast corner?"

It would be nice if she could give him an answer. Who was she kidding? She wished she could give herself an answer. "I haven't a clue. First thing I remember is walking along the motorway and being very, very tired. I didn't have a clue who I was or what I was doing."

"You don't remember crossing an entire country?"

What she remembered was being terrified as she had stood on the hard shoulder shivering in the early morning dew. "I don't even remember waking up that morning," she told him. "A truck horn blared at me, and suddenly I was there." Staring at the trees in a daze. "I was filthy. Disgustingly so." Having heard she may have plunged into a river helped explain why her clothes had looked like they'd been rolled in a wet ball. "My clothes were torn, and I didn't have any identification."

"Dear God," Thomas whispered. His chair scraped along the floor as he scooted closer. She could feel his eyes on her, waiting for what she would say next.

"I didn't know what I was going to do. Fortunately, Chris happened to drive by and recognized I needed help.

He took me to the hospital, who in turn sent me to another hospital in Wick where they came up with the traumatic amnesia diagnosis."

Ironic how those memories were crystal clear. From the moment she'd found herself on that road till now, everything that had happened was indelibly imprinted on her brain.

"I don't understand." Thomas looked more confused than ever, and she suspected she knew why. "If you were at the hospital, why didn't they…"

"Look into the missing persons reports?"

"Surely you knew people were looking for you. Surely your friend, Chris, knew?"

"We did."

"Then…why?"

She paused. When he heard the answer, he wasn't going to be happy.

"I asked them not to."

His eyes doubled in size. "What?"

"I didn't want to be located. Not straight away, anyway."

"For crying out—" His fist pounded the table with a bang so loud it could be heard on the other side of the room. The noise brought Chris to the end of the bar.

"Everything all right?" he asked.

"It's okay," she replied. Collier's reaction could have been worse. Having flung himself back in his seat, he was washing his hands up and down his face. When he finally lowered them, there was no hiding the angry confusion darkening his eyes.

"Why the hell not?" He spoke through a clenched jaw, clearly trying to hold his temper.

"Because I needed time. To figure out what was going on. To see if my memory came back on its own."

"I see." It was hard to decide which was more restrained, his body or his voice. Both were being held tight. "And it never occurred to you that there might be other people whose lives were affected? Who were mourning you?"

"Of course it occurred to me," she snapped. *Though maybe not as much as it should have*, she thought guiltily. "But put yourself in my shoes. I couldn't remember anything—not my name, not how I got hurt. Meanwhile, the doctors are telling me I suffered some kind of horrible trauma. For all I knew, the people I left behind were the cause of that trauma."

Thomas hissed as though slapped. "I would never…"

"I—" Know, she almost said. Even though instinct said the thought was on target, she held back. "I didn't remember you."

"You could have looked. Your disappearance was all over the news, the internet."

"Have you seen where we are? We're in the middle of nowhere. It's not as if we're in a breaking news zone. I looked for missing persons in Scotland and nothing came up. Which only made me more convinced I might be running away.

"Anyway, I asked Chris and Jessica if it would be okay for me to stay here while I got my head together, and they were kind enough to oblige. I've been living upstairs above the restaurant for the past four months."

"Four months? Dear God." Giving an anguished sigh, he dragged his fingers through his hair, leaving the slick black locks standing on end.

Guilt turned in her stomach. Maybe she should have forced herself to look harder, but the truth was she'd been scared of what she might find out about her past and about herself. When Chris found her, the single thought in her head, besides fear, had been the words *I'm sorry*. She'd carried with her a shadow of indefinable guilt that made her wonder if she'd made some kind of horrible mistake.

Now that same shadow had her wanting to run her fingers through his hair and ease his frustration.

"Linus has been dealing with the soap factory since the end of October," he muttered. "October! We could have brought you home weeks ago. Maddie could have…"

"Maddie?"

Her heart seized up. Maddie was the name she'd chosen when Chris had asked what he should call her. The name had sprung to her tongue without a second thought. It couldn't be a coincidence Collier was using the same name. "Who is Maddie?"

He turned his face and looked her in the eye. Son of gun if she didn't hold her breath at the seriousness in his expression. "Maddie," he said, "is our daughter."

Rosalind squeaked. She had a daughter? A little girl?

Stunned, she stood up and walked to the window on the back wall, the one next to the set of deer antlers. Chris liked to tell people the giant horns were from a reindeer, but it was embellishment for business's sake. Scotland didn't have reindeer outside of Cairngorms. One of the weird facts she seemed to simply know.

She knew about reindeer but not about her own child. Might as well stomp on her heart this moment. It had never occurred to her she might have children.

Oh, sure, she would feel a pull whenever a young child came in to the restaurant, but she assumed every woman of childbearing years experienced the same yearning. She'd never dreamed there was someone out there with half her DNA.

"Would you like to see a photograph?" Thomas asked.

"Yes, please." Spinning around, she leaned against the windowsill and waited for him to come to her. In case this was a trick, she didn't want to sound too eager. Although gushing the word *please* didn't exactly exude calm.

Nor did Collier's expression exude deceit.

Rosalind's hands shook as he handed her the phone. She was beautiful. A pudgy-cheeked angel with brown bobbed hair and Collier's eyes. The photo showed her standing on a rock in a flower garden in a sunflower-print dress. Her little arms were stretched high over her head, pointing toward the sky.

"Maddie." Her fingers stroked the screen.

"I took this on her birthday last August."

Rosalind let out a gasp. She'd missed her daughter's birthday? "How…how old is she?"

"Five."

A five-year-old daughter. "I didn't know," she said, as if saying the words aloud would chase away the guilt.

What kind of mother forgets her own child? She swiped left through the photo gallery, discovering there was picture after picture of the little girl. Laughing. Posing with a stuffed dog. Feeding pigeons in the park. And then…

She found a photo of her and the girl together.

Taken when neither were paying attention to the camera, they were kneeling in front of a Christmas tree. The little girl, Maddie, had a box on her lap, while she, Rosalind, was reaching around her to straighten the bow. Longing grabbed at Rosalind's chest.

"I've tried my best," she heard Collier saying, "but she misses her mother. I can only imagine what she'll do when she sees you tomorrow."

"Excuse me, when?" Rosaline let the arm holding the phone drop to her side and narrowed her eyes at him. "Are you saying you want me to go back to London with you tonight?"

His eyes widened. "Are you telling me you don't want to come home?"

"We only just met," Rosalind said. It was too soon. Granted his story was compelling, but it was still a story. "You expect me to accept what you're telling me because you have a phone full of photographs?" Photographs of her, she added silently. They terrified her, because they revealed a life about which she knew nothing.

Shaking her head, she said, "I'm not ready."

She thought about how agitated Collier got when she mentioned not wanting to find herself. It was nothing compared to the look of horror her current answer generated. Seriously, though, wouldn't she be a fool to go along without some kind of tangible proof? Besides photos, that is. After all, photographs could be manipulated.

"Do you really think I would go through the bother of manipulating photographs and then flying all the way up here just to trick you?" he said when she commented as much. "For God's sake, I thought you were dead."

So he kept saying, and if Rosalind were to base the truth solely on his reactions, there'd be no argument.

"Look at it from my point of view. You're a stranger." Her conscience winced at the pain that passed across his face. To her, he was a stranger though, and no matter how handsome and persuasive his story may be, she needed to be sensible. "You come in here out of the blue with hugs and photos and expect me to take you at your word when I can't even remember my own birthday."

"February the twenty-fourth."

"Thank you, but you're missing my point. Would you pick up and leave your safe haven based on a handful of photographs and the word of someone you just met?"

Crossing her arms, she leaned on the sill and waited for her words to sink in. She could see from the way he stepped back that her argument made sense.

"What is it you need?" he asked.

Good question. Answers to what happened to her would be a nice start. "Time," she told him. "You're moving too quickly. I know you said I've been missing for months, but I need time to wrap my head around everything you've told me." As well as she could anyway. "And I need proof. More proof I mean, beyond the photos in your phone."

"All right. I'll have a package sent to you first thing tomorrow. You get email up here, right?"

She couldn't help but chuckle. "Yes. The restaurant has an email account."

"All right, then. You want proof, proof you shall get. Anything you need if it will help bring you home."

With that, she expected to leave. Instead, he moved closer. So close that Rosalind could smell the faint scent of musk on his suit jacket.

"I still can't believe it's really you," he whispered. "I've missed you, Rosie."

He lifted his hand and she tensed thinking he was about to hug her again. The notion wasn't as off-putting as it should've been. Rosalind blamed his eyes. In the shadows, they were like midnight. A woman could get lost in eyes like that if she wasn't careful.

"Space," she managed to whisper just as his fingers were about to brush a hair from her temple. "I'm also going to need space so I can truly think."

Disappointment flashed in his eyes, but he stepped back like a gentleman. "Of course. Take all the time and space you need."

"Thank you." She let out her breath. "I appreciate your patience. Now, if you don't mind, I need to go upstairs and lie down. My head is spinning."

Once again, Thomas fought the urge to chase her as she rushed away. Patience, he reminded himself. Patience and space. He had to remember how overwhelming his news must feel to her. Hell, it was overwhelming to him.

Out of the corner of his eye, he saw Linus strolling toward him, a glass of amber liquid in hand.

"Here. Figured you might need one," he said.

Taking the glass, Thomas took a long drink, savoring the burning sensation as the liquor went down his throat.

"McKringle went upstairs to check on Rosalind. I said I would check on you. Conversation go okay?"

"She needs more proof before she'll believe me," Thomas told him.

"Smart decision."

Yeah, it was, and, as she'd said, one he would've made himself. Once she read her history, he had no doubt Rosalind would realize he was telling the truth.

Thomas took another sip. "I can't believe it, Linus." He might as well be walking in a dream. "How many times did you talk with McDermott about his factory? And she was right down the road." Dear God… "I didn't want to stop for dinner." If not for Linus's insistence, he would never have learned that Rosie had survived. When he thought how close the miss had been, he felt sick.

"How did she get here? Her car was on the West Coast." Linus asked. "Did she say? McKringle wouldn't answer my questions."

"She doesn't know," Thomas said. "She doesn't remember anything prior to meeting McKringle on the motorway."

That included him. Thomas wasn't sure if that was a blessing or a curse. A bit of both, he decided.

So many nights he'd lain awake blaming himself for the accident. *She wouldn't have been at the country house if I hadn't been such a muleheaded fool.*

"And now she'll be home for Christmas." He said the words out loud as much for reassurance as anything. "Maddie's going to be thrilled."

"What about you?" Linus asked.

That was a silly question. "Of course I'm happy. Don't be daft." He drained the last of his drink in one final swallow. McKringle hadn't undersold; the Scotch was superior.

"I know you're happy, Thommy-boy." Thomas winced. He loathed his childhood nickname. "Anyone who saw your face when she walked in would know."

Thomas still couldn't believe the moment was real. That an hour ago he'd been a widower, and with one blink of an eye, his family was returned. It was a dream come true.

Making Linus's question all the more strange. "If you don't mean happy my wife's alive, then what do you mean?" he asked.

His brother leaned against a table edge, bringing them eye to eye. It was rare for the youngest Collier to be serious, so the sober expression made Thomas's pulse pick up. "Are you going to tell her the entire circumstances?" he asked.

"What am I supposed to say? By the way, did I mention I was a lousy husband and that's the reason you were driving around up north in the first place?"

"You weren't a lousy—"

But Thomas held up a hand. He knew at whose feet the blame lay.

"We've only just got her back, Linus. I'm not ready to lose her again."

He looked down at his empty glass at the residual ring lining the bottom. *Brown could have so many shades to it*, he thought. *Amber like the Scotch. Grayish brown like mud. Rosalind's eyes were chocolate with flecks of gold. Darkness dappled with light.*

He'd missed those eyes.

"It's almost Christmas," he said to his brother. "Would it be so wrong to give Maddie a few weeks of family peace?"

"You're staying quiet for Maddie's sake, are you?"

"Okay, for both our sakes," Thomas replied, his cheeks hot. He should have known Linus would call him on the excuse. "Is that so wrong?"

"No." His brother shook his head. "No, it isn't."

Eventually, Rosalind would remember everything. She'd have to remember, wouldn't she? McKringle said the doctors were optimistic as to the outcome.

When she did, Thomas would be there to fill in the blanks, warts and all, including the fact she'd gone to the cottage to contemplate their marriage's future.

In the meantime, the two of them could spend the next few weeks creating new memories. Maybe, with luck, he could show Rosalind that he was willing to change. That he was willing to do whatever it took to make her and Maddie happy again.

Then, maybe, just maybe when Rosalind did remember the past, the problems they'd had wouldn't matter.

After all, as today proved, bigger miracles had happened.

When Thomas had said he'd give her proof, he hadn't been kidding. For the next few mornings packages of documents arrived by email. There were articles. Photographs. A copy of their marriage certificate and her birth certificate. In fact, so much information arrived in such a short time, Rosalind wondered if Thomas had a team of employees working with him. Of course, she did her own research too, since she now had names to search online.

For starters Thomas Collier, she learned, was the Collier Soap Company. Part of it, at least. He became president after the death of his father, Preston. Preston had been a busy man, marrying three times and producing Thomas, his brother, Linus, and a half sister, Susan.

When she read about Thomas online, she found herself unsurprised that he was a successful executive. She'd known when she saw him in the pub that he wasn't an average man. Interestingly, her impression had had little to do with his expensive suit and onyx cuff links.

He would look exceptional in an orange jumpsuit. It

was the way he carried himself when he walked across the room. Tall and regal, the way a man who owned the room would walk.

How on earth had she managed to marry him? From what she could tell, she was the daughter of world-renowned geologists. You couldn't get more removed from Collier's world. When she asked, Thomas said they met at university. Hard to believe a man like him would have given her a second glance. But he had. She saw the wedding photos that proved it.

By the end the week, she knew enough of her life story to believe Thomas even if she still didn't remember a thing. Problem was, being trapped in that nebulous knowing-not-knowing zone was worse than not knowing anything at all. Facts and figures answered her questions, but they couldn't provide the assurance her gut needed to fully commit.

Except, that was, for Maddie. Every time she saw a photo of the little girl, her heart swelled with longing. Maybe because she hated to see such an adorable creature going without a mother. The reason why, however, didn't matter. If she went back to London with Thomas, it would be to give that little girl her mother back.

"I don't know what to do," she said to Chris and Jessica one night after the dinner rush. "How do I go back and be some man's wife when I can't remember him?"

The two of them hadn't talked again since that night. Having agreed to give her space, Thomas limited his contact to the emails accompanying his daily document delivery. While the notes were friendly and upbeat, often filled with anecdotes relating to that day's documents, she could read between the lines his eagerness to have her home. Especially when he included the words "We miss you" in the text.

"Who says you have to?" Jessica replied. "Just because you know your name and identity doesn't mean you have to immediately rush back and start living your former life. You wouldn't rush a baby into walking, would you?"

"No." Sighing, she rested her forehead against the heels of her palms. "If only I could remember him. Reading those papers is like reading a book about someone else. I know facts and dates, but I don't feel real. Does that make sense?"

"You need to give yourself time, sweetheart." Jessica reached across the table and clasped Rosalind's hand between her two pudgy ones. For a woman who spent her days working in a kitchen, her skin was soft as silk—Collier's lavender skin cream. Thomas was everywhere, Rosalind thought. "Eventually, your heart will remember."

"And if it doesn't?" What if she never remembered Thomas Collier beyond his soulful eyes and commanding presence?

"Who says you have to stay with him? You start a new life with your little girl," Jessica replied. "I know you won't have to worry about your feelings for her."

Rosalind blushed. She was already in love with the girl from her photos and, at the end of the day, was the best reason for returning to London. "She deserves to have her mother home."

But Jessica's argument stuck with her. The older woman was right. There was no reason Rosalind had to stay with Thomas if she couldn't remember him.

That gave her an idea.

"What do you mean, a 'trial visit'?"

It was a few nights later and they were walking in the village center, Thomas having shown up unannounced for a visit. Since the restaurant wasn't busy Chris gave her the evening off so they could talk. It was, Rosalind figured, as good a time as any to share her plan.

Needless to say Thomas hadn't embraced the idea with enthusiasm.

"I mean exactly what it sounds like," she replied. "I'll come to London."

"You mean home. You'll come home."

Rosalind sighed. "No, I mean London. This village is the only home I remember. Surely you can't expect me to slide back into my old life simply because you've sent me a few emails full of facts and dates?"

The way he turned away said that was exactly what he expected. Which led to other questions as to what else he expected.

In keeping with the season, the trees on the common had been wrapped in strands of blue and white lights. A patriotic illuminated forest with branches that danced and sparkled in the wind. It was romantic, magical and no doubt the reason why Rosalind was acutely aware of Thomas's shoulder moving beside her.

She looked sideways at his silhouette. He wore the same expensive clothes as before and exuded the same command and self-possession, while she wore flannel and boots. *Night and day. Top and bottom.* Hard to imagine them ever fitting together. They had though. She'd seen the marriage certificate that proved it.

"What about Maddie?" Thomas asked after a moment.

"Maddie is the reason I'm willing to go back at all." Wouldn't matter if Rosalind had a zillion doubts, the notion of that child going another day thinking she'd died was intolerable. "She needs her mother."

"You don't think I need you?"

"You're not a little girl." On the contrary, there was nothing little about him. "And, there's no guarantee you and I will be able to reconnect. I don't want to make promises I can't keep. I'd feel better going in if I knew I had the freedom to..."

"Leave."

"Yes. I mean, no. I wouldn't leave Maddie."

"Just me."

Did he have to say the words in such a flat voice? It left a guilty knot in her stomach. "The plan sounded much better in my head." Certainly less callous. She needed to remember that as far as he was concerned, she was the woman he loved. "I don't mean to imply that I'm not going to try. I'm just…"

"Scared." The softness in his voice allowed the word to wash over her with relief.

"Terrified," she replied. Trading the known for the unknown? Who wouldn't be? "I have no idea what I'm jumping into."

"So you want an end date in case things don't work out."

"More like a potential end date. A point where both of us can step back and reassess. You've got to admit it's not your run-of-the-mill situation."

"No, it definitely is not."

Rosalind let out a breath. He understood. This was the only way she could think of to maintain some control.

"How long do you envision this trial visit of yours lasting?"

"Over Christmas and New Year at least," she said. "I don't want to do anything until after the New Year. Giving Maddie a happy Christmas is my first priority."

"Mine too."

"Then we're agreed. We'll spend the next few weeks focused on our daughter and Christmas and see where things stand in January."

"That gives us three weeks." It was clear he didn't like the idea. To his credit, however, he didn't argue. Their daughter's Christmas clearly was a priority.

"Twenty-one days," she replied. "And who knows? Maybe I'll remember everything as soon as I walk through

the front door, and this whole conversation will be moot."
Stranger things had happened, right?

"Have you remembered anything?"

She shook her head. "No. Not really. A few of the
photos felt familiar, but I think that was more wishful
thinking. I'm sorry."

The ground crunched beneath their feet. "You have
nothing to apologize for, Rosalind."

But she felt like she did. She felt terrible that she
couldn't remember her family and even more terrible that
she wasn't bouncing with excitement over having found
her way home.

"It's not like I don't want to remember. I do." Ever since
he'd appeared in the restaurant, she'd been praying for the
floodgates to open and erase the blankness. The only response she'd received was her heart pounding with anxiety.

"I believe you, and I'll try not to push."

"Thank you." The tension in her shoulders started to
ease.

"But..."

And, tensed right back up again. Stopping beneath a
large blue branch, she turned to look him straight on. Her
heart was starting to race. "But what?"

"I won't push about your memory, but that doesn't mean
I'm not going to try and win you over. You should know
that between now and Christmas, I plan on charming the
socks off you. You'll be too enamored by me to even think
of leaving."

"Is that so?" She crossed her arms and did her best to
sound unimpressed. Difficult since his cocksure attitude
actually was impressive. And charming.

"Oh, most definitely, Mrs Collier." He upped the charm
by saying the moniker with a silky-smooth lilt. "Most definitely. In fact..."

His blue eyes bore into her. Out of the corner of her

eye, Rosalind saw him raise his hand making her think he planned to reach out and touch her. She held her breath.

He kept his distance. His stare didn't waver. "In fact," he repeated, "I'm going to start tonight."

CHAPTER THREE

NO ONE WOULD ever accuse Thomas of giving less than 100 percent. If anything, people accused him of being overly dedicated. When he committed to something, he went all in. Right now, that something was wooing his wife. He intended to do his damnedest to win her over before the New Year. Before she recalled the cracks. Back in the beginning, he'd been a pro at grand romantic gestures. While his inner romantic might be rusty, it was still there. Somewhere.

Taking Rosalind's hand, he led her back the short walk to the town limits where McKringle's sat empty as ever. Honest to God, how the business survived was beyond him.

The restaurant owner, of course, was more than happy to help. He packed a small bag while Rosalind did her best to make him insist she stay to work. Unfortunately for her, the restaurant was nearly empty. The only customers were a pair of short, reedy gentlemen drinking beer at the bar. When the older man rushed Rosalind and Thomas out the door with a cheery smile, she looked practically panicked.

"Relax," Thomas said as they walked to his rental car. "I promise I'm not about to take you into the wilderness and chop you into little bits."

"I know that," she replied.

Could have fooled him. She looked about as excited as a serial killer victim. Seeing her reluctance stung. When had his own wife become afraid of him?

Since she forgot she was your wife, that's when.

As far as she was concerned, he was a stranger, and one prone to impetuous embraces at that. "Would it help if I promise not to wrap you in my arms either?" he asked. Much as he wanted to.

His question got the corners of her mouth to twitch, at least.

"You know, this whole trip would go a lot better if you trust me," he said once they were underway. The rental had an incredibly responsive heating system, so he bumped up the temperature, figuring a little warmth in the air might relax things.

"I'd feel better if I knew where we were going."

Ah, he'd forgotten. Rosalind preferred to control her surprises. All right, he'd tell her. "Have you ever seen the aurora borealis?"

Despite the dark interior, he could feel her stare. The northern lights were visible on most clear nights during this time of year. Every person in the village had probably seen them at least once.

"No," she drawled. "I never have."

"Good. Neither have I. We can see them together."

"You do realize I was being sarcastic."

"Really? I had no idea."

She huffed softly through her nose, the sound carrying in the dark car. "Well played."

"Thank you. I try." The heater appeared to be doing its job. "I probably should remind you that the Colliers are known for their biting wit."

"Are they?"

"Generally, it's only among the other Colliers, but

considering the number of cousins, stepsiblings and half-siblings, we're still talking a sizable group."

"I'll bear that in mind." There was rustling of her nylon jacket as she shifted in her seat. Looking over, Thomas saw that she was leaning against the door and facing him. "Your family is very interesting."

"Our family," he corrected.

Whether she missed his not-so-subtle reminder or ignored him he wasn't sure. "There's a lot of information online. Far more than your files provided."

"I figured you'd do your own research."

"Had to flesh out the narrative somehow," she replied. "Were your father and grandfather really both married three times?"

"That they were. No one would ever accuse them of not being matrimonially inclined. It was the staying married part that gave them trouble. Still, they managed to blend a few families along the way."

"Explaining all the cousins, stepsiblings and half-siblings."

"Precisely."

"Do they all work for the family business?"

If only. He could have used the help these past eighteen months. "No, that privilege fell directly to Grandfather's true heirs. Meaning my father and then me. The rest of the family scattered to the wind with the divorces." To illustrate, he waved his hand across the dash.

"Does that include your mother? She wasn't mentioned in the report you sent," she added when he glanced over.

"A clerical error. My mother died when Linus and I were little."

"I'm sorry."

"It was a long time ago," Thomas replied. Besides, if she had lived, she'd probably have left like the others. At least this way he got to claim an intact family.

"You told me that my parents were dead, as well." In the silence that followed the comment, Thomas imagined her looking down at her lap and plucking at the hem of her jacket. "I'm glad, in a way."

"You are?" What was she talking about? She'd adored her parents.

"Not that they're dead, but that they didn't have to spend the last half year thinking they'd lost their child. Bad enough I put you and our daughter through the nightmare."

"A nightmare that's over," he reminded her. "I take it you researched your family, as well."

"A little."

"Only a little?"

There was silence again. Looking over, Thomas saw she was indeed playing with her jacket. The zipper, not the hem. "There's only so much you can discover online," she said. "Mostly facts and news articles. Doesn't really give you the full picture of a person, does it?"

"But at least you have the framework," he told her. "Something for your memory to attach itself to."

"True."

She didn't seem as excited as she should. "You don't believe your memory will come back?"

"Who knows? I'm more worried…" She shook her head. "Never mind."

"If something is worrying you, tell me. Maybe I can help." He looked over. "Trust, remember?"

Something he'd done in the last few minutes must have broken through her defenses, because she gave a tiny smile. The kind meant to offer reassurance rather than express happiness. "What if I don't like what I find? Or remember?"

His chest tightened.

You opened the door, Thomas.

"Are you talking about things to do with our family?"

"More like things to do with me."

"Oh." Relieved, Thomas dismissed her question with a wave. "You don't have to worry there. I guarantee you'll like what you discover perfectly fine."

"Says you."

"Precisely, says me," he replied. "I'm your husband, and while that might not mean anything to you, I happen to have whiz-bang taste when it comes to wives."

"Whiz-bang?" she laughed. Light and lovely, the sound warmed him from the inside out.

Thomas allowed himself a moment to savor the sensation. "Won't get higher praise than that," he told her.

"I should think not. Thank you. For the compliment."

"Try fact. I wouldn't marry just anyone."

The moment was a perfect time to reach across the bucket seats and give her a reassuring touch. Thomas loosened his grip on the gear shift only to remember his promise to keep himself in check.

He settled for giving her a smile.

She smiled back, and he embraced the moment like a hug. Once upon a time, making her happy had been his greatest priority. That he could please her, even a little, after all these months was a gift.

There were only a handful of cars parked in the lot when he pulled into the point. Thomas offered up a silent thank-you. He'd feared more considering how popular nature's light show was with the tourists. Then again, it was still early. The glow wasn't usually visible until after ten.

But then, that fit his plan.

"Wait here," he told her. "I'll be back as soon as I've set up."

Rosalind watched as he disappeared from view. Presumably to stake out a viewing spot near the beach.

Or near the cliffs, if he was planning to throw her off.

He wouldn't. Strange, really. Thomas thought she didn't trust him, but trust wasn't the issue. Not entirely. That is, she was pretty sure he wasn't a crazy person. At the same time, however, being around him sent her nerves into overdrive. Soon as he said he planned to charm her into staying, she became jittery and self-conscious. He acted as if she were someone special, and that left her off-balance.

Maybe she should tell him to forget London. They didn't have to be in the same house for their daughter. He could as easily bring Maddie to Scotland…

"Ready?" The car door opened and Thomas reappeared, the blue in his eyes aglow in the dome light. In his arms he held a blanket. "This is for you," he said as she stepped out of the car. He wrapped the thick wool around her shoulders. "Wind gets cold off the bay."

"What about you?" she asked.

"I can handle the cold. Besides, that's why God invented Chardonnay."

Using his cell phone as a flashlight, he led her away from the crowds and toward an isolated section, as it turned out, not far from the cliffs. There on a small patch of grass lay another wool blanket along with a bottle of wine and two glasses. "I figured the lights would look brighter if we sat away from the lighthouse," Thomas said.

He sat down, then patted the blanket next to him. "McKringle picked out the wine, so I have no idea if it's good or not. He seems more a whisky man."

"Chris is a connoisseur of most things," she replied. "Far as I can tell anyway." Across the water she could see the silhouette of the Orkney Islands. Black and hilly. The water was black as well, all but a stretch of white from the moon.

"Looks amazing, doesn't it?" she said. "All that darkness."

"Looks cold." Thomas handed her a glass. "This is the

most northern part of the UK. When we were here last week, I told Linus to watch out for elves."

Rosalind laughed. "Why? You think Santa and his minions are popping down for a pint?"

"Why not? Can't the old man enjoy a nip now and then?"

"Of course he can. If he's a real person." And life was as simple as sitting on a lap and making a wish.

"Don't let Maddie hear you. As far as she's concerned, Santa doesn't only exist—he can do *anything*. Including visiting Scotland for a drop of whisky." He touched his glass to hers.

"I'll be sure to keep my blasphemous thoughts to myself," Rosalind told him. Pulling her blanket tighter, she glanced in his direction. "Are you sure you're not cold? I'm happy to share if…" She let the offer drift away.

"Thank you, but I'll be fine," Thomas answered.

Good. She'd hoped that's what he'd answer. Despite the part of her wondering what it would feel like to have those strong arms wrapped around her.

"If Santa was real, what would you ask him to bring you?" she asked.

"Nothing."

"Nothing?" She found the answer hard to believe. Surely there was something he wanted. "Everyone has something on their list, even if they're as rich as Midas."

"Except I already got my Christmas wish. Right here on this beach."

There he went again, treating her like she was some kind of gift. Rosalind's face turned crimson. Ducking her head, she pretended great interest in her wineglass. How she wished she could return his sentiment the way he clearly wanted her to, but her memory remained as dark as the water before them.

"How about you?" he asked. "What would you wish for? Besides the obvious."

"The obvious is a pretty big wish. I'm not sure I could think of another. But if pressed…" She sighed. "I think I would ask for a cottage of my own. Not that I don't like my room over the restaurant, but it would be nice to have a place to call mine.

"Then again, I guess I—I mean, we—do, don't we?" she added. Thomas's body had stiffened at the mention, making her realize her wish was based on having a life on her own. "Apparently, I'm still getting used to my identity. I don't mean to be hurtful."

"You weren't," he replied. "The situation is going to take some getting used to for both of us."

Stretching out his legs, he leaned back on the blanket. Without his body to warm the space beside her, Rosalind shivered.

"Tell you what," he said. "Tonight, we won't worry about our previous lives. We'll be Thomas and Rosalind. Two people enjoying the wonders of nature and Chardonnay."

"Sounds lovely," she replied, the tension slipping from her shoulders. "I'd like that."

For the next hour or so, the two of them talked about nothing and everything. Like any proper first date. When she looked at her watch and saw that ninety minutes had flown by, she could hardly believe it.

"I can't believe we've been sitting out here in the cold for an hour and a half," she said. Other than Chris, she hadn't talked to anyone with such ease since her arrival in Lochmara.

"And we barely touched the wine," Thomas added.

Looking over, she saw he was right. Her glass sat on a nearby rock where she'd set it earlier, still three-quarters full. "Hope it wasn't too expensive a bottle. I'd hate to have wasted your money." She noted Thomas had set his glass aside, as well.

"It's only wine," he replied. "The conversation was far more interesting and well worth the expense."

"Maybe that should be a new measure of success. The amount of wine in a bottle is indirectly proportional to the noteworthiness of the conversation."

"Or the distraction of one's company," Thomas added. The smooth lilt of his voice in the dark made her toes curl. He was definitely charming; she'd give him that. "Are you— Look."

She looked over her shoulder to see a swirl of white light swaying on the horizon. Soon, the ethereal plume was joined by green and pink and together the trio moved in a rhythmic dance. Pulsing and turning to a beat made by electrical explosions.

Rosalind had seen the lights several times, but tonight the colors seemed especially bright and alive. She felt Thomas's body sit up behind her, his proximity creating a different kind of pulse in the air.

"Gorgeous, isn't it?" Thomas's breath whispered across the back of her neck. "And it's only the beginning."

The next morning, Rosalind hugged Chris and Jessica goodbye and crossed the tarmac to the Collier private jet where Thomas stood waiting.

"Welcome aboard," he greeted.

Her "husband" had gone casual for her return, the dark suit replaced by khakis and a gray sweater that accentuated his athletic leanness. *Sleek and graceful*, Rosalind thought. Like a well-toned cat. A warm sensation swirled in her stomach.

"When you said we were flying, I wasn't expecting a private plane."

"Collier's is an international company these days. Saves

us from wasting time in airports." He stepped aside so she could pass, his hand brushing the small of her back as she did so. Barely even a touch, but it was the first physical contact they'd had since their awkward hug, and therefore he might as well have plastered his palm to her skin. She straightened and stepped sprightly into the cabin. Taking in the soft lighting and creamy leather recliners, her pulse kicked up another notch.

She ran her hand along a headrest. "I take it I'm supposed to be used to traveling like this?"

"Actually, you're not. You prefer driving. At least you did before…" Thankfully, he let the rest of the sentence fade off. "Flying two hours is far more efficient than our spending the whole day on the road. This way we'll be home in time to have dinner with Maddie."

At the girl's name, she looked around, anxiously. "Where is Maddie? Who is looking after her?"

"She's spending the day with Linus and my sister, Susan. I thought you and I might use the flight to talk." He motioned for her to take a seat. "Can I get you anything? Water? Tea?"

A good stiff drink? Rosalind settled herself in one of the seats and wished her nerves could settle as easily. "No, thank you. I had too many cups over breakfast. Any more and my bladder might explode. Sorry," she quickly added as her cheeks warmed.

"For what?"

"I don't know. Using gauche language." Being on a luxury jet seemed to call for more genteel behavior.

Thomas laughed. The sound was deep and throaty. "Trust me, you've used far worse. Once you dropped a rock sample on your foot and the air literally turned blue. I'm pretty sure baby trees were stunted."

"They were not," she responded automatically. An

image formed in her head, but it was merely his description. "You're exaggerating."

"A little. Very little." His expression sobered. "You can relax and be yourself, Rosie."

"That might be a problem." She watched as he took a seat in the aisle across from her, far enough away that the two of them couldn't accidentally touch. Seeing his long legs stretched out in front of him, Rosalind was again reminded of a cat and envied his composure. She was a bubbling bottle of nerves. "I don't know who 'myself' is supposed to be." In many ways Rosalind Collier was as much a stranger as he was.

Thomas nodded, understanding. Or so she hoped. "I'm not expecting you to be anything. I promise."

"Thank you." Rosalind hoped he was keeping track of all his promises; they were starting to mount up. In this case, however, the promise meant a lot.

Relaxing slightly, she allowed herself to sink deeper into the chair. The cushions were made of the most supple leather she'd ever run across. In recent memory that was. Although she suspected her forgotten experiences fell short too. Her fingers practically sank into the material.

With her index finger, she traced the double stitched pattern edging her seat belt. "Does Maddie know? About me?" she asked.

A movement caught the corner of her eye. It was Thomas shaking his head. "I thought it best if I waited until you were actually in London and then surprise her."

"I see," she said, with more than a little disappointment. Reading between the lines wasn't hard to do. She wondered if she had always been able to interpret his unspoken thoughts. "Is that your way of saying you didn't want to get her hopes up in case I didn't show up?"

"Yes."

Wow, points for bluntness. Rosalind sat back. How was she supposed to argue with the answer?

"When it comes to my daughter, I don't believe in dancing around—" Thomas explained.

"Our daughter," Rosalind corrected.

"Okay, when it comes to our daughter, I don't believe in dancing around the truth. She's been hurt enough. So long as there was a chance you'd change your mind about Christmas…"

"I would never back out and hurt her like that," Rosalind told him.

Thomas was busy studying his blank telephone, turning it around and around in his hand. "Nice words. But people say a lot of things they end up taking back."

Like the promises he was making?

The captain had sealed the hatch, and they were making their way toward the runway. Looking outside at the tiny terminal, she saw Christopher and Jessica standing in the window, waving. A lump rose in Rosalind's throat. For better or worse, the life she knew at McKringle's was over, and her new life—her new old life—was beginning.

Fearing she might cry if she kept watching, she shifted in her seat. "Tell me more about Maddie," she said. Talking about their daughter would keep her mind focused on happy expectations.

Thomas shifted in his seat as well, so that he was facing her. "What do you want to know?"

"Anything. Everything. I've seen a zillion pictures, but it's hard to know a person's true personality from a photograph. Although, she looks like she has one."

"And then some. When she sets her mind to something, there's very little that can dissuade her. She once spent fifteen minutes explaining to me why she needed to have pudding before bed."

"Sounds precocious."

"Some would say annoyingly so. But she's smart. Not recognize-your-letters-early smart, but able-to-understand-complex-ideas smart."

There was no mistaking his pride. Rosalind wasn't sure which had softened more during the exchange, her heart or Thomas's face. The lines around his eyes deepened with his broadening smile. He had a breathtaking smile, she realized. It was as if his face lit up from within.

"Oh, and she's currently all about puppies," he added. "That's her latest obsession. Puppies and purple."

Closing her eyes, Rosalind tried to merge the girl from the photographs with the personality Thomas described, hoping it would stir something. The vague image of bouncing on a bed flickered in the fog, but without context she couldn't tell if it was memory or her imagination.

"Hey." A hand, warm and solid, covered her fingers. "I thought we agreed we were going to relax."

"I know. I can't help it." The warmth from his hand was seeping up her arm, easing her frustration. Eyes still closed, she let her head fall against the headrest.

"I just wish I could remember more," she sighed. That she could remember anything. "How can a person forget a marriage and a child? I can't even remember my parents."

"Perhaps it's a blessing."

Rosalind opened her eyes. "What?"

"Nothing." The plane lurched as the wheels left the ground. He slipped his hand from hers, bringing a return to the tension. "I was sputtering nonsense."

She tucked a leg under her and sat sideways to better stare him down. "How could you possibly think my not remembering my family could be a good thing?" she challenged.

"It couldn't," he replied. "It isn't. I meant not being able to recall the bad memories like losing your parents or... I told you I was talking nonsense."

"Yes, you were. Just like those people who say 'at least they're no longer in pain' when a person dies after being sick. Of course they're not in pain, because they're gone. Who's to say they wouldn't have taken another day of pain over leaving the people they loved? What?"

He was giving her an odd look. "When your parents died, you said that the platitudes at the funeral drove you crazy. People trying to make you feel better about being orphaned at eighteen," he told her. "You said they would have been better off keeping their mouths shut."

"That sounds about right," she said with a smile. It was an emotional outburst, nothing more, but her insides thrilled all the same. Because if she reacted with the same exasperation now, it meant the core part of her hadn't been wiped away with the memories.

For the first time since her diagnosis, she felt a glimmer of hope. It flared to life in the center of her chest and spread outward, transforming her small smile into a full-on grin.

Her eyes locked with Thomas's. Amazingly, they were a new shade. Neither navy nor gray but the color of the sky right before a storm moved in, when the clouds were dark with potential.

Suddenly, a different kind of energy wound its way through her. The warm, heavy feeling of awareness. The air in the cabin grew thicker. It too, like those storm clouds, hummed with potential.

Too much potential for Rosalind to deal with at the moment.

"I think I might like that tea after all," she whispered.

Thomas wanted to touch her. Here was his wife, for God's sake, two feet away, looking at him *like he was a man* and he couldn't touch her. Couldn't cradle her cheek in his palm and kiss her senseless. No matter how much he longed to do so. To her, he was still a friendly stranger. A man who wanted her more than she wanted him.

Where were the blasted cups? Normally, he would have an attendant on board, but he thought Rosalind would appreciate the privacy. Her return was going to create enough of a stir; he wanted to do what he could to minimize the chaos for both her and Maddie's sake. As a result, however, he was stuck navigating the galley on his own. After opening several random cabinets to no avail, he finally managed to find the supply of Darjeeling, and set about boiling the water. A tricky task at thirty-three thousand feet, but he managed. He found a bag of biscuits, as well. Orange madeleines. Rosalind's favorites. He must have ordered them in hopes she'd someday accompany him on one of his business trips.

She never did.

Distance was a funny thing, he thought as he arranged the cookies on a plate. It built up slowly, the cracks widening subtly until suddenly there's a chasm where one had never been, and you've let your wife slip away. Maybe he and Rosalind could have bridged the gap, maybe not. Thanks to the accident, they'd never know.

But at least he had a second chance.

"I raided the pantry," he said when he entered the cabin a short time later. Rosalind looked up at the announcement with such shy expectancy, he had to clench the tray handles to keep his insides from doing a somersault. "Thought we could use something sweet."

"Are those madeleines? I adore those."

"I know." If there was a hint of smugness creeping into his voice, it couldn't be helped. "Although I swear I didn't stock them on purpose. At least not today."

"Wouldn't matter if you did. I'll eat them regardless." She stacked three of them on her napkin, before taking a fourth and biting it in half. "'S unnerving," she said, between bites.

"What is?"

"Having someone know me better than I know myself."

"I don't mean to unnerve you," Thomas replied. Setting the tray on a nearby table, Thomas added milk to both cups before handing one to her.

"Case in point," she remarked.

"Sorry. Force of habit."

"You don't have to apologize." Her eyes dropped to the contents of her cup. "This situation has to be hard for you too. Maybe harder. At least I didn't have to bury someone. As far as I know," she added cheekily.

Amnesia jokes. Nice. "Is this where I reassure you that it's all water under the bridge?"

She gasped. "I can't believe you said water under the bridge." There was laughter in her voice.

"I can't believe you made an amnesia joke."

Their eyes met for a count of three before they both started laughing. For a moment it was as though the accident never happened, and they were just another couple laughing over inside jokes.

How he'd missed her laugh. Missed making her laugh.

The moment ended with the shrill sound of his satellite phone. Thomas groaned. One of the advantages of a private plane was being exempt from the aviation communications rules of commercial flights and maintaining constant contact with the office.

He let the phone ring.

"Shouldn't you answer that?" Rosalind asked.

"A perk of being in charge is being unavailable," he replied.

"You're not worried it's important?"

Oh, it was definitely important; he had given strict orders to call only if there was a crisis. But he was trying to prove he had changed his priorities. Even if with every ring his blood pressure kicked up a notch.

"What if it's about Maddie?"

Dammit. What if it was? Shooting Rosalind a look of apology, he snatched the phone off the receiver. "Yes?"

It was Nilay Malik, his senior vice president of international distribution. Thankfully, she knew enough not to waste time with greetings and cut straight to the chase. "Mr Ming is threatening to back out of our verbal agreement." Ja Na Ming being the owner of the largest chain of luxury spas in the Pacific Rim and the linchpin to their new products' success. "Somehow he figured out we're using his participation to leverage the European spas and wants a deeper discount."

"Any deeper and we'll be giving him the damn soap for free." Thomas pinched the bridge of his nose to prevent groaning in frustration. Ming had horrible timing.

"All right," he said, "this is what I think we should do." Eager to hang up as quickly as possible, he rattled off instructions regarding a new set of figures that he hoped would satisfy Ming.

"Impressive," Rosalind remarked when the call ended. "You do that a lot?"

"More than I want, but less than I used to." He watched to see if the comment sparked any recollection. Rosalind's expression never wavered. She merely sipped her tea thoughtfully.

"Who knew selling soap was such high finance," she said. "Then again, the plane should have clued me in. Hardly the trappings of a mom-and-pop operation."

"True. Although at its heart Collier's is and will always be a family business. For better and worse," he added, looking down. It was his turn to contemplate his teacup.

"You know," he heard her say, "you never said what you were doing up north in the first place."

"Linus wanted me to tour a soap factory he discovered."

"Do you mean the one in Caithness, near the river? Why would Collier's be interested in them?"

"We're looking for a specific type of soap manufacturer to subcontract a new product. It's a long story. You don't want to hear the details."

"Why not?"

"Because…" Thomas stopped himself. He'd stopped talking about business around Rosalind a long time ago because anything to do with Collier's eventually turned the conversation into monosyllabic terseness. As far as Rosalind had been concerned, Collier's was a rival.

"Because?" She was waiting for him to answer, her head tilted, her hair draping over her shoulder. Unlike the other day, she had her hair down and loose the way he loved. He could make out the soft streaks of dark and light that made the color so uniquely her.

"Thomas?"

"Sorry. I got lost in thought for a moment." Offering an apologetic smile, he took a sip of tea. "We're launching a new line of luxury products this spring. High-end botanicals."

"Don't you already sell a botanical line?"

"Not like this one. These are 100 percent organic, 100 percent environmentally sound, and made from the finest of ingredients. Available only through high-end spas and other luxury distributors. It's our entry into the luxury bath-and-body market."

"But you have a royal warrant. Doesn't that already make you part of that market?"

"No offense to Her Royal Highness, but she's a little older than the customers we're targeting. We're looking for the young, hip crowd with money to burn."

"Nouveau riche millennials, you mean."

Thomas chuckled. "Among others." What he didn't

mention was that Collier's market share had been steadily eroding over the years—a trend his father had stubbornly refused to acknowledge in favor of blind optimism. If the company didn't find a way to reinvent itself and appeal to the next generation, Collier's would gradually fade into extinction.

"And does the soap factory fit your needs?"

"Appears to. Linus is certainly high on them, but he sees things through the eyes of a chemist. We have to run some numbers to see if they can accommodate our production needs… This is strange," he said, shaking his head.

"Why? Granted, ours is not a normal relationship right now, but surely we talked like this before?"

"Actually, when we first relocated to London, we talked about the company often, but over the last year, you'd gotten more and more involved with your own career." Among other things.

He felt a spike of jealousy, the way he did whenever he thought about those "other interests" but shook it away, along with his guilty conscience. Whatever turns their marriage took were his fault. He would bear the blame, and he would take on the responsibility of righting the course.

Hopefully he would do so before those other interests came poking around again.

CHAPTER FOUR

SHE LIVED IN a mansion. Of course she did. She'd flown to London in a private plane. Why wouldn't she live in a stately marble manor across from a park? Her eyes scaled the building to the top two floors that Thomas said held their apartment. "The family used to have an estate in Bedfordshire," he told her, "but after Grandfather's second divorce, he decided it was too costly to maintain. Hard to keep up the grounds and support two wives."

This was their idea of downscaling, then.

The driver pulled into the underground parking garage where they took the elevator to the fifth floor. "We have the fifth, sixth and terrace," Thomas told her. "Fortunately, the building entrances are pretty private, but I've alerted Security just in case."

"In case of what?" Rosalind asked.

"The press. Your disappearance made headlines. Once word gets out that you've returned home, I won't be surprised if someone tries to snag a photo or two."

Rosalind's stomach went the opposite direction of the elevator. "I hadn't thought about the press."

Truth be told, she hadn't thought about the fact that she would be newsworthy. How naïve of her. Dead woman returns home for Christmas miracle? The story would make headlines regardless of her last name.

"Don't worry. I'll do my best to protect your privacy," Thomas told her.

"Thank you." She stole a glance at his profile. Standing tall, shouldering her one small bag of belongings. He was less than a half a foot away, but the distance felt greater. Was it odd of her to want one of his long arms to squeeze her close as reassurance? She hadn't forgotten how soothing his touch had been when he'd held her hand on the plane. If she "accidentally" brushed his hand with her fingers, would he take the hint and hold it again? She could use the grounding. Did she dare?

Before she could make up her mind, the elevator doors opened to reveal a black lacquer door adorned with a giant gold-and-green wreath. "Welcome home," Thomas announced. He unlocked the door before stepping aside.

Giving her space.

Letting her control the moment.

It wasn't too late to turn around and run back to the elevator. She could disappear into the crowds. Looking to Thomas, she saw uncertainty in his smile. He was as nervous as her. Knowing she wasn't alone gave her the courage she needed.

With a gulp and a deep breath, Rosalind crossed the threshold.

Back at McKringle's, whenever she tried to imagine the past she'd lost, she'd pictured living a simple life with a cozy cottage and a postage-stamp lawn. Never did she picture a black-and-white tiled hallway crowned by an enormous crystal chandelier. The grandness of it all made her itch, like she was wearing the wrong skin.

It didn't feel right at all.

"Are you sure we're in the right place?" she asked him, absently catching her arm.

Instantly she regretted the question when she saw a

shadow of a smile, half amused, half something else, flicker across Thomas's face. She'd hurt his feelings.

"The apartment is owned by Collier's. We moved in temporarily when I took over as president. It was already furnished."

That explained why the apartment didn't feel like home. It wasn't. Rosalind felt a little better. "For a moment I was afraid I'd switched personalities when I lost my memory."

"Oh, no. You made a similar comment when we moved in."

"At least I'm consistent, then." Had she hurt his feelings then too? Really, was it all that terrible, being asked to live in luxury?

Something he said struck her. "You said temporarily. Haven't we been here almost two years?"

"Our plans got sidetracked."

Of course. By her accident. If they had made plans to move, Thomas probably set them aside in favor of consistency for Maddie's sake.

The hallway stepped down into a large living room that was flanked by a spiral staircase. Above, the second floor looked down like a balcony.

In the center of the living room, a pair of teal-colored velvet sofas faced one another in front of a white brick fireplace. They were divided by a coffee table on which sat a giant urn filled with holly and fir branches. The arrangement looked like an evergreen fountain.

Propped against the urn's face was a stuffed brown puppy, head flopped to one side.

"Is Maddie home?" She looked one way, then the other. "Is she upstairs?"

"Linus and Susan are bringing her back right now. I didn't want to overwhelm you all at once. Plus, I wanted Susan to be here when I told her the good news. Her being a behavioral specialist and all…"

"Right, right." All the support they could get.

Walking over to the table, she picked up the dog.

"That's Bigsby. Surprised they got her to leave the guy behind. He's been glued to her hand for months."

Explained why the poor little fellow's head flopped. The stuffing was gone from his neck from perpetually being gripped in a tiny little hand for months.

Months. This was Maddie's security blanket. Rosalind imagined her daughter holding him tight while she slept. To keep her safe because her mother couldn't.

Her eyes grew wet. "What if she hates me?" she said.

"Hates you? Don't be silly. She's going to be ecstatic that you're home."

So Thomas kept saying. They were all assuming Maddie would be thrilled to have her mother back. "But what if she knows?"

She turned to look in his eyes. "What if she figures out that I can't remember her?" It was one thing to be drawn to a photograph; it was another to face the child in person. "Children are incredibly perceptive. They know when someone's being fake. What if I can't…don't…?"

"You mean what if you see her as a stranger, the way you do me? It's all right," he said, cutting off her protest. "It's not your fault. It's reality."

He brushed past her and stood by the fireplace with his back to her. Rosalind wondered if the position was to keep her from seeing his expression. Reality or not, her continual reminders had to hurt. As hard as he tried, he couldn't hide all his disappointment, and he was an adult capable of understanding the situation. Maddie was a little girl.

Joining him, she stopped a breath shy of his shoulder. "I don't want to hurt her any more than I already have," she said.

"Neither do I," he replied. "If I thought that was the case, I wouldn't let you near her."

For the first time, Rosalind noticed the photo frames on the mantle. Thomas reached for one and handed it to her. It was of her and Maddie as a toddler, sitting together in an overstuffed chair. They were reading a picture book about a rabbit.

"Call me insane, but my gut says that the kind of bond you two had can't be erased like memory," he said.

"Why not? I forgot you." There she went again, pouring salt on the wound.

"Different case."

"How so?" From what she could see, he was immensely memorable. His eyes had been dogging her thoughts all week. "You're my husband. Don't we have a bond, as well?"

"Sure but, you didn't carry me in your belly for nine months."

He took the frame and set it back in its place. "I know you're worried, but I assure you, the last think I would do is throw you—or Maddie—to the wolves. I plan to talk with Maddie *before* she sees you. I've met with a therapist, and she gave me some tips on how to broach the subject in a way she'll understand."

Some of the weight lifted from her shoulders. "Thank you."

"Not that you need to worry about faking your feelings too much. Our daughter is extremely adorable. You'll fall in love the moment you see her. I guarantee."

"Another promise. You're taking a big risk."

"When it comes to Maddie, there's no risk at all. Our daughter is that lovable. Just like—"

"Bigsby?" she interrupted, his sentence making her nervous.

Thomas nodded. "Exactly. Like Bigsby. Oh, before I forget. I meant to give this to you on the plane." He dug into his front pocket and pulled out an object. "You left this at the cottage."

A wedding band.

She'd wondered why her left hand was bare, but assumed she'd lost the ring during those missing weeks. "I took it off?" That didn't make sense.

"You don't like to wear jewelry when you're doing fieldwork," he told her. "I found it on the bureau when we were collecting your belongings. May I?" He reached for her hand.

It was the contact she'd hoped for, but at the wrong time. Having him slip the ring on her finger felt too intimate, too much like a commitment she wasn't ready to make.

"I can do it." Taking the ring from him, she slipped it over her knuckle. Channel-set diamonds glittered uncomfortably from her hand. "Thank you for keeping good care of it."

"Of course," was his answer. He'd turned again, so she couldn't see his face. The avoidance was a relief, actually; she already felt horrible enough. He was trying so hard to strengthen their connection and falling short every time. If only she could remember something—anything—to mute his disappointment.

"Where is she? Where is she?" Rosalind could hear the high-pitched squeal through the closed doors. Thomas had been talking to Maddie for the past twenty minutes.

Twisting her wedding band, she paced back and forth across the Oriental rug. Any moment now, the doors would open and she would be seeing her daughter.

Please don't let me mess up, she prayed. *Please.*

"Mummy!" The doors burst open and a forty-inch force of nature flew into the room. "Mummy! You're back!"

Rosalind barely had time to prepare herself before the

little girl hurled herself into her midsection. "You're home. You're home. *You're home*," she squealed.

Little arms squeezed her midriff. "I missed you, Mummy," a tiny voice murmured into her sweater.

Rosalind thought her heart might explode then and there as feelings, unfamiliar yet familiar, filled her chest. "I missed you too, sweetie." Her whisper cracked over the words.

Kneeling so they would be at eye level, she combed her fingers through Maddie's brown hair. The photos didn't do her justice. Those eyes. Those cheeks.

Thomas was right; she was precious.

"I missed you too," she repeated, more strongly this time. "I'm sorry I was gone for so long."

"Daddy said you bumped your head and got lost."

The simplified explanation made her smile, even as her eyes watered. "Something like that."

"I also told her you came home as soon as you could."

Looking over Maddie's shoulder, she saw Thomas watching the reunion with a soft wistful expression and felt a flutter in her chest. She caught his attention and mouthed, "Thank you." Thomas nodded.

Meanwhile, Maddie continued to cling for her life. Because Rosalind was kneeling, the child couldn't bury her face anymore, so she wrapped her arms around Rosalind's neck and rested her chin on her shoulder.

"Daddy and I thought you were in heaven with the angels, but I wrote to Santa and asked him if he would let you come home for Christmas," she said.

With each word, her chin dug into Rosalind's shoulder. Not minding a bit, Rosalind pulled her closer. "You did?"

Without releasing her grip, Maddie pulled back, looked Rosalind in the eye and nodded. "Because God and Santa are friends."

She looked so serious about the matter, her deep blue

eyes matching her father's, Rosalind wanted to squeeze her tight. Was it possible to fall in love at first sight? Or was Thomas right and some feelings ran deeper than memory?

"I guess now that I'm back, you'll have to ask Santa for something else for Christmas," she said.

"You can't. Santa only gives you one wish. Jaime Kensington asked for a pony and a racing car and a doll's house, but I don't think that's fair."

"Well, I think in this case, Santa might let you have a second wish," Thomas said. "You've been very good."

She pursed her lips in thought for a few seconds. "You're not going to get lost again, are you, Mummy? Do you have to go back after Christmas? Because I forgot to ask Santa to let you stay longer."

Thinking about the agreement she'd made with Thomas, Rosalind winced. "I promise I won't leave you again. You will always know where I am. Cross my heart." It was as true a promise as she could make under the circumstances and an easy one as well, much to her surprise.

"Yay!" And once again Rosalind found herself in the grips of a pint-sized bear hug. "And Santa doesn't have to bring me anything if he doesn't want to. Except maybe cookies. And a friend for Bigsby."

"Is it all right to come in?"

Linus appeared in the open doorway. Next to him stood a shorter woman with a mass of curly hair. Their sister, Susan, Rosalind presumed.

"Sorry to interrupt the reunion. We promise we aren't going to stay long," Susan said, coming into the room. "I just wanted to say welcome back. I still can't quite believe you're here in front of us."

Whereas Linus had greeted her with warmth, Susan's greeting was far less effusive. She gave Rosalind a quick kiss on the cheek, before drawing back and assessing her.

"You put everyone through quite a fright these past six

months. Thomas and Maddie were crushed when the authorities found your empty car," she said.

"It kills me to think that I put them through the anguish."

"I'm sure. Fortunately, you're back safe and sound. For good, I hope." Although the last line was delivered with a smile, something about it made Rosalind want to squirm. Did she know about the trial period? Was that it?

"And, with that, we are leaving. Come along, Susan. I'll take you to tea." Grabbing his sister by the hand, Linus reached out with his other to ruffle Maddie's hair. "Have fun with Mummy, Maddie-cakes. Oh and, Thomas, turn your phone back on. I've been fielding panic calls from the office for the last hour."

Thomas sighed. "What now?"

"Let's just say Legal's involved and leave it at that," his brother said. He continued dragging Susan toward the door. "Goodbye again, Rosalind. We're glad you're home."

Rosalind watched the two them depart, then turned to Thomas, whose expression had darkened slightly.

"What does that mean? Legal's involved?" she asked.

"Nothing good. Never is when lawyers are involved." Taking Rosalind's elbow, Thomas helped her to her feet while Maddie continued to hold fast, and led them to one of the sofas.

"No, I suppose it isn't." She frowned. "Were there problems between your sister and me?"

"What do you mean?"

"The way she spoke. If I didn't know better, I'd say she was angry with me."

"That's just Susan being Susan. She doesn't do big emotional scenes very well. How are you doing, sweet pea?" He tweaked Maddie's nose. "Happy Mummy's home for Christmas?"

"Uh-huh. Can we put up the Christmas tree now? And decorate it? And put candles in the windows?"

"Whoa, easy does it. Your mummy just got home. There's plenty of time before Christmas yet."

Conversation nicely deflected. She made a note to probe deeper later on. At the moment, she wanted to focus on Maddie who, despite Thomas's admonishment, not only wanted the tree decorated and stocked with presents, but three different types of Christmas pastries baked.

"We don't even have a tree," she pointed out. "Shouldn't that be the first step?"

"We could get one tonight," Maddie replied. "I saw them when Uncle Linus took me to see the Gingerbread City. You said I could put the angel on top this year. And can we have snowflakes?"

Her enthusiasm had Rosalind exhausted, and they hadn't yet started. She could see what Thomas meant about her being persistent.

"What do you think?" she asked Thomas. She needed him to help slow Maddie down. However, he was reading something on his phone and didn't hear her.

"Thomas?"

"Sorry," he said, looking up. "Legal buzzed with a text."

Of course they did.

The caustic thought popped into her head unbidden. Where did it come from? And why did it leave her agitated?

"Tell you what," Thomas said to Maddie. "How about if I call and make arrangements for a tree to be delivered tomorrow? The three of us can decorate it tomorrow night. That will give Mummy time to catch up on everything she's missed while she was gone."

"Did you forget where your room is? I can show you," Maddie offered.

"I'd rather see your room," Rosalind said. "Daddy told me it's a new color."

"Purple! Daddy and Uncle Linus painted it. I wanted purple curtains too, but Daddy hired some lady who made them with orange flowers instead." The little girl rambled on about Linus getting purple paint in his hair.

"Wow. Sounds like Uncle Linus isn't much of a handyman." She looked to Thomas expecting a response, but he was again reading his phone. "If you need to call them back…" she said, checking the sigh that rose with her words.

To say Thomas looked apologetic was an understatement. "It'll only take a second, I promise."

Right. Again, the thought was unbidden. This was obviously not the first time these thoughts had plagued her.

"Don't be sad, Mummy."

Shaking her thoughts away, Rosalind smiled at Maddie. "Why would I be sad? I'm back home with my favorite little munchkin."

"About Daddy working. He doesn't do that anymore."

"He doesn't?"

"He used to work all the time, but then you got lost and now he doesn't." Maddie jumped off the sofa and held out a hand. "Come on, Mummy. Let's go and see my room."

But as they headed upstairs, Maddie chatting a mile a minute, Rosalind couldn't shake the feeling of agitation in the pit of her stomach. The annoyed reactions, his sister's coolness, the missing wedding band. Why did she get the feeling there was a piece to her history that Thomas wasn't sharing?

It was close to midnight when Thomas dragged himself back to the apartment. Nights like this were exhausting, especially when he'd much rather be home with Rosalind and Maddie, but he was committed to securing Collier's future. It was his family's legacy. His daughter's legacy. And, he'd be damned if he was going to be the Collier who led the company to ruin. If he could just get this botanical line launched. It was the first project he'd created from concept to product, the first Collier's product where he was the Collier in charge, and everything rode on its success.

Rosalind never understood...

No. He shook away the thought. He was the one who'd messed up, not Rosalind. This time would be different. He'd show her.

He just needed to get through this launch.

The house was dark as he made his way upstairs. Checking in Maddie's room, he found her in bed, arms flung akimbo in a deep, carefree sleep. He retrieved Bigsby from the floor and propped the dog next to her pillow before kissing her good-night and closing the door. By habit, he walked straight across the hall to his room, his hand just about on the handle when he remembered. Rosalind was in there. He'd relegated himself to the spare room for the unforeseeable future. Out of respect for her condition.

He nearly groaned. How respectful was he now with his body aching to peer inside? For six long months, there'd been nothing but emptiness on her side of the bed. He longed to feel the warmth of her body pressed tight against his.

Soon. He meant what he'd told her. He would do everything in his power to convince her she should stay past the holidays. It would be the best Christmas present he could ever ask for.

He went down the hall to his room.

At first, when he heard the noise, he thought it was Maddie having one of her bad dreams. Half stumbling, half hopping into his pajamas, he headed to her room only to realize the noise came from the master bedroom. Rosalind was the one having the nightmare. Through the heavy door, he could hear her moaning.

Without giving it a second thought, he rushed inside to find Rosalind fighting the covers, her legs thrashing about and getting tangled in the thick duvet. Just as he did when Maddie had her dreams, Thomas sat on the mattress's edge and stroked the hair from her face.

"Shh," he whispered, making sure to keep his voice soft and gentle. "Everything's all right." With his free hand, he pulled the covers away from her flailing limbs. Freed from the tangles, Rosalind's arm swung wide, smacking him on the side of the head.

Oof! He grabbed her wrist to keep her from hitting him again, then curled his other hand behind her head. "Wake up, sweetheart. You're having a bad dream."

As he spoke, he lifted her into a sitting position until her cheek rested against his shoulder. She was gasping for breath, so he let his hand slide from her neck to her spine, gently stroking up and down until he felt her breathing calm.

An arm slipped around his arm to grip his shoulder.

"That's right," he whispered. "You're safe."

"I… I…" Rosalind lifted her head. Thomas could feel the air from her parted lips hitting his. "What…?"

"You were having a nightmare," he repeated.

He wished he hadn't spoken. As soon as she heard his voice, she tore from his grip, hitching backward until she was pressed against the headboard. Thomas swallowed back the punch her panic sent to his gut.

"You were yelling. I heard you crying out through the wall."

"I was…"

The light from the hallway leaking into the room was just enough that he could see her eyes fall to his bare chest.

The man in him took pleasure in her awareness. Lord knows he was painfully aware of her bare legs.

"I was underwater," she said after a pause, "and I couldn't breathe. I kept trying to get my head above the surface, but I was stuck. There was something holding me in place. I think it was a seat belt."

The hair on Thomas's arms started to stand up. "You were dreaming about the accident?"

"I don't know. Maybe. All I know is I was sure I was going to die. Then I heard your voice and…" She combed the hair from her face with her fingers. "Could I have some water?"

"Or course." Reluctant as he was to pull away, he walked to the bathroom. When he came back, she was sitting propped by a pillow with the covers pulled up once more.

"Could you really hear me through the walls?" she asked as he handed her the glass.

"Thought it was Maddie at first, having one of hers."

"Maddie has nightmares?"

"Every now and then. I suspect they'll be better now that you're back."

"I caused her nightmares."

The guilt in her voice stung him. "She missed her mother. It's not your fault. You didn't have an accident and wander Scotland with amnesia on purpose."

"If I did, then we're talking even bigger problems."

"Yes, we are."

Taking the cup from her hand, Thomas placed it on the nightstand. She looked pale and shaky in the dim light. The vulnerability of it all struck him hard. Without thinking twice, he was on the edge of the bed again, brushing her cheek with the back of his hand. "Feeling better?" he asked. She nodded, and his nerves relaxed a little. "Good. Then let's finish tucking you in."

He waited until she lay down before pulling the covers to her chest and molding them to her sides. Same way he did when Maddie needed tucking in.

Though in his mind, he wasn't thinking about Maddie. He was seeing Rosalind's cotton T-shirt and thinking about the long legs exposed below.

I never did like fancy lingerie.

"What's the point if you're sleeping?"

Thomas ducked his head, unaware he'd spoken his thoughts aloud. "So you always used to say."

The air turned awkward as they both fell silent. He should move, thought Thomas. Stand up and let her return to sleep. Instead, he sat on the edge of the mattress with his hands resting on either side of her arms. The closest thing to an embrace he could have.

"Thank you for the water," Rosalind said. "And for coming to my rescue."

"Anytime." He was sorry he'd failed her to the point she'd ended up having nightmares in the first place.

"You must be tired. What time is it, anyway?"

"A little after two, and don't worry. I'm used to not getting a lot of sleep."

"You work late a lot."

Something shifted and Thomas felt a tension that wasn't there before. His guilty conscience, he supposed. "Only in cases of emergencies these days, I promise." Unfortunately, this launch threatened to have a lot of emergencies. "I'm sorry I ruined your homecoming."

"It's all right."

"No, it's not. You deserve special. Besides, I promised you that I would be so charming and debonair that you'd forget all about this trial visit idea of yours."

"Forget?" She gave a soft snort.

"*Discard* then," he replied with a grin. Discard, forget, toss aside. All of those. "I promise that tomorrow I will make everything up to you. We're talking full-on charm offensive."

"Sounds more like a battle than a homecoming."

"Well, you did issue a challenge back in Lochmara, and I never—" he leaned in for emphasis "—back down from a challenge. You won't be able to resist."

With that, he dipped his head, not too far but enough that he heard her breath hitch in expectation. It was a noise he hadn't heard in a long time, and damn if he hadn't missed it down to his core.

If she wasn't in a vulnerable place and if he weren't such a gentleman…

"I'll let you get some sleep," he whispered.

Indulging himself in one more feathery brush of her cheek, he rose and headed to the door.

"Thomas?" Her voice called out as he reached the door. "Would you mind…?"

Closing the door tight behind him? He waited for the command. "What do you need?"

"Never mind. I don't want to put you out."

"Don't be silly. If you need something, all you have to do is ask."

She looked down at her lap, her hands fidgeting atop the duvet. "I was wondering if you wouldn't mind sitting with me a little longer. Just until I fall asleep."

Sit. Her choice of words was obvious as she pointed to the wingback chair in the corner by the armoire. Still, he wasn't one to refuse the opportunity. Pulling the chair closer to what was normally his side of the bed, he sat down with one foot perched on the mattress. "Have you had a lot of nightmares? Since the accident?"

"Back when Christopher found me and I was in the hospital, I had them, but this is the first time in a long time. And it's the first time I've dreamt with such detail. Before they were more vague and foggy."

"That's a good sign. Maybe you're starting to remember."

"Or I looked at too many accident scene photos," she replied.

"You don't believe that's the case though, do you?" He recognized downplaying when he heard it. She was afraid to be too hopeful.

"It seemed so real. I could feel the water closing in on me and the steering wheel…"

Thomas heard the rustling of sheets as she kicked her legs again. Instantly, he put his hand on her knee to stop her from moving. "You're trembling."

"Like I said, the dream was very real."

Forget keeping his distance. He stretched out atop the duvet and pulled her to his side before she could utter a protest. That she went so willingly spoke volumes.

"Luckily for you, there's no water within miles of this bedroom, unless you count the fountain in the park, and I don't think that's in danger of overflowing all the way to the sixth floor. Certainly be interesting if it did though."

She capitulated without argument when he urged her head to his shoulder, sending a surge of pleasure through him. Not sexual pleasure, but happiness that she trusted him. Who knows? Tomorrow they could be back to being awkward around each other, but for now the distance had been breached. A little, anyway.

"Can you imagine? Boats sailing down St. James's Street? Be a sight, wouldn't it?" He combed her hair with his fingers. Slow, methodical strokes aimed at soothing the tremors from her body. Little by little, her muscles began to relax, her breath becoming deeper and slower.

"Tell me something," she murmured, her breath ghosting across his bare chest. "About us."

"Should I tell you about the first time we went hiking? It was right after we met and we decided to climb Cat Bells. Proper city boy that I was, I'd never done much hiking, but I didn't want you to know that. So a couple days before we left for the weekend, I went out and bought brand-new hiking gear. Then I drove over the stuff with my car a couple times to make it look used."

"Your car?" she slurred.

"A couple of pints may have been involved in creating the idea. Anyway, the day of the hike there I was in my brand-new, completely trashed hiking gear all set to impress you and…"

He paused. Rosalind's breath had evened out. Closing his eyes, he concentrated on the sound of his heart beneath Rosalind's cheek. "I got the biggest blisters you've ever seen that weekend, but I didn't say a word," he whispered. "Because you were having the time of your life. I'd do anything to win that smile."

He pressed a lingering kiss to the top of her head. "If it's the last thing I do, I'm going to earn that smile again."

CHAPTER FIVE

ROSALIND WOKE TO an empty bed and a strangely disappointed heart. The latter surprised her. She hadn't asked, or wanted, Thomas to spend the night.

She hadn't asked him to hold her until she fell asleep either, but he did, and Lord help her, she'd liked it.

Or was it simply the comforting shoulder she appreciated? Last night's dream was still in her head. The water rushing around her midsection. The searing pain in her shoulder. The shattering of glass as she smashed…something hard. Against the cracked windshield.

She winced as pain stabbed behind her right eyeball. Maybe it was a memory.

Pinching the bridge of her nose, she closed her eyes and concentrated on better thoughts. Like the rhythm of Thomas's fingers combing her hair. Last night was the safest she'd felt in a long time, an absolutely terrifying thought. How could she feel safe and secure yet still not remember the man?

And then there was the inexplicable annoyance rising up inside her when it came to his business. It was understandable she would find his distraction on her first day home frustrating. But her response felt deeper and almost bitter. Why?

She'd get no answers lying in bed. Where was her bag?

Looking around, she spied it by the armoire, open and emptied. Meaning someone had unpacked her things.

She was officially moved in. Rosalind waited to let the realization sink in.

The clothes she'd brought weren't much. A handful of sweaters and jeans Jessica and Chris had bought for her and a few more she'd bought with her wages. They hung in the armoire with other clothes. Her clothes, Rosalind corrected. She trailed her fingers across the hangers. Like everything in the house, the outfits were familiar and new. A copper sweater caught her eye. It was long and airy, the yarn impossibly soft. A voice in her head said wearing it would be like wearing a hug.

She could use a hug. She grabbed the sweater from the hanger, only to squeeze the fabric in her fist as images flashed behind her eyes.

A tree. White lights twinkling in the snow. An arm in a copper-colored sweater reaching around her waist.

"Will you still want to hug me when I'm as big as a house?"

"Always."

Thomas's breath, warm as he buried his face in the crook of her neck and rained tiny kisses above her collar.

"Always," he whispered again.

Rosalind sighed.

The hanger clattered to the floor, and the images disappeared. She was left in her room with nothing but a bunched-up sweater in her hand.

And a tingling sensation lingering on her neck.

It was clearly a memory. As soon as she finished dressing, Rosalind rushed to find Thomas so she could ask him to add context to the moment playing in her head.

She found him heading up the spiral staircase. Actually, they collided. She pitched into his chest, her hands grabbing on to his shoulders for balance while his ars wrapped around her waist. Smelling the traces of musk and wood on his shirt, she immediately traded the morning's memory for one from the night before. When he'd held her against his bare skin until her nightmare abated. He'd smelled so delicious her body had wanted to melt into the scent.

"Careful there," he said. "Don't need you taking a header over the railing. Everything all right?"

His grip tightened. "You didn't have another nightmare, did you?"

"What?" Rosalind shook herself from her thoughts. Hopefully, he would think the rush the reason for her red cheeks.

"No. Nothing like that," she replied. "Slept like a baby." Thanks to him, but she didn't say that. She hadn't had a chance to process how safe and protected she'd felt in his presence or what those responses meant to her.

"I'm glad to hear. You're up pretty early. Maddie doesn't wake for another hour or so."

"Actually…" She lifted her eyes to his, struck for the umpteenth time over how the blue changed shade depending upon the circumstances. Like right now they were a mix of blue and gray. "I was looking for you."

"You were? Do you need something?"

"Yes, I…" His gaze had lowered to her lips, causing her pulse to stutter and calling attention to the fact they were still wrapped in an embrace. Removing a hand from his shoulder, she pointed to the living room below. "Do you think we can take this downstairs?"

"Certainly." The tiniest bit of red dotted his cheeks as he released her and took a step backward. Rosalind grabbed hold of the railing. She hadn't expected to feel off-balance.

"There's fresh coffee in the dining room. Why don't I pour us a cup and join you on the sofa?"

Giving her a moment to recover. "Wonderful," she said.

"Do you still take it with milk and no sugar?" he called out just as she was stepping off the bottom step.

"You mean you forgot?"

"Not really, but I thought I'd ask so you wouldn't feel like you were at a disadvantage."

Like yesterday with the tea and cookies. She had called the experience unnerving. Considering the entire world probably knew more about her than she did, pretending not to know her coffee preference was a pretty minute gesture. Nonetheless, she warmed from the inside out.

"I bet I could guess yours," she said.

Thomas came walking in carrying a pair of bone china cups and saucers with gold rims. He stopped short of the coffee table and raised the cup a little higher, so she couldn't look at the contents. "You think so, do you? Let's give it a go then."

She looked him up and down. He'd returned to corporate mode albeit without a jacket. His white dress shirt was crisp and perfectly tailored to show off his upper body. His cuff links were simple onyx circles. Elegant and understated. With just the right amount of style, she added, taking in his brightly striped tie. The man was clearly made for sophistication. And to be in command.

"Black, one sugar," she said. Simple with just a touch of sweetness.

Thomas's eyes widened. "Was that really a guess or did you remember?"

"Lucky guess." Although given how the answer had popped into her head with such certainty, maybe luck wasn't as involved as she thought.

She took a sip of coffee and let the caffeine enter her system. The house was quiet, and she took advantage of the silence to catch her breath.

"Speaking of—"

"I have a present for you."

They spoke simultaneously. "You first," she said. "Presents before conversation."

"Sounds like a child I know." Thomas reached into his pocket and pulled out a phone.

"We were fortunate to get the same number," he said. "I had my assistant recreate as many of your contacts as possible, although I'm sure there are a few he missed. Eve from the university is in there though. Sinclair, as well."

Those were the people from the photo he'd showed her the night he found her. Apparently, Thomas wasn't a fan of the gentleman.

"We're working on getting your license, as well."

Rosalind turned the phone round and round in her hand. What would happen if she were to call one of her contacts right now? What would they say? Would they think her a prank caller?

"Do any of them know I'm back?" He'd said yesterday he was trying to preserve her privacy.

"Not yet." He paused to drink his coffee in what looked like a well-crafted delay tactic to gather his thoughts. "I was going to ask our lawyers to make an announcement today—that is, with your permission."

The world would have to be told sooner or later. Much as she'd like to simply resume her life, too much time had passed. "Would I have to talk with the press?"

"You don't have to do anything you don't want to," he told her. "There may be a few reporters trying to snag photos, but we'll do our best to keep them away. The good thing is that while our name is famous, we're not on a par with the Royal Family. Most of London wouldn't recognize a Collier even if they walked right into us."

"Is that your way of telling me people won't be gawking when I cross the street?"

"Precisely. You could walk out of the apartment this

morning and no one would be the wiser as to who you were, unless you wore a sign around your neck."

"Thank goodness for anonymity," she said, still staring at the call screen.

"It does have its moments." Thomas took her hand. "Hey—you're in control. Fast, slow. However you want to return to the world is up to you. If you want to stay locked up in the apartment until Christmas, that's fine with me. It's your call."

Again, his kindness warmed her, even if it wasn't entirely practical. "I can hardly spend the entire month hiding from the world. Sooner or later I'll have to show my face."

Which reminded her. "You've mentioned the university several times now. Do I work there?" It occurred to her that returning to work might be a good way to ease herself back into the world. Give her something outside of herself on which she could focus.

"You...used to." Thomas pulled his hand away. "Your research lost its funding, and you were let go."

"Oh." So much for that idea.

"I'm sorry."

"Why are you apologizing? It's not your fault." The apology, she suspected, was in reaction to the disappointment on her face. She hadn't expected to feel that let down. "So no research. Do I work anywhere?"

Thomas shook his head. "Losing your funding left you at loose ends. You wanted to work but were struggling to find a new research project you felt passionate about. In the meantime, you were staying home with Maddie."

"I bet that made her very happy."

"Maddie? Deliriously so."

Something felt missing from his answer. Rosalind sensed incompletion. She sipped her coffee and waited to see if he'd take advantage of the silence to continue.

Instead, he pivoted the conversation. "Your turn," he said. "Why were you looking for me?"

Right! The whole reason for her excitement. "Something very strange happened to me upstairs."

"What do you mean, 'something happened'?" He scooted closer so their knees were touching. "You said everything was all right."

"Everything is fine. Except that when I was getting dressed I had a… Well, I guess you could say I had a memory come back to me."

"Are you sure? What kind of memory?"

"I'm not sure." *Us in love.* "It came to me in a flash." She told him about the lights sparkling in the window and the tree laden with rustic ornaments.

"Mostly woolen balls and felt animals. And I was pregnant." She left out how he'd nuzzled her neck and vowed eternal devotion.

While he was smiling, a shadow passed across Thomas's blue eyes. "That was in Cumbria. In the cottage."

"The one I was visiting last June." He'd mentioned they'd lived there prior to his father's stroke. "You showed me a photo we took there on holiday. A selfie." Was that why she had pictured the cottage? Had talk of tree decorating and photographs planted ideas in her head?

Then again, their faces had filled the frame leaving very few details for her to remember. If the scene she saw upstairs was from her imagination, she had an extremely vivid one.

"We seemed very happy there," she said out loud.

"We were. You loved Cumbria."

We'll go back, I promise.

Thomas's words sounded in her head, not at the table. She looked over to where he was fiddling with his coffee cup.

"What happened?" she asked him.

"What do you mean?"

"Yesterday, you said we'd moved in here temporarily. We were planning to go back, weren't we?"

"Wow, you really are getting your memory back." He was smiling, but something about his expression felt off. His eyes weren't as bright as they were a moment before. It was as though the mention of Cumbria had dampened his excitement. "You're right. Our original plan was to go back when my father recovered."

"Except your father didn't recover."

"No," Thomas said with a long sigh. "He did not."

So, Cumbria had been postponed because of his father's death. And perhaps again because of hers?

"I'm sorry," she said. "I didn't mean to bring up a bad subject."

"You didn't." Clearing his throat, he repeated in a softer voice, "You didn't. What matters is that you're starting to remember and that is wonderful. In fact, I think this calls for a celebration." This time his face lit up contagiously.

"You're only saying that because you were already planning to unleash a full charm offensive."

And…his smile faded.

"What?" Rosalind asked. She could guess the answer. Thomas was staring at his coffee cup like the contents would disappear if he didn't.

"I arranged to meet with the lawyers this morning so we could finish what we started last night."

Of course he did.

"I didn't expect you up this early," he said. "The idea was to get in and out of the office before you even realized I'd left."

Rosalind nodded.

"I'd only go if it was an emergency."

"I know." She was disappointed. What bothered her was

how strongly her disappointment struck her. With such bitterness and anger. They'd had this conversation before.

"I promise…" Setting both of their cups on the coffee table, Thomas took her hands in his. "I'll wrap this up as soon as I can and then the charm offensive shall be unleashed. You have my word."

She was still disappointed, but she understood. His world didn't stop simply because she'd returned to it. "Fine, but there'd better be a lot of charm."

"Shock and awe. You have my word."

"Are you still here? Shouldn't you be home with your wife and daughter?"

Thomas was in no mood for his brother's cheerfulness. "Whoever invented lawyers should be hung, drawn and quartered."

"I don't think they were actually invented."

"You know what I mean," Thomas snapped. He should have gone home ages ago, but the day just wouldn't co-operate. Soon as he got one fire out, another would crop up.

He tossed his files on the conference table before throwing himself into the head chair. The chair rolled backward, stopping when it bumped into the whiteboard behind him. "Maybe I should call the whole thing off," he said to the ceiling. "Forget the new spa line. Let the company fade away. Two hundred years is a long enough run, don't you think?"

"You couldn't let Collier's fade away any more than you could cut off your head," Linus replied. "If you could, you never would have stopped playing country carpenter and come back."

A fateful decision if ever there was one. "I came back because Dad said he needed me."

"And stayed because Collier's did." Ignoring the chairs in favor of sitting on the conference table, he started straightening the papers that had spilled out of Thomas's file. "On the plus side, you're a hell of a lot better at running the place."

"Than who? Dad? He didn't exactly set the bar very high."

More like laid the bar on the ground. Whatever Preston Collier had done, it hadn't been successfully running a company. The last decade had been a fiscal disaster, and now it was up to Thomas to fix things. Linus, the coward, chose to go into science.

"I'm sorry your reunion last night didn't go as planned," Linus said. "How is Rosalind settling in?"

"About as well as you'd expect." His brother didn't need to know about Rosalind's nightmare or the fact he'd held her in his arms for most of the night while she slept. "She's remembered a few things."

"You're kidding? That's terrific. So why aren't you smiling?"

"She remembered that my return to Collier's was supposed to be temporary."

"I see." Linus stroked his chin. "Does she remember why you stayed?"

"That Dad died and I stayed on to run the company? Yes. But not how opposed she was to staying in London. Give her time though. She'll remember soon enough."

Along with remembering how unhappy she'd been about all the hours he'd worked and how neglected she'd felt. When that happened, how long would it take before they were right back to where they'd been in June? With her walking out their front door.

Groaning a second time, he let his head fall back against the chair. "I promised her we'd spend the day together."

"So why not go do that?"

"Because Ernie messed up the contracts regarding the new shampoo, and now we have to somehow retroactively retain the rights without spending an arm and a leg. That's why."

"So have Ernie and the legal team fix it. There is such a thing as delegation you know."

Thomas lifted his head. "Dad delegated."

Need he say more? Until he was certain Collier's was safely back from the brink, he had no choice but to oversee every detail. Linus was right. He'd sooner cut off his head than see Collier's fail.

Even he had his limits though. "I can't let Rosalind walk away again," he said.

"You don't know if she's going to walk away."

"I know I'll do whatever I have to in order to prevent it," Thomas replied.

Heaving the loudest sigh known to man, his brother pushed himself to a sitting position. "What if she wants you to walk away from Collier's? Can you?"

"I walked away from Collier's before. Carpenter in the woods, remember?"

"That was when you were just out of university and all starry-eyed about being in love. You hadn't actually fulfilled your destiny at that point."

"Running Collier's is hardly my destiny."

"Keep telling yourself that, Thommy-boy." Linus pushed himself off the table and onto his feet. "You were meant to run this company, and you love it. Lawyers and all."

Yeah, he did. But he loved Rosalind too. And unlike the other Colliers in history, if forced to choose, he knew the correct decision to make.

CHAPTER SIX

"I KNOW. I KNOW. I should have been home hours ago. The day started badly and went downhill from there." Thomas rushed into the apartment stripping off his coat and suit jacket as he walked. "Let me…"

Hitting the bottom step, he drew up short realizing he was speaking to an empty room.

Of course he was. Did he expect his family to be sitting on the sofa waiting for him?

That didn't stop his pulse—or his guilty conscience—from kicking up a notch. A better man would have walked out of the meetings and told Legal to hash out the problem on their own. But he wasn't a better man. He was a Collier and it was his name signed on the bottom line, so he'd stayed.

"Rosalind?" He tossed his jackets on the sofa and started working on the tie. "Maddie? Anyone home?"

"The housekeeper took Maddie to the park."

Rosalind appeared at the railing. She looked quite regal looking down on him. He'd always loved it when she wore jeans as they showed her curves.

"She's been beside herself talking about decorating the tree this evening, so we thought the distraction of friends would do her some good," she said.

"You didn't go with them?" He was surprised, since Maddie had been a human barnacle yesterday.

"I was afraid my sudden appearance might cause others to start gossiping and I didn't want Maddie to feel self-conscious. Besides, I didn't know when you would be home and didn't want to leave you in the lurch."

Like he'd left her by running late and not checking in.

He watched as she made her way down the staircase. "You're annoyed."

"No."

Liar. The frosty coating on her words said as much. He was annoyed with himself, so why shouldn't she be? "I came home as soon as I could," he said. But even to his voice the apology sounded lame.

"Really. I understand," Rosalind said, coming into the living room. She paused at the sofa to pick up his coasts and separate them. "You run a major corporation. It's a very time-consuming position. You can't ignore a problem simply to entertain me."

"Yes, I can." Thomas took the jackets from her and tossed them aside. "And, it's not *'entertaining.'* I want to spend time with my family."

When they'd first met, he'd told Rosalind that her eyes were the most expressive eyes he'd ever seen. They spoke volumes—sometimes too much—even when she attempted to school her emotions. At the moment he could see a swirl of hurt and disappointment in their brown depths.

God, he was such an idiot. He'd never wanted to see disappointment in her eyes again.

Which meant erasing the feelings as quickly as he possibly could.

An idea struck him. "Get your coat," he told her.

Rosalind blinked. "Excuse me? You just got home and you want to go back out?"

"Together. Yes. I promised shock and awe, remember?"

"There's no need…"

Oh, yes, there was. If he wanted her to stay beyond Christmas anyway. "No protesting. It might be getting a late start but the full charm offensive gets underway right now."

He tried to shoo her toward the closet, but she didn't move beyond crossing her arms in front of her chest. "What about Maddie? She and Mrs Faison will be coming back soon."

"All the more reason for us to move quickly," Thomas replied. There was paper in the Louis XIV desk in the far corner of the room. "I'll leave a note letting Mrs Faison knowing that we're going out for a couple of hours but will be back in plenty of time for tonight's tree-trimming festivities."

"And where exactly are we going?" she asked.

Victory. Her eyes were staring at him with confusion and excitement. He smiled. "Why, to buy a Christmas tree, of course."

Despite the early hour, Covent Garden was awash with both lights and people. Banners of white lights hung in a row along the street, their tiny bulbs waving gently as, beneath them, hordes of shoppers and tourists, arms laden with purchases, paraded past store windows. Feeling like a stranger in a strange land, Rosalind found herself holding Thomas's arm. It wasn't that she found the streets unfamiliar or even frightening. She simply found the crowds overwhelming. So much noise and commotion. Holding on to Thomas's arm kept them from getting separated.

They'd managed to find a suitable tree fairly quickly— a sturdy Douglas fir a few inches taller than Thomas— which was being delivered to their apartment at that very moment. Rosalind had enjoyed watching Thomas and the merchant haggle over the price. The back-and-forth had been more for the sake of show and pride. Still, seeing the fervency with which Thomas tackled negotiations, with his eyes bright and sharp, had made her pity the businesses who met him across the conference table.

"What do you think?" Thomas asked.

"Of what? The decorations? They're lovely."

With their task completed, Rosalind had assumed they would be heading home, but Thomas, still hell-bent on his "full charm offensive," had suggested they walk a bit. *To get you reacquainted with the city,* he'd said.

"I meant, what do you think of London?"

"Ah. It's very crowded."

More than once, Rosalind found herself stepping out of the way of oncoming traffic. "Feels like I'm swimming upstream," she said. "Only in a river of people." The thought recalled other rivers, and she clung closer to him.

"Sorry about that. Product of the season and the time of day. Everyone rushing to get in a little Christmas shopping before they head home."

As if to illustrate her point, a woman in a green wool coat approached, pushing through the crowds. "Sorry," she apologized with a thick foreign accent every time she wedged herself past someone. "So sorry." When the woman reached them, Thomas pulled Rosalind flush to his side. The scent of his coat grounding her.

"Thank you," she murmured.

"You never were a huge fan of crowds. When we finished university, you couldn't wait to get away from people."

Sounded about right. She didn't like crowds. The noise and commotion drained her.

Bringing to mind a question she'd asked the other day. "Is that why we moved north instead of you taking a job with your family's company?"

"It's why *you* moved north," he said. "I moved because

I'm not a fan of long-distance relationships. Do you want to head back?"

"Depends. Are we heading somewhere in particular?" From the purposeful way he was cutting through the crowds, he seemed to have a destination in mind.

"You'll see," was his reply. "I don't want to play my entire hand."

Rosalind laughed. You had to give it to him—the man was trying. She had been annoyed earlier. The minute Thomas left for the office, an overwhelming rush of anger and bitterness came over her, same as it had the day before. Why drag her back here if he was going to leave her alone all day?

While a logical part of her argued that corporate emergencies were out of his control, the disappointed part of her was mad he'd gotten her excited about spending time together, then let her down.

Then there was a third part of her that was ashamed with herself. Maddie was a wonderful child, and she relished every moment with her, but everything they did together felt like it was taking place in someone else's house. When Maddie wanted lunch, it was the housekeeper who made soup and sandwiches. When the phone rang, it was the housekeeper who answered. It was the housekeeper who took Maddie to the park.

She was in stasis, neither a working mum nor a fully hands-on one, and she was bored to death.

Making Thomas's lateness that much more irritating since he was her conduit to any kind of life.

"Hello? Earth to Rosalind?" A gloved hand waved in front of her face. She blinked and realized Thomas was looking down at her, concern in his eyes. How was it that in the middle of a crowded street in the darkness of the winter's twilight he still managed to have the most mesmerizing eyes? This evening the blue was navy again. The color of the ocean. She could see the illuminated banners reflecting in their depths. Like white caps. Wasn't that what she'd thought the first night she'd stared into them?

"Is everything all right?"

"Sorry. I was thinking about Christmas," she lied, her thoughts better left unsaid so as not to ruin the moment. "Trying to imagine what the day will be like. Do you do a big family celebration?"

"Not usually. The Colliers are too spread out to do anything really crazy. There's the company party, which I pushed to January. For obvious reasons." Rosalind's cheeks warmed. "And we'll host a few family members at Christmas dinner. Linus. Susan. My crazy uncle, Seth."

"What about Christmas Eve?"

Strangely, he looked to the sidewalk before speaking. "Well, up until last year we would make toasted cheese sandwiches and drink mulled wine in front of the fireplace. A Christmas campfire, if you will."

"Really?"

Thomas nodded. "It was a tradition we started our very first Christmas and kept going after Maddie was born."

"Sounds fun." She frowned as his full answer struck her. "We didn't have a campfire last year?"

His eyes were still focused on the ground. "Circumstances got in the way."

What circumstances? Rosalind thought of asking, but suspected he'd pivot the conversation the way he did the few other times something awkward came up. She wished she could remember what it was he didn't want her to know.

"My favorite part of the season was always Christmas morning," she told him, doing a little pivoting of her own. "Waking up and finding all the gifts Santa left under the tree. My mother would insist all the gifts were hidden until

Christmas morning in order to make what was there look extra spectacular."

Thomas's head jerked up and he stared at her, mouth agape. With a thrill, she realized what she'd just said. After months of blankness, she'd experienced two memories in the same day.

"Looks like coming to London might have been what I needed," she said.

He smiled. A gentle expression that made her insides turn topsy-turvy. "I'm glad."

The two of them rounded a corner, and she saw they were heading to a giant iron-and-glass building housing a marketplace.

Guarding the arched structure, in a giant whisky barrel done up with a red bow, stood a behemoth Christmas tree, at least three times the size of the one destined for their living room. "The tree at Covent Garden," Thomas said. "Thought it might provide inspiration for when we get home. There are other trees around the city, but this one has always been my favorite."

"Why is that?"

The two of them stopped to look skyward. The tree was covered with lights, thousands of them. Red, blue and green, all sparkling in the twilight. Glass balls, nestled in the branches, reflected the colors. It was giant and lovely.

"Not sure," Thomas replied. "I think because of where it is. Whenever I visit the market, I'm reminded that people have been selling their wares on this spot for nearly four hundred years. I know, there's history on every street corner in the city, but this spot..." He pointed to the cobblestone beneath them. "My great-great-whatever-grandfather might have very well stood here selling the first bars of Collier's soap. Bit wild when you think about it."

His words had a bit of awe to them, which in turn

made Rosalind feel the same. "History means a lot to you, doesn't it?"

"You wouldn't say that if you'd seen me fall asleep during sixth form Medieval History," he said with a grin. "But I definitely have an appreciation for the passage of time and continuity."

He led her toward the marketplace entrance. Inside was a sea of stalls filled with crafts and goods of all shapes, sizes and colors. Floral scents mixed with patchouli hung in the air.

Looking to the second floor, its railing strung with lights and garland, she spied a little boy not much older than Maddie. He stood with his chin resting on the rail, eyes focused upward. She followed his gaze and spied row upon row of chandelier lights dripping with mistletoe.

She cast Thomas a sidelong glance.

"Would you look at that," he said with mock innocence. "I had no idea they decked out this entire building with mistletoe. However are you supposed to walk through without someone planting a Christmas kiss on your cheek?"

"However indeed."

The greenery was gorgeous, dangling above them with its lights and red velvet bows. A literal mistletoe canopy for as far as the eye could see.

They strolled down the aisle, stopping every now and then to look at a particularly bright piece of tapestry or sparkling piece of jewelry. Every pause led to an enthusiastic greeting by a stall manager hoping to make a sale. One vendor in particular who sold homemade soap caught Thomas's attention and they spent several minutes discussing the properties of the man's product before Thomas purchased a sample pack. Or more accurately, Thomas spent several minutes discussing the properties of the man's product while Rosalind watched with the same interest as when he'd bought the tree.

The entire time she couldn't stop thinking of the mistletoe hanging overhead. Which only increased her awareness of Thomas's shoulder as they walked side by side. The way the wool of his coat brushed against hers with every step. *Swish. Swish. Swish.*

Suddenly, they stopped. "Wait right here," he said, and he stepped in front of her to block her view. "I'll be right back."

"You're going to leave me in this crowd?" She looked around at the people jostling within the stalls.

"I'll only be gone for a moment. Don't leave this spot and I'll be right back."

He disappeared before she could protest.

Now what? She couldn't very well stand stock-still like an idiot waiting for Thomas's return. Taking a quick look around, she saw that they'd stopped at a stall selling wooden flowers and crafts. There was a wooden teddy bear puzzle that Maddie would adore. As soon as Thomas returned, she'd take a closer look. Damn if she hated not having any money.

"Oh, my God! It can't be… Rosalind?" A man in a suede jacket and scarf came rushing up to her. Rosalind backed up. When her bottom came into contact with the craft table, she continued leaning backward, trying to increase her distance from the approaching man. She was about to yell for Thomas when she realized the man looked familiar.

He was in one of the photos Thomas had showed her. The one of her colleagues from the university. *Robert? Randall?*

"My God, it is you. How…?"

"Richard." The name popped into her head and out of

her mouth right as the man wrapped his arms around her in a bear hug.

"This is a Christmas miracle. I never thought I'd see you again." His modulated tones settled welcomingly on her shoulders, like a borrowed cardigan on a chilly day. "They told us you were dead."

"They thought I was." Breaking out of his embrace, she filled him in on what'd happened, ending with Thomas finding her at McKringle's. Richard listened intently, then brushed a shock of silver-blond hair from his forehead.

"You mean, you've been in Scotland all this time and none of us knew?"

She nodded.

"And you don't remember anything?"

"Bits and pieces since I've come back to London, but no. I remember you because I saw a photograph…"

With a laugh, he hugged her again. "I'm sorry. I don't mean to be so effusive, but…you're alive! And standing in the middle of Covent Garden!"

"I know." People were starting to look at them. Rosalind let her hair fall down the sides of her face to avoid the stares.

"Thomas must be beside himself. How is he handling the return? Properly contrite and attentive, I imagine."

Contrite was an odd choice of words. "He's doing everything he can to help and being incredibly patient. It isn't easy having a wife who doesn't remember."

"Although he does get to have a clean start," Richard replied.

"What do you—"

"Hello, Sinclair." Thomas's voice had an edge of possessiveness. He walked up from behind and slipped an arm around her waist. Rather than being annoyed Rosalind found herself feeling a bit tingly. "We didn't expect to run into anyone we knew here."

"Rosalind was telling me what happened. I can't believe you didn't let her friends know."

"We sent word to the authorities and the media this afternoon. The rest, I figured, Rosalind could do at her own pace, when she wanted to contact the world. No sense forcing her into situations before she was ready."

"No. I'm sure you wouldn't. Want to force her, that is," Richard replied.

Looking between the two, Rosalind got the distinct impression their civility was for her benefit. Although why, she hadn't a clue. "Thomas replaced my phone this morning. I was going to call people next week once the news got out."

"Meaning I'm the lucky one who got to know before everyone else. Well, I mean besides your family," he added, stealing a look at Thomas.

"Speaking of—" Was it her imagination or did Thomas pull her a little closer? "—we need to get back home before Maddie tries to climb the Christmas tree."

"She's antsy enough to do it too," Rosalind added with a laugh.

Richard gave her one last hug and kiss on the cheek. "I'll call you tomorrow," he said, "and we can catch up. This is…well, it's unbelievable, that's what it is. My mind is blown."

Rosalind liked his warm personality. He made her feel at home even in a strange building. As Richard walked away, she smiled to herself before stealing a look leftward. Thomas's countenance was the exact opposite. If clenched jaws could crack, her husband's would be shattered.

"You don't like him," she noted. "How come?"

His jaw muscles relaxed as he let out a long deliberate breath. "Who, Sinclair? I don't dislike him."

"Then why the face? And don't ask what I mean because it was clear from your expression you weren't happy about something."

"Because…" He angled his body so that, instead of standing side by side, he held her in a semi-embrace. "I'm not ready to share you with the rest of the world."

Whether from his hips close to hers or the mistletoe hanging above them or the gentle whiff of aftershave on his neck, awareness washed over her. She looked up through her lashes. "Then you shouldn't have left me alone in the crowd."

"Ah, but then I couldn't have bought you this." His lifted his free arm to reveal a brown bag. "Merry early Christmas."

It was a geode. Broken open to reveal the pink crystal formations inside. "You told me once you like the pink ones best. That the color's created by—"

"Magnesium." The whispered answer came to her without having to think. "And it's beautiful. Thank you."

"You're most welcome." She looked up to find his eyes had grown hooded and dark. Her insides started to pulse.

"You know, we are under the mistletoe," he told her.

"I know."

"Be almost sacrilegious if we didn't…"

"Sacrilegious indeed."

His lips brushed against hers. The kiss was soft and sweet, full of the kind of promise that made Rosalind's knees want to buckle.

And then it ended, as a public kiss should. Leaving her tingling and wishing they were alone.

"Let's go home," Thomas said. "We have a tree to decorate."

It wasn't until he led her from the marketplace and the taste of his kiss had started to fade that Rosalind realized he hadn't really answered her question about why he disliked Richard.

* * *

Unbelievable, thought Thomas, as he studied the crowd ahead of them. Eight-and-a-half-million people in London and they run into Richard Sinclair the first day they leave the apartment.

Then again, maybe it wasn't so unbelievable. Sinclair had been like a bad penny last spring. Why wouldn't he show up when Rosalind returned?

He stole a rightward glance. Rosalind's attention was on the crowd, allowing him a chance to study her profile. He loved the upward sweep of her lashes when her eyes were open wide. He loved their downward sweep when they fluttered closed too, which was what they'd done when he'd kissed her.

Dear God, he'd kissed her. Less than two weeks ago, he would have called the idea a dream. She tasted like... He couldn't come up with a phrase that didn't sound hyperbolic. And the hyperbole? It sounded too pale and inadequate.

Why then wasn't his brain reliving that magical moment instead of ruminating about some chance encounter?

Because Sinclair would be around now, that's why.

Thomas had lied about his feelings toward the man. He definitely disliked Sinclair. Rosalind and other colleagues at the university had been always going on about how funny and smart Sinclair was. Thomas found him irritating. Sinclair struck him as the kind of man who needed to be the smartest and funniest in the room. He lapped up the attention. By last spring, he and Rosalind were thick as thieves. The witty, sympathetic shoulder and the unhappy wife.

All right. Thomas was jealous. Every time Thomas had tried to dig himself out of the hole he'd created, there'd been Sinclair competing for Rosalind's attention.

Richard has tickets to a lecture.

Richard joined us in the park.
We ran into Richard at lunch.

The man had been everywhere and anywhere. He absolutely loved having Rosalind—beautiful, intelligent, daughter-of-geology-royalty Rosalind—as his partner in crime.

Thomas half suspected Sinclair had stoked Rosalind's unhappiness so she would continue to hang around.

"You're staring." Rosalind turned her attention from the crowd to look over at him. "You've grown quiet too. Is everything all right?"

Nothing getting rid of a certain archeologist wouldn't help.

He swallowed the jealous thought. Sinclair was a symptom of their problems, not the cause.

"I'm thinking about what to buy you for Christmas. Going to be hard topping a pink rock." He tossed out the term on purpose. It used to be a joke between them that he couldn't identify specimens by their scientific names.

True to form, Rosalind immediately corrected him. "Manganese carbonate." Then she blushed, realizing the instinctiveness of her answer.

"Whatever. It's still pink. Anyway, I've got the choices narrowed down to either a block of marble, a giant slab of slate or a bucket of pebbles from the pathway in the park. Got a preference?" She turned her head away with an exaggerated sniff. "What?"

"Fine. Don't tell me what you were thinking about. I don't want to know."

"Yes, you do," he teased. "But it's Christmas, which means I get to have a few secrets. Besides—" he leaned in so he could whisper against her ear, loving the way she shivered when his lips brushed against the shell "—anticipation is the best part. So, you'll just have to wait."

"If you say so." She looked up from beneath her lashes.

"Guess that means we won't be stopping under any more mistletoe."

Thomas's blood ran straight below his belt. "What?"

"You know, like a penny for your thoughts, only instead…"

The little minx. Putting ideas in his head. He reached for her waist only to have her back away with a giggle.

"Uh-uh-uh," she said, wagging her finger. "You missed your chance. We need to get going home. Someone's waiting to decorate the tree. Besides—" this time she leaned toward him "—didn't you say anticipation is the best part?"

"Looks like one of us is down for the count," Thomas said, pointing to the settee where Maddie lay sprawled on her stomach beneath a blanket. She'd faded while Thomas and Rosalind struggled with the lights. Overloaded with excitement and sugar, she'd crashed hard when the adrenaline wore off.

Rosalind tucked the blanket around her, smiling when the girl mewled and clutched Bigsby closer. "Poor kid. Think she'll be disappointed she missed the finished product?"

"We saved the angel for her," Thomas replied. "Plus, I think she'll be more excited about the possibility of presents under it than stringing lights on the tree." He finished hanging the last ornament, then stepped back. "I have to admit the end result looks quite festive."

Rosalind had to agree. They'd set up the tree in the upstairs library. That was where they always put it. A company-paid decorator did the rest of the apartment, Thomas explained.

The tree, not so tall that Maddie couldn't reach the top from Thomas's shoulders, was set in the corner, hugged by two floor-to-ceiling bookcases. Woolen balls and felt animals—the same ones that had flashed through her mind this morning—hung on the branches.

"It's beautiful," Rosalind said. Simple and homely, unlike the glitzy decorations she suspected would go downstairs. "Explain to me again why we're hiding it up here? Are we afraid of the decorator?"

Her question earned her a chuckle. She'd discovered over the course of the evening that Thomas had a varied and fascinating collection of laughs. There was the amused, from-the-gut laugh he made when playing with Maddie, the slightly mocking laugh he made when he was being sarcastic—that one was reserved for stories about his siblings—and a naughty-sounding laugh that wrapped around her spine whenever they shared a private joke. This particular laugh held a note of question, like he was silently saying, "Maybe."

"The company has hired a decorator to do the president's home for years. Considering we're expected to entertain Collier executives and vendors here, it makes sense.

"Don't worry," he added, sensing how she'd tensed at the idea of playing hostess to a room full of people she didn't remember. "I'd already postponed this year's event until after the New Year due to previous circumstances."

He meant his first Christmas as a widower.

"As for the tree being in the library…it was actually your idea. You wanted a room and a tree more in keeping with your idea of Christmas."

Well, the room definitely fit. The library, while still luxurious, lacked the gilt and glamor of downstairs. The fireplace had a dark mantle, and the overstuffed quarters made the room far more welcoming. She could never picture curling up on the blue velvet sofas downstairs. Yet when taking a seat on the leather love seat, she kicked off her shoes and tucked her legs beneath her without a second thought.

She took a long look at the tree. It too left her with a warm, cozy feeling. The homespun ornaments reminded her of old friends nestled amid the branches.

"Do you think we have enough lights?" she asked.

"Any more and we'll be treading into fire hazard territory," Thomas replied.

He turned off the lights, leaving the room bathed in the glow of hundreds of tiny white points. Rosalind settled back in the corner and sighed. "Gorgeous."

"Couldn't agree more. Though I don't mean the tree." He was leaning in the shadows, drinking her in with a look as warm as the room. "This is the most relaxed I've seen you since we arrived. Being comfortable looks good on you."

"Hard to look uncomfortable when you're surrounded by Christmas."

She turned her face to the fireplace so he wouldn't notice how his flattery affected her. Since their brief kiss at Covent Garden, every word Thomas said left her feeling charged with energy. As though part of her insides had been left dormant and someone—he—had suddenly turned on the switch.

Everything about the evening had been perfect. From the kiss beneath the mistletoe to the crackling fire and carols playing softly on a speaker. The only thing missing was snow falling outside the window.

"Don't the stockings look nice on the mantle?" she asked. Three bright red-and-white knit stockings dangled to the right of the fire.

"I remember how excited you were to hang those stockings our first Christmas." Thomas had moved to the desk where earlier he'd placed a bottle of Chardonnay and a pair of glasses. *Figured we deserved a toast after the tree is finished*, he'd said at the time. Rosalind watched the play of his back muscles as he twisted the corkscrew. When he came home, he'd shed his jacket and tie in favor of another sweater, this one ice blue. The soft wool molded to his frame, accentuating his shoulders. For a lean man, he was surprisingly hard and defined.

Of course, she'd already discovered how defined when he came to her room last night.

"We forgot to buy those holders that slide over the wood, so I ended up hammering a pair of nails into the mantle to hang them up."

It took a moment for her to realize he was still telling the story of the stockings. "Hard to imagine you wielding a hammer." He seemed born to the boardroom.

"Are you joking? I'll have you know I wield the best hammer in the Lake District. Made that table in front of you there."

He had? Looking closer, Rosalind realized the piece was indeed different than the other ones in the room. The sturdy piece was made of darkly stained boards.

"It doubled as a dining room table more than once, especially if you had papers spread all over the actual one. I kept threatening to build you a desk so I could eat my meal without hunching over."

"Why didn't you?"

"Said you didn't want one. You liked working at the table."

"One word from me and you risk becoming Quasimodo? Who knew I had such influence. You didn't mention that in all the information you emailed over."

"Didn't want you getting a big head. Figured you'd find out soon enough." He joined her on the love seat and handed her a glass of wine. "Plus, in case you haven't noticed, you've had your influence somewhat usurped."

"Somewhat, but not completely," she teased. "Means I still have a little power."

"Far more than a little."

As he spoke, he looked at her in a way that made her warm from the inside out. Rosalind sipped her wine and tried not to squirm from the fluttering in her stomach. And who was it that was supposed to have power?

"My papers," she said. "That was my postgraduate work, right?"

"'The cause of graphite deposits in Borrowdale.' Or something like that. I know it was about graphite and Borrowdale."

"Right. Because it's extremely rare to find graphite deposits hosted in volcanic rock. The only other occurrence is in Spain."

She stopped, her cheeks burning. Thomas was staring at her like he was about to burst out in a grin. "Moments like that have been happening all day," she confessed.

"That's fantastic. At this rate, you'll have your memory back before you know it."

It was hard to tell in the shadows, but he looked genuinely happy about the fact. "I'm not sure I'd pop a cork quite yet. It's only been a handful of snippets. I've yet to remember anything of true importance. Like my parents for example." Or their marriage. Or him, for that matter.

Although the latter seemed to be diminishing in importance as time went on.

"I wish I could help you. I never got to meet your parents. Both of them died before we met."

"The articles you sent about my father made him sound larger than life. My mother too." Experts on photogrammetry and laser scanning, they'd apparently traveled the world lecturing and consulting.

"From the way you always talked, I think they were. I know they were highly regarded and spent a lot of time overseas. You used to say they set a high bar."

"In terms of what? Success?" Rosalind leaned in.

"Probably. Although it wasn't as though they placed

high expectations on you. I got the impression the three of you had some wonderful times together."

He turned sideways in his seat and tucked a leg under him in a mirror image of her pose. "I always envied that. Your family connection."

An odd thing to say coming from a man who ran a two-hundred-year-old family business. "You say it as if you and your family aren't close."

"It's complicated," he said, looking down at his wine. "We're more bonded by our family heritage than each other."

"I don't understand."

"The company is the thing that defines and connects us. My father never understood why I moved to Cumbria after graduation instead of stepping into the job waiting for me at the company."

"You said it was because you didn't like long distance relationships." He hadn't mentioned he'd walked away from his place in the company.

"I don't. I also happened to want to make you happy. The house in Cumbria was the only connection you had left to your parents. So, when you wanted to get out of London and take a job up north, I decided Collier's could find another relative to fill my shoes for a while."

In other words, he'd eschewed his family legacy so she could stay connected to her family's memory. Rosalind's heart caught. "That's quite the romantic gesture."

"Hardly. I loved you and did what I thought would make you happy. I like making you happy, in case you haven't noticed."

And when said like that, it became less grand romantic gesture and more romantic sacrifice. "Were you?" she heard herself ask. "Happy?"

He looked at her from across his glass. "I remember you smiled all the time. I loved seeing you smile like that.

Knowing that I was responsible for that smile made feel very proud."

Interestingly, he didn't say *happy*. But they had to have been; they were supposed to move back.

Rosalind watched as he took another drink. Another set of hands as large as his might make the crystal look fragile, but then another set of hands wouldn't look so elegant.

There was an elegance to how he lifted his neck and swallowed too. As she watched his Adam's apple bob up and down, she shocked herself by imagining tracing her finger along his throat.

And then what? She wasn't sure her heart had caught up to her body.

Thankfully, Thomas, having emptied his glass, was too lost in thought to notice. "Hey," he said, looking at her. "Why don't we tuck Sleeping Beauty into bed? I want to show you something up on the terrace."

It was the view he wanted to show her. Rosalind stepped on to the terrace to see London lit up around her. A personal panoramic postcard. Bundling her coat, she made her way to the railing where Thomas stood waiting. While she'd been putting on her coat, he'd brought up the wine and—somehow—a candle. The items were arranged like a tableau on the ground.

"The city's far less crowded from up here," he said, handing her a glass.

And breathtaking, as well. Across the rooftops, she could see the Christmas tree by Nelson's Column, as well as the other trees and lights dotting the city. In the distance, Tower Bridge glowed majestically. She could almost see the traffic passing from one end to the other.

"What is it with you and nighttime skies?" she asked. "Seems like you always have me outside in the cold looking at the view."

"Would you rather go back downstairs to the fire?"

"No, not yet." There was something very simple about being outside alone together. With no questions or missing pieces.

"All right, then. How about we drink a toast? To ending the day better than it began."

"Indeed." This morning's disappointment seemed very far away. She tapped the rim of her glass to his, then turned back to the view. "When you told me you were going to charm the socks off me, I didn't believe you, but I have to admit you've been amazingly charming these past few hours."

"Woe on you for doubting."

The sound of laughter drifted upward. Rosalind looked down to see a group walking on the sidewalk across from them. One of them started singing—a raucous, off-tune carol that had the rest of the group joining along. They unknowingly serenaded them until they disappeared around a corner.

As she listened to their song fade in the distance, her skin began to tingle with awareness. Thomas was watching her with an odd gaze.

"I'm sorry about this morning," he said.

"You rallied late in the day. That's what counts."

"I hope so. Thank you. Guess you could say, I'm working extra hard to keep my promises these days."

"A man of his word." The sincerity in his voice touched her in a way that went deeper than attraction. A part of her was unlocking.

"I'm trying to be," Thomas replied. There was more to the answer. Rosalind could sense the unspoken words and sensed they were important. "I want you to know that there's nothing that means as much to me as our being a family again."

"I know."

A beat passed between them and another part of her unlocked. The world seemed to contract to the two of them and their little terrace.

"Did we really camp out by the fireplace every Christmas Eve?" she asked.

His chuckle was like smoke rising into the darkness. "Those nights are some of my favorite Christmas memories. In fact, I'm pretty sure that's how we got Maddie."

"Oh." Her cheeks burned at the images that came to mind. Wasn't a far jump to go from imagining Thomas stretched out before a fire to imagining...other things.

"Why do you ask?"

"We should do it again this year. Not that," she corrected, earning another sultry chuckle, "but the toasted cheese sandwiches and mulled wine. With Maddie. I don't remember the last time, and I wouldn't mind having the memory again." The fact she was looking at his hands—his strong, capable hands—as she made the suggestion was purely coincidental.

"I wouldn't mind giving you one," he replied with a smile.

Did the man's eyes have to be such a confoundingly beautiful color every time he looked in her direction?

"While we're on the subject..." Without breaking his stare, Thomas set his glass on the railing and stepped closer so that the fog from their breath mingled. "The two of us need to go Christmas shopping for our little angel. Something tells me Santa may want to bring her *slightly more* than cookies."

"Don't forget the friend for Bigsby."

"How could I? We could make an evening of it. Dinner. Dancing. Whatever you'd like."

That his eyes dropped to her lips while he was making his suggestion was definitely not coincidental. Or maybe it was. Rosalind's mouth ran dry regardless. "Are you suggesting a date, Mr Collier?"

"If you're interested, Mrs Collier."

Rosalind ran her tongue across her lips, grateful that he used the moment to bend over and retrieve the wine bottle. How many times had she watched his shoulder muscles flex as he poured liquid? How many times had they bantered? Was it always this natural and easy?

Frustration over her inability to answer clogged her throat. "I wish I could remember when we were dating," she caught herself saying. "I wish I remember a lot of things. Everything, really."

"You will," Thomas assured her. "Look how much has come back just today."

Bits and pieces. And while the flashes were wonderful, they were only glimpses of scenes, not full-blown recollections.

"I know I should be grateful that I'm remembering anything at all. The past months I'd come to terms with the blankness in my head. But now… I want to remember so badly and I can't. I've tried and I can't."

"You always did hate not being in control."

"What?" She started to get angry until she realized he was teasing. His way of keeping her from going down the rabbit hole of frustration. "That is not true," she told him.

"Oh, really? Where do you think our little princess got her tenacious streak?"

"I… That's not the same thing."

Thomas arched a brow.

"It's not," she persisted.

"How hard have you been trying to remember since yesterday?"

Rosalind thought of all the photographs she'd stared at over the last twenty-four hours. Hoping for some glimmer of recognition. "Not that hard."

He chuckled again, the throaty sound pooling in her stomach in spite of her albeit-slight annoyance. "It's all right," he told her. "I happen to like that tenacity. It's why you're sitting here with me tonight. It takes true strength to survive what you've been through. But then you've always been a strong woman. Determined."

His fingers caught in her hair, combing through the strands. "I should have realized rushing water and a damaged car couldn't stop you."

This time she chuckled. Low and shy. "You make me sound like way more than I am."

"Not to me," he whispered.

Rosalind's heart fluttered. He was looking at her with such sincerity and wonder. Like in her dream, she felt pulled under. Drowning in a flood of nerves and awareness. She reached for her wine.

Why? What was she afraid of? They were married. Shouldn't she feel this kind of intense attraction?

Perhaps the answer wasn't to avoid, but to explore?

Thomas's lips glistened from the wine. She brushed at the sheen with her fingers. "Kiss me," she whispered.

CHAPTER SEVEN

HAD HE HEARD RIGHT?

For the past two hours Thomas had been fighting the urge to touch his wife. Every accidental brush of their fingers, every shy sideways glance had him aching with the desire to wrap his arms around her. The need wasn't even sexual. He simply wanted to feel her closeness. The way it had been before everything fell to pieces.

Her request sounded too good to be true.

There was desire in her darkened eyes though. And the fingers tracing a feathery path along his jaw had him stifling a groan.

Who was he to pass up the moment?

Shifting closer, he trailed the back of his hand down her cheek before sliding his fingers into her hair. He'd always loved how easily the strands slipped through them.

"I thought you'd never ask," he whispered.

She sighed, and he touched his lips to hers. Gently. Once. Twice.

On the third kiss, her lips parted and their mouths slanted together as though they'd never been apart. They moved in perfect rhythm.

Rosie, Rosie, Rosie. His brain chanted her name like a mantra. How he'd missed her. She might not remember him, but her body knew. She surged into him, her hands tangling in his hair.

"It's been so long," he whispered. "I missed you so much." He backed her against the rail, pressing into her so she could feel how badly he needed her. In return, she moaned and clutched his shoulders. The soft sound was nearly his undoing. If they didn't head downstairs, he was going to lose it right there on the terrace.

Peppering her face with butterfly kisses, he scooped her into his arms.

"Thomas, wait."

He looked down at her glazed expression. Her eyes were hooded, dark with desire, but something was off. The trembling in her body wasn't from desire.

Slowly he lowered her to her feet. Even in the dark, he knew there was apology in her eyes. "I'm sorry," she whispered.

She needn't be. It was too soon. She'd wanted a kiss, and in obliging, he had forgotten himself. He stroked the hair from her cheek, letting his thumb graze her swollen lips. "You'd better get inside before you get cold."

Rosalind closed the door to her bedroom and shut her eyes. What had she been thinking? Asking Thomas to kiss her. The man had real feelings and memories. Until she was certain she could return them, what right did she have to experiment with their attraction?

Then again, she hadn't expected the attraction to flare so dramatically. When he'd kissed her, it was as if she'd been ripped open emotionally. Everything—his touch, his taste—had overwhelmed her. Flooded her with sensations she couldn't explain. Without context they terrified her.

There were still too many questions. Instinct nagged at her that there was something being left from the picture Thomas painted. Then there was her run-in with Richard.

While 99 percent of her had been consumed by Thomas's kisses, there was a tiny voice whispering, *Contrite, contrite*, in her ear. What had Richard been talking about?

She needed more. Time. Information. Memories. Her brain needed to catch up with her body.

In the meantime, she'd try to forget how Thomas's kiss seemed to reach to her soul. Not to mention the pain she saw in his face when she'd walked away.

Another emergency. Naturally. Thomas threw his phone on to the bed where it bounced off a pillow and became lost in the covers. He was already in a horrible mood thanks to a rotten night's sleep. He did not need another problem dragging him into the office on yet another day he should be spending with his wife. He wanted—no, he needed to see where they stood after last night's kiss. He needed to know if his fears regarding her retreat were real or not.

The question had kept him up half the night. He'd tried to talk to her last night, but when he'd knocked on her door, she hadn't answered.

Did she regret asking him to kiss her? That's what he feared. At the time, he'd hoped the passion might jostle her memory, remind her how good they'd been. But last night, standing on the wrong side of her bedroom door, a different fear had gripped him. What if her feelings were truly gone? Not lost in amnesia but gone. What if she'd given up on them before that weekend she'd spent in Cumbria, and no amount of recollection could bring the feelings back?

Those were the questions he'd hoped to explore this morning until the blasted phone rang. Honest to God, what would this company do without him?

What would he do without Collier's?

Survive, same way he did before. He answered his own question. He didn't *need* Collier's. He needed Rosalind. And he intended to show her how much.

But first, he had to put out today's office fire.

By the time he was out of the shower and dressed, Rosalind's bedroom door was open. He found her in the library with Maddie. The two of them were in bathrobes and were giggling as Rosalind had the little girl hoisted on her shoulders. Although their backs were to him, he could see the angel tree-topper in Maddie's hand. She was stretching to reach the top branch to no avail. The tree had, after all, been bought with his shoulders in mind, not Rosalind's.

"It's no use," he heard Rosalind say. "I'm too short. We'll have to wait until your father's done talking on the phone."

Thomas's conscience pricked and he vowed to get his business done as quickly as possible.

"Looks like someone needs to grow a couple of inches," he said.

"Daddy. We're doing the angel."

"So I see." Catching Maddie by the waist, he lifted her up and over Rosalind's head and on to his shoulders. Stepping as close as possible, he waited patiently for her to arrange the angel.

"Thank you," Rosalind said once they were finished. Maddie immediately ran off to retrieve Bigsby, leaving them alone. "She woke up determined to finish what she didn't get to accomplish last night."

"Funny, so did I."

While she smiled at the remark, Rosalind backed away before he could kiss her good-morning. "Sorry. Last night was—"

Please don't say a mistake.

"—a mistake. I got caught up in the wine and the moment and pushed for something before I was ready."

"It was a kiss," Thomas said. In the sense that Collier's soap was just another soap. But for her sake, he tried to downplay it.

"It's just too soon," she repeated. "Everything is new, except it's not new and I can't tell if a feeling is from memory or if it's happening now. Or maybe it's not a feeling at all—I'm just forcing the emotion."

She turned to him her eyes shining. "Am I making sense?"

Yes, she was. Unfortunately. Hurt like a kick between the legs, but he understood. "I shouldn't have pushed you last night."

She gave him a sideways look. "Appreciate the chivalry, but I was the one who asked you."

"For a kiss. Not an explosion of pent-up need." Seeing her breath quicken and the red seep down her neck and into her cheeks, Thomas knew he'd succeeded in painting an accurate picture.

"Apology accepted," she murmured.

"I promised you before that I wouldn't make you be anything you weren't ready to be. That includes doing anything before you're ready as well. Of course, I might take a few hundred cold showers."

"Only a few hundred?" she asked with a laugh. "I'm insulted."

"Did I say 'hundred?' I meant a few hundred thousand."

"Better." Their eyes connected and they smirked broadly at one another. "Seriously, though," Rosalind said. "You don't mind going slow?"

Unable to help himself, he caught her chin and, even though it probably violated her request, thumbed her plump lower lip. "I'll let a snail beat me, if that's what you need."

"Thank you." To his surprise, she rose on tiptoes to press a kiss to his cheek.

"You look dapper this morning," she said afterward. Since he hoped not to be long, he'd forgone his suit in favor of a jacket and sweater.

Rosalind's hands smoothed his lapel while he focused

on trying to not touch where she'd kissed him, like a teen-age boy.

"I feel underdressed—oh."

It was like a switch being turned off. One moment her eyes were sparkling, the next they'd grown distant and hurt. How many times did that look anger him last spring? And haunt him over the summer?

"I'll be as fast as I can," he said. Inside, he kicked himself knowing how many times he'd said the same line in the past and failed to follow through. As many times as he'd said the next line: "I wouldn't go in if this wasn't important."

In his mind, he heard her familiar reply. *It's always important.*

This Rosalind, the one who didn't remember her lines, shrugged. Then she said coolly, "No need to rush on our account. Maddie and I will find something to do."

Thomas was wrong. She did remember her lines. "This really is important. There's another snag with the new product line." He needed production to recalculate its estimates and personally reassure his European distributors. "Collier's future depends on my making sure this new product is a success."

"I know. It's fine."

No, it wasn't fine. He wanted to be here with them. Did Rosalind realize he wasn't abandoning them by choice? That he had to be the one making the decisions? He was so close to getting Colliers on stable ground. Then things would be different. *He* would be different. If only she could see that he truly had learned his lesson when she walked out last spring.

But then, how could she see anything when it looked like he was repeating the same mistakes? And how could he tell her when doing so would only lead to the one conversation he wanted to avoid?

So he said nothing, choosing to stand in the middle of the room while she needlessly fluffed a cushion from the sofa.

"Why don't I work here?" The compromise smacked him on the side of the head. "I can do my business over the phone as easily as I can in person." For crying out loud, half the business was by phone. It was so obvious he didn't know why he didn't think about it before.

"I'll wrap up as quickly as possible, and then we can spend time together. Maybe take you round to your office and other favorite haunts— Dammit." He'd forgotten.

Rosalind turned around.

"I have to sign off on some documentation. I'll have Andrew bring over the final copy once we're finished." He reached for his phone.

"Don't," Rosalind said. "Don't inconvenience some employee so you can barricade yourself in the library all day."

"It won't be more than an hour or two. Three, tops."

"If that's what you want," Rosalind replied. She turned back to the cushions.

This was not the morning Thomas wanted, with tension hanging thick in the air. They might as well be back to last spring. If only he could close the curtains and bring back last night.

"I'll text and let you know what time I'll be home." Crossing the divide, he leaned in and kissed her cheek. A tiny sigh escaped her lips. "I won't be long," he said, his forehead resting against her temple. "I promise."

With that, he went to find his daughter and tell her the same.

Rosalind waited until she heard Thomas leave the room, then punched the cushion. She was being childish. She was disappointed that he was going into work instead of spending time with her, and acting irrationally. The man ran a company. Corporate emergencies happened. It just felt like emergencies happened a lot since she came home.

Didn't excuse her from acting their daughter's age. What did she expect? First she tells the man she didn't remember him, then that she wanted the right to leave after the New Year. To top it all off, she kissed him, then told him she needed to take it slow. And now she was annoyed he wasn't ignoring his business to be with her.

Like she said, irrational.

What disturbed her most, however, was the intensity of her irritation. Her hurt felt old and festering. What's more, the bad mood was causing a headache to form at the base of her neck. Great. A migraine. Was she prone to them, or were they to be another gift from her accident? She pinched the bridge of her nose.

For crying out loud, Rosalind, what do you expect me to do? We're talking about my family's company!

I thought we *were your family.*

The rest of the argument faded away, leaving anger behind. She was right. Her anger was old. Was she overreacting because of an event in the past?

Pinching harder, she tried to bring the memory back. Nothing. Much as she hated her inability, she couldn't force something before its time.

Deciding she needed a cup of coffee, she left the library and headed downstairs. The change in atmosphere astounded her. From comfortable to cold in forty steps. Her neck and shoulders tensed. The room made her feel like she was wearing the wrong skin.

The dining room table was already set with coffee and her pastries. Someone would come out shortly to see if she needed anything else. There was "someone" to do everything. She'd felt like an interloper baking in the kitchen yesterday.

It wasn't the décor that felt ill fitting. It was the whole lifestyle.

All of a sudden she felt very alone, stuck in a large house with no one to explain her feelings to. *I want to go home*, she thought. Only she was home. That was the problem.

The phone Thomas had given her was in the pocket of her robe. She'd been about to call Chris and Jessica to give them an update when Maddie had asked about the angel. She needed to hear the sound of their voices more than ever.

Voice mail. They must have gone early to the fish market. Chris never missed it. She left a quick message telling them she'd call back later. Hopefully, her voice sounded upbeat enough. She didn't want to worry him.

The phone was barely back in her pocket before it rang.

"I said I'd call back," she laughed. "You didn't have to drop everything."

"Oh, good. You're awake. I wasn't sure if it was too early to reach you."

Rosalind looked at the caller ID, and then smiled. Richard. Nice to know there was someone eager for her company. "Good morning to you too. I'm glad you called."

"The announcement about your return was on the news last night although the story didn't give much detail. Just that you were found in Scotland and the family was only recently notified about your survival. Apparently, Thomas asked for privacy, but I assume that didn't mean friends. Well, maybe he did, but I don't care. I've missed you way too much."

Another person declaring feelings she couldn't recall. "I'm really sorry. There are so many things I don't remember."

"There's no need to apologize. You have amnesia. Ask

me anything you want, and I'll try to fill you in best I can. That is, if you'd like me to."

Oh, would she ever. "Thank you."

For the next half hour, Richard told Rosalind about her job at the university, her research and its demise. "We were all furious when you lost your funding. Losing you was like a giant hole had been carved into the offices. Texting you was not nearly the same as stealing you away for three-martini lunches."

"We had three-martini lunches?"

"Not really. More like one beer and chips at the pub, but they were glorious lunches regardless. Although I'm not sure your husband was too fond of them."

Instinct suggested Richard was right. Clearly, there wasn't any love lost between the men. This was her chance to find out why. "About Thomas," she said. "Why did you say he must be contrite now that I'd returned? What exactly would he need to feel apologetic about?"

On the other end, there was silence as he chose his words. "Well…" he began.

Rosalind listened intently.

"I figured out the Collier curse," Linus announced as he entered the conference room.

"Our lack of doors with locks?" Thomas replied.

"Very funny."

"I'm not joking. I don't have time for your witty insights right now. I have a video conference with our French partner in ten minutes." Then he had to get home with at least part of the day to spare. How was it lawyers could turn one small problem into a multi-day disaster?

Linus being Linus, he didn't care what Thomas had on his plate. He pushed Thomas's electronic tablet toward the center of the conference table and perched himself on the edge. "Genetics," he said.

"I was in the middle of reviewing figures," Thomas replied.

"I'm serious, Thommy-boy. It dawned on me this morning. The Colliers lack the moderation gene."

"You're going to be lacking something else if you don't move. I need to have those figures."

Never mind. He'd walk around to the other side and grab the blasted tablet himself.

"Did you know that I haven't had a day off in over two years?" Linus asked.

"So, take a few days off. No one's stopping you."

"You're making my point. I'm stopping me. I keep telling myself that taking time off is only worthwhile if I take a true break. I'm talking a month or more. And how can I take that much time if the company's in flux?"

"The cost of sharing a name with the company," Thomas replied. "Why do you think I'm here instead of with my wife?" When yours were the shoulders people relied on to carry the burden, there were some luxuries you couldn't afford.

The thought left an uneasy feeling in the pit of his stomach.

"Then how come other executives manage? They manage to have lives. Vacations. Families. And yet, you, me, Susan—we don't. Ergo, the Colliers must be genetically incapable of work-life moderation. That is our curse."

"No," Thomas replied. "My curse is having a brother interrupting my business and preventing me from getting home so I can have work-life balance." This morning's conversation with Rosalind haunted him, and Linus's comments weren't helping.

"As soon as I finish this call, I'm going home. And, for your information, I plan to *stay* home. I'm going to turn off my phone, unplug my email and go dark until after Christmas."

Linus snorted.

"You don't believe me."

"Oh, I believe you."

"Then what's the problem?"

"You proved my point. All in or all out. Genetics, bro. The three of us need to figure out a way around them."

Thomas's fingers curled around the tablet. This morning's conversation with Rosalind haunted him. He was standing at a very important crossroad where he could either repeat his mistakes or work to bring her closer. Now was not the time for one of Linus's theories. Especially one that cut so close.

He needed to go home and spend time with his wife before the distance he sensed this morning grew stronger.

Ninety minutes later, Thomas entered his apartment with renewed resolve. He'd finished his video conference in record time, but he'd made it clear to the entire staff that barring a national emergency he was not to be disturbed. From here on, his focus would be on Rosalind and only Rosalind.

"I'm home!" he called, closing the door. Quiet answered him. "Rosalind?"

Maddie's coat was gone from the closet, as was Mrs Faison's. They must have gone to the park again.

He headed upstairs to find Rosalind's bedroom door shut. Memories of other days with closed bedroom doors caused the hair on the back of his neck to start to rise. Twisting the knob, he opened the door and slowly stepped inside.

"Is everything all right?"

The shades had been pulled, filling the room with shadows. Rosalind lay on top of the covers, a hand covering her eyes. For a moment, Thomas simply stood, taking in how beautiful she looked in the dim light. Once upon a time, he'd have slipped into the space next to her and smoothed the hair from her scalp. Hell, even yesterday he might have considered the gesture. After this morning, however, he found himself rocking uncertainly on his feet.

"Rosie?" he whispered, afraid to speak loudly and spoil the scene.

"I'm awake," came the monotone reply.

He allowed himself to move closer until he settled on the edge of the bed. Although his hands wanted to reach out, he clasped them between his knees. "Migraine?" he asked.

"How observant of you."

"Is there anything I can do?"

"Sure." She opened her eyes. In spite of the dimness, Thomas could feel their chill. A side effect of the migraine. Had to be.

"What do you need? Water? A blanket."

"I was thinking more about answers."

Answers? About what?

"After you left, I had another flash of memory," she told him.

"You did?"

"We were having an argument."

"Oh." He tried to keep his features schooled in a semblance of calm despite the uneasiness creeping down his back. "That shouldn't be a surprise. Married people argue all the time."

"I think this was more than a marital spat. We were arguing about work. About your work and your complete disregard for your family."

There it was, the first brick being pulled from what little foundation he'd managed to build. This was exactly the conversation he'd feared. "I'm not sure what to say." That she was viewing the situation through a small filtered lens? That she was misreading circumstances?

This was what he got for gambling on his charm as a distraction.

Blasted hindsight was always twenty-twenty, wasn't it? Standing, he walked across the room to where the dark brown drapes shrouded the window. He should open them so they could have a proper talk in the light of day, but somehow it seemed more fitting to continue in the dark.

She was waiting for him to respond.

"We did argue about my job," he said. "I told you that when we first moved to London, we planned on the move being temporary. Neither of us were prepared for my father to take a bad turn. Or for how many hours I would have to put in taking over. There was a little...friction."

"More than a little friction," she corrected.

"We—"

"I talked to Richard Sinclair."

Thomas should have known. "And I'm sure he was more than eager to fill in your memory, wasn't he?"

"Why wouldn't he? He's my friend."

A friend who preferred that his playmate didn't like spending time with her husband.

There was a crack in the curtains. He pried the cloth apart and looked down on St. James's Street. Behind him, the mattress squeaked as Rosalind shifted her weight. "Richard told me that before the accident we'd been having problems."

"We were going through a rough patch."

"He said we'd been having problems for quite some time. That after you took over your father's company, you became a completely different person, forgetting everything that was important to you. To us."

"This wasn't about us. I was trying to ensure the survival of the company. For Maddie."

"I'm sure our five-year-old daughter will be thrilled

to know she has money in the bank the next time you're unavailable."

"Don't." Thomas whirled around. "Don't you dare suggest I've been unavailable. I have been available every day for the last six months. I didn't see your friend Richard running over here to help out in your memory."

Rosalind was sitting up against the headboard. She had her arms folded across her chest. "Have you looked at the pictures on the mantle recently?"

The abrupt change of topic threw him, as did her sudden change of tone. She was using the same composed, purposeful tone he used when about to prove a point.

"Not recently. Why?"

"There's one on the far left. A formal shot of the three of us. Maddie's wearing a pastel dress."

"Last year's Easter portrait," he replied, knowing the photo immediately. He kept it out year-round because it was the last shot taken of the three of them together. "What about it?"

"I was studying it this afternoon. Comparing it to the others. You and I look miserable."

"We're smiling."

"We're smiling at the camera." Rosalind looked askance at him. "Our mouths have smiles but we aren't smiling."

Thomas didn't argue. Why bother? He knew exactly what she meant, and she was right.

"I had the same expression in the other recent photos you showed me. From your phone."

The fund-raiser. He remembered it well. Rosalind had been surprised he'd attended, had almost seemed to resent that he had.

"So, I need to ask." She turned so they could look each other in the eye. "How bad were our problems?"

Did he deflect the question? Turn the conversation to a different topic and buy himself a little more time?

After all, avoidance worked so well the last time.

No, he couldn't. They'd exchanged vows. He'd promised to love and honor. Whatever the fallout, he owed her an honest answer.

It was time to face the music.

"Bad," he answered. "Things were very bad."

CHAPTER EIGHT

"I KNEW THERE was something you weren't telling me."

Even suspecting the answer, hearing Thomas say it out loud crushed her. During their call, Richard had reluctantly filled her in on the fact her marriage had been rocky. Thomas was a workaholic, he'd said, who continually placed business over family. He'd eagerly fallen back into his wealthy and privileged lifestyle, completely ignoring Rosalind's wishes for a simple, uncomplicated life.

"Whenever I mentioned Cumbria, I could feel this shadow," she said. "Foolish me, I thought I was bringing up bad memories, but really you didn't want to talk about the place because you were afraid I'd remember wanting a divorce."

Thomas paled.

"Richard told me," she said.

"Of course he did. Good friend that he is."

"At least he told me the truth, unlike my husband."

She was furious. Too furious to rant and rave. How dare he bring her back here and make her think they were some happy little family? Seduce her into kissing him with his soulful blue eyes?

"All that information. Not one mention that we were separated."

"Because we weren't," Thomas shot back. "We weren't separated.

"You said you needed a couple of days alone to think. Without Maddie or me around to distract you. So you went to Cumbria for the weekend. A weekend, no more. You didn't want to leave Maddie for longer. And then you had your accident. But despite what Richard thinks, we— you—never made any decisions."

She looked down at the ring on her left hand. "I took off my wedding ring."

"Which you always did when working in the field. That part is the truth. I'd… I told myself you took off your ring before you drove to Scotland because you thought you might be outside."

Or had she decided they were over? Had she driven north looking for a new home for her and Maddie? Rosalind twisted at the band. The pillow beside her smelled like Thomas. Funny how that was the first detail to pop into her head, but then she had spent the night with her face buried in the scent.

"Two weeks." Her voice sounded flat to her ears. "We've been talking for two weeks. Why didn't you say something?"

"What was I supposed to say? I'd been mourning you for months. Suddenly, I find you in Scotland and I was overjoyed. All I could think about was the fact you were alive."

A tiny bit of her anger leaked away at his answer. Just a tiny bit however, because once the shock had worn off, he still had had plenty of opportunities to fill in the pieces.

What hurt the most was that her heart had started to open to him. There had been so much promise in his kiss, in his eyes.

"Were you ever going to tell me?" she asked. "Or were

you just going to wait until the memory popped back into my head?"

Across the room, Thomas studied the carpeting.

"Great. In other words, you were going to play me for a fool." Again, she thought of their kiss, and her heart cracked a little. Worse, he didn't have a single word of defense.

She lay back down, turning her back to the windows. "I think you should leave."

"I thought if you stayed long enough and we spent time together, you would see things differently. That you'd see that I was different."

His confession wasn't what Rosalind expected.

"Different how?" she asked, rolling over.

"When you went missing, I thought the guilt would cut me off at the knees. It was my fault you went away. I'd made the same mistake my father and grandfather had made, and as a result Maddie didn't have a mother. It made me realize that I should have paid more attention to what mattered.

"When you returned and you didn't remember, I realized I had a second chance. I wasn't trying to lie to you, Rosie. I swear."

No, lying wasn't his style. She didn't need her memory back to know he wasn't malicious. Avoidance of the issue made much more sense. "I believe you."

His face brightened. "You do?"

"Yes."

"You have no idea—"

"But." She stopped him before he could come closer. "It doesn't change anything. That things are different."

"But you just said you believed me."

"Your apology," she said. "But are circumstances truly different?"

"Of course they are."

"Really? What do you call today? Or yesterday? Or the day before that? For crying out loud, Thomas, you couldn't stay away from the office when your wife returned from the dead."

From the way he looked away, she could tell her point had met its mark. "I admit, the past couple of days there have been some emergencies, but I promise there won't be anymore."

"Until there is one," she replied.

"You don't understand…"

A chip of conversation popped into her head. *You don't understand. Collier's needs me right now.* It set her teeth on edge. Her anger returned. He'd dragged her from the home and life she loved, only to abandon them for an executive office.

As far as she could tell, he still was.

"Actually, what I understand is why I needed a weekend away," she told him.

Another direct hit. This time he winced. And, foolish her, she wanted to literally drop everything, to rush and console him.

How could she feel sympathy for him when she was the victim?

"You want to separate. Is that what you're saying?"

Was it? "I need space," she said, déjà vu overwhelming her. "Time to think and learn about my life again. Remember my life again. Or have you forgotten that little problem?"

"I haven't forgotten."

Silently they assessed one another, the clock on her nightstand ticking off the passing seconds. In what was an incredible display of emotional management, Thomas eased the tense set of his shoulders, switching from apologetic husband to a man in control. A company president.

"Nor have I forgotten you promised to stay until after the New Year," he said finally.

So that was his issue. Rosalind keeping her promise. Ironic.

"Don't worry. I have no intention of ruining Maddie's Christmas. I'll stay here until January. After that, I think it might be a good idea if she and I stayed somewhere else for a while. To give us time to bond and for me to:...think."

"Fine," Thomas replied.

"Fine," Rosalind repeated. She was trying not to let the gleam in his eye make her insides squirrelly. "Now, if you'll excuse me, I need to lie down. My head is killing me."

She rolled back over, keeping her eyes closed until she heard the bedroom door shut. Only then did she give a soft sob.

One conversation and they were back to where they were six months ago. Thomas couldn't say he didn't have it coming. He should have been honest about the state of their marriage when he'd found her in Scotland.

Face it. You were too afraid she'd slip out of your life again.

"Aargh!" He scrubbed his hands over his face. How did he let the best thing that ever happened to him get so messed up?

He headed into the living room and found himself wandering toward the fireplace. Next week, the decorator would be in to overdeck the halls. Thomas knew because his assistant had marked the date in his calendar. If it was like last year, that meant lots of draped greenery and candles. In the meantime, the photo Rosalind had been talking about, the Easter portrait, remained where Rosalind said it was. The three of them were seated in the living room, Maddie perched between her parents. It had taken forever to keep her from squirming. Rosalind looked as beautiful as always with her hair swept back and her soft pink dress. Thomas wondered if he would ever look at her and not think she was the most beautiful woman in the world.

Once his heart finished skipping a beat, he took a closer look. And frowned. Rosalind was right: they looked miserable.

"No more," Thomas said to himself as he flipped the photo facedown. He wasn't done fighting. Not by a long shot. It might mean changing his timetable as far as Collier's was concerned, but dammit he would do whatever it took to keep his marriage alive. If that meant risking Collier's legacy, so be it.

CHAPTER NINE

"MUMMY, MUMMY, MUMMY…" Maddie's whisper was more of an excited squeal. Bouncing up and down, she yanked on Rosalind's sweater. "He's here!"

"What?" Rosalind turned her attention from the email Richard just sent her. "Who's here?"

"Santa! He's downstairs. Do you think he's here to check on me? I said he didn't have to bring me anything because you came home."

"Slow down and catch your breath before you turn blue. What's this about Santa Claus?" She swore the little girl was getting more wound up by the day. The abundance of Christmas cookies and the arrival of a fifteen-foot-tall tree in the living room didn't help. At this point, the girl would pop a spring by Christmas Eve.

"He's downstairs," Maddie insisted. "I saw him talking to Daddy."

She sighed. Probably someone Thomas hired to spread Christmas cheer. Since their argument the other day, she swore he was proving some kind of point by being home every day. Of course, being Thomas, he couldn't simply be in the apartment. He had to fill the apartment with his presence. His laugh would insist on drifting down the corridor. The air pulsated with his proximity. The other day she swore she could smell his scent on every piece of furniture, including her bedsheets.

And if that wasn't bad enough, she'd had to spend last night by the fireplace listening to him reading Christmas stories to Maddie. He was marvelous with her. It was obvious the two of them had developed a special bond during her absence. Watching him with her last night, his voice gentle and sweet, her heart had skipped more than a few beats. And now, he'd arranged for Santa.

This was all well and good, but as Richard's conversation reminded her, once he'd proved his point and won her over, Thomas would revert right back to form. *Don't you deserve someone who understands what you need?* he'd asked.

All right, that particular line was a bit presumptuous.

"Mummy. Come on. Before he leaves." Maddie grabbed her hand and started pulling her toward the library door. "I think he's here on a special mission because he's not in his suit, but I recognized him anyway."

"Slow down. What do you mean he's not in his— Chris!" She called the man's name from over the banister.

He and Thomas stood with their backs to the stairway admiring the Christmas tree. Even so, she'd recognize him anywhere. At the sound of his name, he turned around, his bearded cheeks splitting into a giant smile. "Merry Christmas, Lammie!" He stretched out his arms. Rosalind hurried down the stairs and into the waiting hug. He smelled of peppermint and Scotch pine.

"It's so good to see you," she murmured against his chest.

"It's good to see you too. I was just telling your husband that I had business in the city, so I thought I'd come by and see what my favorite waitress was up to."

She drew back in his arms. "Why didn't you say something when we talked the other night?"

"I wanted it to be a surprise."

"Well, you succeeded." As she hugged him a second time, she glanced past him to Thomas who was watching them with a wistful expression.

"Mummy, you know him?" Maddie was looking up at Chris with giant eyes.

"She thinks you're Santa Claus," Rosalind whispered.

"Is that so?" Immediately Chris knelt down, his eyes twinkling merrily. "How are you today, Miss Madeline?"

Upon hearing him say her name, Maddie's eyes grew even larger, if such a thing was possible. Rosalind had to stifle a giggle.

"First time I've seen her speechless," Thomas remarked.

"Your mum and dad tell me you've been a very good girl this year. Is that true?"

Maddie nodded. "No matter what Jaime Kensington says," she added.

"I'm glad to hear it," Chris said with a chuckle. "I came by to see your mummy and make sure she's being good, as well. Is she?"

"Uh-huh. Daddy too. Last night he read me a story about a mouse who saved Christmas, and we had Christmas cookies."

So much for speechless.

"Cookies, you say." He gave a chuckle. "I don't suppose you have any more, do you? I've always had a fondness for Christmas cookies."

"We have tons. I'll get you a whole plate."

"I'll go with her," Thomas volunteered. "I asked the housekeeper to make tea."

"A lovely girl, Lammie," Chris said once they were out of earshot. "Sounds like she's got a bit of a brain in her head too."

"More than a bit," she said. "There are times when I can't believe I could have forgotten…" Damn. She thought she'd pushed past the guilt, but a lump found its way to her throat anyway. "Sorry."

"No need. You've been through a lot. Emotions are bound to creep up on you now and again."

"You can say that again," she replied with a sniff. "Sometimes I don't know what I'm feeling."

"What do you mean?"

"Nothing. I'm babbling is all." The last thing she wanted was to spoil his visit by causing him to worry.

"Now, don't go telling me it's nothing." Chris arched a bushy brow. "I'm Santa, remember? I can tell when someone's not telling me the whole story."

"I thought your powers were limited to judging naughty and nice."

"I have all sorts of powers," he told her. "Why don't you sit down and tell me how you're really doing?"

As briefly as she could, since the others were due back, she told him about the separation. "Turns out we weren't the happy family Thomas claimed we were."

"He certainly seemed happy to see you in the restaurant," Chris said. "Overjoyed."

"Sure, because he'd thought I was dead. But that doesn't erase the problems we were apparently having. According to Richard—"

"Who?"

"A colleague of mine from the university. He's been helping me fill in some of the blanks. What's wrong?"

He was frowning. "Nothing's wrong," he said. "Far be it from me to tell you how to handle your situation, but I have to say I'm surprised you're not asking Thomas to fill in these blanks."

"Thomas has filled in some, as well," she replied, a little more defensively than she would have liked. She didn't want to tell him that with Thomas, every trip down memory lane left her topsy-turvy with emotions.

The sound of footsteps and chatter stopped them from saying any more. A second later, Maddie skipped into the room, a piece of paper clutched in one hand and a cookie in the other. Thomas trailed behind her carrying the tea set.

"We picked out three kinds of cookies," Maddie announced. "The ones with the jam are my favorite."

"They look delicious," Chris replied. "Jessica sent some of her famous shortbread for me to give you, but…" He patted his belly. "It was a long flight."

"We'll tell her they were delicious regardless, won't we, Rosie? Although I think she'll learn your secret when your trousers are suddenly too tight." Thomas winked in her direction as he reached for a biscuit. Rosalind cursed her stomach for fluttering.

"I'm afraid Jessica's been onto my secret for years," Chris said. "I gain weight every December."

No wonder, Rosalind thought as she eyed the stack on his plate. She poured the adults their tea and added a small amount of milk to a teacup for Maddie.

As she was handing Chris his cup—in between cookies— he remarked, "The whole town is buzzing about the soap factory's expansion. Your investment is going to do quite a lot for the community."

Thomas was investing in McDermott's soap factory?

"That was the emergency meeting we had the other day," Thomas replied. "Although to be fair, the bank is putting up the funds for the expansion. Collier's simply subcontracted them to do business with us. I've got to admit I was very impressed with their capabilities. With luck, this expansion will be a good decision for both of us."

"I know Ryan McDermott's eager to prove your confidence right."

"I'm eager for him to prove it, as well. I'd hate to be the Collier who killed the company." He laughed as he made the comment, but Rosalind noticed his smile wavered at the edges.

"Two centuries is a long time for a company to survive, that's for sure." Chris clicked his tongue. "Here I thought my one little restaurant was a handful. I can't imagine keeping a company afloat for that long. Soap must run in your veins."

This time, Thomas's laugh was fuller and less tremulous. "Wouldn't surprise me. I wasn't much older than Maddie when I made my first scented soap."

"Really?" Rosalind was surprised.

Chris took another cookie from his stack. "Pretty young age to be working in a laboratory."

"Oh, no, we weren't in the lab, although my brother Linus probably would have loved if we were. This was the company museum."

"Collier's has a museum?" Rosalind wondered what else about the company she didn't remember.

"A small one. On the first floor of the corporate building. It's mostly articles and newsreels about Collier's contribution through history. Our role in the war efforts and things like that. But there are a couple of hands-on displays, as well. It's very popular with school field trips. My grandfather brought us there to introduce us to the Collier heritage.

"Anyway," he continued, "they had this corner where you could combine different oils and make your own soap scent. To this day, I'm shocked pine-lemon-musk never made it to market."

"Quite a combination," Chris noted.

"The word is *pungent*," Thomas replied, causing the older man to chuckle. "Grandfather said it made his eyes water. After that, it was decided I should stick to the marketing and management side of the business."

Decided? Rosalind frowned at the odd word. "But you were Maddie's age."

"There was never any question we would work for Collier's. When your family's been running a business for a couple centuries, it's more or less a given," he added.

Except that he didn't go to work for Collier's. They'd moved to Cumbria.

"My grandfather used to give this speech about how the company's history was intertwined with England's. A little over the top, but it got the point across."

"That you should be proud of your heritage," Chris said.

"Precisely." Thomas paused while he chewed the last of a cookie. "I don't think I truly appreciated what he was talking about until I had to walk in his shoes.

"Having half a dozen generations stare at you on the way to your office every morning will do that," he added with a smile.

Chris nodded, stroking his beard thoughtfully. "Must be a lot of pressure trying to live up to all those expectations," he said.

"It is, but there's something very satisfying about knowing you're keeping tradition alive. Or trying to."

There was no mistaking the pride in his voice or the passion. Rosalind could see both in the way his eyes brightened, as well. And tension. Like before, there was an undercurrent to his reference to the future. The stress of expectations Chris just mentioned? She shifted in her seat. This entire conversation was leaving her with an uneasy feeling. She was ashamed to say she hadn't realized how deep Thomas's ties to the company ran. Or maybe she did realize prior to the accident, but the discomfort nagging her felt as though she hadn't truly appreciated it.

"Makes me sorry I didn't remember that story," she said out loud.

"You wouldn't have," Thomas replied. "I never told you."

Really? Why not? She tried not to frown in front of their guest.

"Can I make soap smell too, Daddy?"

"You want to make soap?" Grabbing Maddie by the waist, Thomas scooped her on to his lap. "Tell you what. When you're a little bit older, I'll take you to the museum and you can make smelly soap."

"How much older?" Maddie asked.

"Seven. Same age as I was when I went. If it's all right with your mother," he said.

Rosalind resisted the urge to squirm under all three sets of eyes. Why did she suddenly feel like the bad guy? "Two years is a long way off. Shouldn't we be focused on something that's happening sooner, like Christmas?"

With that, the conversation shifted to the festive season and the Christmas present Chris planned to buy for Jessica while he was in London.

Still, despite the change in topic, Rosalind couldn't shake the disquiet left by Thomas's story. Silly that a childhood memory would unsettle her. Her automatic instinct was to chalk it up to jealousy since her current mental state left her childhood slate blank. But it was more than jealousy. It was that Thomas revealed a piece of himself that she hadn't known.

"Oh, my, will you look at how late it's getting?" Chris exclaimed. Two hours had disappeared along with the tea and two servings of cookies. "If I'm going to get those gourmet salts for Jessica, I'd better hurry. It was good to see you again, Thomas."

"It was good to see you again, Chris."

The two men rose and shook hands before Chris bent down to look Maddie in the eye. "And you, Miss Madeline. It's safe to say you've been a very good girl. I have no doubt your friend Bigsby will get that companion he's been wanting."

Maddie beamed. "This is for you," she said.

It was the piece of paper she'd been holding when she came from the kitchen. "I made it while Daddy was making tea. He helped me with the spelling."

Curious, Rosalind peered over and saw the words "Thank you" scrawled in messy red letters.

"For letting Mummy come home for Christmas early and letting her stay."

Rosalind's heart squeezed as she looked from the note to her daughter to Chris. The older man's eyes glistened with the same emotion. "You're most welcome, Miss Madeline," he told her. "It was my pleasure."

"How about me?" Rosalind asked. She was struggling to keep the moment light. This goodbye seemed harder than the last one. "Am I on the good list?"

"Absolutely." He crushed her with his embrace, allowing her a farewell whiff of peppermint and pine. "You've got a second chance with your family this Christmas," he whispered before kissing her cheek. "You can't get better than that."

CHAPTER TEN

"Did you really never tell me about your grandfather and all that?" Rosalind asked once Chris had departed. "Why not?"

"Never came up in conversation," he replied.

"Never? Surely we talked about our childhoods." Hadn't he implied as much the other day? "In fact, you said you envied my family's closeness."

"I did. From everything you described, the three of you were very close."

Nodding to herself, Rosalind walked over to the giant Christmas tree.

Since Thomas's comment, she'd been trying extra hard to remember the wonderful family unit he'd described. Bits and bobs had come to her. She'd remembered her father's sweaters always smelled of cloves, and of hiking in the woods. While each memory filled her with comfort, the recollections themselves were infused with significance, as though they were gifts to be treasured. She supposed they were, since she had only a handful of recollections in her head to draw upon.

Footsteps sounded and Thomas's figure appeared to her right. Immediately, awareness rippled through her. Was she ever going to be able to stand close to him and not have a physical reaction?

"Your family shared a legacy. I would think that made you close," she said.

"A different kind of closeness. Once you got outside the world of soap, the ties got a bit tenuous."

"Is that why you didn't go to work for your father after university?"

"Not at all."

"But you said yourself, you were raised to be part of the company."

"I thought it was obvious?" He poked a set of crystal bells, making them tinkle. "We haven't gone on our shopping expedition yet, you know."

"Shopping?" The comment very nearly sailed over her head; she was still stuck on the story he'd shared with Chris.

"For Maddie's Christmas presents. Now that Santa's told her she was on the nice list, the pressure is on to make sure Bigsby gets a BFF." He poked a different set of bells. The tree was covered with bells of various sizes. This set had a lower tone. "You're still willing to shop for her presents together?"

Like on a date. She remembered. "Of course," she replied. This was about Maddie. "When would you like to go?"

"Tomorrow evening?"

"Um…" Rosalind chewed the inside of her cheek. Richard had suggested he give her a tour of the university. She'd been tempted to go if for no other reason than to escape the awareness of Thomas's overwhelming presence for a few hours.

"Sure." Maddie's Christmas was more important.

Although when Thomas smiled, causing her stomach to involuntarily do a back handspring, she wondered how wise her decision had been.

The sight of his sister drumming her fingers was never good. That she was doing her drumming on his granite counter was even more bothersome.

Thomas held up his index finger while he completed his call, partly because he needed her to wait and partly to irritate her further. He balanced out his actions by moving a platter of sugar cookies to within her reach. "Two people. Seven thirty. By the window." He waited to ensure the hostess had the info correct before setting down the phone.

"Dinner plans?" Susan bit off a snowman's hat.

"Rosalind and I are going Christmas shopping. I figured that we might as well have dinner while we are out." If dinner happened to be at a romantic restaurant, well, he could hardly be blamed for the ambiance, could he?

There was still plenty of time before Christmas. He wasn't letting her walk away from their marriage without a fight.

"Is this part of your grand plan to sweep her off her feet before she remembers the two of you were separating?"

"May have been separating," Thomas quickly corrected. "She'd gone away to think. And to answer your question, it's none of your business. Now, what is the problem that has you invading my kitchen in the middle of the afternoon?"

"What makes you think there's a problem?"

Thomas waved his fingers. "You only drum when you're irritated or you're hungry. I've given you cookies."

"And I've stopped drumming."

But she was, however, still frowning. Which meant she was unhappy about something. "Is there a personnel problem I should know about?"

"Actually, I came by to do a wellness check. You haven't been to work in over a week." She took off the snowman's head and half his midsection before continuing. "Linus and I were afraid you'd died," she said with her mouth full.

"Very funny. I didn't realize my taking a few days off was such an oddity."

"Isn't it? The last time you took a break from the company it was for three years. We were afraid you might have decided to ditch us for the country again."

Ah, so that's what brought her to his kitchen. "You talked to Linus."

"Are you seriously planning to step down from the company?"

Thomas's shoulders grew stiff. He wasn't going to have this conversation. His focus was on convincing Rosalind to stay. "Eventually. Once we launch the spa line and I'm certain the company is stable again."

"The company is stable because you're in charge. You can't leave. Without you we'd still be sorting through the mess Dad made of things. And who is supposed to fill your shoes when you leave? There isn't anyone else in the family qualified to take over. Linus sure as hell won't leave his lab."

"How about you?"

She blinked. "Did you not pay attention when we were growing up? I'm Dad in a skirt. Worse, I'm my mother and Dad in a skirt. Besides, you love running the company. You were meant to run it."

Thomas sighed and reached for a cookie. Thing was, Susan was right. He did love running the company. All those speeches his grandfather had given turned out to mean something when he finally stepped into the head office.

But he also loved his wife.

"Susan, you and everyone else knew when I agreed to help out that it was temporary."

"Because she didn't want to be here."

Wow. For a person with a psychology background, his sister could be incredibly stubborn when it came to a grudge. "You can't hold it against Rosalind for preferring a different lifestyle. I'm the one who told her the move would be temporary and then dragged it out for almost two years."

"She didn't seem to have a problem with you sucking it up while she pursued her research."

"You forget I chose to suck it up." Because Rosalind was happy. And making Rosalind happy used to be enough to make him happy.

Was enough, he corrected.

Susan had gone back to drumming her fingers. He slid the cookies closer, but she didn't take the bait. "Monomania," she said, pushing the tray back.

"Okay," Thomas replied. Whatever that meant.

"It's the obsessive pursuit of a goal to the exclusion of everything else," Susan said. "Linus thinks that's your problem. Actually, he thinks it's a Collier problem." Apparently, Linus was sharing his theory with everyone. "Either way, I think he's wrong."

"No doubt you have your own theory, Dr Collier," Thomas replied.

"It's not that complicated. You're willing to sacrifice everything for a woman who isn't willing to return the favor. Did she even know how bad things were when you took over? Why you were working like a madman?"

"I told her my father had let business slide the last few years."

"In other words, no." She rolled her eyes. "Let me guess, you're not going to tell her now either."

"What would be the point?" It wouldn't change what happened. "I'm far more interested in fixing the future."

His sister pushed away from the island with a loud sigh. "You disagree," he said as she walked away.

"With you playing the villain while she doesn't have to take responsibility for her actions? Hell, yes, I disagree," she said.

He matched her sigh with one of his own. How many times did he have to repeat himself? "First of all, Rosalind doesn't remember her actions," he said. "Second, even if she did remember, it wouldn't change my role. I neglected my wife and daughter."

"Which she made known every chance she got, or have you forgotten how frostily she treated you last spring?"

"She was unhappy." Not to mention that Sinclair was around feeding the fire.

"You're unbelievable," Susan said. "Why does everything have to fall on your shoulders? Shouldn't she have to contribute, as well?"

"When the problems are my fault…"

"That's exactly my point. The problems aren't all your fault!" She leaned against the stove where she'd gone to turn on the kettle. "I love you, Thomas, but honest to God, it drives me crazy the way you treat her like she's this faultless angel."

"Thomas?"

The two of them turned to find Rosalind standing in the kitchen doorway. Dressed in a winter-white sweater and jeans, she looked like a flawless angel. Surely that should answer his sister's question.

"Am I interrupting something?" she asked.

"Not at all. Susan stopped by to share her thoughts on something, but I think our discussion is finished. What do you need?"

"Maddie is upstairs talking about a present she made and that you were going to help her wrap it. She was being very secretive, but apparently I'm not supposed to be involved."

"Perhaps because it's your Christmas present," Thomas replied.

"Well, she's managed to get out the wrapping paper and bows, so you might want to go upstairs before she decides to wrap all of Bigsby's friends."

"Captain Wrapping Paper to the rescue then." Looking

over his shoulder, he narrowed his eyes in Susan's direction, warning her to behave. "I'll be right back."

"What was that about?" Rosalind asked once Thomas had left the room.

"What was what about?"

This was the first time she'd seen her sister-in-law since their short conversation the day of her return. She hadn't given it any thought, but while Linus had stopped by the apartment for a brief visit, Susan had stayed away.

"Thomas's comment," she said. "Sounded as though he was upset."

Susan shrugged. "Difference of opinion."

Noticing the kettle was on, Rosalind walked over to the counter to retrieve a pair of mugs from the mug tree. The air had a definite chill. Odd, but she couldn't tell if it was from December weather or the woman standing nearby. Rosalind heard a tapping noise and realized it was Susan drumming her fingertips against the glass oven front. She was staring at the floor deep in thought, her round face marred by a frown.

"Almost done your Christmas shopping?" she asked, hoping to break the ice.

"Not really. There's always something I need to buy at the last minute."

"Isn't that always the case? Thomas and I are braving the crowds tonight to get Maddie a couple of items."

"He told me. He also told me you're starting to get your memories back. You must be relieved."

"Definitely." Rosalind cradled the box of tea she was taking out of the cupboard. Just that morning while wrapping presents she'd remembered a Christmas from her childhood. "There are still a lot of blank spots, but yes. It's nice to know my brain wasn't completely wiped clean."

"The concept of dissociative fugue is a fascinating one," Susan said. "It amazes me what the brain will do to protect itself from thoughts we can't deal with. Like your accident. I wonder if we'll ever know what happened before you showed up in Lochmara."

"The doctor says I may never get those days back." They certainly weren't on the top of her list of memories to recover, regardless. "Personally, I'd much rather focus on better memories."

"Can't blame you. I'm sure Thomas would like to forget those weeks, as well. He was crushed when you went missing. Blamed himself."

"I don't think anyone's to blame," Rosalind replied. "It was an accident."

"Oh, I know. But you know Thomas. The one time he puts his interests first and it drives you off a bridge. That's how he sees things even though you and I know it takes two to tango."

"I beg your pardon?"

"When it comes to problems." Susan reached for the kettle, which had begun to whistle. "Most issues have two sides."

"You're talking about Thomas and me." Rosalind wasn't overly surprised to hear that Thomas's sister knew about their problems; Thomas probably shared a lot with his family following the accident.

Instead of answering, Susan filled their mugs with hot water. "Did Thomas tell you why he's running Collier's?" she asked.

"He told me some. I know your father had a stroke, and we came back temporarily to help out. Then your father passed away."

"Leaving behind a royal mess. His last few years he very nearly ran the company into the ground. Linus and I aren't involved in the financial side so we had no idea, but if Thomas hadn't taken the reins, there wouldn't be a Collier's Soap Company."

"I didn't realize." Watching the amber trails seeping from the tea bag into her cup, she tried to recall the various memories she had of Thomas and his work. All she could conjure up were arguments about long hours and resentment.

"Our customer base was dying out. Literally. He reorganized the company and ordered a complete rebranding. This spa thing is his brainchild. If it works, it'll bring in the younger and high-end customers we need to keep the brand afloat."

No wonder Thomas's smile had wavered when he'd joked about the line's failure being on his head. It wasn't a joke. "I had no idea he was under such pressure."

"Probably because he never told you."

Rosalind stared at the other woman. "What? Why wouldn't he tell me?" Wasn't that something a wife should know?

"I'm not sure," Susan replied, "although I have a theory. May I be blunt?"

She wasn't being blunt already? "Yes, of course." Seeing how Thomas's workaholism was the crux of their problems, Rosalind wanted to know.

Susan crossed her arms. Although she was shorter than Rosalind, she had the Collier ability to pin a person in place with her stare. The hairs on the back of Rosalind's neck stood on end. "I think he tried to tell you, but you were too busy throwing yourself a pity party to listen."

Talk about a verbal slap. Rosalind stepped back. Pity party?

"It was obvious you hated being in London," Susan said. "The apartment was too big. The apartment was too fancy. From the day you got here, all you did was complain and talk about going home. Would you have cared if the company was going under?"

It's just soap, Thomas.

Rosalind could hear herself in her head. Was it true? Had she shut her eyes and ears to what Thomas was going through?

Or was Susan simply angry and defensive on her brother's behalf?

Carefully, she lifted her mug. "I appreciate your candor," she said over the rim.

"No, you don't," Susan replied. "No one does." She reached for her tea, started to drink and changed her mind. "Look, I know you love my brother."

Rosalind cringed. She hadn't worked out any of her feelings; they remained tangled with too many blank spots. Every time she thought she took a step toward understanding, a new memory or new piece of information held her back.

Like now.

"That's why," Susan was saying, "I thought you should know the entire picture."

In the most passive-aggressive way, of course. "No offense," Rosalind said, "but don't you think that if Thomas felt he was being unfairly judged, he'd say something rather than rely on his sister to speak on his behalf?"

"You would think so," she replied. "Unfortunately, when it comes to you, my big brother tends to think you can do no wrong. He'd give up his soul so long as it made you happy."

"If that was true, we wouldn't be in London."

Did she say that out loud? Dear God, was that how she really felt?

Susan gave a smug smile. "I rest my case."

They went shopping for Maddie's present as scheduled, deciding on a giant stuffed bear to keep Bigsby company and a few other items. As they were walking out of the toy store, Thomas said, "I made dinner reservations."

Dinner had been part of the original plan. But that was before. "I'm not sure it's a good idea," she said.

"It's dinner, Rosalind. We both need to eat, don't we?"

Exactly. She wasn't hungry. Her talk with Susan ate at her the entire time they'd been shopping. Just when she thought she'd had everything puzzled out, Thomas's sister had decided to throw another piece into the mix.

Had she really been as horrible as Susan said? After her sister-in-law left, Rosalind had gone upstairs, stared at her reflection and wondered. The woman Susan had described sounded like a brat. That couldn't be right. Thomas would never tolerate being with a brat. It didn't fit his nature.

Neither did the picture of self-sacrifice Susan painted of him.

So, which was the truth? The workaholic with the long-suffering wife or the long-suffering businessman with the shrew?

"Can I take the silence as a yes?"

Thomas looked over at her, eyes sparkling like Christmas lights.

Hard to think straight when the man could distract her with the simplest of looks. "Sure," she sighed. "Like you said, we have to eat."

"I think you'll like the place. It's keeping with the theme. Plus..." He shoved his hands in his pockets. Unlike last time, Rosalind wasn't holding his arm. "There's something I wanted to talk to you about."

"If this is about asking me to stick around past the New Year..."

"Should I?" Thomas asked. "Ask you?"

Yes.

No.

Maybe.

"You said you wanted space," Thomas continued. "I'm going to respect your request. Do I want you to stay? Absolutely. But I also know that words and promises without substance don't mean anything."

"No, they don't." His respectful acquiescence made her uncomfortable. Shouldn't he be fighting a little harder for her to stay?

Listen to yourself: leave me alone but beg me to stay. Maybe Susan was right about her and she was a shrew. Actually, she sounded like a far worse word.

They walked past Trafalgar Square. Seeing the Christmas tree reminded her of Thomas's comments about respecting history. She tried to imagine what it must be like for him to walk past his ancestors day after day. Did he feel their expectations on his shoulders? Had she ever bothered to ask?

"Was Collier's really on the verge of failing when we moved back to London?"

Her question caught him off guard and his steps stuttered. "Why do you ask?"

"Something Susan said this afternoon."

"Susan can be a pill. What did she say?"

"Actually, I'm glad she said something. When you talked about protecting Maddie's legacy, I thought it was… talk. I didn't realize that you were literally trying to save the company."

Thomas gave a sigh. "I told you, my father made some pretty bad decisions. The company was in dire straits."

Leaving it up to him to bring it back from the brink of ruin. Susan was telling the truth. "There's so much I don't know, especially about the past couple years, that I should. Susan told me that was why you were working so much. I wish I'd known."

"Why?" He stopped, his long silhouette dwarfed by the bronze lion statue behind him. "Would knowing have made you less angry?"

Susan had asked the same question. "I don't know.

Maybe." The idea that the answer might be no made her stomach churn with guilt.

"That's why Susan shouldn't have said anything."

"Don't be too mad at her," Rosalind said. "She's your sister."

"Half sister," he corrected, although she suspected it was a term he used only when annoyed with her. "Suppose I should be grateful she's only a busybody and not a loon like her mother. For once, our father's failure to focus on his wife's happiness worked in our favor. Got Susan's mother out of our lives."

Rosalind didn't comment. Something about his comment picked at her nerves.

He'd picked a rooftop restaurant. She should have known. High atop one of London's tallest buildings, the restaurant had a huge outdoor garden. Nestled among the potted Christmas trees and strings of lights were a series of glass enclosures—private igloos where couples could dine under the winter stars in warmth and comfort.

"I said I wouldn't argue with you," Thomas said as the maître d' led them to their table. "I never said I was going to turn off the charm."

God, but he was trying so hard.

"Besides, this way we can have privacy while we talk."

"There are lots of places we could have privacy." Places that weren't quite such close quarters. Or impossibly romantic.

"But none of them have a view of the Thames. I know," he said when she sighed. "One evening doesn't change anything."

"The problems we had before my accident haven't gone away, Thomas." No matter how natural it felt to sit under the stars together. "We can't snap our fingers and erase them."

"Ah, but maybe we could."

A nice dream, but unrealistic. "How? Make Collier's disappear and go back to the country?"

Thomas slipped into the seat next to hers. "That's what I wanted to talk to you about. What if I did? Make Collier's disappear."

"Are you offering to step down from your company?"

"If it meant making you happy."

Turning, he took her hands in his. "Look, I know that right now, you're struggling to remember your feelings for me. The least I can do is prove that the man you do remember has changed. If that means my leaving Collier's, then that's what I'll do."

Rosalind couldn't believe what she was hearing.

"What about Maddie's legacy?" All the history and heritage he believed so deeply in?

"There's no rule that the company has to be run by a Collier. The company will still be family owned. I'll find someone who I trust to respect the strategic plan I've put in place so that when Maddie gets older, Collier's will be there for her."

"I—I don't know what to say." Stunned, she broke from Thomas's grasp. "You would do that for me? Walk away from your family's company? From a job you love?" For a second time.

"I'd rather have a wife than a company." Gently, he took her face in his hands. Meeting his gaze, Rosalind saw a sheen in Thomas's eyes that squeezed at her heart. "We've been given a second chance, Rosie. All I want to do is make you happy."

He kissed her.

"What do you say, Rosie?" he whispered against her lips. "Shall we go back to where we started?"

Before she could say a word, he was kissing her again, taking her silence for acceptance. Rosalind's eyes fluttered shut.

All I want is to make you happy, he'd said. From everything she remembered, going home was exactly what she'd been wanting.

So why did her stomach feel like lead?

CHAPTER ELEVEN

ALL I WANT is to make you happy.

The damn phrase refused to leave her head. It kept her from enjoying her dinner. Every time Thomas smiled at her, her stomach twisted in a knot. She was getting what she wanted, but the victory—if that's what you could call it—felt wrong.

Once again, she was missing a piece of the story.

The next day she called Richard to apologize again for canceling their plans. His modulated tones were a little more clipped than usual. "I thought for sure I'd get a call telling me he'd stood you up," he said.

"Actually, he's been around every day since...the last time he got called into the office."

"Good for him."

"Seriously." Richard probably didn't mean to sound condescending. "I think he's making a real effort."

"Perhaps you're right. The real test will be if he can continue the effort or fall off the wagon once he's won you back."

Rosalind looked down at the carpet. She was sitting in the library by the Christmas tree while Thomas and Maddie were in the other room. The easy thing would be to tell Richard that Thomas planned to give up his job, thus ending his comments. So why couldn't she?

"I only called to apologize for canceling," she said instead.

"You can make it up to me by having drinks tonight. What do you say?"

"Not tonight," she replied, rubbing her neck. The offer didn't strike her as comfortably as it should. "I'm afraid I don't want to spend two nights in a row away from Maddie. She's still getting over her fear that I might disappear again."

"Next week, then?"

"Maybe." She rubbed her neck again. Nothing Richard was saying was wrong, but her body was reacting anyway. "Next week is awfully close to Christmas."

"That's the point. We need to have a Christmas toast to your safe return. I've missed you, Rosalind. I was hoping we could…"

Could what? An image flashed into her head. A corner café. Maddie coloring on a menu.

None of this would be a problem if you'd run away with me…

Dear God, what had she done?

"Rosalind? Are you there?" Richard's voice sounded in her ear.

"S-sorry, I…" She squeezed her eyes shut, but the image had taken hold.

We could be on a flight by Friday.

The memory widened. She'd removed Richard's hand. Thank goodness. How would she have been able to look herself in the mirror?

"I need to go, Richard." She didn't bother with saying goodbye. She was too disgusted with herself. While nothing might have happened, the fact she'd let another man even think there was a possibility was just as horrifying.

Her head hurt. She needed to lie down and think about

what she was going to do. About Thomas. About her memories.

As she headed toward her room, she heard voices—a voice, really—coming from Maddie's bedroom. It was Thomas. He looked ridiculous with his tall frame folded in a chair at Maddie's play table. His phone was tucked under one ear, while he separated cotton balls for whatever art project he and Maddie were doing.

"You tell Ming that he's got as deep a discount as he's going to get," he was saying. "If he balks, pull the deal. I don't care how many spas he owns, we won't be bullied."

He continued for a few more minutes, confidently rattling off production numbers and percentages from the top of his head while at the same time entertaining Maddie by making faces.

Rosalind watched from the doorframe and felt her heart opening. "Very impressive," she said when he ended his call. "You're very good at that." It was the same compliment she'd offered during their flight home, when she was seeing him through a stranger's eyes.

Finished with the cotton balls, Thomas pushed the pile closer to Maddie before handing the girl a glue stick. "Which one?" he asked Rosalind. He grinned over his shoulder. "Barking about subcontractors or separating cotton balls?"

"We're making Santa a picture," Maddie volunteered. "The cotton's for his beard."

"I'm sure he'll appreciate the effort, and the answer is both," she said. "You're good at both." Every time he looked at Maddie, she could see the love etched in his face.

For that matter, Rosalind saw it whenever he looked at her.

Thomas loved fiercely. Always had. The realization came from her heart, not her head.

And it made her feel awful.

Little by little the picture of her behavior these past eighteen months was becoming clear, and, frankly, it wasn't attractive. Amnesia gave her an objectivity that hadn't been there six months ago. What she saw was a woman who, like a child, had turned her displeasure over their relocation into a months' long pout, demanding Thomas change and that Thomas give in to her wishes. Worse, rather than try and see Thomas's point of view, she'd allowed Richard Sinclair to fuel her bitterness and widen the gap between them.

It hadn't been fair of her. Hadn't been fair at all.

"You can't leave Collier's," she said,

Not surprisingly, Thomas looked at her like she had ten heads. "What are you talking about? We agreed last night."

Actually, they hadn't agreed on anything. Thomas had offered, and she… She'd lost her mind in a fog of his kisses. "Collier's needs you," she said. "It never dawned on me until just now, but you were meant to run Collier's Soap." As his grandfather and father had intended.

Pulling away from the molding, she stood upright with her arms hugging her midsection. "I wouldn't be able to live with myself knowing you'd walked away from your purpose solely to please me."

"There's no better reason, as far as I'm concerned."

Rosalind had no doubt he meant every word. The gleam that flashed in his eyes said so. "It's not right," she said. "You need to stay."

Thomas unfolded himself from the child's chair. He looked over his shoulder to make sure Maddie was distracted before closing the distance between them. "Does that mean you've changed your mind about staying in London?" he asked.

This time the gleam was more than a flash.

"I…" How was she supposed to answer? She still hated the city. In fact, the more her memory improved, the more she disliked the crowds and noise. She wanted to raise her daughter the way she'd been raised. In a small village where there was green and hills.

She looked away. "No," she said. As much as Thomas belonged here at Collier's, she belonged elsewhere.

"I see." His shoulders sagged, her stomach sagging with them. "Where then does that lead us?"

Where indeed? Much as she hated to admit it, they'd come full circle, to the place they'd been six months earlier.

"I think I need some space," she said.

CHAPTER TWELVE

I NEED SOME SPACE.

This couldn't be happening. Not again.

Thomas grabbed the doorframe, his nails digging into the wood. He was trying his best to look composed while inside he was shattering. Surely he'd heard wrong.

Last night, they'd been on the same page—or so he'd thought. "What happened?"

"Nothing happened." Turning away, she crossed the hall to the iron railing where she stood looking down on the living room. "That's the problem. We're back where we were six months ago."

"No, we're not," Thomas replied. "Six months ago I hadn't decided to walk away from Collier's."

"Which I've already said I don't want you doing. It's not right. Your company needs you."

"Susan said something to you?" Saying how much the company needed him was something his sister would do.

"Susan has nothing to do with this."

"Then…Richard." Someone else who liked to stir the drama and keep the two of them at odds. "He said something."

Her shoulders immediately stiffened. "What does he have to do with anything?"

Thomas didn't know, but the little busybody meant something. Her rigid posture said so.

"Can't you see that we're at an impasse? I don't want to live in London and you…"

"Said I would move."

"But you don't want to," she said, turning back around. Seeing the resignation mixed with the dampness in her eyes killed him. She was giving up the fight. Giving up on them.

"Don't you see?" she said. "All we would be doing is trading one person's unhappiness for another's. It's not right."

"I wouldn't be unhappy." Not really. Not completely. He would find…something. He did before.

"Yes, you would. You're giving up your legacy."

"So I'll work from home."

"Run a company from hours away?"

"Why not? Linus is always telling me I need to work on finding shades of gray. I could divide my time."

"Sure, and then before we realize, the two of us will be arguing over how much time you spend away from home." She shook her head. "I don't think so."

"So…this is it? You're going to walk away without trying to find a solution?" There was more going on. Thomas could sense it. Feel it hovering in the air between them. But what? What'd happened between last night and now that changed her mind? "Without giving me any kind of explanation?"

"I just gave you an explanation," she replied.

"No, what you did was run a scenario through your head and make a decision. That's not an explanation."

"What more do you want me to say?"

"You could…"

Thomas rammed his fingers through his hair, frustration mounting. For the past eighteen months he'd been fighting a battle where the rules kept shifting and no matter what he did, he was wrong. Save the company. Save his marriage. Go to London. Leave London. Stay in London. Mourn his wife. Reconnect with his wife. Lose his wife. It was all too much to keep track of. Every time he took a step in one direction, he was asked to turn around and choose another.

"Just tell me what I'm supposed to do, dammit."

"I don't…"

"To win you back. To save our marriage. To make things right. Anything." He was tired of trying to trying to read minds. "I'm trying, Rosie, but I can't do all the work alone."

"I know," she replied. Tears shone in her eyes. "I know, and it's unfair."

As he watched one break free and run down her cheek, Thomas kicked himself.

"That's another reason I need the break," she said, wiping the tear away. "I need to think. About us."

It was six months ago, all over again. Despite fearing the answer, he had to ask. He had to know where he stood. If he stood anywhere at all. "Do you even want to try?"

Taking a deep breath, she closed her eyes, preventing him from seeing the emotion in their depths. An answer in itself, really. "I have some things I need to work out. Memories…"

He didn't need to hear anymore. Fists clenched against the pain tearing through him, Thomas focused on the one thing that mattered. "What about Maddie? We were supposed to be giving her a family Christmas. Are you planning to cut me out of that too?"

"What? No. Never." She lifted her hand toward him, only to change her mind and pull back. "We'll be back for Christmas Eve. I'm only taking her now because I don't think she could handle our being separated again. Her and me."

"But I can."

"I didn't mean—"

"Don't." There wasn't an argument she could make. Plus, she was right. Maddie needed her. Whether Thomas did too was inconsequential at this point.

"Just be back by Christmas Eve. That's all I ask."

"You have my word."

Like he had had her word that June's trip was going to be only for a few days? Apples and oranges, he knew, but he feared the outcome would be the same.

Suddenly, he felt very, very tired. Too tired to fight the inevitable. "I have some phone calls to make. I'll be in the library."

"Thomas."

Her call stopped him.

"I meant it earlier. You can't resign. You're too good at what you do. Collier's needs you."

At least someone did.

She'd told Maddie they were going to Cumbria to have a mummy-daughter adventure. In reality she'd picked Cumbria because it was where everything began. Both for her and Thomas, and for her before that. She'd hoped the cottage might spur on more memories and help her process her thoughts.

The cottage wasn't fancy. She knew it wouldn't be. A simple two-bedroom building with a living room and a dated kitchen.

There was a fireplace though and, two nights into the visit, she stood, cradling a cup of hot chocolate and watching the flames as they crackled and popped. Earlier in the day, she and Maddie had decorated the mantle with evergreen branches they cut from the backyard. Same way Rosalind and her mother did when she was a little girl, she realized. For an added bit of festive whimsy, they'd hung heavy woolen socks on the nails. Three, because Maddie insisted Thomas needed one too.

A tiny tree sat in the corner as well, strung with popcorn and paper snowflakes. Compensation for the trees they left behind.

All and all, it was a sweet setting, exactly the setting that had flashed through her brain in bits and pieces, and about as far removed from the London house as you could get. Weight pressed on her shoulders as she sipped her hot cocoa. You'd think, after all her discomfort in London, these surroundings would relax her, but she felt as uncomfortable as ever.

Since arriving, more and more memories had come rushing back. Some were of her childhood, the images from photographs she'd studied growing details. Like the time her parents returned home from a conference in Switzerland and, declaring a personal holiday, whisked her away from school to come here for a weekend full of camping.

What about my legacy? she'd tossed at Thomas during one of their arguments. She'd been talking about this cottage. The place where her family went to be a family when her parents weren't in the field or lecturing on their findings.

Now though, most of her memories were about recent events. Like sitting at the kitchen table studying samples while Thomas stood by the window, a bright red dish towel slung over his broad shoulder. There was a very ornate, very expensive cradle in the spare room in which she remembered placing Maddie down to sleep.

A gift from Linus, she realized, the memory hitting. They hadn't exactly been cut off from Thomas's family while out here, had they? Nor had she gone to London not knowing the world she was entering.

Truth was every time a memory struck she felt more and more ashamed. The other afternoon, when Thomas pressed her for an explanation as to why she was leaving, she couldn't tell him the truth: she wasn't sure she deserved a reconciliation. Here was Thomas, ready to give up everything—again—while she…

Because there's so much call for geologists in London.

She'd wallowed like a child. Pouting when her research project got canceled. Demanding they move back to her childhood home. So wrapped in self-pity had she been that she couldn't see—hadn't seen—the pressure Thomas was under. Instead, she'd turned him into the villain. Laid everything at his feet rather than tried to see the situation from his point of view.

And Richard… Her stomach lurched with disgust. What right did she have to ask Thomas to give up anything?

God, she missed him though. In just a couple weeks he'd become an integral part of her. Her present, not her past. She and Maddie would be busy doing something and her mind would drift to what Thomas might be doing. Was he hurting over what she'd said? Was he working himself too hard?

She missed his laugh. His smell. The sound of his voice.

And then the guilt would hit her once more.

Looking to her lap, she eyed the phone Thomas had given her. Time to pay the piper. She snatched up the phone and hit Autodial before she could lose her nerve.

"This is a surprise. After the last time we spoke I didn't think I'd hear from you for quite a while." Richard's normally melodic voice sounded petulant and clipped.

Rosalind rested her mug on her thigh. Her legs were twitching, making the liquid slosh against the sides. "I'm sorry about the other night," she said.

"You hung up on me and didn't call back for three days."

"I know. Something came to me that I needed to process. I, um, may I ask you a question?"

"A quick one. I'm heading to a friend's party. Where are you anyway? The reception is awful."

"Cumbria. I came up to the cabin to think."

"Again."

"Yes, again." Glancing around her, Rosalind saw herself pacing the floors in June. She'd come to a decision…

"What was your question?" Richard asked. A closet door opened in the background.

"I need to know if… That is, did we…?" She took a deep breath. Best way to do this was to ask all at once. "I keep having this memory of you putting your hand on my knee."

There was a pause, then Richard's deep laugh floated through the receiver. "And you think something was going on between the two of us?"

"Was there?"

"Seriously?" He laughed again. "You're too funny."

"This isn't a joke, Richard." Gripping onto the phone, she glared at his invisible expression, which judging from his earlier laugh was probably a smile.

"Of course it isn't," he replied. "But then, it is. You and me… Sweetheart, I'm gay!"

What?

"But that day at lunch in Canary Wharf. You said we should run away together."

"On a geo-archeological adventure, not as a couple."

We'll go to Angkor and find the road to Battambang.

Oh, God. She remembered now. The mythical road across Tonle Sap, one of their favorite points of discussion. Rosalind's entire body turned crimson. "I was complaining about not having a purpose and you suggested I join your expedition."

"And you told me a month in Cambodia wouldn't solve your problems…"

But that she would think about it.

"I'm an idiot."

"Yes, you are," Richard replied. "I love you, Rosalind, but you are so not my type."

Thank God. For the first time in days, she felt like she could breathe. "Then why were you always on me about Thomas? Saying I deserved better?"

"Because. That's what you wanted to hear."

Was it? "But we're friends," she said. "Shouldn't you have told me what I *needed* to hear?"

"Would you have listened?"

The words "Of course" sprang to her lips, but she bit them back. They tasted wrong.

At least, she thought as she hung up the phone, she could wipe one crime from her record. But knowing she'd misread the Richard memory didn't erase her other actions. She'd still been a stubborn child, wanting everything her way without any sort of compromise.

Funny how in forgetting what had happened, she was finally able to see the situation more clearly.

Question was, how did they solve the original problem without Thomas giving up everything or her being frustrated and miserable?

The problem with taking a good look at yourself is that there was a good chance you wouldn't like what you would see. In Rosalind's case, the more she looked at the pieces, the more she began to realize that she shared the blame for whatever problems had befallen her marriage.

Sure, Thomas worked endless hours and had in the past reneged on promises to his family. But from what Rosalind could tell, after her grant fell through she'd done nothing to improve her situation. Instead, she'd played the martyr.

Insisting that Thomas give up everything so she could go back to the life she preferred. She hadn't even attempted to see circumstances from Thomas's point of view or seek some kind of compromise.

Rosalind sighed. For nearly two days she'd been pacing the entire house assessing the breakdown of her marriage with nothing to show for it but a pad full of doodles reflecting her jumbled mind. And not even current doodles at that. Most of them were from a previous visit.

The more she thought, the more she realized it was no wonder that she and Thomas had gotten to the verge of separation. They were two people unable—or unwilling—to find middle ground. Their whole marriage had been one sacrificing for the other. First Thomas, giving up his career to live in Cumbria, and then her moving to London. Although in her case, the sacrifice had been made far less willingly.

Marriage was supposed to be about working together, not surrendering yourself. Yet martyrdom was exactly what both she and Thomas had done. A person could sublimate themselves only for so long before they became bitter and angry. It was what had happened to her. It's what she feared would happen to Thomas if he carried through on his plan to leave Collier's.

So what should she do?

If the last weeks had shown her anything, it was that beneath all the stubbornness, she and Thomas had something worth saving.

She loved him.

Not the memory of him, but the man who'd been moving heaven and earth to charm her these past few weeks.

The man who'd messed up more than once, yet in the end did everything he could to keep his promise.

The man who negotiated contracts while helping their daughter glue cotton balls on a picture of Santa Claus.

That kind, earnest man, so desperate to do right by his family.

Now it was time for her to do right by Thomas, but how? She didn't dare go back to him without some kind of handle on the changes she was going to make in order to give their marriage a fighting chance.

Sighing, she stared at the doodles in front of her, hoping for some kind of inspiration. Unfortunately, one couldn't find much inspiration from a bunch of scribbles. She'd be better off…

Rosalind blinked. Turned the paper forty-five degrees and blinked again.

Turned out the answer had been staring her right in the face the whole time.

"Call her. You know you want to."

His eyes glued on the behemoth Christmas tree, Thomas shook his head. "I promised to give her space."

He heard the sound of footsteps as Linus came up to stand beside him. The two were in the living room because it was the only room besides the spare bedroom that Thomas could stand being in. The only room besides the spare bedroom that didn't have memories of Rosalind attached. Current memories, that is. Lucky him, he got to deal with two sets.

"It's been a week," his brother said. "How much more space does she need?"

"Tomorrow's Christmas Eve. She'll be back then." If there was one thing he was certain of, it was that Rosalind would want to give Maddie a family Christmas like they'd promised. He ignored the anxious voice pointing out that he'd been certain she'd return in June too.

"And you're still planning to quit?" Linus asked.

"I am." His resignation notice was typed and ready to be distributed to the company. As of the end of January, he would no longer be Collier's president. He boxed in his sadness about departing with his anxiety. He'd walked away from his legacy before and survived. Life would go on again. What was a legacy anyway if he didn't have someone with whom he could share it?

"Didn't you tell me Rosalind asked you to stay?"

"That was her guilty conscience talking," he replied. "She was asking for space and didn't want me prematurely giving up anything."

A third voice he needed to ignore suggested her guilty conscience was over knowing she planned to leave for good. The box in the back of his mind was getting very crowded.

"When push comes to shove, though, whether I give up Collier's is my choice." An easy one to make too. He poked at one of the silver balls that dangled from the tree's branches, making it sway. "I'd cut off my own arm if it meant saving my marriage."

"Surprised you haven't."

"What?" He whipped his head around. Linus's remark had a distinctly derisive drawl. "What are you suggesting?"

"Nothing," Linus replied. "Only that it's painfully obvious that you'd sacrifice anything for Rosalind. You always have."

"Of course. It's called making a marriage work, Linus. I know it's a foreign concept in this family, but sometimes you have to put your partner's needs before your own."

"You know what else is a foreign concept? Compromise. I need a drink. You want one?"

Again, Thomas shook his head. "Alcohol will only make me maudlin."

"More maudlin. You've been maudlin for days."

"Can you blame me?"

"Didn't say I did."

Mrs Faison had arranged glasses and several bottles of

spirits on the credenza in anticipation of holiday entertaining. Not that Thomas had been in any kind of entertaining mood. He turned his back on the tree and watched as Linus studied the different labels.

"For your information, I compromise." He knew where his brother was trying to go with the remark. "I am more than capable of seeing shades of gray in a situation."

"In business, maybe. When it comes to your marriage…" Shrugging, he unscrewed the cap on a bottle and sniffed. "I think you'd rather cut off your arm."

Thomas changed his mind about the drink. Crossing the space, he started dropping ice cubes, loudly, into a glass.

"I'm not sure I like what you're implying." His brother made it sound like he was being some kind of martyr. "Not to mention that you're completely wrong."

"Am I?"

"I wasn't exactly amputating any limbs the last eighteen months, was I?" In fact, maybe if he had, he wouldn't be in this situation.

"Instead, Collier's would be in receivership and you'd be pretending to enjoy being a country carpenter."

Thomas hadn't realized he'd spoken aloud and resented Linus's comeback. He glowered while Linus filled both their glasses to the halfway mark with gin.

"Well, aren't you quite the expert this evening? I didn't realize we had a clairvoyant in the family." How did he know what Thomas enjoyed and didn't enjoy?

"Are you telling me you enjoyed what you were doing?"

"Of course I did."

"As much as you enjoy running Collier's?"

"Apples and oranges. You can't compare the two." There was a meaning attached to Collier's that didn't exist with carpentry—or any other job for that matter. And carpentry didn't come with the same kind of excitement or rush of satisfaction that he felt when the business was clicking on all cylinders. They weren't the same kind of fires. The stakes weren't the same.

All right, so maybe he didn't love being a carpenter. What did that matter? "My wife wasn't miserable when I was a carpenter."

"Rosalind was definitely miserable here. That's for sure."

"Yes," Thomas replied, snatching the bottle of tonic from Linus's hand. "Because of me."

Letting out a long sigh, Linus set his glass down. "You know, I'm beginning to think Susan was right. Subtle isn't the answer."

"Don't even mention Susan. I haven't forgiven her for whatever it is she said to Rosalind the other day."

"Probably the truth. Although knowing Susan, she was a little too blunt." Taking back the tonic water, he began to pour. "Remember the other day when I shared my theory about the Collier curse? That the Colliers lacked a moderation gene? I was wrong."

"I could have told you that."

"Says the man who coined the phrase 'Collier curse.' The three of us do suffer from an inability to see beyond black and white, but that's not where I went wrong. My mistake was thinking you'd pick up on the hint about your behavior. *You're* the one with tunnel vision. You seem to think you can have either Collier's or marriage but not both."

"You don't know what you're talking about." Thomas turned back to the Christmas tree. None of this talk had anything to do with his marriage or his decision to leave Collier's. Linus and Susan had never been married. Who were they to pass judgment?

"Maybe I don't," Linus said. "But I am a scientist by nature, and as a result I do a lot of observing. And over the last five—no, seven years—I've watched you act as though there were only two choices. People balance marriage and career all the time."

"Not in our family," Thomas replied.

"Grandfather had an ego the size of the British Empire. And Preston...he married Susan's mother. Doesn't that say enough?"

He returned to his spot by Thomas's shoulder. "All I'm saying is that there might have been more at play than their dedication to Collier's. You just weren't looking at the whole picture.

"Same way you might not be seeing the past couple of years as accurately as you should," he added, clapping a hand on Thomas's shoulder. "The truth bomb our Susan tossed at Rosalind the other day? She let her know Rosalind wasn't so innocent in the whole debacle as you were leading her to believe."

Thomas shrugged away from his touch. "What are you talking about? Of course Rosalind's innocent."

"I think your guilt over the accident gave you amnesia too, Thommy-boy. Have you forgotten how much complaining Rosalind did?"

"Of course she complained. I asked her to give up her life, and then practically ignored her."

"Really? I seem to remember you trying to appease her. Granted, you didn't do too good a job..."

I'm trying the best I can, Rosie.

It was an argument he'd given over and over. He was trying his best, but there were thousands of jobs and two hundred years to save.

And God help him, he enjoyed it. For all the headaches and stress, he enjoyed the job.

That was the biggest part of his guilt. If he'd enjoyed his job less, he might have saved his marriage and saved Rosalind six months of missing time.

His shoulders sagged. "Doesn't matter." What mattered

was having Rosalind in his life. Having his family together. He was nothing without her. "I have to save my marriage."

"No one is telling you not to, Thommy-boy. All I'm saying is that it took two to create the problem. Maybe it should take two of you to create the solution."

CHAPTER THIRTEEN

HAVING TWO PEOPLE solve the problem was easier said than done, especially if one of the people wasn't there to talk.

Christmas Eve came and there was no sign of Rosalind or Maddie. At first, he told himself they'd gotten a late start. Maddie could be a handful when she didn't want to cooperate. Rosalind's phone must have died, which was why she hadn't called or responded to his texts. No news was good news. The police called when there was an accident; he knew from taking the call in the past. As long as the phone didn't ring, everything was okay.

They would be home soon.

But, as twilight fell, so did his hope. The belief that they would be home soon became the knowledge that maybe they were simply staying away. Funny how the threat of abandonment became preferable depending on the circumstances.

He stood in the library watching the snowflakes begin to fall, his heart in his throat. He was alone. His phone had been ringing all afternoon. Linus, Susan, a host of business calls. He'd ignored them all. If his world was going to break apart, he wanted to be alone when it happened.

Outside, the Christmas lights were coming on. Traffic was getting lighter. People were starting their festivities.

Someone on the street was ringing sleigh bells.

He squeezed his eyes shut. "Please," he whispered. "She doesn't have to stay but let them come home for Christmas."

"Daddy!"

Thomas's eyes flew open. "Maddie?" He rushed to the hallway. Sure enough, his daughter was running into the living room.

"Daddy! It's Christmas!" she was screeching. "It's Christmas!"

He practically slid down the stairs to hug her hello. "Merry Christmas, sweetheart," he whispered as he squeezed her tight. Tears of relief burned the inside of his eyelids.

"Santa brought us home and he gave me cookies," she said, wrapping her arms around his waist.

From over Maddie's head he saw Rosalind come toward him. She had snowflakes in her hair and on her jacket. When she saw his moist eyes, a hand flew to her mouth.

"I'm so sorry. I dropped my phone in a puddle and killed it," she said. "Chris tried to call a couple times but you didn't answer."

Chris?

Sure enough, Chris McKringle came stomping down the steps into the living room. "Merry Christmas!" he greeted as he shook the snow from his red knit cap. "I happened to be in Cumbria just as these two lassies were getting ready to head home. Since it was snowing, I thought it might be a good idea to follow and make sure she came home."

"I told him he didn't have to, but he insisted," Rosalind replied.

"No sense in tempting fate a second time. Especially since I wasn't sure how comfortable she'd be driving in the weather."

"Looks like we owe you yet another thank-you." Thomas let go of Maddie so he could extend his hand.

"You don't owe me a thing. Jessica would have my head if I didn't make sure our Lammie got home safe. We're mighty fond of her."

"So am I." Thomas cast Rosalind a look, only to find her eyes cast downward, hidden from view. His spirits flagged, but he tried his best to keep the worry from showing as he shook Chris's hand. "I'm sorry it's costing you Christmas with your wife though." No way he'd make it back to Lochmara until the middle of tomorrow.

"No worries there. She's used to me being out and about. We're spending the holidays with some friends a little way north of here. I'll be seeing her soon enough."

After a few minutes more of conversation, the Scotsman stuck his cap back on his head and said his goodbyes. Thomas and Rosalind walked him to the door. "Merry Christmas to you both," he said, giving Rosalind a giant hug. "Go and make the most of your Christmas Eve. It can be one of the most romantic times of the year, you know." Then, giving a wink and nod, out the door he went.

Leaving the two of them standing face-to-face.

"We need to talk," they said in unison.

Thomas held up a hand. "Sorry. You first." If he was going to hear bad news, he'd rather hear it now so he could have time to put on a good face for Maddie. He steeled himself for the news.

Rosalind took a deep breath to calm her heart. Where to start? There was so much she wanted to say. She'd spent the entire drive practicing but now that the time had come, all the words were rushing to come out at once.

"I'm sorry I worried you. I really did break my phone." She couldn't believe how it'd slipped out of her pocket straight into the one random puddle at the gas station.

"What matters is you're home now."

"I'm sorry I wasn't home sooner. I'm sorry I took so long to think things out." She paused. Carefully choosing her next words.

"I was wrong," she said. Slowly, so they would have time to resonate. "All the problems we were having, I put them all on your shoulders, and I shouldn't have. I... I remember now. I remember a lot of things. How harsh and unhappy I was because life wasn't how I wanted it, and I took that unhappiness out on you."

He shook his head. "I didn't help matters. I was never around..."

"No, you weren't." But she wasn't going to let him shoulder all the blame anymore. "But I should have talked to you more. I mean, really talked," she said when he went to disagree. "About what I was thinking and feeling. Instead, I complained and expected you to do all the work to solve my issues. I never stopped to think about the pressures you were under."

"Because I didn't talk to you either," Thomas replied. "I was afraid to admit how much Collier's meant to me or how much I liked running the company."

"I knew. I could see it in your eyes."

The revelation came one night while she'd been watching the fire. She'd remembered pieces of a dinner party and Thomas sitting at the head of the table. He had the glow of pride about him. Of command. And she remembered realizing it was from being in his element.

"And I was jealous," she said. "You'd made your whole world about me and suddenly I had to share it with your legacy."

"I swore I'd never be like my father or grandfather."

"You're not." Having confessed her fear, Rosalind felt lighter. It was as though all the months of hoarding her emotions had weighed her down.

With lightness came bravery. Only a few inches separated them, and she stepped close, cradling his cheek in her palm.

"When I think of all the times you put my needs first during our marriage…"

His hand reached out to cradle hers in return. "Not nearly enough. I should have worked harder to keep my promises."

"And I shouldn't have put so much pressure on you to be the answer to my happiness. I love you, Thomas Collier. So very, very much."

Thomas didn't say anything. He didn't have to. Instead, he kissed her. Before she could answer, he kissed her. Slowly and purposefully. A once-in-a-lifetime kiss or, in her case, maybe twice in a lifetime. The kind of kiss that spoke what words couldn't. Closing her eyes, Rosalind wrapped her arms around his neck, giving herself to the moment.

When the kiss ended, Rosalind lay her head against Thomas's lapel and listened to his heart beating against her ear.

"You know…" Thomas kissed the top of her head. "Linus says that we need to work on learning to compromise."

"Linus is a very smart man," she said. "Do you think we can?"

"I'm willing if you are. But then, I'm crazy in love with you."

Smiling, Rosalind closed her eyes and held him tight. This wasn't the end of their problems, but it was the beginning of a solution. Life had truly given them a second chance, and she intended to make sure they didn't waste the opportunity.

"Guess that makes two of us," she told him.

Six months later

"Admit it, we're lost." Thomas looked over at his wife who was wearing the cutest frown on her face as she poked at the touch screen of her phone.

"We are not lost. The GPS on my phone froze. I'm almost positive this is the correct road though. I remember those rock formations."

"Naturally." He laughed when she reached across and swatted his arm.

They were on a second-honeymoon-slash-research trip to the Scottish Highlands and had decided to pay Chris and Jessica a surprise visit. Having not connected with the older couple since Chris had followed her home Christmas Eve, Rosalind was eager to say hello and share their good news.

They'd spent most of the winter talking and learning how to truly communicate. Much as Thomas hated to admit it, Linus had been right. It took two to solve their issues. Together they'd laid out their desires and their fears, and created a compromise. While it took some time, Thomas came to realize he could delegate tasks without Collier's falling apart. Right before the botanical line's launch, he hired hired a second in command. Someone who could deal with the day-to-day crises while he focused on steering Collier's toward the future.

Meanwhile, Rosalind had realized that a large part of her issues were that she missed the stimulation of research. Turned out, she told him, that she'd discovered that part of the answer right before her accident. Two words scribbled in the corner of the notepad had jarred the memory: glacial erosion. It was why she'd gone to western Scotland. To refresh her memory on a couple of key points about the landscape. She was now happily soliciting funding for a new study on glacial erosion in the Highlands.

And they'd moved from London. Not to Cumbria, but to a house in a small town within commuting distance of London. A town that held no connection to either family and could truly become the connection to theirs.

Because it was expanding. That was the real reason for their visit to the McKringles. Thomas looked at Rosalind's midsection and grinned.

"Are you going to stare at my belly from now until Christmas?" Rosalind asked.

"Probably." Shifting gears, he rounded the corner. There were days when he thought he might burst from being so happy. "When I think of the hell I was going through a year ago, and how things are now…"

They weren't done working. Successful marriages always took work. But today, as he drove down this Scottish country road, he was happier than he'd ever imagined. He had his wife, a lovely daughter and a child due Christmas Eve. It was a miracle, that's what it was.

"There's the marker." Rosalind pointed as the sign reading Lochmara appeared a few yards ahead. "The restaurant should only be a mile or so. Around that bend in the road."

"Unless you misremembered the rock formation."

"Thomas Collier, I may have forgotten many things, but I never forget a rock. Look, there's the building."

A building, yes, but not McKringle's Pub. It was nothing but a broken-down, old icehouse.

Exchanging a look, they stepped out of the car. Most of the windows were boarded up as was the faded front door, making it impossible to look inside. Didn't matter. It was obvious that the building had been vacant for a long time.

"Hate to break it to you, my love, but it looks like your rock memory is slipping," Thomas said.

"But I could have sworn…" She was frowning again.

It was strange, he had to admit. The building looked the same. Exactly how many other back roads with icehouses could there be in this area? "Why don't we drive into the town and ask for better directions?"

He turned to lead her back to the car when he spotted something by the bottom of the door. A tiny Scottish flag had been wedged in between the door and the board. Just like the ones that had decorated McKringle's wreath.

There was a piece of paper wrapped around the staff. Thomas unrolled it. "It can't be," he muttered.

Rosalind knelt down. "What does it say?"

"You're not going to believe it."

He wasn't sure he did. Although in a weird way, maybe it made sense. A warm sense of contentment washed over him.

Leaning over, he kissed her. "Have I told you today how much I love you, Mrs Collier?"

"I love you too. Now, what does the note say?"

"The note says, 'Merry Christmas. PS: Have you considered the name Noel?'"

* * * * *

THE MAJORS'
HOLIDAY HIDEAWAY

CARO CARSON

This story about a family is dedicated to my family.

Many military families must spend some holidays apart. I know I'm very lucky to have never spent a Christmas apart from Richard, Katie and William.

May all your Christmases be bright.

Chapter One

It began with the note taped to her door.

Or rather, the note was the end.

Major India Woods, US Army, stood in the hallway outside her apartment in Belgium and read the note. Her feet were killing her after a ten-hour day in black, high-heeled pumps, but the note was taped right at eye level, so she read it on the spot.

Her boyfriend, Gerard-Pierre, had very neat handwriting. His words, lovely loops of black ink that formed perfectly parallel lines across the white paper, spelled the end of their relationship.

He just didn't know it.

He'd written in French, of course, although his English was nearly as good as hers. Ostensibly, he preferred to use French when communicating with her because she'd once said it was her weakest language and he was, therefore, helping her. Considering her English, German, Dutch, Flemish and Danish were better than his, she believed he preferred to use the one language that made him superior—but she'd known that for almost as long as she'd known Gerard-Pierre.

It wasn't the language in which he'd written that signaled the end of their relationship.

They needed to talk tonight, Gerard-Pierre had written. He had to work late, but he'd be home after dinner. This was Europe; after dinner could mean ten or eleven at night. India was an American and an army officer to boot; her workday started as early as six in the morning, something Gerard-Pierre had always considered uncivilized. His schedule as a university teaching assistant might be more sophisticated than hers, but expecting her to wait up for him tonight was a thoughtless way to treat a woman who had to get up before dawn to run three miles with her military unit.

But that wasn't why she was going to have to bring things to an end, either.

It wasn't her boyfriend's insistence upon communicating in French, and it wasn't the fact that his hours conflicted with hers far too often. It wasn't the fact that they hadn't found the time to take any of the weekend excursions around Europe that they'd once planned. Heck, they hadn't found the time to take an excursion to the bedroom for months.

Months? India frowned, trying to remember the last time they'd had sex. Yep. Months.

Still, India wouldn't have called off the relationship. Maybe things had cooled down between them, but they got along just fine. At long last, they were going to take one of those excursions and catch a train to Paris over Christmas. If that didn't revive any passion, India knew she would have let their relationship drift along into the new year, maybe indefinitely—after all, sex wasn't the be-all and end-all of a relationship—but now...

She jerked the note off the door. Now, she had to take action.

India used her hundred-year-old, oversize brass key to turn the old lock in the door. The moment she was in her apartment, the first action she took was to kick off her pumps. Since her current duty assignment required her to work in an office in NATO headquarters, she wore the army's service uniform every day, a blue suit with epaulettes on the shoulders and military insignia on the lapels. In a straight skirt that was tailored precisely to midknee, India worked in her dream position, using her linguistic skills while living in a European capital, but sometimes she longed to be stationed back in the States, where nearly every soldier wore the roomy camouflage uniform and comfy combat boots, even in an office setting.

Still wearing her sheer pantyhose, India scrunched her toes into the Turkish carpet she'd lugged from, well, Turkey, which had been her last duty station. She'd worn her blue service uniform daily in the embassy there, as well. She missed combat boots. She missed…

She looked at the French writing on the page and felt something like homesickness. How irrational of her. This apartment, created out of a few rooms in a building that had existed for a hundred years longer than the United States itself had existed, was her home. There was no childhood home back in the States to miss. Her mother was a nomad, a happy nomad who had circumnavigated the globe by sea and rail and camel caravan twice in the eleven years India had been serving in the military. Her mother was on round three, somewhere in Australia at the moment.

It was tomorrow in Australia, around four in the morning. India plunked her messenger bag onto her little high-top table, which served as her dining room and work desk in one corner of the apartment. She took

out her cell phone, opened an app that enabled international video chats for free and pinged her best friend
in the United States. It was before noon in Fort Hood,
Texas. Maybe Helen was on her lunch break.

Captain Helen Pallas answered, all smiles at her desk
in the brigade headquarters of the 89th Military Police
Brigade. The camouflage collar of her uniform was
visible. And, as she waved into the camera, so was the
diamond band on her finger.

That vague feeling of missing something turned
into a sharp longing, a sudden stab of pain that took
away India's breath. It couldn't be homesickness, but it
couldn't be jealousy, either—India wasn't in the market for a husband. She must be feeling envious of that
comfy camouflage.

But gosh, Helen sure had looked happy for the past
year as a newlywed.

"What's up, roomie?" Helen asked. They'd been
roommates as young lieutenants. India had been a first
lieutenant who'd already completed two years of service
when Helen had been commissioned as a new second
lieutenant. They'd split the rent on a two-bedroom house
outside of Fort Bragg for a while, until promotions and
assignments had sent them off to different corners of the
world. Now India was a major and Helen was a captain,
just a couple of years away from being a major herself.
They hadn't been roommates in the past seven years,
but the *roomie* nickname still stuck.

"What time is it in Brussels? After dinner?"

"I wish. Hang on for a second—I've got to set the
phone down. Enjoy the ceiling." India put the phone
faceup on her table and shrugged out of her suit jacket.
Her rows of hard-won medals and badges clinked in
a muted, metallic way as she hung the jacket over the

back of the bar stool. She picked up the phone. "Okay, I'm back."

"I love your ceiling. Those beams look like they belong in a medieval castle."

"This was a medieval stable, I think, before they divided it into apartments."

"Still cool. There's nothing like that in Texas. There's nothing like that on this *continent*. So, what's up? You said you wished it was after dinner. Is your man taking you out on a hot date? Do you wish the meal was over and it was time for a little somethin'-somethin' else?"

Her man. That sounded kind of sexy, to have a man. India pictured someone strong, someone tall, dark and handsome—even devilish. Devoted. Maybe even protective. While she was at it, someone her age, early thirties; maybe an American, for a change. Someone financially independent, with a career. Someone…not Gerard-Pierre.

"No hot date. My, uh, boyfriend—" India winced. She couldn't bring herself to call him her *man*, but *boyfriend* sounded so crushingly juvenile. "My boyfriend wants to have a big talk after dinner tonight."

"A big talk? Like, *the* big talk? This is so exciting. You're finally in love, and I'm finally going to see Europe because I will *not* miss your wedding. You'd better invite me."

"Actually, I need to break up with him, ASAP." India kept her expression pleasantly matter-of-fact during the pause as the phone app sent her words from Belgium up to a satellite in outer space and back down to Texas.

She heard Helen's voice a second before the video showed her friend wrinkling her nose in disappointment. "Oh, India. What's wrong with Jerry-Perry?"

"Gerard-Pierre. But close."

"It sounds better when you say it. I can't keep up with your exotic European men. But seriously, hasn't he been your only exotic European man for forever?"

It was India's turn to wrinkle her nose. "Only a year. Just about as long as you've been married. Happy anniversary, by the way." She knew the satellite would beam her a delayed image of a much happier expression on her friend's face.

It did. A second later, there Helen was, beaming like a new bride. "Thanks. It's flown by. We still haven't gotten a chance to take a honeymoon."

"But the new house?"

"We just moved in. There's still some work to be done, but it's livable. I love it so much. We've got acres of land. It's so quiet, you can hear the babbling brook. The dog is in heaven. Now stop trying to distract me. What did Gerard-Pierre do?"

"He wrote me a note."

"Uh-huh."

India held up the note.

Helen leaned into the camera. "You're going to have to help me out here. Number one, this video isn't clear enough for me to read it, and number two, I bet it isn't in English."

"It's *French*."

"The man's name is Gerard-Pierre," Helen said dryly.

"He knows English, though. He just refuses to use it. I bet *your* man writes you notes in English."

"Well, yeah, but his name is Tom Cross, and he's an American. Are you breaking up with Gerard-Pierre because he wrote you a note in French, or is it because he said something awful in French?"

"He wrote…" India scanned the note. "That he wants to talk to me tonight after dinner—that's after *his* dinner—because he just found out that his parents and his sister and his nieces are going to be here for Christmas. He says this affects our holiday plans." India waited as the satellite in space did its thing.

And she waited some more.

Helen tilted her head, and looked like she was waiting, too.

"Is our connection frozen? Did you get that?" India asked.

"No, I only heard that his family is coming for Christmas."

"Yes, that's it."

"What is?"

"That's why we need to break up. I can't do the family thing." India tugged at the black tab tie at her throat until the Velcro closure gave with a satisfying little ripping sound. She unbuttoned the top button of her white blouse. "No family. It never goes well."

Helen shook her head slowly, like she felt sorry for India. "It could go well. His family could love you. You could love them."

That's what I'm afraid of.

"No family scenes for me. I have to call it off. I'm just better at being alone."

Major Aiden Nord stared at the note in his hand. He'd never felt more alone.

He hated being alone.

Once upon a time, he'd been happy enough to be on his own, swaggering his way through the army as a bachelor officer, spending time with women who enjoyed spending their time with him. He vaguely remembered being free to schedule his off-duty hours without worrying about anyone else's wants or needs, without worrying about whether or not anyone else liked what he'd chosen for dinner, or whether or not he was staying up too late and the volume of his television was keeping them awake.

Whether or not the fairy book had been read more times than the puppy book.

Whether or not the sandwich should be cut into triangles or squares.

Aiden was a family man now. Four years ago, his wife had given birth to their fraternal twin girls, and Aiden hadn't stopped worrying about other people's needs since. Two years ago, his wife had died—the unfairness of her shortened life still maddened him, would always madden him—so he shouldered all those worries himself. Were his daughters hungry? Tired? Happy? Scared? It all mattered now, far more than his own wants and needs mattered.

Aiden worried about Poppy being on the small side of the pediatrician's height-weight chart, although his wife had been petite, and the doctor thought Poppy was simply taking after her. Aiden worried about Olympia, who was turning out to be tall with darker coloring like his, but who would surely stunt her own growth by refusing to eat practically every food in existence. He worried about things he'd never known parents worried about until he'd become one himself. It was constant. It was exhausting.

He loved it.

He loved them, and he loved being with them, but the note in his hand included the address of the vacation beach house where his sister had taken his daughters for the week to visit with his parents. An entire week lay before him without constant negotiations, constant questions, constant little fingers reaching for things they weren't supposed to touch. An entire week without his children.

In black ink on white paper, his sister had written "Enjoy being a bachelor for a week."

Not likely. He didn't remember what it was like to chug milk straight from the carton rather than pouring it into purple sippy cups. He didn't remember how to swagger through work without keeping an eye on the clock and the day care center's hours in the back of his mind. He didn't remember what it was like to take a woman out on a date without checking his watch to make sure he still had time to get the teenage babysitter home before her teenage curfew.

He didn't want to remember. He wanted his family.

"Would it really be so awful to meet Gerard-Pierre's family?"

India unbuttoned another button on her blouse and cleared her throat. "It's hard enough to tell someone that you no longer want them in your life. It kills me when I've met the family. Do you remember the guy I dated in Germany? His *oma* made me a whole cake to take with us when we left her house. His baby sister drew me a birthday card. It was awful."

"India, that's not awful. That's a loving family."

"When I broke up with him, I had to reject a sweet grandmother and a cute little girl, too."

"You had to talk to them? They were there?"

"No, but he reminded me how much the whole family had loved me. I told him his family was wonderful, but that only made the breakup harder for him to understand."

That wasn't exactly true. It had made things easier for him to understand. India could still see Adolphus standing there, handsome in his quiet way, hands in his pockets and tears in his eyes. *I see*, he'd said. *My family is wonderful, but I am not wonderful enough to make you want to be part of us. They will be very disappointed in me for losing you.*

The guilt had just about killed her. She still thought about it sometimes. Somewhere out there, a little old lady with a Bundt pan and a girl with crayons thought she had rejected them personally. She wasn't going to add Gerard-Pierre's probably adorable nieces to her list.

"It's better when I date a man to keep things just between the two of us."

"But people have families. That's life." Helen leaned a little closer to the screen and lowered her voice. "Tom's family isn't easy to deal with, I have to say, but my parents love Tom and he loves them. He says that's icing on the wedding cake. He gets an extended family along with a bride. You've been with Gerard-Pierre for a year. Why not meet his family? If you love someone, you'll probably love the family that made him who he is."

Ah, Bernardo. Before Adolphus, there'd been Bernardo. He'd been loud but affectionate, and when she'd met his family, she'd immediately seen why he was the way he was. The Italian language had stormed all around her as his extended family talked over one another, cheered for one another, cooked for one another. They'd been appalled she was an only child, but they'd lovingly demanded that she bring her parents with her on the next visit. Since Italian wasn't one of her languages, she'd awkwardly and accidentally said she'd become an orphan that year, when what she'd meant was that her mother had left her for her first trip around the world that year. Bernardo had cleared up the misunderstanding, but his family had kept their real concern whether or not a girl who had no family would know how to make a family with their precious son. Bernardo had started worrying, too.

They were right. I wouldn't know how.

"I enjoy being just two adults who share some time together, you know? Nice and simple. Meeting the family is always the kiss of death. I'd rather not go there with Gerard-Pierre."

"It's just sad that you're breaking up with a man you enjoy sharing time with just because his family is visiting for Christmas."

"We haven't shared a lot of time. Not lately. We were going to try to get to Paris for the holidays, but now that his family's here, I'm guessing that's off." She waved the note again. "That's probably what he wants to talk about after dinner, which could be midnight, by the way. I wish he'd just say he has to cancel Paris. It's not a big deal."

In fact, it was a relief. The prospect of reviving their sex life in a hotel near the Eiffel Tower had been a little intimidating. She didn't know why he'd lost interest, but she'd had a feeling Gerard-Pierre was going to use this trip to list all of her shortcomings as a sexual partner—neatly, and in French.

"Canceling plans for a romantic trip to Paris is no big deal to you? I'd be weeping."

"It's only a train ride from here. Maybe an hour and a half. Maybe a hundred bucks. I didn't really want to go."

"Honest, roomie?" Helen pointed at her through the screen, wagging her finger in warning. "Are you telling the truth? I don't have to worry about you being lonely at the holidays?"

"Honest, roomie." But as India looked at the extra

sparkle in her friend's eyes and that sparkle on her ring finger, that pang of longing for that *something* sharpened.

Aiden folded his sister's note and slipped it into one of the pockets of his camouflage uniform. Two pennies in the pocket jingled together, one from Olympia, one from Poppy. He used to carry a penny from their mother. There would never be another penny from her; it made the other two pennies all the more priceless.

There would never be another penny from any woman. He dated now and then, when there was some event that was clearly for adults only: a rock concert, a wine tasting. But he couldn't imagine loving another woman enough to turn his little family of three into a family of four. She'd have to be so special, impossibly special, someone he wanted very badly, someone who loved his daughters as much as she loved him.

He stood and shoved in his desk chair, then left his office to head for the battalion headquarters conference room.

He couldn't imagine it…but if he could, what would that be like?

The pang of longing that hit his heart was sharp.

Unexpected.

There was plenty of love in his life. He'd be a greedy man to want more.

He strode into the conference room, tossed his binder onto his seat near the head of the table, then headed for the window. He had four minutes to get his mind back on work before the battalion commander arrived and expected him to conduct the meeting.

The view was boring: square army buildings on flat Texas land. The grass had turned brown for the winter, but there was no snow. They never got more than flurries in Central Texas. It was just as well; there was nothing to remind him how close to Christmas they were.

The reason his sister had been able to take his daughters for a week of fun was that her employer had given her the time off for the Christmas holiday. The reason Aiden had watched them leave for the airport without him was because he was an officer in the army; he didn't get to decide when he got time off with his family.

That came with the job. In his twelve years of service, he'd missed family holidays before, twice while deployed to combat theaters. But today, it chafed. The reason he had to be parted from his family wasn't something critical, like combat overseas. It wasn't an essential task, like security or law enforcement here on post. There was no natural disaster to respond to, no citizens who needed immediate help.

Instead, Aiden was looking at a week without his girls because of a training exercise. A pretend deployment. That was what the army did when they weren't at war: they pretended they were at war.

Bad attitude, Nord. Check yourself.

They rehearsed their wartime missions.

Better.

But the week before Christmas was just about the worst time to schedule a monster-sized training exercise that could have been scheduled for any other week of the year.

That's not a bad attitude. That's a fact.

It wasn't his call to make. The schedule had been set by someone much higher up. He would stand at this window and get his head in the game because today's meeting mattered. It was their last opportunity to fine-tune their plans before the simulation began tomorrow at dawn.

Those plans were Aiden's responsibility. He was the battalion operations officer, known as the S-3. The S-3 wrote the orders. The S-3 designed the training that kept the entire battalion in readiness for future missions, and the purpose of this week's exercise was to test that training.

The battalion consisted of four military police companies here at Fort Hood, including the 584th MP Company, where Aiden had first served as a young lieutenant. Back then, he'd led a platoon of thirty soldiers. Now, twelve years and six other posts later, he was once more at Fort Hood, serving as the operations officer for roughly six hundred soldiers.

Out of six hundred soldiers, the order of command responsibility went from the battalion commander to the executive officer to him, the operations officer. The CO to the XO to the S-3. Put bluntly, if the commander and the executive officer were to die, Aiden took over command of the battalion. That had never happened, never come close to happening in real life, but during these training exercises? Yeah. They'd pretend to kill off the CO or the XO at some point, and Aiden would take over the battalion.

In other words, he had to be here.

His children did not. It was better for them to go have fun with his sister than it would be for them to stay in the house with a sitter, wondering why Daddy didn't come home for ninety-six hours straight. He'd done the right thing by letting his sister take them away.

Aiden looked out the window at the dead grass and jingled the two pennies in his pocket.

Chapter Two

"Okay."

"Okay?" India asked, just to be sure Helen meant it.

"I agree you should break up with Gérard-Depardieu-Pepé-Le-Pew, but not because he wants you to meet his family. It's because you can live without going to Paris with him. That is proof that he is not a man with whom you will ever be madly in love. You might as well end it now."

"Thank you very much for your approval."

"It's what you called me for, isn't it?"

India was startled into silence. Maybe it was.

"I should go," Helen said. "We're starting a monster-sized training exercise tomorrow. I won't see daylight for a while. Show me the view before I hang up. Pretty please. Make me jealous."

This was the traditional way they ended their calls. Helen was crazy for all things European. Ironically, her friend was also one of the few soldiers whom the army had never stationed in Germany—not yet, at least—so she used India to get a little peek at Europe now and then.

India held her phone up as she walked toward her

window, a rectangle cut out of stone walls that were almost two feet thick. The square beyond was a mix of old and new, eighteenth-century spires soaring into the sky with the flashing green cross of a modern pharmacy sign below. It was a great view. If India squinted to block out the modern traffic that rolled over the old grey stones, she could imagine herself living in a past century, looking out this same window.

Undoubtedly, other women had looked out this same window in past centuries. Other women would do so for a century after India left, too. She was just a brief visitor, one who would leave nothing behind. Buildings lasted. People disappeared. She was just passing through.

India stood by the two-foot-deep stone casing and felt small.

"Bye now," Helen said. "Fun talking to you."

"Wait. I just—I just—" India's heart was beating a little too fast. She felt so insubstantial. Insignificant. But everyone was just passing through, weren't they? Everyone looked out their window and felt a little… untethered.

Not her friend. Helen was part of *something*.

"I want to see your view for a change."

"Mine? A boring army base in Central Texas? It's just brown in December." But Helen obligingly turned her phone so that India could see out of Helen's second-story, modern office window. The view of brown grass and miles of flat land was anything but boring to India. Soldiers in camouflage and absurdly comfortable-looking combat boots were walking on the sidewalk below. A civilian pickup truck drove by on the smooth asphalt road. Then another pickup truck. Another. Texans sure drove a lot of pickup trucks.

India felt herself beginning to smile. She'd forgotten just how big American trucks were compared to European vehicles. She hadn't been home—or rather, back to her native country—in four years.

Helen turned her phone back around. "It's pretty sad compared to a medieval town square, isn't it? I swear, India, I'm going to show up on your doorstep with Tom one of these days and surprise you."

"I'd love it, but I don't know where you'd sleep. My place isn't even big enough for two people." Not that Gerard-Pierre had let that stop him from moving more than a few of his things here. He kept clothes here, toiletries. Books. A laptop. He liked to work at her hightop table and enjoy her view of the old city square. He liked her television. Since her job meant she always needed to go to sleep before he did, he'd stay out on the couch and watch shows. More often than not, he'd fall asleep on her couch. In the mornings, she had to tiptoe out of her own apartment with her pumps in her hand, so she wouldn't wake the man who found her apartment more convenient than his own.

She looked at the note again. It had been written on her notepaper. It had been taped to the door with her tape. The tape dispenser had been left on her high-top.

Her *man* was a mooch.

"Actually, if you wanted to visit, you and your husband could take the bedroom. It won't hold a queen-size bed, but I do have a full in there. I could sleep on the couch."

Because Gerard-Pierre will no longer be sleeping on it.

"I couldn't put you out like that."

"Three would be a crowd for a honeymoon, wouldn't it? But the offer stands."

"It's sweet of you, but we won't put you out any-time soon. To actually take a honeymoon, we'd have to be done with the contractors in the house, and we'd have to find someone to watch the dog for a couple of weeks, and—hang on." Helen tapped on a keyboard. "Got an urgent message from the brigade CO. Let me read this real quick."

India marched the three whole steps from the window to the sofa. Gerard-Pierre's red sweater was thrown over the arm. Feeling like she was reclaiming her home, she whipped it off the sofa. It left red lint on the creamy-beige upholstery. A bit of teal peeked out from between the cushions, too, Gerard-Pierre's shirt or scarf or some-thing. He favored flamboyantly fashionable French scarves with his winter wear.

She yanked on it. The cloth turned out to be a strap. The strap turned out to be part of a lacy, teal bra. It was darling and daring and so very French.

It wasn't hers.

She sank down onto the beige cushions, a little dazed. A little nauseous.

Helen's voice penetrated her thoughts. "Oh. My. God."

"I know, right?" India said, but her voice sounded funny. "Talk about three's a crowd…"

"This is the single best message I've ever read in the United States Army. That monster training exercise? Canceled. They decided the planning phase was a suc-cess and canceled the execution. We're standing down. A training holiday has been granted instead. Wait until Tom gets the word. Hang on—he won't get the word if I don't pass this memo down to battalion."

India stared at the lacy bra. Gerard-Pierre was cheating on her. *They* hadn't had sex in months, but *he'd* had sex. In *her* apartment.

"India? Hello? Can you still hear me?"

"Fine." Why would he put so much effort into it? He wasn't very exciting in bed. He'd take a fine glass of wine over a round of sex.

"Are you okay?"

He'd wanted her to cancel her holiday vacation so he could present her to his parents as his accomplished, multilingual girlfriend. And then what had been his plan? To take up with his side piece again in January? To keep cheating until he got caught?

Of course.

Then, when his infidelity caused their breakup, India would have known there was another family out there wondering why she'd decided to break up with their son after they'd had such a nice visit. Hadn't she liked them? Had they scared her off in some way?

The shock was quickly being replaced by anger.

There was an even worse scenario possible. *Tom loves my parents*, Helen had said. What if India had spent Christmas with Gerard-Pierre's family and *loved* them? She would have lost them when she lost her cheating boyfriend.

She clenched the bra in her fist. This was why Major India Woods, US Army, was thirty-two and single. She didn't do families. She didn't do complicated. She didn't do *any* of this.

"You're looking awfully serious," Helen said.

"I…" She dropped the bra on the floor. The truth was too humiliating. She lied. "I reread that note while you were sending your message. There was more to it. I'm really, really ticked off."

She was ticked off at herself. This was her home, an

impermanent rental unit, but the only home she had, and she hadn't protected it. She'd let someone use her home, she'd let someone use *her* and now—

India stood up. She didn't want to sit on the couch. She didn't want Gerard-Pierre's stuff to be in her apartment. Most of all, she didn't want to be here when Gerard-Pierre came over tonight. He didn't deserve an audience for his excuses or his accusations—and that was all there would be. Certainly, he'd offer no apology. He'd still probably expect her to play hostess for his family, anyway. It wouldn't be civilized to cause a scene so close to the holidays.

"I want to go somewhere," she told Helen. "My leave was approved. Just because Gerard-Pierre decided not to go, that doesn't mean I can't have a Christmas holiday, right?"

"Right. Where do you want to go?"

Home.

The pang was strong enough to cut through her anger. She wanted to go home, to a place where she was part of something. To a place where she belonged.

It didn't exist.

"I want to come back to the United States," she said, the words surprising her even as she spoke them.

It would feel familiar. There'd be all the foods and the stores and the street signs she'd grown up with. She'd be surrounded by American accents and over-size vehicles. She wanted to eat in a McDonald's that did not serve *gazpacho* or *koffiekoeken*, in a KFC that served tea on ice without asking, because they didn't even sell hot tea.

Her friend laughed. "The grass is always greener on the other side of the pond, then. You want to come to the United States, and I'm dying to go to Europe."

There was a pause, and then, despite the satellite's relay delay, the old roomies spoke in unison. "We should swap places."

India seized on the idea. "We really could do that. We could swap houses."

"Now?" Helen asked.

"Yes. You could spend Christmas here."

"My reflex is to say 'No, I couldn't,' but Tom and I just got extra days off. *Minutes* ago."

India looked at the bra on her floor. A lot had happened in the past few minutes.

"It's like fate," Helen said, half-serious.

India pressed her point, trying not to sound frantic. "It would be perfect for you. My place could be your home base for your honeymoon. From here, you could catch trains to Paris or Rome. You could take a ferry to England. You could drive to Amsterdam or Luxembourg."

"Stop, stop. I'm sold. I've been sold since you first pointed that phone out your window last year."

Thank God. India really needed to get out of here. What she wanted was…

Well, it wasn't here. What she wanted was time away, time to herself to decide what she wanted.

Helen was apologetic. "It's great for me, but what would you get? An unfinished house and nobody to talk to except our goofy dog."

"Do I have to meet the dog's family?"

"No."

"Sounds like heaven."

This is going to be hell.

Aiden brooded at the brown, barren view. He'd been through worse, of course. Combat tours, with their eternal stretches of boredom flavored by the underlying knowledge that monotony could explode into a life-or-death situation at any second of any hour. There'd been the extreme sleep deprivation for months at Ranger School. The steady, prolonged pressure of four years at West Point. Those had each been their own sort of hell, but he'd made it through each one because he'd had a sense of purpose during them.

He also hadn't been a father during any of them.

He wasn't feeling particular purposeful this week. Nobody in the battalion seemed to be. As the staff arrived one by one, Aiden glanced at the array of expressions: resignation, anger, glumness. Plain old bad moods—and this was the senior leadership. The barracks full of eighteen- and nineteen-year-old privates must be a real barrel of laughs. Dragging an unmotivated unit through an unnecessary exercise? Yes, that counted as a kind of hell, when it took his children away from him.

He'd survive it, of course. He could survive anything, and he'd learned that not overseas or in a Georgia swamp or in the granite-walled environs of a military academy. He'd learned that in a hospital, by his wife's bedside. He could survive anything, even if he didn't want to, even if it was grossly unfair of the universe to expect him to take another breath.

He closed his eyes, blocking out the brown flatness, and missed the unsullied joy of his daughters. They gave him breath. They gave him purpose. They gave him happiness. They were gone until Christmas Eve. He rubbed the two pennies between his fingers.

"Good morning, ladies and gentlemen." The battalion commander entered the boardroom with energy, clapping his hands together and rubbing them in anticipation. It was entirely too much cheer for the start of a three-hour meeting.

Aiden turned away from the window and took his seat.

"The preparations for this exercise have been executed in an outstanding manner," the battalion commander said, then he turned to Aiden. "Major Nord, well done."

"Thank you, sir."

It was an unexpected way to open a meeting, but Aiden supposed he couldn't ask for better than that. The commander went around the table, congratulating each staff officer and each of the four company commanders, including Tom Cross, Aiden's new neighbor. Captain Cross and his wife, Captain Helen Pallas, had bought the acreage adjacent to Aiden's. Their new house was not quite complete. They'd moved in about a month ago, anyway.

"Which brings me to the highlight of this meeting."

Aiden exchanged a look with the executive officer, who raised his brow and shrugged. Neither of them had been informed there was going to be a *highlight* of this meeting.

"The powers-that-be have completed their review of the plans and preparatory work we've submitted. They are certain that we have prepared for every contingency."

A few of the officers and senior NCOs gave appropriately restrained, indoor *hoo-ahs* in response.

"In fact, they are so certain we'll ace this exercise, they have decided not to hold the actual exercise."

Silence.

The lieutenant colonel seemed to enjoy it. "Please, ladies and gentlemen, try to control yourselves. I know you were looking forward to ninety-six hours of no sleep and delicious MREs, but you're going to have to find a way to cope with a training holiday instead."

A training holiday? Time off without having it counted against his annual leave? Time off when he'd been expecting to work around the clock for days? *Time off?*

The stunned silence held. It was like they'd all just witnessed a Christmas miracle.

Aiden didn't trust it. "The entire exercise, sir? The brigade as well as the battalion?" If the brigade was still a go, then he would still work. The brigade S-3 would want input from the battalion S-3.

"The whole enchilada. I don't think it takes a genius to realize that, in addition to reviewing our plans, someone higher up also reviewed the amount of fuel the exercise would require and the amount of fuel *budget* they had left for the year. They don't have a burning need to deploy hundreds of vehicles across Central Texas's highways this week, after all."

All around the table, faces were starting to smile.

The commander was openly laughing. "Frankly, I wouldn't be surprised to learn that some of their spouses reviewed the calendar with them, too. This level of exercise being conducted this close to Christmas while all the kids are out of school was guaranteed to piss off some very important spouses—or entire organizations of spouses."

No kidding.

Aiden's surprise was wearing off. Anger was taking its place. Couldn't they have foreseen the blow to morale among the military families? Couldn't they have counted their damn money and their damn fuel and canceled the whole damn enchilada sooner? *Before* he'd promised his sister that she could have his girls for the week?

The three-hour meeting was over in five minutes.

The battalion commander stayed, wishing each person a happy holiday as the team cleared out with alacrity, everyone dialing their cell phones as they left to give their families the good news. Aiden was in no hurry. He had no one to dial.

Only one person came in the door instead of out, and that was Captain Helen Pallas, who'd no doubt sprinted over from the brigade headquarters building to see her husband.

They were both in uniform, so they could not share any newlywed hugging and kissing—thank God, because Aiden couldn't leave before he gathered up the papers it turned out he didn't need—but their high five, a hard slap of victory, made up for it. Just the sound of that clap made his hand sting.

"Pack your bags," Helen said. "We're going to Europe, baby."

"We're *what*?" Tom asked.

Aiden stacked papers and listened as his new neighbor explained that she'd set up a house swap with an old friend in Belgium.

"How long before *I* knew the exercise was canceled did *you* know?" The laughter and approval in Tom's voice as he spoke to his wife gave Aiden another pang of…wistfulness. He remembered what that had been like, to have a coconspirator. A friend. A lover. Long ago—it felt like a million years ago.

Helen made a show of checking her watch. "About fifteen minutes."

"You set all this up in fifteen minutes?"

She pretended to dust off her fingernails on her camouflage lapel. "That's right. One European honeymoon, arranged in fifteen minutes. We're already on the list for a Space-A flight to NATO headquarters tonight. If we don't get a seat, then we're going standby on a commercial flight to Amsterdam out of Austin, and we'll rent a car and drive to Brussels. Colonel Reed already signed my leave form. Any questions?"

Tom looked past her to the battalion commander. "Can I get a leave form signed in the next half hour, sir? I hope the answer is yes, or else I'm apparently going to miss my own honeymoon."

Helen turned to Aiden. "Major Nord, I hate to impose on you. My friend India will take care of our dog once she gets to our house, but there's going to be about ten hours where we're passing each other over the Atlantic. Could you come over and feed Fabio in the meantime?"

Aiden had already met Fabio, a golden retriever with long, flowing hair. Aiden and the Crosses had already exchanged house keys, too. Not only were they all in the same brigade, theirs were the only two houses along half a mile of road.

"If you're not going anywhere yourself, sir, that is."

"I'll be home." *Rattling around an empty house.*

"Great. Can I leave your name and number for my friend, just in case she has any questions?"

"The name is India?"

"Yes. I've known her a long time. She's…well, she was my mentor, really, when I was first commissioned."

"She's some kind of weird savant with languages," Tom offered.

Swell. A mentoring, motherly, older lady who studied foreign languages and took vacations alone, in houses that were out in the middle of nowhere.

"I doubt she'll need you," Helen said, "but just in case."

"Sure. Give her my number."

At this rate, a call from Tom and Helen's house sitter would probably be the most exciting thing that would happen to him all week.

Chapter Three

She was running on empty.

International travel was always draining, but this trip had been especially so. India had only fallen asleep for little fifteen-minute, neck-straining naps on the plane, despite spending the hours before her flight not sleeping, but instead gathering up every single thing Gerard-Pierre had littered around her house. The books she'd stacked neatly in the hallway outside her apartment door. She respected books; they hadn't done anything wrong. The rest she'd dumped into a pile in the hallway.

The bra she'd hung on the century-old doorknob. Explanation enough in any language.

India checked the pickup truck's gas gauge. Her body wasn't the only thing rapidly running out of energy. She'd found Helen and Tom's pickup waiting for her at the airport, right where their text had said it would be. The tank had been almost half-full, surely enough to cover the distance from the Austin airport to the countryside beyond Fort Hood. She'd passed a dozen gas stations leaving Austin. A half dozen through Georgetown. More in Killeen…but when Helen had said her house was out in the middle of nowhere, India had forgotten how big nowhere could be in the States. She'd been driving for ninety minutes, enough to have gone to another country from Belgium, but she was still in Texas, driving past miles of land occupied only by grazing cattle and the occasional barn. Sheesh.

She had just decided it would be wise to turn around and head back to the last gas station she'd passed when she saw a mailbox, the standard American kind, a black metal shoebox with a rounded top, mounted on a wood four-by-four. When she'd been a little girl, she'd thought the shape looked like the Road Runner tunnels that the Wile E. Coyote was always trying to enter—with no luck. He was shut out, denied, every time.

Gold letters on the black metal read *489*. Who opened this mailbox every day without even thinking about how easy it was? India slowed the truck as she passed the driveway. Its single lane of asphalt ran for at least a quarter mile, unwaveringly straight, to a classic two-story brick home. The colors of the bricks were distinctly Texan, though, gold and beige and cream that reflected the afternoon sun, which was bright even in December in this part of the world.

She didn't need to turn back, after all. Helen's house number was 490. Her mailbox was up ahead, a little sentry on the side of the road. India hit her turn signal, then scoffed at herself. Who was there to signal? Her truck was the only vehicle on the road. But as she slowed and started to turn, she looked down Helen's straight driveway—and tapped the brakes.

Someone was there.

The garage door was open and, even though a red pickup blocked most of her view, India could see that someone was moving around. A thief.

She didn't turn in, but kept driving. Tom and Helen

had a dog, but Helen had texted her that the dog would be at the neighbor's house, so India could sleep off her jet lag without having a dog wake her. A barking dog might have scared off a thief, but the house was empty.

Don't be crazy, India. Why would a thief go to an empty house when the owners are out of the country?

Not so crazy. India could dial 911. Maybe. She'd turned off cellular data on her phone to avoid astronomical international roaming charges. Wasn't 911 supposed to work from all phones, regardless? But she didn't have an American phone. Maybe it wasn't programmed for that emergency service. How long would it take a sheriff to get out here, anyway? The thief would have plenty of time to help himself to whatever he wanted and then drive away with a flat-screen television in the back of his pickup.

She stopped the truck on the road's shoulder. *Think about this, India girl; stay awake.* She scrubbed her hands over her face, then dug in her bag for a peppermint. The bracing flavor woke her up. She turned the truck around and drove by one more time, slowly. The parked red truck was awfully nice, shiny and new, hardly the getaway vehicle of a criminal.

She pulled in the driveway of 489 to turn around and head back, feeling exceedingly stupid. She was just tired. And emotional—she'd failed to protect her own home. Hadn't that thought been relentlessly circling in her head as she'd kicked out Gerard-Pierre? Well, kicked out his stuff, anyway. That was why she was thinking of homes being invaded.

Damn. She'd passed her own driveway again. With a sigh, she made a U-turn in the middle of the empty road. Helen's house wasn't finished yet. The truck probably belonged to the general contractor who'd been building the house, supervising all the subcontractors. The truck could belong to one of the subcontractors, too. Maybe to an electrician. A tile layer. Who knew?

She was getting so sleepy, she didn't care. If it did turn out to be a thief, she'd at least get a license plate number as the truck drove away, before she fell asleep waiting for the sheriff to show up.

She drove up to the house and debated parking behind the truck to block it in, just in case this person had no reason to be here. But then she caught a better view of the man in the garage. His back was to her, but the width of his shoulders was enough to make her decide to park out of his way. She was a soldier, but she'd spent the last four solid years tied to a desk. She was super rusty when it came to close quarters combat. She wouldn't want to take on this guy, anyway, not without a stick or a bat or something. *Gee, I'm fresh out of ninja staffs.*

He wasn't a thief, anyway. He wasn't moving in a sneaky, furtive way. As she parked, he walked calmly over to a refrigerator in the garage. She'd forgotten how Americans not only had giant fridges in their kitchens, but they often kept one out in the garage, too, the good old beer fridge that held the leftovers when holiday dinners called for a mammoth turkey. The man with the buff shoulders opened the door and took out a beer. He wore a leather tool belt around his waist, a hammer hanging from it. Someone in construction, of course.

She was an idiot and she wanted to go to bed, but she supposed she'd have to make small talk with this contractor and hope he was almost ready to leave for the day. She opened the door and practically fell out of the cab, dropping the foot from the cab to the ground, landing with all the grace of a tired elephant. She slammed the door. This man was all that stood between her and a soft bed with fluffy pillows.

The man in the tool belt turned around.

Oh, my.

India abruptly felt awake and alert. Just the sight of that man, that tall, dark and handsome *man*, sent a jolt through her system better than a whole roll of peppermints.

Aiden had shaken his head as he'd watched his neighbors' pickup drive by, drive by and drive by again. She couldn't read the numbers on the mailbox, maybe. *Poor little old lady*, he'd thought.

Aiden looked at the woman standing in the driveway. *Poor drop-dead gorgeous woman.*

He didn't let the beer bottle slip out of his grasp. That was something, anyway, but he sure as hell was knocked speechless. This woman was the definition of a knockout. Literally, the sight of her knocked the sense out of his brain—because she looked rumpled and sleepy, and all his brain could think about was that he'd like to be rumpled and sleepy with her.

Enjoy being a bachelor, his sister had written.

He'd thought about milk cartons and sippy cups.

He wasn't thinking about sippy cups anymore. He was thinking about the brunette standing in front of him, looking at him with gray eyes. *Gray.* Beautiful. All grown-up and beautiful.

Okay. Right. He should speak now. Right.

"Are you almost done here?" she asked. "I'm dying to get in bed."

The beer bottle in his hand slipped an inch.

Okay. Right.

She tilted her head at his silence. "I'm going to be

staying here while Tom and Helen are on their honeymoon. Did they tell you that?"

"Right." One word. He sounded like an idiot. It may have been a long time since he'd been a bachelor, but he was thirty-four years old and a battalion S-3, not thirteen and in middle school. He gestured toward her with the bottle in his hand. "Would you care for a beer?"

He'd meant there were more in the garage fridge since he'd just put a six-pack in there, but she huffed out a tired sigh and plopped her overnight bag on the concrete floor, then took the beer from his hand. "Actually, I would." She wiped off the mouth of the bottle with a quick swipe of her sleeve, then tilted her head back and chugged the whole bottle right down that graceful, womanly throat with long, sure swallows. She finished it and gave him a polite, sleepy smile. "Thanks."

Okay. That was…provocative. "I take it you like beer."

She scrunched up her nose a bit. "Actually, that tasted horrible. I just ate a peppermint."

He laughed.

Her smile turned a little more genuine, but still tired. "I needed the calories. I haven't eaten much more than airplane snacks for the past twelve hours. That beer was my dinner, because I will be asleep in two minutes. I suppose Tom and Helen gave you a house key?"

"Right."

She pondered that for a moment. "I won't ask for it back, but could you make yourself scarce for the next ten hours?"

"Okay."

"Make that twelve." She turned her head away and put the back of her hand to her mouth and burped the tiniest, ladylike burp. "Sorry."

He laughed—again—and took the empty bottle from her. She was all grown-up and beautiful, but also surprising and adorable. And rumpled and sleepy, which was a sexy damn look on her. *Oh, hell yeah. It's all coming back to me now.*

She picked up her overnight bag. "I'll be here all week, so even though you have a key, knock first. I'll let you in."

"Promise?"

"I— Oh." She looked at him, startled.

He winked. *Just joking.* For now.

She looked away, but her lips quirked into a smile. She had just a touch of a dimple in one cheek. How easy it was to imagine her smiling at him as they shared a pillow.

"So." She gestured toward his truck. "If you're done here…?"

"I can come back. I just have to have this project finished by Christmas." He nodded at the planks he'd stacked on the floor.

"What are those for?"

"Bookcases."

"Nice. Well. Goodbye."

But they stood there, staring at one another. He unbuckled his tool belt without breaking eye contact. She bit her lip.

He shook his head to himself a little bit as he turned away to set the belt on the stack of planks, trying not to be bowled over because a sexy woman had done a sexy thing like biting her sexy lip.

He'd been asked to leave; time to go. He stopped at the small security box on the wall just outside the garage and punched in the code that lowered the double-wide door. It started rolling down. He looked over his shoulder at her, savoring his last glimpse of rumpled and sleepy. "I'll see you later."

The chain and motor were loud as the door lowered, but Aiden could have sworn he heard a one-word answer: "Definitely."

Chapter Four

The contractor was so hot. Like…lava hot.

Helen hadn't even dropped a *hint* about that. Maybe she'd thought India would be heartbroken over Gerard-Pierre. She hadn't sounded heartbroken when they'd chatted, had she? But fresh from a breakup or not, a woman would have to be dead not to notice that contractor. And he'd *flirted* with her.

She curled her toes into the plush carpet of the master bedroom. She felt great. She'd slept without the sounds of a TV coming from another room. She'd slept without having her service uniform all laid out on the chair by her bed, a fresh white blouse and sheer nude hose ready to make their demands the second her alarm clock went off. India wriggled her pantyhose-free toes. Without setting an alarm, she'd slept until seven in the morning in this time zone. Fifteen blissful, uninterrupted hours.

That would probably not happen again, though. She had to get the dog back from the neighbor's today. She was no expert on dogs, since she'd never owned one, but she doubted any dog would let her sleep for fifteen hours without needing to go out. She wandered into the kitchen, where Helen had left her a long note with all the information she'd thought India might need. Wi-Fi password—check. Veterinarian's phone number—check. Neighbor's phone number—check—followed by a list of the workers that had already been scheduled before Helen had said it was fate that they could swap houses.

Helen had left the general contractor's name and number as the person to call if anything went wrong with the house. *Nicholas Harmon.* The boss. Nicholas practically oozed testosterone. She had no doubt he could keep a bunch of subcontractors in line with ease. He was probably former military. He had that posture. The haircut, too.

Nicholas had the dark coloring of many Italians, the square jaw and strong bone structure that made her think of Germany, but he was unmistakably American. There was something about Americans that she'd never been able to put her finger on, but she could always spot a countryman without hearing their accent first. She herself was rarely mistaken for any other nationality anywhere she went, although she couldn't say what, exactly, made her look American.

In short, he was perfect, this Nicholas. When Helen had said *your man*, this guy had been who India had imagined. Helen had also said, *It's like fate.*

India felt her stomach twist.

She needed food. There was half a loaf of bread in the ginormous new pantry. She put a couple of slices in the toaster and pressed the lever. She glanced around the brand-spanking-new kitchen with its brand-new appliances, then she turned back to the toaster and stared at the bread. There was nothing else to do, nothing to distract her from her thoughts.

From thinking about the way he'd laughed. That wink.

Her stomach twisted a little more.

Fate seemed kind of heavy. It was more like a *wish* that had come true. A fantasy had materialized in her friend's garage. A sexual fantasy, no mistake about it, which had awakened parts of India's body and brain that she'd been content to let hibernate while she'd fallen into an undemanding, platonic routine with Gerard-Pierre.

Her body was making demands now. She wanted to see Nicholas again.

And then what?

Good question. She was only here for a week. On Christmas Eve day, she was going to drive three hours to San Antonio to a bed-and-breakfast. Helen had booked it for herself and Tom, and she'd insisted India use their reservation. San Antonio was a great little tourist town, Helen had assured her, with the Alamo to visit and the River Walk to mosey along for shopping and dining. The morning of the twenty-fourth, the contractor was having some polyurethane work done on the floors and grout, and they'd need to leave the windows open to let out the noxious fumes, even though it was winter. India would be warm in the B&B instead.

India would be stir-crazy after a week of isolation, anyway, and Helen had known it.

But first, India would be here for a week. A week wasn't long enough to develop a relationship with a man. India didn't sleep with a man unless she was in a committed relationship.

Really? Because you were in a committed relationship, but you still weren't sleeping with Gerard-Pierre.

Things had cooled off with Bernardo after she'd met his family, too. And Adolphus? They'd slept together, of course, after a few months of coffee conversations in bookstores. He preferred Saturdays, when he could spend the night without worrying about making it on time to work the next day. They'd had some nice Saturday nights, but frankly, he'd been more excited about exploring the possibility that she was his intellectual soul mate than he'd been about actually being a bedmate.

It had been okay. Sex was not the most important part of a relationship. India was certain that was true, but…

She'd had enough relationships without any sex. What would it be like to have sex without a relationship?

Knock first. I'll let you in.

Promise? He'd winked at her, six feet of masculinity with a wicked smile.

India stared at the toaster for a few more seconds before she realized it wasn't toasting anything. Feeling ten kinds of stupid, she *plugged in* the toaster.

Nothing happened. She moved the toaster to the other side of the stove, where there was another outlet. That one was dead, too.

She went into the garage and took a quick peek at the fuse box. None of the switches had been tripped. That meant the electrical outlets were dead for some other reason, and the problem was going to require a professional to take a look at it. Like, say, the general contractor.

What a perfect twist of fate.

India went back into the kitchen and dialed the contractor's number. *Oh, Nicholas? Come over and knock on my door.*

A woman answered, but she sounded like a secretary. *Please be a secretary.* "Could you ask Nicholas to stop by 490 Cedar Highway today? The electrical outlets in the kitchen are dead."

Then India abandoned the cold bread in favor of a hot shower and fresh clothes and a touch of makeup, because her outlets might be dead, but her libido no longer was.

Fabio was trying to kiss him.

No—he was trying to make out with him, hot breath and slobbery tongue dragging Aiden out of his sleep.

Aiden pushed away the dog's head. "No means no, Fabio."

The dog backed up a step on the mattress but kept staring at him, panting.

"Don't look so hopeful. I've never had a thing for blondes." Hadn't he been dreaming of a brunette? Aiden squinted at the clock by his bed. Nine o'clock?

He stared at the numbers a moment, as if they couldn't be right. Aiden hadn't slept until nine o'clock in…hell, in at least four years. Even when he was stationed stateside at a staff job, as he was now, the army required him to be up at an earlier hour. He was awake, dressed in his PT uniform and ready for PT—physical training—by six on most mornings. If there was no PT, he was in the office by seven. On the days he was off, Poppy and Olympia were bright-eyed and bushy-tailed by seven o'clock, too, clambering onto his bed and chattering about whatever they were thinking about that minute, perhaps wondering if a teddy bear could be rainbow-colored or if Daddy could make pink grapes instead of green grapes. *I don't decide what color grapes can be.*

Why?

They grow on vines. Daddy can't make vines do things.

Why?

Because I'm not the boss of plants. Let Daddy brew some coffee.

Nine o'clock.

He'd forgotten about sleeping in. He hadn't known his body was still capable of it—but it sure was. He rolled onto his back and ruffled the dog's ear. It was the first silver lining of this week of enforced bachelorhood: sleeping late. He wouldn't set an alarm for a week. He'd take the dog back to the neighbors' house today and see if he slept later than nine tomorrow.

The neighbors' house. India. Beautiful, gray-eyed India.

An awareness traveled over his skin, crossing his chest, his stomach, lower. He could call it lust, but it wasn't anything as base as simply getting hard. It was a sense of electric anticipation, a sizzle of energy washing over all of his skin, waking up every inch of his body—his fingertips, his eyelids, his scalp. It was as if the image of her in his mind's eye had all his senses reaching out, all the cells in his body searching for her.

He caught his breath at the foreign sensation. Too electric. Too aware. He sat up and pushed off the sheets.

The dog jumped off the bed and faced him, tail wagging in excitement.

"Let's just call it lust, okay?"

Aiden could handle that. *That*, he remembered how to do. He'd taken a woman he'd known for a while to Dallas for a weekend…when? Months ago. She liked to say they were friends with benefits, but he'd still insisted on paying for the tickets to the Aerosmith concert. The dinner. The hotel room. Lust was basic—he could definitely handle that.

The dog barked once in approval. Aiden had sat up, so the dog wanted him to stand up. "I hear you, boy.

Let's get you fed and walked, and I'll take you to meet your new house sitter."

If anticipation prickled down his spine, touching each and every vertebra, it was simply lust.

He could handle it.

India was beside herself with anticipation.

She was on alert, ears tuned with almost painful eagerness to any sound in the driveway, until, at last, she heard the low sound of an engine, the slam of a door. *Wait for it...*

When she heard the metallic sound of a tailgate being lowered, she hit the button to open the garage door. Why make the man walk up the bricked path to knock on the formal front door? He was parked by the garage, and she was already certain he was going to want to test her fuse box. The question was, would she test her courage and flirt her way to a little more? A lot more? Would she? Could she?

The garage-door opener turned a heavy chain. The door lifted slowly, its new wheels rolling smoothly in their tracks. India hastily gave her hair one last fluff and tried to strike just the right pose: casual, yet sexy. She was wearing jeans, yet her hoop earrings were sized to be stylish, not subtle.

I can do this. Why not? Consenting adults, safe sex. I'll never see him again after a week. No embarrassing scenes with a former lover. No awkward evenings avoiding each other at an embassy dinner. No running into him at a café as he dated the next woman. A perfect holiday fling, if Nicholas was willing and able.

The rising door revealed the toes of cowboy boots, then denim that bunched a little at the ankles. More denim—up, up, revealing that hot body inch by inch. The man had certainly looked *able* yesterday.

I can't do this. Wasn't this how porn movies started? The electrician came over and the lonely housewife greeted him at the door, her hair fluffed up and her lip gloss on? *Oh, dear God, I'm imitating a porn movie. I can't do a porn movie.*

India held her breath. Flirting. She was just going to flirt a little, see where it went. *That*, she could handle.

As the garage door rose, the denim got a little wider at the waist. The shirt covered a little bit of a paunch…

Wait. No.

The rising door revealed narrow shoulders, a weathered face and a white beard. A friendly smile. "Mornin', ma'am. I'm Nicholas Harmon. Pleased to meet you."

"Nicholas Harmon," she echoed, her voice a little high-pitched as arousal and disappointment stretched her nerves to the limit. "Of course. Nice to meet you, too."

"Let's see what's going on in the house."

Nothing.

Glumly, she followed him into the kitchen after he pulled a toolbox out of his truck bed. It was a good thing she hadn't been trying to recreate a porn movie; she would have given the man a heart attack if she'd been standing there in lingerie.

Lingerie. Good one. She didn't own any lingerie. She wore skin-tone bras with lightly padded cups to ensure her nipples never showed through the white business shirt of her uniform.

The memory of a lacy, teal bra sent a little lick of anger through her system, shaking her out of her glum state.

Nicholas stuck some kind of metal probe into the outlets, informed her they were dead—*yes, I'm well aware of that*—then started unscrewing outlets.

India leaned against the marble kitchen island and read Helen's note again. A landscaper was coming two days from now to plant a pair of cypress trees, one on either side of the front door. That couldn't be her man; hers had been working on bookcases. The same day, a shower door was going to be installed in the hallway bathroom—allow three hours. A gutter hadn't been installed correctly on the west side of the house. They were coming to reinstall it three days from now. Helen had written that India didn't need to be home for that one.

India ran down the list, frowning. There was no mention of bookcases, no trim carpenter scheduled to spend a day this week. Maybe he was supposed to have finished yesterday, before she'd arrived.

After Nicholas fixed the wiring and screwed the outlets back into the wall, she walked him out to the garage and gave her best nonchalant nod to the stack of planks. "When does the carpenter come out to finish the bookcases?"

"I don't know anything about bookcases. There's nothing in the plans about built-in bookcases."

"But the carpenter was here. Yesterday."

"He wasn't one of my subcontractors." His friendly face got a little less friendly. "I'll be calling Tom and Helen about that. There aren't supposed to be any workers in here that I didn't hire. That's very clear in the contract. I hire all the subcontractors."

Great. Some house sitter she was, getting the general contractor all riled up so he'd call the homeowners on their honeymoon. "They must not be built-ins. That was my assumption. I'm sure Tom and Helen didn't

hire anyone to work on the house behind your back."
Then she pinned him down with her don't-screw-with-
me glare. She was, after all, an army officer. "Tom and
Helen aren't the kind of people who'd dishonor a contract with you, are they?"

He looked away first. "You're right, you're right.
Well, I'll be off now."

"Thank you for coming out so quickly."

Nicholas left.

India returned to the kitchen.

The silence settled in, broken only by the hum of the
fridge as it cycled on. A kitchen clock with an art deco
pendulum ticked steadily.

She sat on a bar stool at the cool marble countertop.
Thank goodness she hadn't laid out a little Bloody Mary
station here. She'd considered putting out the Tabasco
and Worcestershire sauce that she'd seen in the fridge,
the tomato juice and the vodka, so the hot bookcase man
could make his drink as hot as he liked it.

*Oh! Do you like Bloody Marys? I was just going to
make myself one when you drove up. Help yourself to
whatever you want.* In her mind, she sounded like a seductress. *Show me what you like.*

In reality, she wasn't that kind of seductress, and
she knew it. Fortunately, before Nicholas had arrived,
she'd decided to put away the two glasses she'd placed
rather obviously by an outlet. At least she hadn't had
to awkwardly offer a glass of tomato juice to a general
contractor who resembled Santa more than a hot guy
in a tool belt.

The clock kept ticking.

India had already unpacked. She'd showered. She'd
eaten. She had time on her hands, time to be alone with
her own thoughts. It was what she'd thought she wanted,

but now it didn't seem like much of a holiday. A holiday was supposed to be a change from one's normal life, something different, something exciting to explore. But she was alone and, as she stared out the kitchen window at empty land, she realized that was nothing new.

Brussels was such a lively city, it was easy to feel like she was connected to people. She was surrounded by people. She ate at sidewalk cafés that jammed little chairs so close together, she sat shoulder to shoulder with people. She went to the market with a crowd of people. She crammed into the elevator with other people at NATO headquarters. She had a boss. She had subordinates. She even had a boyfriend.

But she'd been alone, just as alone as being the only human for miles, sitting in an empty four-bedroom house on acres of empty land. She had no one to share her thoughts with here, but she didn't share her thoughts with strangers at sidewalk cafés, either. The only thing she talked about at the market was the price of endive. At work, she addressed her superior as "sir." Her own team called her "ma'am." Her boyfriend was awake while she slept, and now she knew that when he slept, it was with someone else.

Her stomach churned.

Was she so desperate for a human connection that she would have offered sex to a stranger this morning? A total stranger?

She dropped her face into her hands and wallowed in her own foolishness for a moment.

Foolish—but she'd been undeniably excited as she'd waited for him to arrive. So alive with *hope* for…something.

Whoever he was, he'd said he'd come back to finish before Christmas. He might not return until Christmas

Eve day, when she'd be on her way to San Antonio and
the house would be full of cold air and noxious fumes.
Nicholas had said the workers wanted to get started by
seven in the morning, so they could finish by lunch,
what with it being Christmas Eve and all, ma'am.

The week stretched ahead of her, six more nights.
Helen had warned her there would be nothing to do
here, hadn't she? It hadn't even been twenty-four hours
yet, and India was already feeling stifled in a house big
enough to hold four of her apartments.

She supposed she could start perfecting her own
Bloody Mary recipe. *Sure. Drinking alone wouldn't
be depressing at all.* She could add some salty tears in
there for flavor. Ha ha ha.

Outdoors, the weather was about ten degrees warmer
than Brussels, but the sunshine was ten times as bright.
Texas was known for blistering hot summers, but that
meant it had sunny winters, too. India checked the coat
closet and found Helen's red, double-breasted peacoat.

She might as well go out and be lonely in the sunshine.

Chapter Five

The only sign of civilization was a bridge.

The house sat on two acres, India knew from all the conversations she'd had with Helen this past year, but the view from the flagstone patio sloped away for miles beyond the property line. The undeveloped land really did look the way Texas looked in cowboy movies. The ground was mostly brown; the sparse trees were struggling to hold on to their green despite the approaching winter. India wasn't certain what sagebrush actually was, but she assumed it was the random shrubs that dotted the landscape. There was a single tumbleweed, too, off in the distance, a slow-rolling ball of sticks that could have been a movie prop.

The open land under the blue sky would give a person a sense of serenity, perhaps, if that person wasn't her. She was feeling small and lonely. Wilderness didn't exactly chase that feeling away.

India headed for the bridge. The classic wood structure was only wide enough for people on foot, like her. It crossed a creek than ran down the length of the property. The golden-beige brick house stood somewhere beyond the other side of the bridge, she was certain.

Helen's note said the neighbors had taken the dog overnight to give India a chance to sleep off her jet lag. That
meant the neighbors must be experienced with jet lag
themselves—and must be very kind, as well. How lucky
for Helen to live near people like that. How lucky for
India last night.

Then again, maybe it wasn't rare luck. Maybe neighbors like that were common here. There were a lot of
ex-military people in an army town, and military folks
understood travel, deployments, hardship tours. They
understood how far a kindness like watching a pet could
go. At home, India was the only soldier in her apartment
building. If she lived here, she would be surrounded
every time she went into town by military and former
military—like the bookcase guy.

She turned over the memory of him in her mind, pin-
pointing the details that had made her assume he was
former military. Military haircut, physical confidence,
physical *fitness*. Broad shoulders, capable hands that offered her a beer, that unbuckled a tool belt...

India walked faster, taking longer strides, trying to
clear her head after the morning's disappointment. *You
mean the morning's sexual frustration.*

She was still a good distance from the creek when a
sudden streak of golden fur flew across the bridge toward her, a large dog that was running full speed, so
fast that he slipped and skidded right past her when he
tried to put on the brakes. She laughed.

He didn't care. He came bounding up to her—no
other way to describe it—pink tongue hanging out, tail
wagging, sides heaving.

"Are you Fabio? Are you, boy? Are you?" The dog
was deliriously happy, and India felt her mood lifting
as she enjoyed the antics of the golden retriever. He

seemed to expect her to break into a full-speed run with him. He ran away five yards or so, then checked over his shoulder to see if she'd followed. He came back to her, then he did it again, as if he was demonstrating the proper action for her.

"Not this morning, sorry."

But maybe the energetic dog would enjoy fetching a stick. She looked around her feet. No sticks here, but there were a few trees along the creek that must have dropped a stick or two. She turned back toward the bridge.

There was her fantasy man, standing sentinel by the railing.

Her breath left with an *oof*, a punch to the stomach.

Phone calls and propositions, lingerie and Bloody Marys—none of that would be overboard. Any way she could get more time with this man was worth a try. She felt rooted to the ground, frozen in place as he crossed the bridge and strolled toward her, a sexy saunter in the sunlight that made her cheeks burn, but she didn't look away. The view was too spectacular: blue jeans and bomber jacket, brown eyes and brawn.

The dog bounded between them, back and forth, until the man stopped just an arm's distance from her, leaving the dog turning in the tightest of circles.

"Good morning." He nudged the dog out of the way with a gentle knee.

"Yes. You must be the neighbor." Her thoughts were making her blush, but her cheeks were probably red from the chilly air, anyway, and the red coat was probably bringing out the color, too, so she hoped she looked more bold than bashful. "I thought you were the general contractor."

"No, I'm not."

"No. The real contractor showed up this morning and he definitely wasn't…" She let her eyes take a quick dive down the placket of his button-down shirt to the lean waist revealed by the opened bomber jacket. More slowly, she lifted her gaze back up to his tanned throat, his face. "He wasn't you."

He hesitated at that, then tilted his head a bit as he studied her, his eyebrows lifted a little in surprise, his mouth suppressing a smile. "And you were disappointed?"

"Maybe a little." She stuffed her hands in the coat pockets, feeling the heat in her cheeks, but he wasn't mocking her. There was nothing about him that was arrogant. Confident, comfortable—but not arrogant. Unlike her, he wasn't flustered in the least.

India pictured Helen's note in her mind, with its hastily scribbled addendum at the bottom: *Fabio at Nords' first night*. That sounded like there were multiple Nords. Had Helen meant to write *Nords'* or *Nord's*? Was there a wife?

Oh, what the heck. You only have a week. Just ask.

"So…" She nodded in the general direction of the golden-bricked house. "Is there anyone else at your house? Maybe a wife?"

His reaction was a little surprised again, a negative shake of his head with a bit of a smile, but his eyes were watching her with an expression that was a little…sad?

"No," he said. "Just me."

She felt butterflies in her stomach—better than a punch in the gut. She took her left hand out of her pocket and held it up, wiggling her ring-free fingers.

"You don't have a wife, either, huh?" He managed to keep a straight face as he asked.

She laughed. "No—and no husband. I'm definitely the kind of woman who is into men."

The way his smile escaped to lift the corners of his lips could not have been sexier. "What a coincidence. I'm the kind of man who is definitely into women."

Fabio crashed into her from behind, catching her behind the knees and making her legs buckle. One hand was still stuck in her coat pocket. She felt that moment of helplessness before an inevitable fall.

Her fantasy man was fast. "I got you."

She was caught against a strong chest, held up with strong hands on her upper arms.

"You got me," she repeated, sounding all breathy.

He didn't let go.

The leather of his bomber jacket was cool where she'd grabbed it with her ring-free left hand. His expression was warm as he looked at her, only inches separating them. She stood, but he didn't let go, and since their faces were so close, his voice was a quiet rumble of delicious, deep bass. "Fabio was dying to come over to see you sooner, but I'm a man of my word. I promised you twelve hours of sleep. Did you get it?"

"Fifteen, actually."

He still didn't let go. "You didn't get hurt just now? Nothing sprained?"

"Not at all." Her breathy voice sounded about a thousand times more Marilyn Monroe than normal.

"In that case," he said, as he looked past her shoulder to the frolicking dog, "thanks, Fabio."

He let go of her then, but he didn't step back. The look of approval on his face was obvious and so very welcome. He liked what he saw.

"I hope I'm not dreaming this," India said, tucking her hair behind one ear and letting her finger trace the copper hoop earring. "Did I really house-swap my way into being neighbors with a handsome, unattached bachelor?"

She was being too bold, moving too fast, but he was keeping up with her. His smile deepened, crinkling the corners of his eyes, spreading over his whole face, spreading to *her*, like a rising sun spreading light over her day.

"I can vouch for *unattached* and *bachelor*. You get to determine the *handsome* part."

She dropped her hand and very nearly sighed. "In that case, neighbor, would you care to come over? I happen to have everything a person needs to make a great Bloody Mary."

Fabio was a perfect chaperone: he got distracted easily and stayed out of their way.

Aiden walked with India, side by side, toward her temporary home.

He very nearly reached to take India's hand in his. Walking hand in hand seemed as natural as imagining her face on his pillow.

Too soon. You remember how to do this. First, you talk. You flirt. You go out to dinner. Then you know her well enough to hold hands.

"I don't know if Helen told you, but my name is India Woods. What's yours?"

Right. First, you tell each other your names.

"Aiden Nord."

"So, Aiden Nord, why are you building bookcases in Helen's garage?"

She didn't know. Of course she didn't, but it took him by surprise, because if there was anything that anyone knew about him, it was that he was a widower with two young daughters. He was building something for one of his daughters. Who else did he have to build anything for?

Olympia had used the pause button on the remote control during one of her preschool TV shows, a live-action show with a little girl as the star. Aiden remembered being surprised, and then telling himself he shouldn't be surprised that his four-year-old knew what the pause button was and how to use it. She'd paused the show to look at the TV girl's bookcase, one shaped like a tree. Aiden was building it for Olympia in the neighbor's garage, to keep it a surprise for Christmas morning.

If he told India this, she would be impressed. *You're such a good father.*

Women were always impressed. *It's precious, the way you take care of those girls. I can't believe you know how to braid hair.*

Braiding hair wasn't rocket science. No one was amazed with the dozen types of rope harnesses he could tie for rappelling; of course he could braid his daughters' hair. If he didn't care for them, who would? *That poor man. His wife died, and he's been raising those two precious little sweethearts all by himself.*

"I was borrowing Tom's power sander to prep the boards." The lie came out brusquely, but easily enough. He had his own sander. He was only using Tom and Helen's garage as a secret Santa's workshop to hide a gift for his child. Tom and Helen were nice enough to let him.

The last woman he'd dated had been nice enough, too. *An Aerosmith concert in Dallas? I'd love to go. You never get to leave your children overnight, do you? You poor thing. If you want to just get a good's night sleep for a change, I'll understand. I remember when my kids were that young.*

He hadn't wanted to sleep, damn it. Was it really necessary to have a woman stripped, sweaty, satisfied on a mattress, before she saw him as a man instead of that poor widowed father?

Yes. Every damn time.

You must miss your wife. You know, I could come over and cook dinner for you and your girls a couple of nights a week.

His wife had loved life, but hers had been cut short unjustly, unfairly. The idea that Aiden missed having a *cook* was so offensive, there wasn't enough lust in the world to override that. *No, I can't come in for a drink. It's later than I thought. The babysitter has a curfew.*

"You don't have a sander?" asked the woman whose hand he wanted to hold. "I assume you're a carpenter. A power sander sounds like a very carpenter-y thing to have."

"No, I'm in the army."

"Me, too."

He glanced at her, not really worried about fraternization rules, because she was a friend of Helen's, and therefore probably an officer. Officers could only date officers. Just to be safe…

"Major Aiden Nord."

"Major India Woods."

He laughed softly, almost to himself. She was his equal. Her striking gray eyes were alight with interest in him—as interested in him as he was in her. She didn't feel sorry for him. She didn't pity him. Her heart wasn't melting at the idea that he pulled little ankle socks over little feet every morning. She wasn't calculating how much time had passed since his wife had died, and whether or not it had been *enough*.

She was looking at *him*. Major India Woods was looking at *him*, evaluating him as a man whom she might like to get to know better, and suddenly, powerfully, he wanted to keep it that way.

"How long will you be in town, exactly?" he heard himself asking, a man with ulterior motives.

"Until Christmas Eve day. And you? Oh—never mind. You live here. Do you have to work this week?"

"My battalion declared a training holiday."

"Wow. I need to get stationed back in the States. Helen and Tom got a training holiday, too."

"Same battalion. I'm the S-3."

"Ah. That's cozy."

"It is. I didn't have to think twice about exchanging house keys with them."

"Helen planned a European honeymoon the same day your exercise was canceled. What plans did you come up with?"

"She wins. I'm not going anywhere. I have…family for Christmas."

"And between now and then?" she asked, and Aiden felt his pulse speed up, because she bit her lip as she waited for his answer.

They were almost at the back steps. He'd refrained from holding her hand for an acre, but now he let his hand rest on her lower back, escorting her unnecessarily as they ascended the flagstone steps behind the enthusiastic dog. "I have a week of free time. No prior commitments."

"Well, Major?"

"Yes, Major?"

"We're both uncommitted until Christmas Eve. What neighborly sorts of things could we put on the agenda?"

"I'm not sure," he answered her honestly, "but I'm pretty certain it all begins with a Bloody Mary."

Chapter Six

"Is this a test of my manhood?"

Aiden raised the Tabasco bottle in question. India had stopped skewering olives on cocktail picks to watch him when he'd picked up the hot-pepper sauce. "I ask because it seems like you are watching this pretty closely."

She blushed at his question, even as she tossed back her hair with a flash of sexy, copper earrings. For such a bold woman, she sure did blush easily. It was a conundrum: was she ashamed of her own boldness?

Despite her pink cheeks, she looked up at him with a come-hither look, although she didn't actually bat her eyelashes…but she came close. "I'm just curious to find out how hot you like it first thing in the morning."

That was bold, all right. Aiden leaned over the marble island toward her and lowered his voice to something quieter, a tone of voice pitched only to carry across a pillow. "Tom mentioned you were a language expert. He didn't tell me you spoke double entendre so fluently."

Her blush turned to a flush—but she smiled. Truly, she was a puzzle.

"But maybe it's a recently acquired language?" he asked. "You speak it well, but you're not entirely comfortable with it, are you?"

"I'm only certified in German, Danish, Flemish and Dutch. The rest I pick up on my own by spending time with…native speakers."

He chuckled at that. "I'll do my best, but I may not be any better at it than you are."

She did that thing again, that appraising look as her gaze drifted down his body, followed by a little showing of that dimple in one cheek, warmth in her approval. Or burning heat.

She twirled an olive on a pick. "It's hard to believe that you're new to this."

You've got no idea how rusty I am at the game. "Since a gentleman would never kiss and tell, I can neither confirm nor deny anything."

As he was still leaning over the island toward her, she leaned over the island toward him. It gave him an outstanding view down her V-necked shirt of curves and cleavage, but he wasn't certain she realized it. He glanced but he didn't stare, just in case it wasn't an intentional invitation to look.

He was certain, however, that her purr was intentional as she spoke. "My question was, how hot do you like it in the morning? I'm talking about the Bloody Mary, of course."

"That depends how good the vodka is," he answered honestly. *Let's pace ourselves here, no rush.* "What are we drinking?"

India opened a door in the island and pulled out a bottle of Russian vodka.

Aiden tipped the Tabasco over his glass. "One dash. That's excellent vodka. I don't want to kill my taste buds." He waited a beat, until her gray eyes met his. "I'll have to prove my manhood some other way."

India snorted when she giggled. Aiden had to laugh. In fact, he'd laughed a lot this morning, since Major Woods had met him at the bridge.

She came around the island to stand close and raised her glass. "A toast."

He raised his. "To what?"

"To…"

That blush really gave her away. She was telling him she was interested, but it wasn't something she did very often with men she'd just met—if she'd ever tried it before at all.

If she was new at this, Aiden didn't want her to put any pressure on herself. He tapped his glass to hers gently. "Let's keep it simple. To Bloody Marys in the morning, hot or not."

The tension left her shoulders. "To Bloody Marys."

They sipped their drinks. He didn't want to even attempt to calculate how long it had been since he'd had vodka before lunch. Rarely in the evenings, either. He'd rather head straight home to see his children than spend time at a bar with other adults. Poppy and Olympia weren't here, though.

India was.

Aiden leaned against the island. "Nothing says you're on vacation quite like having a cocktail before noon."

"To vacations."

They tapped glasses again, took longer drinks.

India sucked in a breath of air through pursed lips. "I might have made mine a little too spicy."

"Let me see." Aiden leaned forward with the vague idea of tasting her glass, but instead he kissed her lips. Softness. India was softness.

What the hell *are you doing? That isn't how it's done. First, you ask her out to dinner.*

India looked as surprised as he felt that he'd kissed her.

Damn, you're rusty, Nord. Get your act together.

"Could you...?" She cleared her throat and set down her glass. "Could you do that again?"

More and more surprising...but she didn't need to ask him twice. He kissed her soft lips once more, took an extra second to savor the sensation. Just a second.

She took a little breath against his lips and he barely, just barely, kept himself in check. They weren't lovers. Her parted lips were not an invitation for him to taste her deeply, to make love to her mouth.

But that little breath hadn't been displeasure, either. He set down his drink and very intentionally cupped her face in his hands. He kissed her softly on the corner of her mouth before he tilted her head back and kissed her chin. He smoothed his lips just an inch farther along her jawline, breathed her in. Another inch, and then he had to taste her skin on his tongue, just a taste, before placing another soft kiss there.

Her fingers fluttered a little bit on the island next to their drinks. He needed nothing more to know that she was enjoying his touch. He pulled back just far enough to see her face, anyway. Her eyes were closed. She looked relaxed, languid, lips just barely parted, a sleeping princess in a fairy tale.

He closed his eyes, too, and kissed her mouth once more. She made a little hum of a sound, and then she was kissing him back—harder. Mouths opened, heat built. Her arms were around his neck now, her body plastered against his—surely that had been of her own initiative, because he didn't remember pulling her close—ah, those lips were so soft in a shorter, sweeter kiss, a pause before a second round of hotter, sexier kisses. He must have pulled her close because his arms were around her now, anchoring her to him as she kissed him like she wanted him.

He wanted her, too. Too much. Too intently. It was too easy to see her naked in his arms, on his pillow. He should stop this. He should slow things down.

"Aiden," she whispered. "This is going to sound crazy, but..."

He kissed his way across her cheekbone to her ear, feeling her turn to liquid in his arms, her body heavier as she leaned into him, pliant under his touch. "But what?"

"But, I'm only going to be here for a week, and I know we just met, but..."

"But what?" He took her earlobe between his teeth gently, let go, nuzzled her hoop earring out of the way to kiss the soft spot just under her ear.

He felt her throat work as she swallowed, felt the vibration as she spoke. "Would you like to have sex with me?"

He was the one who turned to liquid. It was astounding, really, that he was still solid on his feet, standing on the kitchen tile.

"Just for fun?" she added. "I know it's only lust, but..."

"Lust." He smiled against her neck. He could handle lust.

"I know we're strangers, but I've known Helen for ten years, and you've known her for...?"

"One."

"For one. So, I'm pretty sure Helen's battalion S-3 isn't a serial killer—"

"India…" But he had to taste her again, taste this mouth that was his fantasy, the mouth that was saying words he wouldn't have dared to dream she would say.

She was panting lightly as she broke off the kiss. Her hand at the back of his head kept his forehead pressed to hers. Did she think he would ever, ever back away as she whispered to him?

"And," she whispered, "you have a safe bet that Helen's good friend isn't going to steal your wallet after she gives you an orgasm so great that you'll have to sleep it off."

Liquid: all his bones, all his muscles, melted with the rush of desire her words released, but he was taking her down with him, because he was never going to let her go. He cursed, one word, softly against her ear, as he fell back, only a foot until the hard marble edge of the counter cut across his backside. He slid a little lower and spread his legs a little wider, pulling India to him so she stood in the V of his legs, very close—God, he was hard and she was soft. That was right, that was good, and he was going to drown in it, gladly.

She was pressing him backward now, angling herself over him. He let her, because he loved the weight of her, the way she stayed when he let go, so he could bury his hands in her hair and tilt her head and kiss her fully, no holds barred, unrestrained. He made love to her mouth, and she met his passion, tasting him as boldly as he tasted her. Her fingers were clutching his shirt, digging into his right shoulder, his left biceps. He was aware of every little thing about her; he was lost in a wave of sensation.

"I've got—" she panted a moment "—a bed, just, just, just down the hall."

Her difficulty getting out the words made him smile,

too wide of a smile to keep kissing her. "Well, good, because this marble slab isn't getting any softer."

She took his hand, leading the way down the hall, her palm warm against his, her fingers sliding into place between his. Holding hands; he felt a small squeeze in his chest.

He pushed away the sensation and focused on the curve of her shoulder as she walked before him, and he imagined the way her hair would brush over that curve when her shoulder was as bare as he was going to make it in a moment.

"I'm using a guest bedroom," she explained. "This one."

Good. He wouldn't have to wonder if it was polite to make love on Tom and Helen's bed, although he was certain he would have overcome any etiquette issue in about a nanosecond.

He gave her guest room a quick glance. Moving boxes were still stacked in a tower in the corner. Pictures and a dresser mirror were leaning against the wall, waiting to be hung. There was a suitcase, a bed—a queen-size bed, its sheets rumpled from a sleepy woman.

"I didn't make the bed this morning," India said.

Aiden wondered why she'd think that was something to apologize for. He bent to kiss her quickly, reassuringly. "Waste of time, anyway."

Impatient now, he smoothed her shirt up her body, dizzy with the sensation of her skin on his palms, with the sight of her skin being exposed to him. The shirt was pulled over her head and dropped to the floor. He gazed at her breasts, rounded and lifted by a smooth, nude bra, and he felt weak. He longed to reach behind her, to undo the clasp and cup those breasts with his hands, but his muscles wouldn't obey his brain. She was too beautiful. He was helpless. Liquid.

He rested his forehead against hers.

She undid the buttons of his shirt with hands that trembled. He watched her fingers work, glad her arousal made it a little difficult, glad her arousal made her determined as she worked her way down to the last button, then pushed the shirt off his shoulders. He brought his wrists behind himself to tug off one cuff, then the other. If the motion made his chest and arm muscles flex, she seemed to like the show, because when the shirt hit the floor, she turned her face away from his and dropped her head to press her forehead against his collarbone instead. She exhaled, a sigh he felt on his skin, and his muscles were no longer liquid, and he was the furthest thing possible from helpless.

He lifted her face from his chest with one hand under her chin, then held her in place with a kiss as he unbuckled his belt and unzipped his jeans, freeing an erection that had grown painful in the confining clothes. She wore no belt, so he unzipped her jeans with ease, exposing a V of smooth material, nude to match her bra. Not nude enough. The curve of her waist looked beautiful and felt beautiful as he slipped his fingertips under the elastic of her underwear. He smoothed his palms over her backside to push her jeans and underwear to the floor.

She inhaled, a tiny gasp of breath. He pulled her into him, nude woman against his unzipped jeans, and she gasped again. He'd thought to undo her bra next, but to hell with that, he needed to shuck off his own jeans. As they kissed—she tasted amazing, this woman did, like heat and life—he went to take his wallet out of his back pocket to toss on the dresser, an automatic motion from years of habit, but his back pocket was empty. Damn it, he'd been out walking a dog, not out on a date.

"India," he said, but she kissed any further words away.

"India." This time, he placed his hands gently on either side of her neck and smoothed his thumbs along her perfect jawline. "Not only do I not have a wallet for you to steal, I don't have a condom, either."

"I have an IUD." Then her hands were caressing their way up his bare back, over his shoulders, but he didn't move. He was struck still at the thought, the incredible thought, of being inside India, bare.

He couldn't do it—he shouldn't. He had annual physicals, he knew he was healthy, but they were strangers and it just wasn't done. If a man respected a woman at all, if he respected himself, he used protection. He protected *her* and gave her some peace of mind. He always wore a condom.

The only exception: his wife.

He pushed away the thought—not now, not when everything India was all around him, her scent, the sound of her breath, the taste of her mouth, the softness of her skin. She'd gone still now, too, maybe realizing the implications of the words she'd just blurted out in the heat of the moment. He kept holding her neck gently between his hands as she opened her eyes, and the impact of those serious, silver eyes obliterated any thoughts outside of their two-person world. He cared for her. He wouldn't take advantage of her; he gave her time to think.

"I may have a condom," she said, and the blush was back. "Let me go see."

He dropped his hands as she turned to go, but she realized her jeans were around her ankles and giggled, but it was a nervous giggle, no snort. He held her arm for balance as she kicked off the jeans. He was glad she hadn't pulled them back up, although why he'd think that had been a possibility, he didn't know.

She went into the bathroom, and he heard the distinctive sound of a woman sorting through a makeup bag, the clinking of plastic compacts and lipsticks and things.

Such a feminine sound. It made him smile as he laid on the bed and kicked his own jeans the rest of the way off, still letting the anticipation and arousal build. Even if she didn't find a condom, he was going to enjoy her, savor her, learn her as he touched all of her soft skin. And, if her boldness held true, he'd feel her soft hands on him.

She came back in the room, naked but for her bra, a condom packet in her hand. When he saw it, the spike of anticipation was outright painful. Within the same fraction of a second, her gaze fell on him, the man who was stretched out on her bed, which made her stop and breathe an *oh*, and put her hand over her heart as if she was startled that he was there.

The foil packet touched her breast. She recovered quickly and smiled just a shade too brightly. "I did have one. I don't know why. It's from…a long time ago."

He shook his head at her blush. "Major Woods?"

"Yes?"

"How old are you?"

She was surprised. "Thirty-two."

He pushed himself up to reach for her hand and tugged her down to the mattress. "Then you don't have to explain why you have a condom in a travel bag. I'm not expecting a virgin. I wouldn't know what to do with you if you were."

Yes, you would. The thought whispered through him as he watched her ease herself onto her side, facing him. There was something vulnerable about her.

You'd know what to do. If this were all new to her, he'd be deliberately gentle. He'd talk to her. He'd go slowly—but he'd be thorough. He'd make sure she loved her first time with him.

This *was* her first time with him, virgin or not.

The thought didn't diminish his desire for her, but it changed the tenor of it. Fun? Yes, but this wasn't anything like a game. That vulnerability called to something in him. *Handle her with care.*

She sat up again. "Oops. My bra." She started to reach behind herself to unclasp it, but she had the condom packet in her hand. "Oh. I just—" She tried to laugh at her own clumsiness.

She didn't strike him as a normally clumsy woman; she was nervous. Aiden gently took the packet out of her fingers, then deliberately kept his eyes on her face as she undid the clasp and her bra fell away. As she laid down again, he took in her reddened lips, her flushed skin, the way her breasts peaked, the way she slid her thighs together restlessly. She was aroused, without question, but she wasn't touching him. Aroused, but nervous.

He reached over her head to set the condom packet behind her, next to the pillow, out of the way for now. Her eyes widened a little bit. "No rush," he said. "We're on vacation."

"That's true." Her smile was a reward. He'd read her correctly.

Take your time with her. Talk to her.

But he had to touch her, this beautiful woman lying nude beside him. He put a hand on her waist and pushed with just enough pressure to let her know he wanted her to roll onto her back. He remembered to speak only after she'd already laid back, already understood his touch, but he explained himself, anyway. "You're very beautiful. I want to see you. I'm glad it's daylight."

He stayed on his side, letting his gaze sweep down her body, a completely feminine body, nothing like his own, the yin to his yang.

His hand followed. *Gently, slowly.* Chest, breast, stomach. Brushing over curls, sliding down a thigh. He listened to her shallow breaths, watched her stretch one leg and point her toes, felt the rustle of movement as she lifted her arm and set her hand on his shoulder— and pulled him toward her.

He obeyed the pressure of her hand, rolling onto her gently, only half his body covering half of hers—and he just about lost all of his mind. Her skin against his skin short-circuited his brain. It was the extreme version of the feeling he'd had when he'd first thought of her this morning, that electric awareness, every cell of his body seeking her, wanting her.

Here she was. She fit against him, she was made for him—that grunt of desire came from him. That convulsive thrust was his.

She made a sound, too—desire, or fear? Her hand stayed on his shoulder, but he felt its fine tremor. Lust, or nervousness?

He opened his eyes, desperate for some sense of control, and fell into the silver-gray of hers, for she'd been studying his face. She bit her lip—sexy or second-guessing herself?

Rules of engagement. That was how to maintain sanity. The rules of engagement had to be decided ahead of time, because during combat, decision-making was at the most rudimentary level: go or no-go. Soldiers had to know in advance which actions could trigger a battle, which responses were acceptable. Aiden needed to know the rules of engagement *now*, because he was being overwhelmed by an onslaught of sensation. He didn't want to lose track of what was too fast for India, what would be too far for her. Go or no-go?

The condom packet was beside her on the mattress. The ends of her long hair, spilling off the pillow, nearly touched it. *She has to reach for it. If she really wants this, she will tear that packet open. She has to reach for it herself.*

That was it.

With the decision made, he could lose himself in the pleasure of the moment and stop second-guessing every bite of her lip or tremor of her hand. He lifted himself on one forearm, stroked his other hand up her body more firmly, watching her eyes as he did. She closed them—shy. But then she pushed against him luxuriously, catlike under his caress—bold.

They would go as far as she wanted to go. They wouldn't go as far as he wanted to go, not unless she grabbed that foil packet herself.

He looked his fill of her breasts now, scooped his hand around the rounded shape of one, bent his head to enjoy the impossible softness of the other with his mouth. At the touch of his tongue, she sucked in a breath and pushed at his head a bit—he'd hurt her? She giggled, a lovely sound. He was charmed by the shyness, but he was cheering for the boldness.

Please, India—trigger those rules of engagement.

Chapter Seven

Aiden's warm brown gaze captured hers as they looked at one another over the curve of her breast. "Ticklish?"

"I'm not." But India was biting her lip and laughing because it *had* tickled. "At least I was never ticklish there before, not with—" She stumbled. "W-with anyone else."

He raised an eyebrow at her stutter, and she blushed. Again.

I'm thirty-two. He's not expecting a virgin. Still, she was embarrassed to have even mentioned previous partners.

Aiden licked her like she was a piece of candy, with a firm stroke of his tongue. "Does that tickle?" he murmured against her skin.

"Not as much."

He looked back up to her and smiled. That sight alone stoked the pressure that was building, the pleasurable pressure that was rapidly building to a point where it would become pain without a release. By the time they got around to actual intercourse, she was going to be ready to explode at the first stroke.

She felt like a virgin in some ways. She'd never quite

done it like this before, never had so much pleasure building up. Aiden was so into touching her. Everywhere. Not just *going for the good parts*, as what's-his-face had announced he was doing, as if that had been some kind of genius game plan.

India had her fingertips resting lightly on Aiden's head. He turned away from her breast and kissed the inside of her wrist. She shivered with pleasure.

He moved up the mattress a bit, teasing her with a smile. "Your *wrist* is ticklish?"

She shook her head, rustling the pillowcase. "No, it's just that you're finding parts of me that no one's ever… That I didn't know were so…happy to be touched."

Something flashed in his eyes, an emotion a little darker than they'd shared so far. Her heart pounded.

"Beautiful India," he said, his tone not quite as light as before, "then I'm sorry to tell you you've been sleeping with idiots."

That startled a laugh out of her. *No, that's not it. I'm just not very good at this.* The words were on the tip of her tongue, an automatic excuse for lackluster sex, but Aiden had closed the inches between them to kiss her lips again, then her cheek, a slow descent down her throat, her collarbone, a lick on her shoulder. Her *shoulder*. She loved it, all of it.

"Maybe you need something that won't tickle." Aiden's jaw was slightly rough with the earliest stubble of a beard—he probably hadn't shaved on this first morning of his vacation. Quite deliberately, he ran his jaw a short way across her chest. It left behind a little burning wake, a sensation only a man could give a woman. As that sensation faded, he slid a little lower, keeping his eyes on her face, and did it again, a gentle abrasion down the curve of one breast this time. She held her breath as he lightly rasped over the peak, but before the sensation could fade, he closed his mouth around her, his tongue extraordinarily cool and soothing in contrast.

She gasped and sucked in her stomach, a contraction that made her bring her knees a little closer to her chest, as if her whole body wanted to curl up around this one source of pleasure. Her fingertips had been resting lightly on his hair; now her whole hand cupped the back of his head fiercely.

He rested his forehead on her chest and made a sound like he had to catch his breath, too. "India..."

Do you see what we have here? That was the rest of the sentence that came after her name. She knew it.

This, *this* was what she'd been missing. This piece of the puzzle had been missing from her life, and because she hadn't known how it could feel, she hadn't minded the predictable Saturday nights. She'd been content with a man who'd been able to leave her bed forever at the first sign that his mother might not approve of her. She hadn't understood the teal bra and a man's willingness to risk a routine that benefited him. She'd let those relationships go. She hadn't fought for any of them, because none of them had had *this*. This spark. This joy.

Aiden placed soft kisses down her body, a kiss on each rib, warm breath on her stomach, as he slid lower still on the mattress. She reached for him, stroked his hair with two hands as she discovered her left hipbone was sensitive to a man's mouth, her right knee to his trailing fingertips.

It felt wonderful, this new source of joy. This was sex, good sex with a giving partner. How had she lived without this for so long? *I'm thirty-two years old...* She felt a quick sting of self-pity: why couldn't she have had this in her life before now?

With his hands, Aiden brought her back to the moment as he touched her with care, the most intimate exploration yet. Intimacy. Connection. She'd found it here, paradise in bed with Aiden Nord.

Finally. She'd found it now because she was with *him*.

Then Aiden bent his head and she felt the strong stroke of his tongue. She arched her back at the sensation, so much pleasure from her lover—finally, everything was right. She was in the right place at the right time with the right man. Finally. When she squeezed her eyes shut, tears ran down the sides of her face to wet her hair. She didn't care; let them fall.

He shifted again, a slight lifting of his mouth, but she didn't feel him breathe. She didn't feel him move at all for a long moment. When her eyes fluttered open, he rolled away from her and laid on his back.

"Everything's okay, India."

"It is?" She didn't know what he was talking about.

"It really is. Just give me a moment."

Was she not supposed to touch him for a moment? That couldn't be right. She ate up the sight of him, the way the muscles of his arm moved as he laid his forearm over his eyes, every motion by this man a thing of strength and beauty. She rolled toward him, wanting to touch him, to explore him, but when she slid her hand down his stomach, he caught it with his own.

"You don't have to do that. We'll go out to dinner. I'd like to take you out to dinner tonight, okay? Really. I just need a minute." He drew one knee up, and she had the intuition that he was trying to master his breathing.

"Give you a minute to do what?" she asked, but suddenly, she knew. "A minute to cool off? Don't you dare. You can't—"

Neither one of them had climaxed. Nobody was satisfied. He couldn't just stop everything now.

But he could, of course. He wasn't obliged to have sex with her.

She laid on her back and stared at the ceiling. Her heart hurt. Every single beat hurt. Something had happened; she'd done something wrong again. Why was sex always so hard?

She might have been content to let another man give her a pat on the shoulder and leave the bed when he'd decided he'd had enough of trying with her, but not this time. This had been so different. Aiden had been so different. This time, she would ask.

"What did I do wrong?"

"Nothing."

"Am I a bad kisser?"

He only laughed, a short sound of disbelief.

She wasn't joking. "Am I... Do I respond...funny? In a funny way? Am I odd?" She kept her gaze on the ceiling, her blush burning her cheeks more painfully than anything his rough razor stubble could do. She could feel him looking at her, but she could not look at him. These were the hardest questions she'd ever asked in her life.

"India...don't cry."

"I'm not crying."

Oh, God. She was crying. It just didn't feel like it because there were no gut-wrenching sobs, but tears were sliding from the corners of her eyes to the pillow. It irritated her. More than that—it angered her.

She sat up and turned toward Aiden, dashing the unwanted tears away as she tucked her legs under herself to kneel beside him. She sat on her feet, a yoga pose, or that of a geisha girl. Which was more fitting? Frustration and embarrassment and anger warred within her. She'd had a taste of something that she now wanted desperately. She'd been missing out all these years. She'd had something; she couldn't go back to nothing.

"If someone doesn't tell me what I'm doing wrong in bed, I may go crazy. You're it, Aiden. I'll never see you again, so you're the one who can do me this favor. Just tell me, please. *Why did you stop?*"

He took his forearm off his eyes. "Didn't you need to stop?"

"Are you kidding me? I've never wanted anything more than to keep feeling what you were making me feel."

"You were feeling *sad.*"

She shook her head in quick denial. "What made you think that?"

"India, *you were crying.* You said something about another guy, I said he was an idiot, and a minute later, you were crying. I don't mind being the rebound guy, but I won't make love to a woman while she's literally crying over a breakup with another man."

"That's it?"

"That's enough."

He was looking at her like she'd lost her mind. She was looking at him like—like he was the best man she'd ever looked at. He'd stopped in the middle of sex because he'd thought she was unhappy. He had standards, this man did. Empathy, an innate kindness. He knew how to worry about someone else before himself.

She had to explain fast, because he was worried about something he didn't have to worry about. "I wasn't thinking about anyone but you. How could I?

You're so…" She could never fill in that blank quickly, so she kept going. "The last idiot was never— Jeez, I can't even think of his name right this second, that jerk. If I was crying, those were tears of gratitude, because I was enjoying the best sex of my life. The best. I'll tell you what I was thinking. I was thinking that finally, *finally*, I found a man who knows how to touch me. This felt so…essential."

Their eyes were locked on each other. Silence stretched between them.

"Tears of gratitude?" he finally asked, and he raised one eyebrow skeptically.

She bit her lip. "Too melodramatic? But yes. It's so amazing with you, I was so happy to be with you…" She gave up. "Tears of joy, then?"

Aiden began to smile, that devastatingly appealing quirk at the corner of his mouth. "The best sex of your life, huh?"

She blinked at the change in attitude. "Well…it would have been. We were definitely on the way to a grand finale, but you had to go and turn all gentlemanly on me and get concerned about me and decide to *stop*." She gritted out the word *stop*.

"I apologize for interrupting the best sex of your life." His hand settled just above her knee so naturally, it was possible he wasn't even aware he'd reached out to touch her. "How long has it been since the *last* sex of your life?"

She shook her head again. "I thought you didn't approve of kissing and telling."

"Yes, but you already kissed and told me enough to make me wonder."

"Months. He just stopped being interested, but I didn't know why."

"You didn't ask?"

The truth was so clear in hindsight. "I didn't care."

He squeezed her thigh.

"It was never..." She gestured around them, at the tumbled sheets, the crooked pillows. "It was never like this. But it turns out he didn't stop. He's been having sex with someone else."

Aiden winced. "When did you find that out?"

"That has nothing to do with this."

He rolled his eyes. "C'mon, India. When?"

"Day before yesterday."

He didn't wince again, but India knew that sounded awful. Because her ex was awful, this wonderful morning now sounded awful.

"That has nothing to do with this. I'm telling you, I was crying *tears of joy* just now. Because I loved everything you were doing, damn it. Now I'm really ticked off, because I did not want to waste a minute of something great by discussing something that was not. A whole wasted year of *not this*."

She was tied up in knots now. Not only was she sitting on her feet with her thighs pressed tightly together, but her hands were clenched together, tucked under her chin, which brought her arms in front of her chest, hiding some of her nakedness from him. This was all wrong.

"See? I told you I'm the rebound guy." He squeezed her thigh—and winked at her.

He didn't seem unhappy to be the rebound guy, but she couldn't let him think that was how she felt about it. "I wasn't thinking that. You're so much more than that."

"Best lover, then?" he asked, sounding boyishly hopeful. He sat up halfway.

She sat back, a little exasperated with him. She

unclenched her hands, but she crossed her arms over her chest, still hiding herself. "I can't award you Best Lover, because you stopped before some key required moments." *So there.*

"I'm in the running for the Best Lover award, though. That makes me one hell of a rebound guy." He laid back down, but he tugged on her wrist with one hand as he did. "Come here."

She let him have her arm. "That sounds so awful. *The Rebound Guy.*"

He laughed even as he kissed the fingers of her hand, then set her hand on his shoulder so she was leaning over him. "Or it sounds like a great way to spend a vacation."

Her mouth dropped open at the outrageous remark.

"Now come here." He pushed one of her knees, encouraging her to spread them apart. Then he was tugging on her ankle, like he wanted her to move that leg to straddle him. She settled onto him, one knee on either side of his waist.

"You seem a little eager to be my rebound guy."

"I wonder why." He hadn't cooled off at all. His body was thick and hot beneath her. His hands stroked up her, sure and firm, like he had the right to feel all of her skin from her hips to her waist to her chest. Hot hands cupped her breasts for a moment before smoothing over her shoulders. She watched him as he watched his hands. He looked very *satisfied* with the path his hands were taking, like he was doing some kind of primal survey, taking ownership of the woman he'd invited to straddle him. Or maybe that was how she felt, like he was reestablishing the connection that had been building from all their touching, from skin sliding over skin.

With a gesture that seemed too civilized given their

current state, he brushed her hair back from one shoulder, gently pulling a few strands out from the hoop earring. Survey over, he rested his hands on her hips, a loose grip. His hands were so large, his thumbs rested so very close to *there*.

She'd never wanted a man so badly in her life.

Conversationally, he said, "I am also available this week for revenge sex."

"Revenge sex?" She couldn't grasp the meaning of the phrase, of any phrase, because her reality was entirely physical at the moment, centered on the man underneath her, between her *knees*, and such a man—

"That's when you know your ex is with someone else, and you're determined to outdo them and have more sex than they're having. To have better sex than they're having."

"That's revenge sex?"

"That's revenge sex." He reached up and pulled her head down to kiss her on the mouth as if they were the lovers they should be.

She panted over his lips for a moment, until she was sure she could speak very clearly. "Then *hell, yes*, you are the rebound guy, and no person I've ever slept with or ever dated at any point in the past or even *looked* at in the last decade will have better sex than I do this week."

She tossed back her hair when she sat up, but Aiden's knowing grin made her grin, too. She felt a bubble of joy in her chest—it would come out as a laugh any second—as she lunged a little past the other pillow to grab the condom, which brought her hair forward again, all around her face and shoulders. She sat up to tear open the packet. It would be easier to use her teeth to get the tear started.

But Aiden had gone very still. Every muscle in his body had tightened underneath her, as did his grip on her hips. He was watching her with an intensity that pushed aside the playfulness.

"What is it?" she asked, tearing the packet halfway with her teeth. She tore it the rest of the way with her hand and scooted back so she could sheathe him. Aiden couldn't be surprised by this. He couldn't be. As she smoothed her hand down his length, she leaned in to purr in his ear, "Did I not make it clear that I was taking you up on your offer, starting now?"

"My beautiful India," he said, a growl instead of a laugh, "we are a go."

Then she was flipped onto her back and Aiden took over. India forgot about revenge sex and rebound guys. She couldn't think about anything or anyone except Aiden, about any other time of her life except now. Everything fell away, and she surrendered herself to the best lover she'd ever had.

She was falling asleep on him.

"Hey," Aiden whispered to the woman he'd exhausted. "Didn't this start with you bragging that I was the one who was going to need to sleep it off?"

India stayed on her stomach, her arm stretched over his waist casually, strands of her hair clinging to his chest and stomach as he propped himself up by stuffing an extra pillow behind his neck. It jostled her a little bit.

"Go to sleep, baby," she mumbled into the mattress.

Baby. No one called him baby; it sounded sexy, tacked onto the end of an order like that. Aiden smoothed a few of the wayward strands of her hair back into place as her breathing slowed. *Rumpled and sleepy.* He smiled to himself. *Far beyond rumpled, and sleeping like the dead* would be more accurate. He wished he could obey her order to go to sleep, but he had to get home to his kids.

No, he didn't.

He was so used to thinking that way, but they weren't here. Poppy and Olympia—his chest hurt a little at the thought of them. He hadn't forgotten them—they were always a part of him—but they'd been relegated to the back of his mind while his focus had been on India, all on India.

Guilt warred with the afterglow of hot pleasure, which was absurd, because it wasn't as if he'd abandoned his fatherly duties. His girls weren't even in the state.

But Poppy and Olympia…he saw their little faces in his mind. He missed them.

He looked at India's face. He brushed her hair off her cheek, so it wouldn't tickle her nose and wake her. He slid a little lower, making himself at home in her bed. There was no babysitter getting paid by the hour, no clock ticking. He could take an afternoon nap with the woman he'd made love to all morning. There was nothing he'd rather do.

The novelty of being able to go where the day took him was striking. It was hard to believe he'd been walking a dog just hours ago, completely unaware that he was about to start one of the best days of his life.

Best day? Part of him felt guilty. Outraged, even. *How can you think such a thing?*

He had children; his children had given him the best days of his life, moments of pure love and pride—holding them for the first time, watching their first steps—moments that could not be equaled. He'd been married, had enjoyed many great days with his wife. Carrying her over the threshold of their first house. The sonogram with two heartbeats. Their wedding day—that had been one of the best days of his life. Of course.

Of course.

All of that was true: his children, his wife, his life.

Aiden looked at India's face for a long, quiet moment. She'd revealed so much to him, her sexiness, her shyness. She'd made him laugh. She'd told him off. And then, there'd been those moments of hot silence where they had felt like one and moved like one, with only one need, one desire. Now she was peaceful. He felt peaceful, too. It had been a miraculous morning, unexpected and perfect. He kissed her very gently, letting her sleep, his lips light on her forehead.

"And this day, too," he whispered, "is one of the best days of my life."

That ringtone was the worst.

Her phone wasn't even in the room, but it was so high-pitched, it invaded her sweet dreams.

The phone stopped ringing. Relief. She could fall asleep again if she didn't move a muscle, and she really wanted to fall asleep again, because she was dreaming of sleeping next to Aiden. She was actually sleeping next to Aiden, but she was dreaming it, too. Her brain didn't want to miss a minute, apparently.

Don't move a muscle. But she couldn't resist. She opened one eye to see her dream man in real life. Sculpted muscle, warm skin, tan body against white sheets.

Her phone rang again, down the hall in the kitchen, so obnoxious. It didn't stop ringing for at least ten rings, which meant it was probably her video app, the one she used in place of international phone calls. It might be Helen, having an issue with the apartment. Helen would forgive her if India explained later that she'd been sleeping with this paragon of manhood.

Paragon. A fancy way to say "the best." India smiled to herself. He'd won that Best Lover award decisively.

Her phone rang again. Maybe Helen had run into a really serious problem. India supposed she had to get up and answer, especially because that high-pitched ring might wake up Aiden, too, and he deserved to sleep.

She couldn't answer the video call while she was stark naked. She'd love to slip into Aiden's shirt, but that was too obvious, and the man had no other clothing here. It would be no hardship for her if he walked around shirtless, but he might get chilly. She wouldn't want him to catch a cold. She had plans for him this week.

She tried not to laugh at the thought, because she had an unfortunate tendency to snort if she giggled, and she really didn't want to wake Aiden. She tiptoed out of the bedroom and went to raid Helen's room for a bathrobe. One was hanging on the back of the master bathroom door. It was silky and lacy, providing modesty without making the wearer look very modest. *Perfect.*

India was tying the sash when she caught her reflection in the mirror.

Oh, my God. Who is that woman?

Her hair was wildly messy, but her skin positively glowed. There was a red mark on her neck from a kiss that had held her in place for an extra moment of demand. Her lips were a little puffy, but she couldn't force them into a frown, not when she felt like she was going to laugh at any second, for no reason at all. She was just *happy*.

The woman in the mirror looked thoroughly... ravished? Radiant? That woman had been satisfied in every physical sense—and that made her heart sing with satisfaction, too.

She smiled at her reflection. "Someone looks like she's having the best time of her life."

Her phone rang.

She did not want to answer that phone. Helen would guess in a second why India looked so merrily disheveled—or else Helen would give her bad news, like her car had been stolen. India walked briskly down the hall to silence it.

Naturally, her phone stopped ringing just as she picked it up. Missed Call: Gerard-Pierre.

That took her glow down a notch.

There was another notification of a missed call from him. And another.

Oh, garbage. She knew him. He wouldn't stop calling. If he felt it was time for him to talk and for her to listen, then that was that.

India sank into a chair at the kitchen table and tried a few drop-down menu options, but it wasn't easy to find a way to block his video-chat requests on the app. The phone rang again in her hand.

Garbage, garbage, garbage. She couldn't talk to him now. It was a *video* chat, and right now, she looked like—

She looked like a woman who'd had some world-class revenge sex. That's what she looked like. There was a French term for it: *en déshabille*.

She remembered the shock of that teal bra, and answered the call.

Gerard-Pierre was too indignant to be shocked at her appearance. *"Enfin, tu m'as répondu. Où étais-tu?"*

"Did you call me just to yell at me for not answering when you called me?" India kept an eye on the video of herself in the upper right corner of the screen. She made a little show of fixing her mussed-up hair, then rested her chin on her hand, feeling very proud of herself.

Gerard-Pierre demanded to know who the man in her apartment was.

Ha. India could just imagine Gerard-Pierre banging on her door, and the shock of having Helen's husband answer it. Tom Cross was a good-looking man, an officer and a...very good person to be vague about.

India shrugged. *"C'est important? C'est un ami,"* she said, because French was very good for sounding blasé. *Does it matter? He's a friend.* India hadn't actually met Tom in person yet, but he was a good sport every time he got stuck in one of her video chats with Helen.

"He took my key," Gerard-Pierre said in French, his tone getting more indignant by the second. "Right out of my hand."

It sounded like Tom had been a *great* sport about getting stuck between his wife's friend and her ex. Kudos to Helen for marrying a hunk who automatically backed up anyone his wife backed up.

"I hope you didn't put up a fight. Tom's a military police officer. He's got...moves." She was speaking double entendre and doing it in French, too. Aiden would be so proud.

India propped her phone against the napkin holder and sat back a little bit. She didn't have to fake her slow, sleepy blink. She had a man in her bed whom she wanted to get back to.

"Where are you?" Gerard-Pierre demanded. "What are you doing?"

Her slow, secret smile wasn't fake, either.

"Who is he to you, this Tom?"

Obviously, Gerard-Pierre had no idea India was out

of the country and Helen was in her apartment. He could assume what he wanted to assume about Tom. India owed her ex no explanations, but he sure owed her one.

"You're not going to tell me, India? You want me to guess?"

Her name had always sounded odd, coming from his lips. With his soft, slurry French surrounding it, the three short syllables of *In-di-a* were too obviously not part of his language.

He scowled. "I can't believe you let another man into your apartment."

She snorted—a disgusted snort, no giggle—at his imperious tone. "I can't believe you let another *woman* into my apartment and slept with her on my couch."

Gerard-Pierre tried to switch to an imploring puppy-dog-eyes expression. "This is why it is important that we talk. This is why I had to keep calling until you answered. I must explain my heart to you. I must."

He was crooning to her in French, laying it on thick, preparing to deliver a monologue on his heart and soul and his feelings and life and his dreams and...yuck.

She decided to never speak French to the man again; she tried to forestall him in English. "I'm not interested in your heart. Your heart didn't screw another woman on my couch. I put all your stuff in the hallway. You returned your key. I think that concludes this relationship." She glanced at herself in the little corner screen. She was losing that drowsy, glowing look. She wanted it back. She wanted Aiden.

"I didn't know, India. I swear it to you. I didn't know my own heart until my family told me they were coming for Christmas to meet the woman with whom I'd been sharing my life for over a year. That was the moment I knew I had to leave you."

Likewise.

"Because when I imagined my family meeting the woman I loved, I thought of *her*. Not you. She has to be, she must be, the woman they meet this holiday."

Ouch. She'd assumed his note had meant he wanted to introduce her to his family. He hadn't wanted them to meet her at all. That shouldn't have stung, but it did. A whole darned year, after all…

Gerard-Pierre was still continuing his monologue in the slurry, blurry French he spoke after a few glasses of wine. "I could not pretend to love you in front of my family. They would have seen through the *charade*. They would want me to follow my heart, and my heart chose her. There was no other option. You understand, *mon amie*, don't you?"

She kept her English short and crisp. "Yes. Your heart chose to boink someone in my apartment, and your family will be very happy to meet your side chick. A very merry Christmas for everyone."

Boink didn't have a French equivalent. Like the language expert she was, she could conjugate it for Gerard-Pierre: *boink, boinked, boinking, has boinked.*

"*Cherie*, it is tragic that you don't know true passion. I could not bear to wait a minute longer to make love to her when she came to me at your place and gave me her heart," he said, patronizing and pitying her at once. "Maybe you'll find that out yourself, some day. I understand that you are hurting right now, but when enough time has passed and you think you are ready to take another lover, you should try being more— Who is that?"

Qui c'est? India looked at her video self in the screen's corner. Behind her, Aiden was walking into the kitchen, jeans on, shirt off. *Oh, my.*

She turned around. Aiden strolled to just outside of

the camera range. As he started to get himself a glass of ice water, he met her gaze and winked.

I am also available this week for revenge sex. He'd done that hot walk on purpose.

Her blasé expression was slipping. All the happy-glowy-ness had returned to her face—and Gerard-Pierre's face was looking far less smug.

"Who is that?" he repeated, his French higher-pitched. "Where are you? That's not the same man who was in your apartment. Is it?"

"That's my rebound guy. Now, you were about to give me some advice, weren't you?"

But Aiden's strong hand was suddenly onscreen, passing her the glass of ice water—"Thank you," she said—then his profile was visible as he kissed her temple—"I was so thirsty," she lied—then his strong jaw was on the screen as he placed his mouth very close to her ear and asked, "Are you ready for more?"

India's eyes opened as wide as Gerard-Pierre's at that. She sat very still, holding up the ice water as Aiden lowered himself to one knee, kissing the silk lapel of her robe as he sank down, his head slowly disappearing from the phone screen.

She and Gerard-Pierre were left staring at each other for one second, and then India burst into laughter. Aiden was crouched under the table, but he was cracking up, too—silently.

"Qu'est-ce qu'un rebound guy?"

At Gerard-Pierre's demand to know what a rebound guy was, India laughed so hard that she spilled a little ice water in her lap. She squealed at the cold and put down the glass hastily, but Aiden started tugging on her robe, pulling her down to the floor. She could only gasp, "Okay, bye now, Gerard-P—" before Aiden tickled her waist and she squealed again and tried to dodge his hands, which made it a challenge to tap the phone's disconnect button as she fell out of the chair and landed on top of Aiden.

They continued to kiss and laugh and tickle until they were lying on the floor, half under the table, smiling at each other like a couple of teenagers who'd just pulled off a prank.

"Much better," Aiden said.

"What is?"

"Your smile."

"How did you know who he was? Do you speak French?"

"I didn't like his tone of voice. I could tell everything from that."

"Wow, really?"

He squeezed her waist and gave her a little shake. "No. You were answering him in English, you know. It wasn't hard to figure it out. 'Your heart chose to boink someone.' Great line."

"The way you sank out of the screen—the look on his face! That was priceless."

Being under the table gave her a cozy feeling, like they were in a kid's fort, hiding away. She propped her head on one hand and trailed her other hand over his muscled chest. He was strong—when he let go during sex, breathtakingly so. When his body had covered hers, she'd reveled in it, even then not realizing just how much power it contained, not until that final second before his release, that last stroke that had pushed her whole body up the mattress. It had been thrilling.

She wanted to feel it again. With a sigh, she stopped tracing his muscles with her fingers and settled her head onto his chest.

"He wasn't good enough for you," Aiden said.

She laughed softly. "You are such a good rebound guy. Tell me more."

"You didn't need him. You'll find someone much better."

I already have. The thought was so clear—and so scary.

This was just for fun. Just a few vacation days.

It won't be long enough.

Too clear. Too scary. She needed to distract herself. She started kissing her way down his body.

He kept up his rebound-guy reassurances, barely stumbling over a word as she kissed her way lower and lower, and his hand began to smooth her hair gently. "They say it takes two, but it doesn't. He's the one who screwed up."

"Good one," she whispered over his navel.

"It was definitely him, not you, because you're... *damn*...terrific."

"Mmm-hmm."

"India—" A sharp inhalation, and then all he could say was *India*, repeating her name in their cozy hideaway, each syllable sounding like it was part of a language he'd always spoken.

Chapter Eight

Aiden crossed the bridge, heading back to his house twenty-four hours after he'd first followed Fabio over this same bridge and walked straight into India's arms.

Straight into her arms—that wasn't an exaggeration. How long had he spoken to her yesterday morning before he'd had his hands on her? Two minutes? No more than three, before Fabio had bumped her into him, like the world's best canine wingman.

From that moment, Aiden hadn't wanted to take his hands off India—and, incredibly, that was the perfect attitude to have, because India wanted to have her hands on him, too. He was drunk on sex with India, high on the constant contact with her skin. She'd asked him to stay for supper last evening. He'd shrugged on his shirt, she'd stayed in her robe, and they'd talked until the pizzas had baked their way from frozen to deliciously hot. A bottle of wine…back to bed.

How can life go from hell to heaven in a day?

He was so aware of himself this morning, of where he was, how the air felt cool on his neck, how the sun felt warm on his face. Inside, too, he felt like he was seeing himself differently for the first time in ages.

In front of a new gas fireplace, he'd been drawn out by questions that had reminded him of the life he'd lived outside of the past four years. India had wanted to know about the sports he'd played in high school—football, but the coach had required them all to run track and field in the spring, and Aiden had ended up being more dedicated to the discus and the long jump than football.

She'd wanted to know about his first year away from home. He'd been homesick at West Point and unable to admit it to anyone around him, barely able to admit it to himself, because they were all trying to be tough, invulnerable cadets in Dress Gray, wanting to prove they deserved to walk in the hallowed, historic footsteps of generals and presidents and astronauts. Eighteen and homesick had been a hard thing to be in the same barracks where Schwarzkopf and Aldrin had slept.

He'd forgotten so much.

He'd forgotten his own origin story.

Ah, Aiden. There you are. I remember you now.

He watched his boots as he strode across the bridge, each step striking the planks, each plank acting like a sounding board, amplifying the sound as it bounced off the surface of the water below. Even his footsteps sounded better. They had more depth, a satisfying resonance.

Last night, when he and India had eventually fallen silent in front of the flames, she'd taken his hand and led him to her bed. She hadn't asked him if he'd like to spend the whole night; he hadn't asked if he could. They'd fallen asleep like a couple of innocent puppies piled together, arms and legs and noses all on top of each other, all touching, all night.

And this morning? Her shy confession that she was out of condoms had charmed him. She'd come into the bedroom this morning with the empty box. They'd used three and the box had originally had…three.

It had been a brand-new box the day before? He'd teased her: *I thought you said these were left over from a long-ago trip. It must not have been a very good trip.*

But her chin had gone up, a little defensively: *I decided I didn't trust him enough to sleep with him. But I'd been prepared. There's nothing wrong with that.*

No, there isn't. He'd sat up as she'd sunk onto the mattress next to him. *What made you decide you could trust me?*

She'd tugged on a corner of the pillow, then fallen still. *I don't know. What made you decide you could trust me?*

I don't know, but I do.

Yes. I do, too.

He'd left her while she showered. At his house, he had a box left over from a less satisfying weekend, too. While he was home, he would shower and shave and bring back a change of clothes to take her out to dinner tonight. He *was* going to take India out to dinner. It might be out of order, but it was a step he didn't want to skip.

He walked up his back steps, walked into the empty living room of his own house—and got blindsided.

Poppy's tower of blocks stood abandoned, unfinished. Olympia's mini beanbag chair was still indented with the shape of her. The sudden weight of missing his children dropped on him, nearly driving him to his knees.

He took the hit standing, ambushed by his own emotions, the ache of longing killing the joy that had compelled him to come here.

Another emotion, another hit: guilt. How could he

have been thinking of heaven when his children were so far away? He'd walked across that bridge while rejoicing that his life had taken a turn for the better, but how could anything that excluded his daughters be for the better?

He had no easy answer—he didn't want to think about it.

Move out, soldier. He'd come here with specific objectives. A shower, a shave, a change of clothes—a box. Lines from the Ranger Creed had been ingrained in his mind years ago: *move further, faster.*

But as Aiden walked through his house toward the stairs that led up to his bedroom—and Poppy's bedroom and Olympia's—he snagged a plastic toy vacuum and set it by the colorful play kitchen. He picked up Olympia's dinosaur-print nightgown and Poppy's Batman cape and carried them upstairs, each move ingrained by four years of fatherhood.

He tossed each article of clothing on the appropriate bed. This was who he was: a man with a family. He was a man who constantly fought clutter and laundry. He had children, and that would never, ever change. Only the type of toys and the size of the clothes would.

Ah, Aiden. There you really are: you're a single parent.

He stopped again, just inside his own bedroom, and heard his wife's voice: *Let's make this an adult oasis.*

Ah, Melissa. After reading enough parenting books for the two of them, she'd been determined that parenthood wouldn't cause their marriage to erode, only to strengthen. They'd set inviolable date nights—and they'd actually done pretty well keeping those dates, although they'd quickly learned that no schedule was *inviolable* with infant twins.

Once the babies were sleeping longer stretches through the night, they'd been moved to their cribs, the bassinets had been banished from the bedroom, and Melissa had reclaimed the master bedroom as an *adult oasis*. The decor was a sedate, soothing navy and gray. The bed had never been used as a surface to fold laundry or to sort through bills. The door had been kept shut during the day, so toys and pacifiers didn't creep in.

And at night…

Well, unless they were actually making love on those nights they weren't both exhausted, the door had been left open, so they could hear if their children were in distress. And, despite all the books' warnings about not letting children get in the habit of joining them in bed whenever the whim struck them, they'd let the children climb up in the mornings for family cuddles before breakfast. That hadn't been bad for their marriage; those had been some of the happiest times they'd had.

We should have had more.

But they hadn't.

For the past two years, his bedroom had just been a bedroom, not an adult oasis. Nothing close to adult activity took place here. He'd never brought a woman into this bed, because he had two little girls who made very effective chaperones. He couldn't imagine the awkwardness of having a rumpled and sleepy, sexually satisfied woman sitting at the breakfast table, mystifying his daughters with her presence.

If he was being brutally honest—*what the hell, as long as we're filleting my heart open*—he didn't want to have a lover watch him lose a battle with Olympia over food or with Poppy over her choice of clothing. Maybe some small part of him worried that it would be a little emasculating to fill those sippy cups in front of a woman he wanted to seduce.

A woman like India.

The thought of her set him in motion. He took off his jacket and tossed it on the bed, then unbuttoned his shirt as he crossed the room and kicked off his jeans in the master bathroom. He didn't wait for the water to heat up, but stepped into the shower while it was still punishingly cold. He stayed there after it turned too hot.

An adult oasis. That had not been part of his life, not for two years. There'd only been casual nights at a hotel or at a woman's home, now and then. But the last twenty-four hours...

The combination of a willing and beautiful bed partner and absent children had never happened before. It was little wonder he'd overindulged. Cold water, hot water—none of it dampened his body's primitive determination to keep indulging.

He could bring India here, tonight after dinner. In the morning, she could eat breakfast in that silky bathrobe, and nobody would be here to be shocked. No little girls would ask questions. India could eat in the nude; it wouldn't matter at all, as she sat at the kitchen table in one of the chairs that didn't have a booster seat strapped to it securely. The toy vacuum, the block tower—she'd know the minute she walked into the house that his life revolved around preschoolers.

He slammed off the shower and shook the water out of his military-short hair.

No.

Yes. You're a father.

He knew that, damn it, but on the walk here, he'd felt different. Still himself, but a version of himself he hadn't caught a glimpse of in years. He wanted more time to rediscover the man who'd been a whole and complete person for thirty years, before children had entered his life.

He wanted to keep discovering India, too. He wanted to laugh over Best Lover awards, and he wanted to make her laughter stop by taking her breath away. Desire for her simmered like lava under the surface even now, waiting for another opening, for a chance to expand, for oxygen. He was so effortlessly learning how she liked to be touched, how to soothe her, how to excite her— how to bring her to a second orgasm when she'd been limp from the first. She'd sounded awed as she'd whispered in his ear, *It's like you're the master of my body.*

Once she saw him as a dad, once she had to step around a tricycle on the back porch and over a scattered tea set on her way to the master bedroom, she wouldn't see him as a master of anything anymore, except the master of preschool chaos.

That poor widowed father...

He towel-dried himself roughly. *Not happening.* Not today.

He counted the days as he shaved. India was leaving the morning of the twenty-fourth. Including tonight, he had five nights with her, total. That was all. He'd been alive for thirty-four years; he hoped he'd be alive more than thirty-four more. Out of his entire lifetime, taking five nights with India Woods didn't make him a bad person. It didn't make him a bad father.

He wouldn't have planned anything that excluded his children, yet this time with India did exclude them, and it was good. Good for him, good for her. No one was going to be hurt by a few days of happiness. These unexpected days were a gift out of the blue, a chance to reconnect with himself, a chance to connect to a woman as a man, not as part of a three-person unit.

He pulled a fresh shirt over his head, and immediately imagined India pulling it back off. She *would* pull it off him, and she'd do so today, and he would feel lighthearted in a way that he'd almost forgotten how to feel.

Don't forget that box of condoms.

Not a chance. They weren't in the nightstand by his bed, because the adult oasis had long been only the place where a tired single parent slept. Instead, he dug in a bathroom cabinet for the civilian toiletries bag he used for overnights with women who understood that was all the time he could spare them, because they knew he had children. He threw on his jacket, stuffed the box in a pocket and headed back out of his house without stopping to straighten a damn thing.

This week was different. This time with India was different. He looked up as he crossed the bridge to see her walking toward him—then running toward him. He scooped her off the ground and spun her around and kissed her in the bright sunlight.

If the stars had aligned to give him an early Christmas gift, then he intended to enjoy it. He would take India out to dinner tonight, to an intimate cantina. He'd spend their dinner date not talking about children, not being given advice on how to handle upcoming stages of development, not commiserating with a woman over the way the county had redrawn the elementary-school boundaries.

Instead, he would watch India without watching the clock. He would tell her she was beautiful. He would feed her a bite of his own food from his own fork when she asked for a taste, watch the way she savored the flavor as the candle on the table flickered. India would ask him about his hometown. About his likes and dislikes in cars, in movies, in books. About him.

He would answer her honestly. He wouldn't be lying to her. He would be enjoying time with her, and she would be enjoying time with him.

It all happened just like that. And afterward, as they were falling asleep together, skin to skin, he told himself there was nothing between them, nothing between them at all.

They couldn't be naked all the time.

For one thing, that shower door had been scheduled to be installed. A three-man crew had arrived in a truck designed to carry panes of glass. Aiden had spent the first hour in the garage, painting the boards for his bookcase a clean, crisp white. India had checked on Aiden as often as she'd checked on the installers, because Aiden had looked absurdly sexy as he'd wiped paint off his fingers with a clean rag. He looked absurdly sexy now, chilling out on the opposite end of the couch from her, reading a book.

She'd put on a red sweater with her black jeans. Every time she looked up from her book to see him with his nose in his, she felt her cheeks flushing. The sweater made them look a little redder to start with. It was camouflage for stalking a man who would probably look too hot for words in camouflage.

She'd never see him in uniform. He was only her lover while he was on vacation.

The glass installers continued to call measurements to one another. They'd cursed up a storm when their first attempt at installing the custom pane of glass didn't work, pretty hard-core cursing at that. It was a good thing there weren't any children around.

Aiden had set aside his book and walked down the hallway to check on their progress about half an hour ago. Male voices had murmured in the hallway, then Aiden had come back in with a can of sparkling water for her and retaken his seat on the opposite end of the couch. But now it hit her: she hadn't heard any swearing in a while.

"You told them not to curse, didn't you?"

He looked at her over his book. They were facing each other, backs against their respective sofa armrests, jeans and bare feet sharing the center cushion.

"I really am an army officer," she said. "I can handle cursing. I've been known to do it myself."

"Should I tell them to resume? Do you miss it?"

He made her laugh, all the time.

"No, but I—" *No, but I'm going to miss you.* She'd almost said it out loud.

He was looking at her, so she concentrated furiously on the page before her, just so he wouldn't ask her what she'd been about to say.

It wouldn't have been appropriate. This was a fling with a definite end date, and they'd both known that from the beginning. But she couldn't help wondering what would happen after December 24. She was heading to San Antonio, then on to the beach town of Corpus Christi. She'd be missing Aiden the whole time. There'd be another guy someday, she supposed, once she was back in Belgium…but she couldn't imagine a man generating enough interest for her to get in the vicinity of a bed with him.

The rebound guy after her Rebound Guy was going to be a disappointment. It might be easier to just give up sex after Aiden.

She peeked at him. He'd gone back to reading, so

she returned to staring at him more than at her book. He flipped a page, calm and comfortable despite the installation crew in the house. She was glad he was here, to be honest, although it made her feel like a wimp to admit she wouldn't have liked being outnumbered by these men if she'd been here alone. They were loud, which wasn't the same thing as dangerous...but she would have kept her phone nearby.

When she'd talked to Helen and imagined her ideal man, hadn't one of her criteria been *maybe even protective*? She was going to upgrade that to *definitely* protective. The man who was casually keeping her foot warm with his own made an excellent bodyguard. His presence alone was enough to keep the crew from getting too loud and too disrespectful. Aiden was in his early thirties, an obvious athlete, a man in his prime, and he would never let her come to harm while they were together. She knew that like she knew the sky was blue.

What about when they were no longer together?

She was thirty-two and single. She handled the world on her own; this was a vacation from the ordinary. Having a protector was a change from the ordinary, but she shouldn't get used to it. This wasn't the first time she'd felt like she was overdue for a refresher course on close-quarters combat. She needed to get out of her high heels and back into her combat boots now and then. Maybe she could arrange to get herself sent back to Fort Hood when it was time to requalify on her weapons.

They'll send you to a range in Germany, and you know it.

Her future did not include Aiden. How could any rebound guy replace him? She wouldn't want to make Bloody Marys with another man. She wouldn't want to walk a dog with another man or eat dinner in a candlelit Mexican cantina.

It hit her again, just as hard the second time: *I'm going to miss you—and not just in bed.*

But it was easier to focus on sex. She wished the shower installers would hurry. She wanted to get naked with Aiden and stop *thinking*. This week wasn't supposed to involve thinking. It was supposed to be a vacation from being alone with her thoughts. A week of bliss with a man who wasn't an ass.

"What are you reading?" Aiden asked.

The question forced her to come out of the brooding silence into which she'd unintentionally fallen. He'd intentionally broken that silence. He was too observant.

"I'm attempting to read *The Girl with the Dragon Tattoo* in its original Swedish."

"Right." Aiden shook his head a little bit. "There's an answer I never expected to hear. Is Swedish another one of your certified languages, or is it just another one you happen to speak fluently, like French and Spanish?"

"I wouldn't say I was fluent in Spanish. Those were just common phrases at the restaurant last night. Easy enough."

But he'd noticed that she'd lapsed into Spanish around Spanish-speaking people. He was impressed with her language abilities, and it made her feel as good as a child being given a ribbon for winning a spelling bee.

"I'm certified in Danish. Swedish is close, though, so I'm trying to identify the similarities and differences."

"So, you're working?"

Yes.

"No, it's just fun, like a crossword puzzle. I like languages. It's kind of my thing."

"You're an interpreter at NATO?"

No.

"Yes, and a speech writer. If one of our generals has to give a speech to a university in Denmark, guess who writes out every word for him phonetically?"

"You."

"Yep. Hoo-ah, right? Combat translation." She was less of a soldier and more of an office geek, and she knew it. "I'm Airborne certified, though, believe it or not. Kind of a waste of the army's money, it turns out, but I guess the army didn't know I was going to turn into a desk weenie when I was a brand-new lieutenant. I know I didn't expect to."

He studied her again for a moment, his gaze steady. "There are tens of thousands of people who can hump a backpack and fire a rifle and fall out of a plane. I've never met someone who serves her country by being a savant at languages. Don't disparage yourself."

"A savant?"

How casually he soothed her with the sole of his foot, an easy slide of his masculine weight down her shin. "That's what Tom told me about you. He failed to warn me I was going to be knocked out by your gray eyes. I was completely speechless when you first walked into the garage, you know."

I love...this.

He knocked her out, too. Knocked her sideways with these casual compliments. This was their third day together, and she was so sadly addicted to his style of conversation. She loved his ability to make her laugh, his generosity in bed and out, his...his everything.

She had to stop thinking about how much she was going to miss him. They had four whole days ahead of them, a ton of time. "Well, for starters, he may not have mentioned it because I think Tom only has eyes for Helen's eyes."

"As it should be."

"I agree. It's rare, isn't it? Once in a lifetime stuff."

He returned to his book. She thought their conversation was over when he said, so very quietly, "Don't settle for less, India. It's out there."

It's right here.

Her heart broke at the thought, because she could not remain here. She tried for a perky tone of voice. "Well, I hope it's in Europe. I'll never be stationed anywhere else."

He looked at her sharply.

I'm too valuable in Europe. She could never tell him that. She couldn't tell anyone that.

She was certified in far more than German, Danish, Dutch and Flemish. Those were her cover. She didn't just write speeches for the highest-level commanders; she traveled with them, serving as an aide-de-camp when were meeting with officials from certain nations or traveling to certain countries.

Being an aide-de-camp was her cover, as well. She wasn't an interpreter on those trips, just a staff member, one who had to make sure the transportation would show up at the right building, at the right entrance. One who had to make sure the hotel rooms were ready, the restaurants were reserved. During summits, she waited in antechambers with the staff of the leaders of the countries that were hostile to the United States. She pretended she didn't understand their languages. She listened, sometimes while simultaneously talking to a hotel's waiter about how the American general preferred his coffee.

She gathered intelligence. She was not trained as a spy—nor was she paid as a spy—but that was essentially what she did, when asked. She'd been able to alert the American contingent when the prince of a Middle Eastern nation had decided to abandon talks early, because she'd overheard his aides confirming runway availability at the local airport. They'd foolishly used their phones to set up the logistics while the female American officer was pretending to listen to music on her silent headphones, tapping out an imaginary beat on her skirt, lounging in a window seat in the staff break room with her pantyhose-clad ankles crossed. She wasn't James Bond, but she traveled across Europe and kept her ears open to a dozen languages in the service of her country.

I'll never be stationed here in Texas with you. We can't hope for it...but would you hope for it? Are you hoping for it?

Her smile felt weak. "The army doesn't need someone who speaks Danish here in Texas. It would be nice, though, to come back to a line unit. I do all this embassy office work, while you're in leadership positions. You're the battalion S-3? Before that, probably a company commander."

He nodded.

"Leading troops directly. That's what being an officer is all about. It's what I thought I'd be doing. I started as a platoon leader, but then I got sidetracked with all these language degrees—"

"India."

She was skilled at pretending she understood nothing. There'd been that checkpoint in a hostile country when she'd been detained too long. For hours, they'd tested her, trying to ascertain whether or not she really didn't understand their language. The heavily armed men had sharpened their knives as they'd described how they were going to carve their initials in her skin if they raped her. She'd just checked her watch as if she was bored, then mimed that she was thirsty, while praying that the ambassador would quickly realize his convoy was missing one lowly officer. Her acting skills had passed the test. She'd been released.

She'd gotten a medal for something else, officially.

"It's not very high speed," she said, "but someone has to know the difference between Dutch and Flemish, right?"

She worked in any country except her own. She had very little family, just a mother who traveled constantly herself. It made India perfect for her position. She wasn't tied down to a husband. She had no children. She was…untethered.

Whether she was standing at her medieval window or sitting on a modern couch, she was just passing through. She was not part of something—except for the US Army.

In service to her country, she was sent on missions with no notice. She bluffed her way through dangerous situations several times a year, but to most of the army, to practically every other soldier of any rank or station, she was just an officer who'd lucked out and gotten a lot of free advanced degrees in foreign languages, courtesy of Uncle Sam. She couldn't say a word about her real service, and for years, she'd told herself that didn't matter.

It mattered to her what Aiden thought of her. Just once, just once, it would be nice if—

"You have a rare skill, India. You use it in service to your country. I respect your dedication."

Down the hall, a nine-foot custom-cut pane of glass shattered.

The cursing resumed.

Chapter Nine

Sex with a sensual woman was great.

Sex with India Woods was more than sex—and it was more than great.

Aiden was too experienced, too mature and, he hoped, too brave to pretend otherwise. He recognized *more* when he saw it. He didn't want to lose it.

That meant he needed to look at their situation in the cold light of day—reason enough to literally open his eyes. It was full morning. Bright light forced its way through every seam in the bedroom's closed shutters, unstoppable, illuminating a sleeping India. Aiden lay still and appreciated the way the sun kissed the curve of her bare shoulder.

Her face looked so peaceful. He was grateful for every smile he'd received from those lips, for every touch from her fingers. He loved the way the corners of those eyes crinkled with laughter when she got his jokes. He was humbled that so much beauty was only the exterior of a woman who had a mind that grasped so many more languages than he ever could, who had a heart that had chosen a life of service like he had. In the bright light of day, the truth was easy to see: India Woods was not a vacation fling.

From that first moment he'd laid eyes on her, he'd known, hadn't he? It had been so easy to picture her sharing his pillow. He should have known when they'd spoken by the bridge; his first instinct had been to hold her hand. Simple lust didn't make a man want to hold a woman's hand as they walked in the sun.

Every leadership cliché he'd ever heard seemed to mock him now. *Begin as you mean to go on.* He *had* begun as he'd meant to go on. He'd meant to spend a selfish week enjoying himself as the object of a beautiful brunette's attention. He'd reveled in the way she saw him as a man and not as a widower and parent.

It wasn't the beginning he wanted to change. He would never choose to go back and undo those Bloody Marys.

It was the *going on* part he wanted to change. He did not want to say goodbye to India on the morning of Christmas Eve. He could persuade her to stay—he was arrogant enough to believe he had that ability—but staying meant she'd find out he wasn't the man she'd thought he was at the beginning.

Too late for that cliché.

Honesty is the best policy.

Too late for that one, too. He hadn't lied, though. She'd never asked him if he had children. He'd so easily slipped into the prefatherhood version of himself, it had never occurred to her to ask, perhaps.

He could have offered the information. He hadn't.

Practice how you'll play. His high school coach's favorite. If the track meet would be held outdoors in the heat, then practicing indoors in the gym was poor preparation. Then there was army's version: *Train the way you'll fight.* Since battles could be fought in mud, soldiers trained in the rain. Battles could erupt in the middle of the night, so units trained at night. If they'd have to hump twenty pounds of gear on their backs during a battle, then each soldier had to hump twenty pounds of gear during road marches across a safe, stateside post.

Aiden knew this. He trained six hundred soldiers in accordance with that principle. He needed to apply it to this situation. Any relationship he had with India beyond this week would be with the Aiden who dealt with real life, the man who lived for two little girls who shared their deceased mother's green eyes. If he was going to sleep with India on Christmas Eve, he'd do it at his house, with his children tucked in their beds, just down the hall.

He could almost imagine it. Almost—but there was some fear there, some anxiety about having four people around a table that held three. But four could happen. For the first time since he'd lost Melissa, it was a possibility. How it would look was still hazy, but he could envision something where before there had been only a blank.

He watched India sleeping, then reached out to move a strand of hair off her face, so that it wouldn't tickle her nose and wake her up. He'd done that the very first time they'd slept together. He wanted to do that for a very long time to come—and that meant he'd have to do it with children tucked into their beds in the rooms next to his.

Practice how you'll play. Train the way you'll fight.

If he continued to build this relationship as a bachelor with no family, then neither of them would be prepared to handle the reality of life with his children. The race would be lost before it began, the battle lost before a shot was fired.

Losing India had become an unacceptable outcome. Aiden needed to tell her about his daughters. The clock was ticking, after all. Their third night was over.

India rustled around a little bit, then opened her eyes to look at him over the pillow. It was more like a squint, actually. She wasn't a morning person.

"What time is it?" she mumbled.

He cupped the back of her head. "It's time for me to tell you how beautiful you are. It's time for me to tell you how lucky I am to spend the day with you."

She closed her eyes, but now she was smiling. "You really are the most amazing rebound guy."

She came willingly when he pulled her closer. He tucked her head against his chest and held her, knowing she was going to fall back asleep for another five or ten minutes. Then she'd be a little more awake—not completely, but enough. He'd learned three mornings ago that he was not the only person who woke up aroused.

She drifted off. He could feel her breathing change when she came back to him, surfacing for the second time. He certainly could feel her hand as it drifted down his body. Lazily, sleepily, she rolled onto her back as he rolled on a condom, her thighs parting as she turned her head to kiss his shoulder without opening her eyes. He covered her body with his own, settling onto her, sliding into her, making love to her, bringing her with him into the bright light of the day.

"Good morning," he said, his voice so husky with emotion, it came out as a whisper.

"This is the best way to wake up, ever," she said against his throat. "So much better than an alarm clock. I wish I could take you back to Belgium with me."

"I do, too."

She pulled away to look at him, her gray eyes now awake and alert, and he knew she'd heard the regret in his voice. "But you can't?"

"I can't." He needed to explain why, and he would. Today.

But they'd begun the day as they'd meant for the day to go on. He didn't want to change course, not yet, not when she climbed out of bed and tugged his hand, bringing him into the shower with her.

Honesty is the best policy. There was nothing more honest than this, than the way he worshipped her body and the way she lost herself in his. The honest truth, communicated in her kisses and her words—*I wish I could take you to Belgium*—was that neither one of them would be ready to part three nights from now.

Things had to change. He would take her to lunch, explain everything, and they could begin again, once they agreed that they would be going on together for far more than three nights.

She would know that the man who was kissing her now under the rainfall of a new showerhead would kiss her like this whether he was raising children or not. Their desire wouldn't change when she found out the man who was driving her wild with his wet hands was also the man who dealt with clutter and laundry. She'd know he was still Aiden. She'd still want him for more than three nights.

Wouldn't she?

He had no choice. He was going to have to tell her—

She lowered herself to kneel before him.

Later.

Lunch.

Lunch would come soon enough.

Aiden closed his eyes, turned his face up to the falling water, and let India take him where she wanted him to go.

"McDonald's? You want to go to McDonald's?"

India laughed at Aiden's expression. "It may not be a big deal to you, but I've been living in Europe for the past four years. I want to go to an American McDonald's."

She intended to drive him there, too. Tom's pickup had been okay, and Aiden's red pickup had looked new when she'd arrived in all her jet-lagged glory, but Helen had a Jeep, deliciously orange, with the kind of windows that could be removed and a top that could be put down. It was sixty degrees and sunny right now. India was taking the Jeep.

"But…" Aiden took the rear window from her and set it down in the garage. "I know the closest McDonald's has a big kiddie area. It's always busy."

She wrinkled her nose in distaste. "We'll sit as far away from it as possible. Other side of the restaurant— *all* the way across the restaurant."

Aiden was loosening the passenger-side window. He paused. Scowled.

"What's the matter? Is the window sticking?"

He shook his head and hauled the window all the way out of its tracks in one swoop.

India undid the latches near the windshield so they could pull back the canvas top. She kept one eye on Aiden as he carried the passenger window into the garage. He was still scowling.

"It won't be that bad," she said. "Kids are like most critters. If you don't bother them, they won't bother you."

He laughed at that, a single *ha*. He was amused. Wasn't he?

"You know what? It's no big deal. We don't have to hit McDonald's. I can go in San Antonio or Corpus Christi. I'll probably pass one every ten miles on the way to the coast." The names of the next two cities on her vacation itinerary stirred more dread than anticipation. She didn't want to be anywhere except 490 Cedar Highway. *Three more nights...*

Aiden was right before her, close enough to touch, smiling at her now. "You just surprised me, that's all. If you want McDonald's, then I'll take you to McDonald's."

"Actually, I'll take you." She patted the orange metal. "I'm driving this machine. You can ride shotgun."

"Want to go cross-country for part of the way? I know some land we can cut across."

"Hell, yes, let's do some mud-dogging," she said, possibly the most American thing she'd said yet since coming back. "At least we can go off-road on the way there. I don't know if my stomach will be able to handle getting bounced around once I stuff it full of fries." *Ugh*, she sounded like such a wimp. "But it'll be fun on the way there, getting windblown and jarred to pieces. It clears the mind."

Aiden kissed her before going around the vehicle to jump in the passenger seat. "Sounds good. Let's arrive at McDonald's with clear minds."

The french fries were everything she'd remembered and more.

"Delicious." She dragged a salty, golden piece of nirvana through her puddle of ketchup, then placed it on her tongue.

"If you keep groaning like that, we're going to get thrown out for public indecency."

She grinned at him. "The last time I ate at McDonald's, I was in Barcelona. Do you know what they served there? Gazpacho."

"They don't serve fries?"

"Well, they do, but the ketchup isn't the same." She picked up another ketchup packet just as she realized a family with little children was heading for the booth across from their table. "Shoot. We didn't get away from them after all."

"From who?" Aiden turned.

"Don't look," India said, feeling like she was in a school cafeteria.

The family settled into the booth. The dad was in the army, obvious by his camouflage uniform, so this was probably his lunch break. The mom was trying to sort out which burger was destined for which child. The children apparently thought it would be helpful to announce their likes and dislikes: *No pickles! I don't like cheese!*

She looked to Aiden with a grimace and an apologetic shrug—it had been her idea to eat in a place that was almost guaranteed to be full of families, after all. "Sorry," she said under her voice.

He cut his gaze back to her. He'd been looking at the children like they were cute or something, she belatedly realized. "For what? They're just kids."

Had she imagined a subtle rebuke in his tone? "Maybe we'll luck out and they'll be the kind that don't scream."

"There's no such thing." Aiden smiled at her as he said it, not chiding her at all. She'd imagined it. "They're kids. What's your excuse? You were screaming along with the radio on the way here."

"That was *singing*, and I still think you're a lot of fun to be with, even when you refuse to sing along with the radio."

"I know my skill level." He finished off his hamburger.

She loved this, this normalcy. They were having an everyday conversation, as if they didn't have a limited time together and had to make every moment count.

"Aerosmith is hard to sing along with," he said, "unless you're Steven Tyler."

"True, but you have to blast hard rock when you're driving off-road. It's mandatory."

"Country music is mandatory for mud-dogging."

"Uh-oh." She ate another fry. "I think we're going to have our first disagreement."

"No, I love Aerosmith. I just can't sing it." He gave her *such* a look before he winked. "Neither can you."

"Aerosmith was my very first concert, did you know?" She caught herself. *Listen to me, just talking away like he would want to know every little detail of my life. Like we're dating.*

Like this was an open-ended relationship, like they were seeing how far it would go, how long it would last.

"Tell me about it." Aiden laid his hand on the table between them, palm up, inviting her to take it.

She did, of course. She *loved* all this touching. Who would touch her when she returned to her real life? She touched no one. She didn't even shake hands with people at work. She saluted, was saluted, returned salutes. Tears pricked at her eyes.

Don't ruin what time you have with him. Don't lose your next three nights.

She told her story brightly. "I had to sit with my mother. In fact, she wouldn't let me go without her. I think she thought Aerosmith was too hard-core heavy metal for her little baby girl. She was ready to whip me out of there if anything got too adult." India leaned back in her chair and gave his hand a squeeze, ready to deliver her punchline. "I was nineteen."

Aiden was, unsurprisingly, surprised. "You had overprotective parents, then?"

"Parent. It was just me and Mom. Anyhow, Aerosmith and I go way back. I feel like I have the right to sing along whether it's above my skill level or not." She didn't want to talk about her family; it got too embarrassing. It was time to steer the conversation into safer waters. "What's the last concert you saw?"

"Aerosmith. A few months ago."

She wanted to shiver at their like-mindedness, but she forced herself to laugh at the coincidence—and gloss over it. "Not with your mother, I hope?"

That question had been a mistake. She didn't want to talk about his mother, because then she'd be expected to talk about hers. Her mother always came off as weird in comparison to everyone else's. Even the mother in the booth across from them had managed to settle her little brood in. She was now eating her fries like a normal woman.

India couldn't remember her mother being so calm in public. Her mom was the weird one compared to practically every other mother in the world. If India wasn't careful and told too many stories, everyone would start looking at her differently, as though her upbringing must have made her weird, too.

Everyone, this time, meant Aiden. She did not want Aiden to know how weird her family—or lack of it— was.

She rushed to fill in the space before he could answer. "You took a date to the concert, didn't you? But you're not going to kiss and tell."

"I wish it had been you."

Her world stopped. For one second, there was no chatter, no bustle, nothing but Aiden and his warm palm against hers, his steady gaze holding hers.

The next second, she tried not to panic. They'd agreed to be a couple for one week. He wasn't supposed to say he wished she'd been part of his life before this vacation. How had this conversation become a minefield?

She pretended he hadn't just blown up the boundaries they'd set. "Well, since I was in Belgium at the time, I can't really be upset that you took another woman on my dream date. Now, if I'd been in town and you'd taken someone else…" She attempted a saucy, sexy shrug. "Then I might be jealous. I do so love… Aerosmith."

He laid his other hand on the table, palm up. Not a demand, but an offer. *My hand is here if you want to hold it.*

Funny how it would be easier to get naked and play in bed with him. In the middle of a busy McDonald's lunch hour, she placed both of her hands in his, and felt vulnerable.

"When you're in town," he said, "you are who I will be with."

He shouldn't make her want things she couldn't have. She would not be in his town again. She had no reason to return to Fort Hood. She would never be stationed here.

"Could you come to Belgium?" Now she was the one blowing their boundaries.

He shook his head sadly, but he leaned in. "India, we need to talk."

Those words were ominous, whether Gerard-Pierre wrote them or Aiden said them.

"Change of plans? You can't stay through the week, after all?" Her questions sounded casual. Her hands clutched his.

"I can stay. But then it will be Christmas Eve, and my family will arrive. I'd—I'd like you to meet them."

Oh, no. Not this. "I'll be in San Antonio."

"You don't have to go."

"I do. They're doing this sealant on the floors and the windows have to stay open for a day. It'll get freezing cold. Helen got me a place in San Antonio because the fumes are—"

"Or you could stay at my house."

"Or you could come to San Antonio."

His silence was just surprise, wasn't it?

"It's a romantic bed-and-breakfast. Come spend Christmas with me." *Please, Aiden. Choose me. Aren't we good the way we are?*

He dropped his chin to his chest for a moment. "I really can't. I have to be with my family for Christmas."

The children in the nearby booth had started getting wound up again, but the mother had produced crayons from her giant tote bag of a purse. *Crayons.* Adolphus's sister and her adorable, handmade card. His grandma, patting India's cheek and telling her she was such a pretty girl. Bernardo's entire family, so concerned because she didn't have one. Every man's mother, every boyfriend's sister…

India was single, because she'd failed them all, hadn't she?

"I understand." She let go of Aiden's hands. "You only had this one week. I knew that. We've both known that from the start."

"I want *more* than a week, but my family will be here."

"I don't do families."

He went still. "What does that mean?"

She didn't want to go through this, not again, not with Aiden. She shouldn't have to. They had such a wonderful thing going. Why did he want to change it?

Obviously, he didn't think it was as wonderful as she did.

Tears pricked her eyes again. *Don't cry, India.*

She smiled. "What we have right now is perfect. Consenting adults. Nothing complicated. That's all I do. It's all I'm good at."

"You've never met a boyfriend's family?"

Crayons were hitting the ground now, rolling into the aisle. She watched them instead of Aiden. "Of course I have. I don't know what it is, but meeting the parents, the grandparents, the brother or sister… It's the kiss of death. It kills the relationship every time."

They don't like me, and then my boyfriend doesn't like me anymore, either.

Except for Adolphus. The reverse was worse: his younger sister had wondered why India didn't like her enough to keep dating her brother.

"What about children in a boyfriend's family?" Aiden asked. Such a quiet question.

She flinched as if a drill sergeant had shouted it. "I know my limits. My skill set in that area is nonexistent. I won't compete with a child for a man's time and attention."

I won't, because I'm not a horrible person. God knew she'd hated being the child who was neglected by the father. She'd been very young, but she'd known she couldn't compete. Adult women had won her father's attention, every time. Neighbors had called the police when her father had left her home alone in favor of those adult women, again and again.

The third time, her mother had been called back from her first attempt at a trip around the world. She'd been angry at her ex for neglecting their daughter and ruining her lifelong dream. *I'm sorry, Mommy.*

India had known she'd failed to keep her father's attention, and so she'd had to change houses, change primary parents. Her mother had been so angry, forced to settle down, forced to rent an apartment near a good elementary school. *Not your fault, Indy. I'll just put my life on hold while he has fun with his women.*

Now India was the adult woman. "It'd be like stealing candy from a baby. I'd be stealing a father from a baby. I don't date fathers."

Aiden was looking at her, *watching* her, analyzing her. If there was one subject India wanted to broach less than her mother, it was her father.

She rushed in to fill the silence again, smiling too brightly. "Besides, everyone says that having children kills their sex life. What would be in it for me, then? Consenting adults need something to consent to."

But Aiden was looking so utterly serious, and she was feeling so utterly miserable, that she gave up trying to steer the conversation anywhere at all. She started crumpling up paper wrappers, consolidating the trash. Her emotions were balling up in her chest, tighter, bulkier, something like hurt. Something like anger.

Aiden wanted to see her past the twenty-third. That ought to have made her happy—from the beginning, her heart had been warning her that their week would never be enough. But Aiden only wanted to keep seeing her if she could fit in with his family over Christmas. She didn't want to take that test.

She'd fail.

The soldier across the aisle had given up eating in order to chase crayons. He'd awkwardly kicked them out from under the table with his clunky combat boot and was half off the bench seat now, bending down to retrieve the crayons. He smacked his head on the table; a mighty warrior laid low by a preschooler's toy.

India stood with her tray of crumpled paper, causing Aiden to stand, too. She led the way to the giant trash can by the door and dumped the remains of their lunch date.

She pushed her way through the glass door, out into the sunshine. She'd drive home cross-country, after all, with Aerosmith blasting the whole way to drown out any more mine-filled conversation with Aiden. She didn't want to think about December 24. She didn't want to even imagine meeting his family and screwing everything up, as she inevitably did.

Maybe she'd arrive at the house with a clear mind. She was going to need it to deal with her foolish heart.

Chapter Ten

Aiden watched India's profile as she pulled into Tom and Helen's drive. She had driven hard to get here, yanking off her hoop earrings when the wind had tangled her hair in them. The wind and the drive hadn't cleared her mind. She was frowning. Still.

A work truck was in the space where the Jeep was usually parked. Two ladders were angled against one side of the house, one man topping each.

"Gutters today," India said. It was the first thing she'd said since lunch.

Worst goddamn lunch of his life.

How can you even think that? Remember eating in the hospital cafeteria?

He sighed and looked at his ringless left hand. That was one thing about being a widower: he'd always have a heart-wrenching loss to compare all other losses to. It pissed him off most of the time, but right now, it gave him perspective. He wasn't any worse off than he'd been before lunch. This morning, he'd had three more nights with India ahead of him.

He still did.

He lifted his gaze to her profile. She was beautiful,

windblown, healthy. She was a pleasure to spend time with out of bed. She was ecstasy in bed. If the timing had been different, if this was a different year and he'd never been anything but a single man, they wouldn't have talked about meeting families yet. They wouldn't have talked about children at all, not on their fourth day in one another's lives. They were lovers and becoming friends, but he'd tried to switch tracks as if they'd already become more. Perhaps they hadn't, not yet, but she was still his—for three more nights.

If she'd speak to him.

She did, turning to him, perfectly polite. "Do you want to come inside? They could be hammering on the roof awhile. If you needed time at your own house to get anything done, this is probably a good time for it. You'll avoid a headache. I could drive you over, if you don't want to walk the bridge. I'm sorry. I should have asked you that sooner."

"Do I want to come inside?" *How can you even ask that?*

They had three days. He'd been trying to get more, but the bottom line was that only so much more was possible, whether she dated fathers or not.

Testing things out as a couple with his children had been a pipe dream. Working toward becoming a family of four instead of three? Foolish.

His children weren't the only obstacle. Even if he and India could be a couple instead of a family, their future was limited. Aiden didn't believe for a minute that India spent her days writing speeches for generals in Danish. She was too sharp for that.

She had some kind of extraordinary language skill that the US Army valued, and she would not be able to move here. She'd be in the service at least another eight years. With her skill set, she could remain on active duty longer if she chose to, almost certainly.

They'd be apart for eight years after this week. He would be able to leave the girls with his family for a week, maybe, each year. No more. One week of bliss every year—would he still be addicted to her eight years from now? Pining for her? Waiting for her?

He was afraid the answer was *yes*.

The answer would be *yes* if he returned home right now, and the answer would be *yes* if he stayed and made love to her for three more nights.

There wasn't a choice there at all. He would take the three nights.

"India. Do I want to come inside?" He picked up her hand from the steering wheel and brought it to his lips. "How can you even ask that?"

Her fingers jerked a little in his. "That lunch conversation made it pretty clear that you aren't comfortable with things the way they are. If you need to go… If this isn't working out for you…"

"Baby, wild horses couldn't make me miss the next three nights of our lives. I won't miss the chance to spend more time with you, ever."

"Oh." Her silver-gray eyes were on him as he kissed her knuckles. She looked away, blinking rapidly, but he saw the tears she was trying to hide.

"Don't cry, India. Everything is going to be okay." It had to be. There was some way it was going to be. He just needed more time to figure out how to make a handful of days this year and every other year suffice.

She recovered enough to shoot him a bit of a skeptical look. "The last time you said that, you were quitting on me in the middle of sex."

"I'm a fast learner, India. I'm not quitting on you."

* * *

December 23 was a cool, sunny day. Perfect weather.

For lunch, Aiden had taken India to his favorite barbecue joint, something she couldn't find in Europe, and they'd been able to enjoy brisket and corn bread on an outdoor patio, because the day was not too hot, not too cold. A perfect meal.

Working in the garage was easy on a day like today. The double door was raised, the sky was blue beyond it. Aiden was nearly done with his daughter's bookcase. He'd designed it, then measured and cut the boards. It had been sanded, painted, assembled—the only thing he had left to do was use a nail punch to drive each nail head just below the wood surface, so nothing would scrape or catch on a person in passing. A perfectly smooth finish.

He placed the tip of the punch precisely on the head of a nail and tapped lightly to sink it. It was precision work, when he wanted to drive nails hard with a hammer. Hell, he wanted to take a sledgehammer and smash a wall, tear it down, destroy it, because this perfect day was his last day with India. This perfect day was one of the worst days of his—

How can you even think—

Shut the hell up, already. I don't want to lose India.

But he would lose her. Tomorrow morning, his sister would bring back his daughters. He couldn't wait to see them, to hear their voices, to hold them, to *smell* them. If he hadn't had India this week, he would have gone crazy from missing them.

He tugged off one leather glove with his teeth and tossed it into his toolbox. He dug in the pocket of his jeans and pulled out the two pennies. He let them sit in his palm a moment, then he closed his hand around them loosely and shook them a bit, letting them jingle together. Poppy and Olympia would be back where they belonged, thank God, because without them, he might go crazy from missing India.

While India drove to San Antonio, while her borrowed house was being filled with noxious fumes, he would assemble his artificial Christmas tree. Melissa had bought it the year she was pregnant, declaring that she couldn't run a vacuum to suck up any falling pine needles that year, not when she was so big. Of course, Aiden could have run the vacuum for her, but Melissa had still wanted the artificial tree because the following year, she'd said confidently, it would let them avoid worrying about two babies picking up pine needles and putting them in their mouths.

That had been before they'd known anything about real babies, of course. The next year, two real-life babies had crawled over a safety gate and pulled off an entire artificial branch. He and Melissa had been shocked by their determined little teamwork. Aiden smiled a bit at the memory. He jingled the pennies some more.

Real life. Real babies. Tomorrow, things would go back to normal.

Oh, that poor widowed father...

Women would continue to pay attention to him, melting with sympathy at his situation, expecting to take him to bed, wanting to offer the widower gentle comfort. It occurred to him, for the first time, that he'd probably been the object of more than one mercy screw.

Sex offered out of pity. He tossed the nail punch into his toolbox and hooked his hammer on his leather belt with a little savagery. If they'd started their dates expecting him to be grateful for their mercy in bed, they'd ended by trying to catch their breaths after a climax for which they were always the grateful ones. *Surprise, surprise, ladies.*

He couldn't go back to that.

After tonight, that would be all there was. Again.

He left the bookcase and yanked open the fridge, grabbed one of his beers and downed half of it in one go. It didn't help. His future love life looked exactly like the past two years; a murky jumble of carrying on with life, enjoying pleasure where he could, getting by with less. There were only two bright spots: Melissa and India. The time between them? Nothing he wanted to go through again.

How long ago did his wife die? He must be lonely, raising those girls by himself...

"Here you are. I was looking for you to let you know my secret-recipe spaghetti sauce is almost done. We can eat anytime." India's voice washed over him, clearing away the ugliness of his memories.

He didn't look at her, not yet.

"Penny for your thoughts," she said.

He laughed to himself at nothing remotely amusing as he jingled the pennies in his hand.

India came up to him, touched his hand. "You actually have pennies? Two thoughts, then."

Emotion kept Aiden silent. He watched India's thumb smooth over the black-domed onyx of his West Point ring as he held the pennies. The sight stirred something in him, an awareness of the stages of his life: his schooling and career, his first wife and their children...and the stage he wanted to move to next.

I'm not quitting on you, he'd said.

I won't compete with a child for a man's time and attention, she'd said, so unaware that it was the only future they might possibly have.

"Oh, wow. This is the bookcase? It's so cool." She left him to run her hand over the tree's branches, in no danger of catching herself on a nail because he was a father who took care of things like that. "When you said a bookcase, I had no idea it was going to be a tree. You're so creative."

"I saw one on TV and copied it." But it was a warm feeling to see her admiring his work. The tree was like a child's drawing of a Halloween tree, leafless branches angling every which way from a central trunk. The books that would be lined up on each branch would be the leaves.

"This is a Christmas gift?" She turned to him suddenly, her fingers suspended in the air over a branch. "For the family that's coming. You made somebody a bookcase from scratch? I wish I had relatives that made me something this cool."

"It's for a little girl." He watched India carefully, aware of every nuance in her expression. Her eyebrows lifted a little, mild surprise, and then the look came over her. *That* look.

"Oh, that's so sweet." She tilted her head and practically cooed over him. "She'll love it." *It's so precious, the way you care for those girls.*

God, he hated it.

He didn't want it, not from India. Her hands were touching her heart now—did she know it? She was melting, same as all the others.

He and India hadn't started like all the others. They'd been equals, stripping themselves down the first morning they'd met. She hadn't pitied him. She'd been angry with him, clenching her hands together under her chin, kneeling over him, angry that he'd pitied *her*. Furious that he'd think she didn't want the heat that had been burning them up in bed.

She was looking at him now like he was some kind of adorable puppy.

That is not me, damn it. You know me. Remember me.

Whatever the look on his face was, it made her smile fade and her eyes open a little wider. "What—what's up?"

He looked into those gray eyes as he yanked off the other glove. He threw it on the cement floor just as he reached her, crowding her back against the wall. For one suspended second, they stared at one another, and then he was kissing her hard, taking her mouth, swallowing her gasp. She made a sound in her throat, a little surrender, and then her tongue was smooth against his.

He raised his hands to hold her head, to angle her face the way he wanted it, but he had the pennies in one hand. Greedy for her, impatient, he dropped them on the floor, barely hearing their metallic *pings* as she whispered his name against his jaw.

She knew him now, and he knew her, every breath. Knew those fingers digging into his right shoulder. Knew what she wore under those black leggings: nothing.

She shifted sharply when his hips pressed into hers—he was wearing his tool belt. He backed off a few inches, still kissing her, shorter tastes, letting them both catch breaths between kisses as he jerked down the waistband of her black leggings a few inches, then slid his hand where it wanted to go. She was all heat, smooth and slick. "Already wet," he murmured over her lips, a lover's compliment.

"Because you're with me."

"Good." He pressed her against the wall once more,

giving in to a darker, possessive feeling. "I'll be with you all night."

He forced himself to let up, to ease back and keep himself and his damn belt far enough away so that he wouldn't hurt her—but he made demands with his hand. She gasped, a sound of anticipation. Her eyes were open, unfocused, looking at the blue sky beyond his shoulder as he played her with his fingers. She was going to look rumpled and sleepy, right here in the garage where he'd first laid eyes on her—right here, right…about…*now*.

"Aiden," she breathed as she shuddered against the wall, as she pulsed against his hand. "Aiden," she breathed afterward, as if his name was all she could think of. "Aiden."

He kissed her softly. "Yes, this is me."

But when she went back in the house to check on her farewell dinner, he bent to scoop up his pennies once more, and finished the bookcase.

Twilight was turning into night.
Not yet. It's not dark yet.

India rested her cheek against Aiden's shoulder. He was sitting in a teak deck chair, and she was sitting sideways across his lap, like a child. She wasn't little, but she didn't care. It was cozy to have his arms around her, to feel his warmth against her.

It was very chilly this evening. Even Fabio had chosen to stay in the warm kitchen, but neither of them had wanted to break the mood and go inside for a blanket. With a long reach, Aiden had snagged one corner of the patio table's vinyl tablecloth, and he'd pulled it over them. The flannel backing was actually soft and warm, but the red-and-white checked vinyl made crinkling, wrinkling noises whenever they shifted positions. It should have been ridiculous. They should have been laughing about it.

They weren't.

The landscape undulated toward the setting sun, reminding her of an ocean. "It's like we're on a cruise ship."

"What is?"

She had a hand tucked under her chin. She held it out and made a little wave motion. "The land. See the waves?"

"I do now."

She tucked her hand back under the tablecloth, out of the cold. "It's really like a cruise, isn't it? This week has been our vacation. We've had a shipboard romance."

"The best one."

India watched the waves turn gray in the gloaming. "We can't stop it from being over. The ship is going to dock and the passengers must disembark. It's inevitable. All good things come to an end."

"Vacations do. Lives don't."

"Lives return to normal. You'll go back to your normal, and I'll go back to mine. Our houses. Our jobs. Our routines."

Aiden was silent as he set his cheek on her hair. She guessed that he knew what she knew: it was time to say goodbye.

Sadness made her head too heavy to lift from his shoulder. "Maybe I'll be able to bear this better if I tell myself it was a lovely cruise, but it couldn't last forever."

"What if we wanted it to?"

To last forever? Her heart thudded. He couldn't have meant forever, but maybe he wasn't ready to say goodbye, either.

"Can you come to Belgium?"

"Once a year."

It wasn't forever, but she'd take what she could get. "I can come back here next year."

Aiden took a deep breath, sighed it out. "Two vacations a year. Six nights each? Five, depending which flights we catch."

"We can talk in the meantime. I'd rather see your face on that video app than anyone else's."

"We won't really be part of each other's lives, India. A face in an app doesn't give you the full picture. We'd only see what we wanted to show each other."

"Like having a perfect life on social media." She hated that he had a point.

"I've looked at this every way I can," he said. "Trying to keep this shipboard romance going after the vacation is over won't work."

"But we could write. And—and text."

But Aiden was shaking his head, shifting their positions, sitting her up so that she faced him as an adult and not as a helpless child.

"My beautiful, beautiful India, we could do all that, all of it, and we want to, because nobody wants their vacation to end. It will help, for a little while. A few weeks. A few months? How long will it be, before we realize that we're pretending we're still involved, when we aren't? It will hurt, and we'll be mad at the world or mad at the circumstances that keep us apart. Then we might start being mad at each other, for being the reason we hurt. Mad at each other for being so wonderful that we couldn't prevent ourselves from falling in love this week."

"*Aiden.* Is that true? Do you think we've fallen in

love with each other? Because I think— I was afraid to think it, let alone say it, but…"

He waited, his dark eyes unreadable in the darkening night.

"But I think it's true," she said, but she didn't sound confident, not when he was so grave.

"And then," he continued, his voice calm and even, "eventually, I'd be mad at myself, furious at myself for being so shortsighted about it all that I'd set myself up for all that pain in the first place."

That sounded true, coming from a man who knew himself. All the qualities she'd recognized on that first morning—his empathy, the way he could put others before himself—came with maturity. He was being brutally honest with himself, and with her, because he didn't want to ruin what they had.

He was right. Trying to force a vacation to last after they resumed their real lives would not work.

"I don't want you to be mad at yourself," she said. *Because I love you.* "The cruise ship is arriving at port. We can't stop it."

He seemed to exhale a little bit, as if he was disappointed that she'd accepted his wisdom. He couldn't have expected anything else. They had no other choices.

"What time do you disembark?" he asked.

"Seven in the morning."

She was going to let him go. She had to. She rushed her words a little bit, so he wouldn't feel obliged to fill in the silence. "You know I'm not much of a morning person. Maybe this should be goodbye. What good will it do to sleep in the same bed tonight, really? It will just make tomorrow morning all the harder, when I have to go around opening windows a few inches and locking them into place with this pile of screwy things Helen left for me. That wouldn't allow for a decent goodbye, not with workers pulling into the driveway…and stuff."

He was silent in the dark.

"Plus, I've got to pack. So…"

He nodded, but he didn't say anything to make this easier.

"So I guess this is goodbye." Tears—she wasn't sobbing, but she felt the tears. "I'm going to miss you so very much."

She leaned toward him and kissed him, and the thought of never feeling his lips against hers again just about killed her. He raised his hands to hold her face as he kissed her back, his thumbs touching her wet cheeks.

"Don't cry, India. We knew this was how it was going to end."

He stood, careful not to step on her toes as they both came to their feet. He set the tablecloth on the chair, then turned and walked away.

She couldn't watch him for long because the darkness swallowed him up, but she stayed and stared until she imagined that she heard his boots on the boards of a faraway bridge.

Chapter Eleven

One hour.

Aiden had been home for one hour, and he still didn't have the Christmas tree assembled. It had seemed like a good idea to put it together tonight instead of in the morning. India had said goodbye; his children's tree would distract him.

But tonight, it was Melissa's tree. The memory of Melissa—hell, his heart hurt so damn bad, anyway, he let himself think about her. When he thought about Melissa, really thought about Melissa, he missed her hard.

It was painful. Usually, a weighty ache. Sometimes, a sharp pain, like when he'd pulled the tree box down from the rack in his garage.

Now, he would miss India, too. Differently—she fit in a different part of his life—but with that same sense of longing. Of emptiness. The lack of someone who should be there. Another person to remember and wonder what might have been.

Pain made him angry. There was no help for it with Melissa. She was gone from this life. He had to deal with that pain.

India was not gone.

The difference was so blindingly obvious. He stood in his living room with a half-built Christmas tree and wondered how he could be so stupid.

India is not gone. She would be in the morning, but right now, at this very moment, he didn't have to miss her. They might not have forever. They might not say *I love you*, and he would absolutely miss her tomorrow and every day after that, but right this second, he didn't have to hurt. He could be with India.

He tossed the last branches on the floor and headed for the back door. For God's sake, what was wrong with him? The woman he wanted was alive and well and only an acre away, and he was wasting time missing her before he had to miss her.

He slammed the porch door behind himself and took the steps two at a time to the grass. There was just enough moonlight to see where he stepped as he covered the distance as quickly as possible. Why wasn't he with India? Just because she'd made a little speech and said goodbye? She'd had tears running down her face, *tears*, but he'd walked away as if it would hurt any less if they were apart.

The only way the hurt would lessen was if he was *with* her.

He looked up from the uneven ground to see how much farther it was to the bridge. On the far side, coming toward him, was the beam of a flashlight, bouncing with every step of the person who carried it. *India.* He could make her out as she crossed the bridge. *India.*

She was on his land before she saw him. She broke into a run and called his name, and then he called hers like they were in some sappy movie, *India* bursting from his throat, and he started running, too. The impact when she crashed against his chest felt like the best thing on earth—a hard chest compression to jump-start his heart into beating again.

"I'm so stupid—"

"I don't know what I was thinking—"

"*God*, India."

"I know."

He couldn't even kiss her. He could only stand in the moonlight and drink in the face he loved while she held him tightly, two arms tight around his chest to keep him from falling or flying or doing anything at all without her.

"We don't have to start missing each other yet," he said. "Not yet."

"It's not even ten o'clock. We have hours and hours until tomorrow."

They walked back to her house, but they didn't hold hands. Instead, she kept her arm around his waist and he kept his arm around her shoulders, and they held on to each other as if they never would let go.

Nine hours.

For nine hours, Aiden had not missed India, because he'd been with her. For nine hours, they'd made love and talked and catnapped and snacked before making love again. He'd had nine hours to fall further in love with her—but she'd had her arms wrapped tightly around him, so he must have taken her down with him as he fell.

Now, because of those nine hours, missing her was going to hurt even more.

She was taking Tom's truck. After her week's tour of the Texas coast, she'd leave his truck in the parking lot of the Austin airport, back where she'd picked it up, and she'd fly all the way to Brussels. That hadn't changed.

No matter how many extra hours they'd had, their vacation was over. No matter how much they might want to, they could not sustain this shipboard romance for years to come.

The workers had arrived very early, eager to be done so their Christmas holiday could begin. One of their trucks had blocked in the pickup.

Aiden waited with India for someone to come and move the truck. They looked at one another in the early morning light, spending their extra fifteen minutes standing apart, hands in their coat pockets, listening to workers shout at one another about truck keys.

That was stupid. Aiden took his hands out of his pockets and pulled India close.

"It's going to be so hard to leave," she said.

"Yes." It was already hurting. Worse pain was waiting on the horizon, ready to knock him out when she drove away. *Not yet, not yet.*

"Maybe it wasn't such a good idea to spend last night together," India said. "It only makes this worse."

It was going to hurt anyway. Aiden held India and thought of Melissa. Not once, even in the darkest days of his grief, did he ever regret any nine hours he'd ever spent with her. His life was only better for every hour he'd had with his wife. He'd never wish he'd had less time with her. He'd never wish he'd had less time with India, either.

He kissed India's forehead. "Don't wish you didn't experience happiness. Nine hours of happiness is no small thing. That's what we had last night. Nine fewer hours of missing each other in this life."

"*Aiden.* You can't say things like that and let me go."

Behind him, men shouted. "'Bout damn time you got out here. Move that truck so the lady can leave."

The clock was ticking. Minutes left.

India looked devastated. Aiden didn't know how to make it better for her. "Baby, I'm so sorry."

"So am I."

"You know the phrase 'Begin as you mean to go on'? We began as a vacation romance. We're ending as a vacation romance. It's just…it's harder than we thought it would be, but it's what we decided to have. It's what we invested ourselves in. We had ourselves one hell of a vacation romance."

Nothing more, because I screwed it all up from the beginning. If I had it to do over again—

What would he do? Would he have handed her a beer in that garage and introduced himself as the man next door with the dead wife? Would he have showed her photos of his twins' birthday party as she watched to see how much Tabasco he put in his Bloody Mary?

They would never have gotten this far. *I'd be stealing a father from a baby. I don't date fathers.* They wouldn't have had this week, not one hour of it.

"Then let's make our vacation last longer," she said. "I know you have family coming for Christmas, but after that, I'll be at the beach. Corpus Christi. Padre Island. Come and be with me there."

"I can't. My family will still be here." *They will always be here, because I'm a widower and a father, and everything that turns you off.* "You don't want to get involved with another man's family and have it be the kiss of death for yet another relationship. You won't risk yourself like that."

She frowned at that and tilted her head as if she wasn't certain she'd heard him correctly. "I won't risk it? You make me sound like I'm a coward."

The construction truck began to back out of the

drive, beeping with one of those shrill reverse alarms. He was going to have one of the most important conversations of his life while an alarm drowned him out. Perfect.

"You didn't answer my question last night, when we were sitting on the porch," he began. "You said it was a great cruise, but it couldn't last forever. Do you remember that? And I said, 'What if we wanted it to?'"

She was hanging on his every word, staring at him with those luminous eyes. He could drown in those silver-gray eyes. Happily. Forever.

"What would it take, India? What would forever look like?"

"Forever?" she repeated, as the truck shrieked its warning. "Us?"

He felt that same disappointment from yesterday. He hadn't been expecting more, he really hadn't, and he had no right to, but…well, part of him had hoped, he supposed. He stopped hugging her close, but he couldn't let go of her. He kept one hand on her arm. He touched her face.

The truck had backed up all the way and fallen silent. She could go now.

Aiden managed one more smile for the only woman he'd wanted in a long, long time. The only one he could foresee himself wanting for a long, long time. "Forever would look messy. It would get complicated, very complicated, and it would involve families, from grandparents to kids. It would be everything that you've ever run away from before. That's what it would take, my beautiful India. That's what it would take, if you stayed."

"But that's not the woman I am. That's what you're thinking, isn't it?"

"Am I wrong?"

She pressed her lips together. She lifted her chin—
she was hurt.

"It's okay, India. It really is. I like you just the way
you are. I'm crazy about you, just as you are."

"I'm crazy about you, too, just the way you are."

The guilt was his. This was not just the way he was.
This was Aiden Nord on a child-free vacation. She
didn't know the real him. She wouldn't like the real him.
But even now, he couldn't explain that. Instead, he held
the door open for her and she climbed into the pickup.

She rolled down the window after she started the
engine. "This vacation is really over." But she looked
to him for confirmation.

"I'm afraid so. Even if we could have pulled off another week on the coast, the one thing that wouldn't
change is NATO. You'd still be needed in Brussels.
We'd still only see each other for a few days each year.
We'd still end up unhappy."

"But we shouldn't regret having been happy this
week?"

"Right. A week of happiness is a gift. I'm glad we
met." *It's going to kill me later.* "Drive carefully."

Then he stepped back and watched her go.

His heart was still beating. He was still standing.
Poppy and Olympia would be home soon.

He walked into the garage, up to the wall where he'd
demanded with his hands that India remember him as
her man, not as a little girl's sweet bookcase-building
relative.

What had he been thinking?

The bookcase wasn't overly heavy, but it was awkwardly shaped. He hefted it onto his shoulder and
started walking back to his house, Fabio at his heels.
Today was Christmas Eve. He could hide the book-

case in his closet for a few hours, then put it by the tree while the girls were sleeping, a gift from Santa Claus. Their joy and excitement would be everything good about Christmas.

India would be in San Antonio. She wouldn't know what she was missing, because he had never told her.

His vision blurred, but he took a breath and blinked until his vision cleared. No regrets. He'd had a wonderful week with a wonderful woman. Nothing to regret at all.

Aiden made it all the way to the bridge before the pain broke through, a hard hit that threatened to bring him to his knees.

He staggered home with the bookcase on his back.

She was a coward.

She was a fool.

She was in love.

She was in San Antonio.

Go back, go back. Tell him you love him.

But…he knew that. He'd practically taken it for granted that they'd fallen in love with each other. He'd said so, sitting in that teakwood chair, but it had been only part of what he'd said. The rest had been about other things. He wanted other things besides love. She couldn't remember every word, yet every word had been important.

She twisted her hands on the inflexible steering wheel in anxiety. It didn't matter if she couldn't recall everything. She was miserable without him. She'd started crying in Round Rock and had to get off the road when the worst sobs had struck south of Austin.

You shouldn't be in San Antonio right now.

She needed to concentrate. The navigator on her

phone's map app was trying to get her to her B&B in an impersonal, BBC-British voice. "Make a left turn on Alvarez Boulevard."

India complied.

"In one quarter mile, make a U-turn."

She hated directions like that. It made her feel like she'd done something wrong, when she'd only been following orders. The geography didn't change. The app should get it right.

The geography…

She'd left with Aiden's assurances that she had nothing to regret, because geography would have kept them apart, regardless. NATO wouldn't move, and they'd end up being mad at the situation, mad at their careers, and eventually mad at each other for being unhappy and apart. *That* was what he'd said.

"In one half mile, the destination will be on your right."

He'd been kind. He'd given her the perfect excuse: she should not feel guilty about leaving as she had planned to do since the first day, because the geography was difficult and the geography was out of her control.

But was it?

The light up ahead turned red. She slowed to a stop.

NATO headquarters might never move, but that didn't mean she'd stay there for the rest of her career. Officers generally retired after twenty years of service. She had twelve years of service. Aiden had even more, probably fourteen. Their posts would surely change in the next six or eight years. If they were married, they'd be considered for joint domicile, and the army would try to station them together on their next assignment.

If they were *married*. The army didn't move boyfriends and girlfriends around the world together.

The light turned green, but India didn't move for a second.

Married.

Why not? They were both single, both in their thirties, both well established in their careers. They were in the perfect place in their lives to get married. At thirty-four, most people would say Aiden was a confirmed bachelor, but she was a confirmed bachelorette herself. That didn't mean she couldn't change. She wasn't set in her ways or too inflexible to live with someone else. Aiden wasn't, either.

She stepped on the accelerator, drove only a block or two, and saw the flower-laden sign for the B&B ahead on her right.

Marriage. That meant families would be involved. It would be messy, complicated, Aiden had warned her. He didn't even know about her family, and he was worried about her willingness to meet his.

Could she handle it? She'd been evaluated and found wanting by Bernardo's crowd. She'd been unprepared to be smothered by the grandparents and siblings surrounding the coolly academic Adolphus. So many others…she hadn't even wanted to try to meet Gerard-Pierre's.

But this was Aiden. Bernardo had never spent six hours, let alone six nights, being alone with her and only her, being interested in what she thought, enchanted by the way she did even the simplest things, like drinking a beer. Adolphus had never touched her so much, never held her hand just to walk through a restaurant's parking lot, never shared a pillow when they were dreaming. Those men had been so much less than Aiden, and yet, she'd made an effort to blend in with their families. She'd met their families, at least. She'd *tried*.

Aiden had so generously consoled her with geography, but he'd been disappointed that she wouldn't take the first step toward a messy and complicated forever. She wouldn't stay for Christmas and meet his family.

"You have reached your destination."

India parked the pickup truck and walked into the Spanish Mission home. It was historic and gorgeous, with white stucco walls on the outside and colorful Mexican tiles on the inside.

She'd never seen the inside of Aiden's house, had she? But he'd told her she could stay with him for Christmas. He'd said that at McDonald's. *My family will arrive... I'd like you to meet them...you could stay at my house.*

"Ah, you've made it," her hostess said. "*Feliz Navidad*, and welcome."

"*Gracias*," India said, feeling a little disoriented. "But I think I must leave. Yes, I think I should. There's somewhere else I'm supposed to be."

Chapter Twelve

India had been less nervous in the underground tunnels of the Kremlin.

This was 489 Cedar Highway. She was petrified.

India turned into Aiden's long driveway. *Everything's okay. It really is.* That's what Aiden would say. He was going to be surprised when she knocked on the door, but he wasn't going to yell at her to go away or call the cops on her for trespassing. She had no reason to be so nervous. She was only going to tell a man she loved him, and crash his family Christmas.

She'd dressed for the occasion, stopping at a Mc-Donald's—oh, the irony—to change in the bathroom from her jeans to the one dress she'd packed. It was a jewel-toned purple wrap dress, not too dressy, not too casual in style, suitable for day or night in color. She didn't know if Aiden's family had a big dinner on Christmas Eve or Christmas Day. They might go to a Christmas Eve church service. She was prepared for anything, for any size gathering. Really, she was.

There might be a chance Aiden was alone. He'd said he had family coming for Christmas. This was Christmas Eve day. There might be no family here until to-morrow.

Please, let there be nobody here until tomorrow. Please.

She didn't see his truck. It was possible his big red extended-cab pickup fit in his garage, she supposed.

Please, let Aiden be home. And nobody else.

She hadn't wanted to arrive at a family gathering empty-handed, but it was Christmas Eve afternoon and stores were closing, so she'd done some quick gift shopping at a mammoth twenty-four-hour grocery store. She'd bought wine, a bouquet of flowers and one of those blue tins filled with supposedly Danish butter cookies, probably a poor offering during the season of homemade Christmas cookies. Aiden would tell everyone she was visiting from out of the country, that she was an army officer on vacation. His family wouldn't expect her to be Betty Crocker, would they? She hoped not, because her mother had never passed down any family cookie recipes.

It was going to be okay. She'd placed her little offerings in a bright red gift bag they'd sold in the school-supplies aisle, so she held that in one hand and gave her hair one last fluff with the other. She rang the doorbell.

The door cracked open, only as far as a security chain reached. Aiden's face appeared in the crack. "My God. India."

She smiled. "Surprise."

He didn't do anything.

"Merry Christmas."

Still nothing.

I am not a coward. She stood tall in her dress and black pumps, slipping into the posture of an army officer in uniform. She spoke about love. "I had a lot of time to think this morning while I was driving. I thought, at first, that you were disappointed that I lived in Belgium, but that's not true. You're disappointed in me, for not even trying to meet your family. I don't fit in easily with families. They intimidate me, to be honest, but if I'm going to be brave for anyone, I should be brave for you, because I love you more than I've loved anyone else. May I come in?"

He closed his eyes briefly, a look of—not of relief, actually. Not happiness.

"Right," he said. "Okay."

He shut the door. She heard the slide of the chain, and then he opened it again, but not much wider. His body blocked her from being able to see anything inside the house. "So…how are you?"

"I'm fine."

I think I might die.

Her military confidence fled. She was just a girl in a purple dress imposing on a man whom she'd terribly, horribly misread. "Did I come at a bad time? I could just go home— No, I couldn't. The fumes. But I could just…go. Come back later?"

A little voice piped loudly. "I want to see!" Then a little face popped into the inch of space between the bend of Aiden's knee and the edge of the door.

"Oh." India couldn't have been more surprised, which was silly, because Aiden had made a bookcase for a little girl. This must be his niece or cousin, someone who was going to be excited very soon by a cool tree bookshelf. "Hello."

"Hi," she said, her face so cherubic, it could be on a Christmas card. "Who are you?"

But then a second little voice preceded a second little

face, although India could only see the button nose, really. "Move over. My turn. I want to see."

Aiden sighed, an unmistakable sound of defeat. He stepped back and opened the door wider. The two girls immediately filled in the space. One had reddish hair, one had almost black, but they both had very green eyes. They had to be related. Cousins, maybe sisters.

They were cute. The strawberry-haired one wrapped her arm around Aiden's leg and put her finger in her mouth, but she kept staring holes through India.

"Your dress is purple," the dark-haired one said.

"Yes, it is." India bit her lip, trying to be serious. Polite. How did you make conversation with a little girl? "You, ahh…you know your colors."

"I know my colors," said the clingy one, speaking around her fingers.

Aiden looked down at her and brushed his hand lightly over her hair. "Take your fingers out of your mouth."

India's heart squeezed. His gesture sparked some emotion—yes, he'd done that to her, too, that brush of his hand over her hair, so many times. She looked at him as he looked at the little girl. He looked so, so sweet with a child. He was big and broad, filling up the door frame, masculine—a *man* in a dark knit shirt that clung to muscled shoulders and biceps—and still so, so sweet to these girls.

Fabio joined the party, nosing his way in between the girls, who barely noticed him as they continued to unabashedly stare at her.

"Hi, Fabio," she said. In the house, she could hear more voices. A family gathering was happening, after all—but Aiden clearly wasn't going to let her in. She remained standing on the porch, facing the three of them, wondering how she'd misjudged Aiden's invitation so badly.

"Are you here for Christmas, too?" the dark-haired girl asked.

Too? What other woman had already arrived? A new possibility hit India so hard, it hurt: she hadn't accepted Aiden's invitation, so he'd invited someone else. Some other woman, someone less family-phobic than India. *Are you here, too?*

"I'm not sure." She met Aiden's impassive gaze. "Am I?"

"Sure. Come on in." His words were polite. His expression was resigned as he stepped back and opened the door wider.

She had to step across the threshold to be close enough to speak to him under her breath. "I can go. I should have called." *I thought you'd be happy.*

"No, it's better this way."

What is better? But the dog was turning circles, and the little girls were still right in the mix. The voices India had heard were coming from a television in the next room, not from a big family, although she could see the back of a man's head, someone sitting on the couch. He could be the father of at least one of the girls. There were probably more family members in the kitchen.

"Daddy, tell her my name."

So gosh darned cute, the way the cherub said *Daddy*—India froze. The child wasn't talking to the man on the sofa. She was looking up at Aiden.

"Tell her it. Tell her my name is *Poppy*."

"Okay, I will." Aiden put his hand on the child's head as she continued to squeeze herself against his leg. "This is Poppy."

"Poppy," India repeated, staring at the little girl,

looking for any resemblance. Fair skin, red hair, green eyes. She must have heard wrong.

"Dad-*deee*," pleaded the other girl, "tell her my name."

Daddy, *again*. India looked up at Aiden.

He returned her look with much less shock than she felt. "And this is Olympia. Poppy and Olympia. My daughters."

"We're twins."

"Fraternal," Aiden said, as if he knew that was going to be the next question.

"How…?"

How could she not have known this? How could she possibly not have known this?

A car door slammed in the driveway. Fabio went bounding out the door, and India turned around to prepare herself for whatever was going to hit her next. Fabio was jumping around a woman as she walked toward them. A woman who was probably her age. She was telling the dog to shoo and holding a child's suitcase and a gallon of milk out of his reach. She was…

Oh, my God.

She whirled back to Aiden and spoke under her breath again, through fiercely gritted teeth. "Is that your *wife*?"

"That is my sister."

Her relief was short-lived. "But are you *married*?"

"No, I'm not."

"Hey, you, did you bring us a present?" the dark-haired one—Olympia—asked.

"Olympia," Aiden said sharply. "That's not polite."

Aiden sounded like a father. Aiden *was* a father. His sister was coming up the walk, his daughters were staring at her and India's heart was pounding out of her chest.

"I brought cookies." She sounded desperate, but after she set the bag on the floor, she backed away in a controlled and careful manner, like she'd just plunked down a raw chicken in front of a couple of lion cubs. Cute lion cubs.

When the cubs pulled out the blue tin, the flowers came out, too, and hit the floor with a splatter of petals. Little Olympia picked up the bouquet and put it back in the bag, blooms down. Aiden reached down and snagged the wine bottle before it could suffer a similar fate. He stood there so casually, bottle dangling from his fingers, as if nothing here was a big deal at all.

India could handle this. She had five seconds to handle this while the girls were chatting with each other, five seconds before his sister walked in the door. "Okay, let me get this straight. You're divorced. Sharing custody. This is your weekend with your children."

His children. That was going to take her a while to get used to, but *thank God* he wasn't married. She couldn't live with herself if she'd slept with a married man, even if she'd been duped into sleeping with a married man. She didn't think Aiden was the kind of man to dupe a woman—but he had duped her, hadn't he? Just not about a wife. Thank God.

Aiden let the bottle swing from his fingers, back and forth, back and forth, hypnotic—easier to focus on than all of these people with all of the emotions they churned up. India had to force herself to look away from it, back to Aiden's eyes. He'd been waiting for her to look at him, she realized, before he spoke.

"I am widowed, and I have full custody, and they're all mine, every day."

She couldn't speak. She couldn't look away.

Fabio came bounding in, the woman from the car—Aiden's *sister*—following behind.

"This is the last one." She set down the child's suitcase. "Got the milk before the store closed."

Aiden finally looked away from India to glance at the suitcase, then his sister.

His sister looked between the two of them. "Aren't you going to introduce me?"

Aiden gestured toward the woman who shared his coloring. "This is my sister, Debra."

India smiled politely and nodded, totally on autopilot while her inner self ran around screaming and pulling her hair out. "Nice to meet you."

Debra looked at her brother. "And...?"

Aiden set down the wine bottle on a little hall table with a decisive *thunk*. "And this is India Woods. She's... the girl next door."

"Are you dating that woman? You are, aren't you?"

His sister was whispering to him in the kitchen. Terrific. Neither of the women in his house could speak to him in a normal tone of voice.

"You're the one who told me to enjoy being a bachelor." He dried the spatula Debra handed him and stuck it into the crock he kept by the stove because Melissa had kept it by the stove.

"Did you two get busy this week? You did. I can see it on your face."

He didn't want to discuss his sex life with his sister. "Get busy? Is that what the kids are calling it these days? Or is that what the grandmas are saying?"

"You did. You got jiggy with it. You did the wild thing. You—"

"What decade are you in?" He shoved the cutting board in its drawer and slammed it shut.

That killed the conversation for an eternal second.

"You like her, don't you?" Debra's tone of voice had changed in that second, which only annoyed Aiden more.

"Of course I like her. I wouldn't sleep with a woman I didn't like." He dried the glass measuring cup and placed it carefully on the shelf, bracing himself for Debra's crow of victory, because he'd just inadvertently confirmed that he'd slept with India.

"No, I mean you *like her* like her, don't you?"

He stared out the window over the sink, seeing nothing. He liked her, yes, and she liked him. They'd broken up and parted ways, and there'd been no reason to tell her anything more because he hadn't expected anything more. Now she was back, telling him she loved him as she wore a purple dress, a knockout, a single woman who intended to stay that way, a single career officer—currently sitting shell-shocked on the sofa in the family room. He exhaled, dully aware that meant he had been holding his breath.

Debra kept her voice quiet. "She doesn't look anything like Melissa, does she?"

Aiden frowned at his sister. "Is she supposed to? Since I loved Melissa, the next one should look like Melissa? Is that how it works?"

"No, I— Oh, Aiden. The next one? You're thinking of her on the same level as Melissa? She's not just the hot chick next door, is she?"

"Hot chick? Come into this decade, Deb." He threw the dish towel on the countertop. The macaroni and cheese was in the oven, the pots and pans were washed and put away. There was no reason to stay in the kitchen and play Twenty Questions about something that hurt his soul.

He turned to go, but he couldn't just walk out on his sister with no explanation. She'd been with him through the worst times of his life. He hoped he wasn't heading for more darkness now.

He spoke over his shoulder. "She didn't know I had kids. She didn't know any of it, nothing about the whole sorry situation. She just liked...me."

Deb was silent.

"So much for that, right?" Aiden asked, suddenly wanting to know what his sister thought.

"Well, she hasn't turned tail and run out the door screaming yet. That's something."

"I suppose it is."

"It is. Good luck. You're going to need it." Debra was the one who turned to walk out this time, but after she passed him, she stopped to toss one more comment over her shoulder. "Next time, don't be such a block-head with a woman you might really like."

"Next time?" It made him angry, her casual assumption that if India didn't work out, he'd just move on to someone else. "There's no next time."

"Then you better not blow this one."

Chapter Thirteen

"India, you really blew it this time."

She whispered the words to her reflection in the bathroom mirror.

She could hardly freshen up her makeup, she was scowling at herself so hard. This was an epic screwup.

Remember that time you thought this guy was in love with you, and you chased him down at Christmas in his own house, and his whole family didn't know who you were, and you found out he had kids and he'd been married and he hadn't told you anything about it? Remember that one? Epic.

And yet...

She was still here.

Aiden had looked at her. For one second their eyes had met, and she was still here, because she was a lovesick idiot.

It had happened in the kitchen. She'd met Debra's husband, who seemed more than ready to give Aiden his children back. She'd made some vague attempt to help Debra salvage the flowers, but she hadn't known where the scissors or the vases were kept, so she'd just kind of stood by and watched an efficient woman do everything efficiently. It had all been a farce; India wasn't part of the scene. She was entirely superfluous, unexpected and unwanted. She'd shown up at Aiden's house without knowing the most basic facts about him: *I am widowed. These are my daughters.*

He hadn't told her anything. He'd kept her in the dark.

She should have left.

Instead, she'd been invited to stay for Christmas Eve dinner, or rather, it had been assumed she was staying. Debra had told her the plans as she'd set the flowers on the kitchen table that India noticed had been set for five; they'd added a sixth place setting for her. *We'll be leaving after dinner, but then you and Aiden and the girls can get the tree decorated before Santa Claus comes.*

India should have bowed out gracefully. She could have said that she couldn't stay for dinner. She'd only come by to wish Aiden a merry Christmas and give him the wine and flowers for helping her with the dog and the shower installers this week—a very reasonable lie—and then she should have bolted. Aiden had not planned on her staying for supper and being part of his Christmas with his children, because he hadn't even hinted that he had children. He hadn't wanted her to know.

Instead, the girls had gotten so excited at the talk of tree decorations and Santa Claus, they'd been jumping around, and the dog had barked, and India had continued to stand silently in the kitchen without agreeing or disagreeing to Debra's plans, because she hadn't really been asked if she'd like to stay for dinner.

Christmas Eve dinner was not going to be a turkey or a goose or a ham, but macaroni and cheese. Debra and Aiden had done the work and put the casserole in the oven as the girls got in the way and talked about Santa Claus incessantly. It got loud.

The girls have been fast asleep by nine every night, Debra had told Aiden. *Then you'll have some peace and quiet to...you know...talk.* She'd laughed, and her husband had laughed as he looked in the fridge for juice boxes for the children. India had felt overwhelmed and out of place, and she'd just resolved to pretend to notice the time, make her apologies and leave, because she was not part of this family she hadn't known existed.

One step toward the door, *one*, and then her eyes had met Aiden's.

She'd caught him watching her, but he didn't look away. He wanted her, a raw hunger in his eyes that she recognized, a trace of pain that she didn't.

He still wants me.

He wanted her the way he'd wanted her since she'd propositioned him over a Bloody Mary, and she wanted him, too, like she wanted to breathe.

So here she was, hiding in the bathroom until the macaroni and cheese could finish baking, because a man who had not shared the most essential part of his life with her still wanted her in his bed. Six nights hadn't been enough. She was apparently so desperate for one more night, she was willing to disrupt his family tree-trimming tradition.

No, I'm not. I'll leave after dinner.

There was a knock on the bathroom door. India paused in the middle of unscrewing the cap of her lip gloss. She'd have to stop stalling and let someone else use the bathroom.

"Just a minute," she said.

More knocking. She could tell it was coming from

low on the door, little knocks made by little knuckles. Insistent.

Well, she was done in here. Her clothes were fastened, her hands washed. She couldn't imagine what the girls wanted, but her instinct was to avoid the children. She'd spent a four-day weekend with Adolphus's family before his little sister had gotten so attached to India that she'd cried, according to Adolphus's report, when India had left. India would only be here for a few more hours, at most. How much damage could she really do in just a couple of hours?

Knock, knock, knock.

"Come in?" *I guess?*

The door opened. A little face appeared at the door, all eyes. The littler one—Poppy.

"What are you doing?" she asked, hanging on the doorknob with two hands.

What did she think a person did in a bathroom?

"Are you putting on lipstick?"

Olympia's face pushed Poppy's face out of the way for a second, until the door just swung the rest of the way open and two girls crowded right up to India. Jeez, they were cute. Aiden dressed them so cutely, too, from the little ankle socks and Mary Janes on their feet to the sparkly barrettes in their hair.

"Lipstick," Poppy said.

India held out the squeeze tube for inspection. "It's lip gloss, actually."

"Glossss." Poppy said the word with such satisfaction.

"What's it called?" Olympia asked.

"Lip gloss," India repeated.

"No, what's it *called*?"

India had no idea what Olympia was trying to ask.

Poppy came to her rescue. "Aunt Debra's lipstick is called 'mixed berry.' What's your'ses name?"

Both girls were just so interested in the plastic squeeze tube of gloss. Their little hands were on the sink counter. Their little faces were reflected in the mirror, and India realized with a jolt that their eyes were focused on *her*, not the gloss. They were studying her avidly, waiting for her to reveal one of the mysteries of the world.

"Oh. Well, let's see." India squinted at the tiny font on the tube. "This is called...fifty-one."

"Fifty-one?" Their disappointment was palpable.

India felt the need to make things better. "Yes, but do you know what that means? That means there are fifty other colors of lip gloss, too."

"Whoa..." Poppy was suitably impressed. India felt proud of herself for that spin.

Olympia was not so impressed. Her little nose scrunched up. "But why?"

"Why what?" India asked.

"Why did they make fifty colors?"

"Well..." They were even more inquisitive than they'd been at the front door. India suspected Aiden dealt with this all the time, on every subject. "Well, I suppose because fifty different women won't all like the same color, so they make a variety to choose from."

"Why do you like fifty-one?"

Why, why, why. "It makes my lips shiny."

"The other numbers aren't shiny?"

This is crazy. "I assume they are. I only use this number. I like the way it looks."

"I like the way it looks, too," Poppy said.

"I like it, too," Olympia said.

They were both on their toes, trying to get closer to

the mirror and the reflection of the tube of lip gloss. If they were puppies, they would have run up to the mirror and left little nose prints everywhere.

The thought made India smile. "Would you like to try it?"

They responded like she'd asked if they'd like ice cream and ponies and cotton candy. Their little faces didn't just light up; their whole bodies did. What a joy, to see so much joy in a person that it couldn't be physically contained. Poppy bounced on her toes, like the happiness was going to lift her right off the ground.

India laughed—and remembered laughing as Aiden had lifted her right off the ground, remembered the happiness as he'd carried her into her house.

That kind of happiness was different than this, of course. That had been adult. Sexual anticipation. There was no comparison.

But she'd felt…

She looked at the bright eyes and smiles of two little girls who were enchanted with lip gloss. She looked at herself in the mirror and remembered how she'd looked just before a night with Aiden: like she'd been anticipating ice cream and ponies and cotton candy.

Aiden was her lip gloss.

India cleared her throat and crouched down to little-girl level. "Okay, it only takes the tiniest bit. You're so pretty already, the gloss is just for fun." She held the gloss up and squeezed until a little bit appeared at the slanted tip of the tube.

"Ohhh," the girls said in unison.

India almost laughed, but she didn't want them to think she was mocking them. She used the tip of her pinky finger to transfer the dab of gloss to Olympia's lower lip. Her mouth was so tiny, her lip so impossibly soft.

"Go like this." India demonstrated how to smack her lips together to spread the gloss.

Poppy bounced on her toes. "Me, me, me!"

They were all three smacking their lips when Aiden appeared at the door, a masculine presence in the corner of India's eye as she remained crouched down with her little lip-gloss fan club.

"There you are, girls. Don't bother—"

His sudden silence made India look up. He looked shocked. He looked at her like he'd never seen her before. What had she done that was so terrible?

But he recovered quickly enough. "Girls, you don't bother your guests while they're in the *bathroom*. People want privacy in bathrooms, remember?"

"But she said come in."

"Because you didn't stop knocking, did you?"

Two little lip-glossed mouths pouted.

"Did you?" Aiden repeated sternly.

India did not have a good enough poker face for this parenting stuff. It was kind of hysterical. She did her best to look at the girls with one eyebrow raised, asking silently if they were going to tell the truth.

"Poppy knocked," Olympia said.

"Olympia knocked," Poppy said at the same time.

Aiden sighed. "No more knocking, either one of you. Dinner's ready."

"Carry me. Carry both of me's."

"Both of *us*." Aiden knelt, scooped up a child in each arm, then stood.

Oozing testosterone, India had thought when she'd first laid eyes on him. His masculinity was even more obvious now, his size and strength such a sharp contrast to his daughters' delicacy. He used that testosterone to make two girls feel safe and loved.

Her father had used his to make it with two girls at once. India hadn't known what sex was at the time, but she'd known that her father was leaving her alone in the house again and walking out the door with each of his hands on a woman's butt, and she'd known you weren't supposed to touch people's butts. Aiden would never act like that around his daughters.

She followed him through the house, crossing the family room. Aiden was behaving like a gentle giant; her gaze fell on items that told another story. As an army officer herself, she recognized them all. The long, rectangular shadow box holding a slim, silver sword that was a cadet saber from West Point. The framed certificate that featured a black arch with the bright yellow *Ranger* designation was a letter for—she wandered a little closer as Aiden set the girls in booster seats while Debra put a bowl of green beans on the table—a commendation for placing third in the Best Ranger Competition.

The Ranger competition? The annual army-wide, military-wide event was infamous. Two-person teams faced round-the-clock testing of military skills for three days. It was brutal. It was voluntary. He'd excelled at it.

The man who was pouring milk into sippy cups had another side, all right, another use for all that testosterone: he was a warrior. She watched the way he smiled with his daughters, the way he laughed at their little jokes, and tried to imagine him channeling the ferocity and furor needed to conquer— *Ah*.

She flushed, because she could easily imagine it. She'd tasted it herself, as his lover, the change that came over him when playfulness and teasing turned serious, when stark need drove everything else away. That one, raw second of conquest before climax—

"India should sit here. This is the girls' side."

India sat with a father and his children and family, and she tried not to think about sex.

His arm was practically at her eye level when he lifted the lid from the casserole dish. She watched the play of biceps and triceps as he reached across the table to put a scoop of macaroni on Poppy's plate.

When India went back to Belgium, would Aiden miss the sex as much as she would?

Yes. He'd told her so. He enjoyed having sex with her, but he hadn't told her about this, about the most essential, most elemental part of his life. She'd blundered into it.

If she hadn't convinced herself that their great sex resulted from love, she would not have turned around the pickup in San Antonio. In a week, she would have ended up back in Belgium without ever having met Poppy and Olympia. Her lover's daughters. His heart. His soul.

She had known nothing about them.

Because he'd wanted it that way.

She was on the outside, looking in, and the pang of longing was too much like pain.

His children made damn good wingmen.

India was on edge, ready to bolt for the front door at any moment, but over macaroni and cheese, his children locked up his plans for the night with India.

Olympia started it. "Hey, um, hey you. Where is your house?"

"Her name is Miss Woods," Debra said.

"It's Major Woods," Aiden said. "Don't shrug, Debra. It matters. This is a military town. Olympia, who is Janice's mom?"

"Captain Smith."

"I know Captain Smith," Poppy said, never one to let someone get credit for something she could do, too.

"I rest my case. It's not any harder to address someone by rank than by saying mister or misses."

Debra made a face at him, then turned her attention back to India. "So, Miss Major Woods, where is your house? It's next door?"

"Not Miss Major," Aiden said, "just Major. Don't be such a civilian."

"Miss Major," said Poppy.

Aiden nearly growled in frustration before he heard India's soft chuckle. It was the first sound of anything remotely resembling happiness that he'd heard from her since he'd opened the front door and she'd said *Surprise*.

Well done, Poppy.

"I live in Belgium," India said.

"Oh," Debra said, with such blatant disappointment it would have been laughable, had Aiden not shared the disappointment.

"Belgium is far away," he explained to the girls. "Across the ocean. You have to take an airplane to get there."

"But where is your next-door house?" Olympia asked, bringing the subject back around like a little champ.

"It's my friend's house," India said. "Fabio's house."

"Fabio has to sleep here for Christmas," Olympia said. "His house smells bad."

"Polyurethane," India told his sister. "The house has to be vented for twenty-four hours."

"Do you have to sleep here for Christmas?" Poppy asked.

"I don't have to. I didn't realize…when I got here…"

Aiden knew the rest of that sentence: *I didn't realize you existed.* It was a miracle she hadn't thrown the flowers in his face and driven away.

India was blushing, which made him feel like hell. She hadn't done anything wrong. She shouldn't be embarrassed—but it wasn't stopping her from trying to decline his invitation to spend Christmas with his family, now that she knew just what his family involved. It also didn't stop him from feeling a compelling need to prevent her from running, not when they hadn't had a minute's privacy to talk yet.

She was shaking her head. "I didn't realize that there was going to be a big Christmas here. You're going to be so busy. I want you guys to enjoy it with your father, not with—"

"You can sleep in my bed," Poppy said. "It's for big girls."

Damn, his girls had mad skills.

"That's so sweet of you," India said. "But where would you sleep? You need to sleep in your bed."

Olympia waved her fork in an adult's dismissive gesture. She was apparently done with the topic. "Daddy has a big bed. You can sleep with him."

Olympia, my sweet, I love you.

But since India was now blushing pretty hard and his sister and brother-in-law were about to choke to death from suppressing their laughter, Aiden put an end to the discussion.

"The adults will figure out the sleeping arrangements. Right now, we've got a tree to decorate."

India stared at the artificial tree and panicked.

She couldn't do this. The tree was lit up, but the bare branches were waiting for ornaments to be taken out of the boxes that were waiting neatly to one side. Aiden had set it up while she'd been driving to San Antonio and back. While she'd been convincing herself that a week of great sex meant she was in love, Aiden had been arranging a Christmas for the people he truly loved.

Not that she resented his love for his daughters, of course. The girls were so precious. Infinitely precious. India couldn't take their father's time away from them tonight, not one minute. Poppy was still literally clinging to him, and India had heard Debra and Aiden discussing how their week apart had been harder on Poppy than Olympia. The girls needed their father's attention tonight. And tomorrow, too—it was *Christmas*. What was India doing, stealing their father's attention on Christmas, when they were clinging to him after a week apart?

Still, when Debra announced it was time for her to leave, the girls shifted their clinginess to her, the aunt who'd been the main adult in their lives all week. It was an emotional farewell. Had India ever clung to her mother like that? Her father?

Debra kissed her brother, wiping away her own tears and laughing at them. "Oh, my goodness. How about that? But we'll be home in a couple of hours, and that will feel good, right? There's no place like home."

Had India been staring? She must have been, because Debra explained to her, as if it were her business, "We live in San Antonio, so it's not like we aren't going to see the girls again for a year."

We'd only see each other a few days each year. Everything Aiden had said to her on their deck chair had more significance to her now. When people really loved each other, a few days weren't enough, not even enough for an aunt to see her nieces or a brother to see his sister.

But India hadn't known that. She saw her mother a few days every two or three years. It was enough.

She didn't know how real families, how close families, acted. She couldn't do this, couldn't *deal* with this.

"San Antonio?" she asked Debra. "That's where I'm supposed to be. I have a room reserved at a bed-and-breakfast place. I could follow you—"

"No." Aiden stepped right between her and his sister. With his hand on her waist, he spoke into her ear. "Don't even think about it."

It was the first time he'd touched her since he'd held open the door of Tom's pickup truck for her this morning—a lifetime ago. She hadn't realized how badly she'd been missing his touch, craving that touch, not until she felt it again.

Aiden smoothly turned to face his sister and brother-in-law, keeping his arm around India's waist, and all that banked strength, all that ambient warmth, reminded her of why she'd turned around that truck and come back. Sex might be a pretty basic motivation, but it was a strong one.

As his sister and brother-in-law listened, Aiden explained that *no* to India in a perfectly civilized way. "You can't go now. The girls will be devastated if they don't see you in your pajamas tomorrow morning. Once they've got an idea in their heads, that's that."

"That's the truth," Debra said.

"Since they've decided you are going to see all of their presents on Christmas morning, I'm afraid that means you are going to see each and every part of each and every toy. I'll make lots of coffee."

Everyone chuckled. India spending the night was so

wholesome, even cute, the way Aiden handled it. Once they all said their *goodbyes* and *thank-yous* and *it was nice meeting yous*, India was alone with Aiden. Finally.

"We need to talk," he said.

"Don't you think we needed to talk a week ago?"

A direct hit; he didn't try to defend himself. He even nodded slightly. "I'm sure it doesn't—"

"Daddy."

The wail of grief made India's hair stand on end. Olympia was absolutely devastated.

"I want Aunt Debra."

"I know, I know…shhh…" Aiden scooped up his daughter and continued to murmur soothing-sounding things into her ear.

"M-m-make her come back."

Poppy came running in and plastered herself to his leg again.

India just stood dumbly, helpless to ease anyone's pain, and watched Aiden take care of everything. He stood with Olympia clinging to his chest and Poppy hugging his legs, and he looked like he was just covered in little girls. Half of her heart thought it was unbearably sweet, half of her heart thought it was unbearably sad. Her heart just broke in two for them, for this absolutely loving, tight-knit family.

Olympia's sobs subsided enough that India could hear what Aiden was saying. "It's okay. Everything is going to be okay. It really is."

She knew those words. They'd soothed her, too.

She wiped her eyes, but unlike Debra, she couldn't laugh when she saw the tears on her fingers.

Chapter Fourteen

The three Nords recovered much faster than India did.

She still felt so raw inside. She was silent as she took ornaments out of their storage boxes and hung them on the tree. Silent, but keeping a pleasant expression on her face, because there were children involved. Not just children, but Poppy and Olympia, with their unique personalities and their Christmas Eve excitement.

She couldn't hurt them, not in any way, so she stayed far away from Aiden, and she smiled as she picked up another ornament. *Our First Christmas Together.* Porcelain wedding bells, with the year written in gold. Six years ago.

She thought she might be sick. It was too much loss. Aiden hadn't been married very long. The twins were four. They must have been conceived after Aiden and his wife had been married for only a year or so. When had his wife died?

Even if she'd died yesterday, she would have had no more than six years with Aiden. She. *His wife.* The woman he'd pledged his life to. The woman who should be hanging this ornament right here, right now. The woman who would have known how to soothe her children when they missed their aunt.

Aiden's wife should be here, but instead, India was the one who would watch her children open presents from Santa in the morning. What had India done to deserve this honor? She'd boinked the woman's husband. That was all. India hadn't even bought her daughters a present.

I didn't know they existed.

But she did now. Her throat hurt from the tears clogging it. Her face hurt from trying to smile. Her hand trembled as it held the wedding bells of a dead woman.

I have no gift for her. I have no gift for them.

"I have to go," she said, shocked at the steadiness of her own voice, even as her hand shook.

Aiden was beside her in an instant. "Don't go. Please. We haven't had a chance to talk."

She looked at him, a little confused. "I have to go to the store."

"Now?"

"Yes. I have to go. I don't have any presents for the girls."

"It's okay. They're going to have so many gifts, they won't notice."

She glared at him then. "I have standards. I won't show up at someone else's Christmas without at least having a gift for their children." She set down the ornament and walked with shocking calm to the foyer, where she took her coat off the rack.

She nearly knocked Olympia over when she turned around. "Oh! Sorry."

Olympia looked up at her with those emerald-green eyes. Aiden's wife must have had emerald-green eyes. *Oh, God. This hurts.*

"I'll be back in an hour or so, okay?" The nearest twenty-four-hour grocery store was a good twenty minutes away. She touched Olympia's hair, tentatively—it was black, like Aiden's hair. At least that came from someone who didn't haunt her. "You get that tree decorated. You're doing a great job. I just need to run to the store."

"Do you need a penny?" Olympia asked.

It was a cute question, but Aiden closed his eyes as if it was…not cute.

She kept one eye on Aiden as she answered. "No, I have enough money. Thank you, though."

He didn't open his eyes. "She means, do you need a penny because you are going to be apart from her? When we can't be with each other, we give each other a penny." He opened his eyes and they were bright with emotion. From his pocket, he took out two pennies. She remembered them from the garage. Two pennies: Poppy and Olympia. He never lost touch with his daughters. He'd had that piece of his real life with him all along, even during a shipboard romance.

But he'd kept it a secret from India.

He gave her one penny and put the other back in his pocket.

Somehow, she managed to smile at Olympia. "Thank you. I'll be back as soon as I can."

Aiden had lost her.

In the quiet of the night, while his daughters slept, India sat with him on the sofa, leaning into him a little bit as he kept his arm around her shoulders and they stared at the Christmas tree, but everything had changed.

She didn't remember him, her lover. She was all tangled up in his children and his widowhood. Her sorrow doused her inner light, her joy in their relationship, her passion to find out if they had more than passion.

All gone.

All his fault.

His real life had been too much of a shock for her.

He wanted to ease that shock, if he could. He broke the silence. "What would you like to know? You must have questions."

"What was her name?"

"Melissa." He was vaguely surprised. That wasn't one of the most common questions, certainly never the first one. *That poor man, losing his wife with their children so young...* He'd never heard someone say, *He lost Melissa so young.*

"How did you meet her?"

He had to think about that one. For a fraction of a second, he drew a blank—no one ever asked him that. But, of course, he remembered. "A friend's party. Halloween. She was dressed like an M&M. Yellow. I couldn't tell much because of the costume, but I guessed her body would be as cute as her face."

Why in the hell had he said that? What a horrible memory to share with another woman, to admit that he'd hoped his dead wife had had a hot body when he'd first met her. He turned toward India to apologize.

But India's lips actually quirked in a brief smile. "Typical guy. You get credit for not ignoring her and going after the sexy nurse costume."

"Mmm." He was going to remain neutral on that one. Sexy nurses had tended to be eye-catching when he was a young lieutenant. But when he'd been a 27-year-old captain, the yellow M&M with the cute smile had made an unforgettable impact on him. That had been *it*, from that first conversation. They'd dated for half a year, been engaged for another six months after that and gotten married, but really, that party had been it. There'd been no one else after he'd talked to that yellow M&M.

Not until he'd been standing in a neighbor's garage, missing his children, holding a beer, and a woman with gray eyes had stepped down from a pickup truck, looking rumpled and sleepy from an international flight. Sudden impact. The beginning and the end at once.

But he'd been stupid, and he'd let her go. She'd come back, but only to discover he'd kept so much of himself separate from her.

Shouldn't age have made him wiser? He'd gotten more stupid instead.

"How did she die?" India asked.

He couldn't hold back his sigh. *Here we go.* This was why he'd tried to keep part of himself from India. He hadn't wanted to do this.

He took a breath. Cleared his throat. *Let the recitation begin.* "It's easy to see it in hindsight. She had a blood clot in her leg that broke loose and traveled to her lung. She died of a pulmonary embolism."

Next: Was it quick? Did she suffer?

"I don't know anything about that," India said. "Is it rare?"

He had to think about that one, too, for a second. He was so used to a certain soundtrack. That question wasn't the one that usually came next.

"They say it's common, but I don't know anyone else who has dealt with it. We didn't know she had the clot in her leg. We'll never know what caused it. I had to consciously accept that. Flying is one risk factor, and we'd flown with the twins to Connecticut to see my parents, so, of course, they blamed themselves. They still blame themselves, but the doctors said it could have been a clot still left over from the pregnancy. She'd also had a recent bike wreck that bruised her leg. A little bit of everything, probably.

"There were no symptoms, until she noticed one foot was more swollen than the other. We thought it was nothing at first. Her feet had gotten swollen when she was pregnant, and it was like that. We even joked that when she'd had both feet swollen, she'd had twins. If she was pregnant again and only one foot was swollen, maybe it was only one baby this time." He looked up to the top of the Christmas tree, the very top, shaking his head in disbelief, still. "We *joked* about it."

"Was she pregnant?" India barely got the question out, she'd gone so tense under his arm.

"No. We hadn't been trying, but they tested her at the hospital, anyway. They would have had more concerns about the blood thinners if she'd been pregnant." He tapped India's shoulder. "Breathe."

She exhaled in a *whoosh*. "I didn't realize I was holding my breath."

I did. I know your body, I know your breaths. I know you, India, intimately. Have you forgotten?

He plowed through the rest of the story. "She called the doctor and made an appointment for that Wednesday. But on Monday, she couldn't catch her breath. She didn't feel well, so she slept most of the day. On Tuesday, she was sweating. It wasn't hot or cold, she just was sweating. We called the doctor to see if she could come in a day early, and they told us to go straight to the emergency room. We had to get a friend to come watch the girls. They ran all the tests, started the blood thinners. It was an emergency, but treatable, they said. And the next day, too. But the next day... I could tell

the doctors were thinking this wasn't a routine case.
They said we might need surgery. I sat by her bed all
night instead of going home to check on the girls. We
watched some TV. Neither one of us could fathom what
the hell was happening. She was fine. She was healthy.
She was only thirty-one years old."

A little squeak escaped India.

"Breathe."

He didn't want to share misery with India. *I'm sorry,
India. I thought I could spare us this.*

"On Friday morning, she died. She was just so tired.
I told her to get some rest, and she went back to sleep.
I read a book. I know she thought she was just going to
take a nap. I know she did. We were scared and worried in general, but she didn't think she was going to die
in the next half hour, you know? I'm grateful for that."

He stared at the lights on the tree and let the numb-
ness settle over him. It was so unreal sometimes, to tell
the story, like it had happened to someone else. He still
couldn't believe they'd been through that. *They*—he
and Melissa had gone through it together, but he was
the only one left who remembered it.

He wasn't hurting, just numb.

"How long ago did she die?"

Ah, the real question. *Are you over it? Are you dating again?* That was what people really meant, questions Aiden hated, questions he'd been so happy to skip
with India.

Now he felt it, that sharp stab. It wasn't pain; it was
anger. He was sick of this scenario, sick of these questions, sick of the way his history made everyone view
him now. Everyone, including India.

He pushed himself off the couch and stood by the
fireplace. "Two years."

"I'm sorry," she said.

He'd said *two years* with too much venom. It wasn't directed at India. It wasn't even directed at the universe this time. It was fury at himself.

Are you ready to fall in love with someone else now?

I'm not looking for love. He'd known that was the right answer, time after time, but this week, love had moved in right next door. She had moved in, and he had kept secrets from her.

"Am I your first since then?" she asked.

He turned around. "What?"

"Am I the first person you've slept with since she died? It would only be fair, if you were my rebound guy, that I would be your rebound girl."

"No, you're not the first."

"Oh." She frowned a little at her interlaced fingers in her lap. "Aerosmith."

He looked away. "Among others."

"Was it hard to sleep with someone else again?"

Not that night. But the next morning, on the drive home, I wept. I felt like I'd cheated on Melissa. Logic didn't help much, that first time.

He put his hands on his hips and looked up at the ceiling. "You're killing me, India. These aren't the usual questions. It was long enough ago. Does it matter?"

"It… I… Yes, it matters. Is it hard to sleep with me? Do you think of her when you sleep with me?"

His outrage made it impossible to answer her. How could she think that? How could she possibly think that? Were they not having the same sex at the same time?

Bad attitude, Nord. Check yourself.

What kind of terrible, horrible lover was he, if India wasn't sure that he was thinking of her when he was utterly *lost* in her?

He stopped standing like an arrogant jerk and turned to face her.

"I'm asking," she said, "because maybe that's why you didn't tell me you'd been widowed. Maybe you were being kind, and you didn't want me to know I was a substitute." She couldn't look at him. She bit her lip. She blinked. She was hurt.

There was the pain again, the sharp stab, but it had nothing to do with his past. He hurt because India had been hurt, wondering if she was a substitute. The pain brought him to his knee, but that was fine, because he needed to take a knee in front of India to apologize.

"That's not it, baby. When I'm with you, I'm *obliterated* by you. Nothing else matters but you. I'm wild for the way you make me feel. I'm wild to make you feel as good. I'm—" He remembered lying with her under the kitchen table after the video app, and he smiled. "I'm having fun with you sometimes. Other times, I feel like I'm going to die if I have to wait a second longer to be inside you. I've been making love to *you* every single time, and I'm so very sorry to have made you doubt that."

She touched his face, smoothing her fingers along his cheekbone—it was the first time she'd initiated any touch since she'd walked through his front door and gotten ambushed by the truth he had withheld.

"I'm so very sorry," he said again.

She gave him a small smile. "It only just occurred to me this afternoon. I couldn't have thought it all week, could I? I didn't know you'd been married."

"I'm sorry you thought it for even a minute today." He dropped his head and kissed her hands as he smoothed them with his own, so she was no longer lacing her fingers together so tightly.

"You didn't want me to know," she said softly. "Ever."

"Not at first, not until I realized I was going to want you for far more than a week. I was going to tell you everything at McDonald's."

She looked confused for a moment, but he saw it in her face when she remembered their conversation over burgers and fries.

"Right. You told me that you don't date fathers. I could have lost you then and there, or I could have stayed with you another three nights before losing you. I was selfish. I took my three nights."

She nodded, far too understanding.

"Is there anything else you want to ask me?" He let the silence settle between them for a moment. "Any names you want to call me? Any coals you want to rake me over?"

There was, there had to be, but she only shook her head.

"You're letting me off easy." He kissed her hands one more time and stood, then tugged her to her feet, too.

"It's Christmas Eve," she said, and her smile was a ghost of its usual self, but it was genuine. "We can say it's your present. I didn't get you anything else."

He laughed—faintly, but it was genuine. After saying goodbye to her this morning, after seeing the shock on her face this afternoon, after answering her questions tonight, he could still laugh.

It was a Christmas miracle.

Or it was India.

They were pretty much the same thing this year.

"Then it's time to play Santa Claus. That's nothing kinky, that's just putting out the bookcase and filling the stockings. Then I have to find you some kind of pajamas to wear tomorrow morning, because the girls were quite clear that all gifts would be opened in pajamas, and I happen to know you don't have any."

"Yes, I was told the dress code several times." But as India moved past him to get started with their tasks, the tree lights brought out warm browns in her hair and highlighted her face. He caught her gently. "I didn't tell you about one of the best Christmas gifts I ever received in my life."

"What's that?"

"You came back and knocked on my door." He kissed her forehead. "And you stayed even when you got way more family than you bargained for." He kissed her nose. "Thank you." He kissed her lips.

"Merry Christmas," she whispered.

India only watched as Aiden set out the tree bookcase, but she helped him assemble a plastic dollhouse taller than Poppy. The dollhouse took two army officers a solid ninety minutes to puzzle out, so it was late by the time she and Aiden had succeeded in making it match the photo on the box. Aiden held out his hand as he had so many times that week, his half smile saying so much that words weren't necessary. She placed her hand in his, and he led her upstairs.

Aiden gently shut the door to Olympia's room. At Poppy's door, Aiden held India's hand a little tighter as he closed the door. Then they stood outside his bedroom. This door was shut; he had to open it.

India walked in and panicked. This was not their room, the new guest room with no history but their own. This was the room that he'd shared with Melissa, the woman with the cute smile and cute body hidden by an M&M costume, the woman who'd died too soon.

"I can't."

She'd backed away from the king-size bed, right into Aiden's chest. He caught her, he soothed her. "It's okay."

"No. I can't."

"Okay. Then we won't."

She was not cut out for this. This wasn't lust; this wasn't a romantic vacation. This was...

I don't do families.

"It's been a hell of a long day," Aiden said quietly. He wrapped his forearm over her chest and held her securely. Surely, he could feel her heart pounding. "We can just sleep, baby. Everything's going to be okay. Let's let it all sink in. We'll get some sleep, then we'll enjoy Christmas morning, okay?"

She nodded. Sort of. It was a jerky move.

He hesitated. "Or I can sleep on the couch. Am I making you nervous?"

"The bed is fine," she said.

But as she laid too far away from him to feel his warmth, she stared into the dark and knew this was the beginning of the end. This wasn't her bed, her family, her life. Aiden wasn't her man.

But it had been a beautiful shipboard romance.

Chapter Fifteen

If she hadn't already been in love with Aiden, she would have fallen hard Christmas morning.

He was the best father in the world. He admired the wings on fairy dolls, and he kept a screwdriver and a pack of batteries by the tree to make those wings—and every other toy—light up like magic. He was so very handsome, ridiculously so, in his snug T-shirt and plaid flannel pants. He put cinnamon rolls in the oven and orange juice in sippy cups. Poppy and Olympia wanted him to sit on the floor with them as they opened gifts, so he did. While he was down there, they ambushed him with hugs and kisses after every toy.

He loved it. He was having a wonderful Christmas as a parent. India couldn't keep her eyes off him. He looked like the man she'd fallen in love with, but now he was more. Looking at his smile now, it seemed incredible that she had thought he was happy with her. This Christmas morning with his daughters was his true happiness.

He so clearly loved those girls. There was a lightness about him, now that they were back in his life. The girls were so secure with him. They could ask him a question and he'd answer it. They could bring him a toy and he'd make it work. They could climb right over him and he'd hold them up. He made it look so effortless.

India sat on the floor, too, in a pair of Aiden's pajamas. She'd cuffed up the sleeves and the pants. She was completely bowled over by the little-girl hugs and kisses she got in exchange for humble grocery-store gifts of candy and picture books. She ate a cinnamon roll.

It was not effortless for her.

She tried not to cry, because she didn't want to ruin Christmas. Every sweet moment made her throat tight with tears, though. Every moment proved to her that this would be her one and only day as the fourth wheel to this perfect three-person family. She didn't do families, because she *couldn't*.

She didn't date fathers, because she was not a horrible person. She would not compete with these girls for their father's time and attention. Because she loved the father and, by extension, the father's daughters, she was going to do the right thing and go back to Belgium.

She was only the girlfriend. Her week was up. Her role had become obsolete. Lust and sex and desire, everything that had bound her to Aiden when she'd thought he was as single as she was, had no place in this house. This house was about parents and children. One parent had been lost, but it was still a beautiful family. A girlfriend who'd only been fun in bed for a week didn't fit in, not at all.

She hugged the girls back. She smiled. She choked down her cinnamon roll.

The twins had been up at dawn and charging full speed for hours. Aiden seemed to know that magic moment when they were just groggy enough for him to carry them upstairs with a pile of new books. He laid them both on Poppy's bed and started reading.

India listened in the hallway. She'd never know how the story of the little elephant ended, because Aiden stopped reading halfway through and left the room. He grinned at her, that half smile that said so much, as he pulled the door shut behind himself slowly, silently.

"I can't," she whispered.

The light went out of his expression.

"I have to leave," she said. "You know I do."

He stilled. "Next week."

She swallowed hard. "No. I have to leave now. It's Christmas, and you have your children. I'm just in the way."

"You're not in the way. You're part of it all." He stepped closer and raised his hand to her cheek to smooth a piece of her hair back.

She flinched.

He stopped. "Couldn't you feel how you were part of it all?"

"It was nice of you to include me. You are such a good father. It was nice for me to see you with them."

"Nice." He hissed the word, a little burst of impatience.

She dropped her gaze. "Not nice. It was *humbling*. Humbling to see what a good father you are. What a full life you have."

"It's not full enough."

She breathed, just breathed, *just keep breathing*.

"I need you, India. Nice has nothing to do with it. Being a good father has nothing to do with it."

"I know it doesn't. That's the problem. You *are* a father."

The way his eyes narrowed as he looked at her broke her heart. "And you don't date fathers."

"No, I don't. Don't look at me like that."

"I was about to say the same thing to you. Don't look at me like I'm only a father." He reached to cup her cheek in his hand again, but this time, he wrapped his other arm around her and pulled her close, as well. "Remember me, India?"

He kissed her, softly, his lips gentle on hers, lingering until she relaxed, until she responded. When she swayed toward him, pressing a little closer, he stopped kissing her to whisper quiet words over her lips. "Remember me, baby, please. I'm the man you said you loved. I'm the man who fell in love with you this week."

"I know. I came back to steal another week of your time, but—"

"So steal it." It was an order. It was a plea.

It would be so selfish of her, to take his attention away from the children who needed him. Why was he asking her to be so selfish?

"I can't. This vacation is going to end, Aiden. This romance is going to end with it. I should leave now, while we're still at least a little in love."

"At least a little? Yesterday you showed up on my doorstep and told me, so bravely, that you loved me. Full stop. Not a little."

"But then, last night…" She gestured toward his bedroom door.

"I'm not going to pressure you into sex. Is that what you think? I know it must be a lot, to find out about Melissa and Poppy and Olympia, but if you give us a chance, if you give us this week—"

She backed away from him, sad that he was tempting her to do something that would ultimately split his time and attention until he came to resent her for competing with his daughters. His first instinct, to keep his real life a secret from her, had been the right course to take.

"I have to go back to Belgium sooner or later. If I go sooner, I can tell myself we never fell out of love. I can tell myself it's just geography that kept me from you, not anything else. Let me have that. Let us both have that much."

"I'm supposed to live like that? When I'm *raw* inside because I miss you, I'm supposed to imagine you in Belgium and be content with the knowledge that we never fell out of love?"

"Yes." She had backed up against the wall, she realized, gasping for air like a fish out of water. "I need that. I know we'll really be missing only sex, but it would be nice to think it would have ended differently if we hadn't lived so far apart."

"Only sex." He sounded angry.

Then she was angry, too. "You let me go to San Antonio with only the memory of a vacation romance. If I don't leave soon, then even the memory of that week is going to go bad. Please, let me leave."

He was looking at her less and less like a lover with every beat of her heart. "When?"

"Now."

"While the girls are sleeping? They're just supposed to wake up and find that you've left without saying goodbye to them?"

He was angry that she might do something that would make his girls sad. She only loved him more for that anger. It proved that he was a better father than hers had been. Aiden's priorities were straight. His daughters mattered more than a girlfriend. That was good, even when she was the girlfriend.

Do you see? Being a father has everything to do with it.

"I don't know how this works with children. Am I supposed to stay for turkey?" She was going to cry. *Don't cry, India.*

"The girls only eat chicken drumsticks, so that's what I'm making. Dinner will be around six. It's up to you if you leave before or after that."

He left her standing in the hallway, panting against the wall, staring at the door that led into the bedroom he'd shared with the woman he should have gotten to keep.

It was nearly six. Dinnertime.

She was still here.

Aiden and the girls were still in their pajamas. Aiden had been cooking. The girls had been playing with the new dollhouse. Only India had gotten dressed, but she was still here.

She used the bathroom to wash her hands before dinner. There were some suspicious shuffling noises on the other side of the door, but no knocking.

Such good girls. They were obeying their father, learning their manners.

Then Olympia belted out at the top of her lungs, "Miss Major, we're not knocking."

India laughed, actually laughed when she'd been trying not to cry, but she laughed silently, with her hand over her mouth. Jeez, she loved those girls.

Her laughter died. They weren't hers to love.

"Come in."

They burst through the door.

India held up her empty hands. "Sorry, no lip gloss here."

"Santa Claus can bring you some," Poppy said.

"He only brings toys," Olympia said. "Why are your earrings big today?"

India turned to look at herself in the mirror. She'd put on the copper hoops, the ones she'd worn when she'd invited Aiden in for a Bloody Mary. Why had she worn sexy earrings when she was only going to drive away? Sex wasn't the same thing as love. She'd learned that much. Hadn't she?

If she would never be more than his sexy vacation romance, then she supposed she had worn the earrings to remind herself of her proper place in his life.

"They're shiny," Poppy said.

Ah, shiny again. No higher compliment.

"I love them," Olympia said.

"Thank you." India had loved the way Aiden had toyed with them. She'd loved the way he'd placed them on the nightstand...

They were all three looking into the mirror together, looking at the earrings from two totally different angles. The children loved something shiny, she loved something sexy—but they loved the same pair of earrings.

"Oh, my God," India whispered to her reflection.

"Oh, my God," whispered Poppy.

"Don't say that. I shouldn't have said that."

India stood in front of a bathroom mirror with two four-year-olds and felt like she was on the verge of understanding something important. She'd been dividing love into types and then assigning each thing—no, each person—the one kind of love she thought they should have. Her father had loved his harem of available women, so he hadn't loved India. Her mother had loved her, so she hadn't been able to have the traveling lifestyle she also loved, not until India had joined the army and moved away. Aiden should have the love of his daughters, therefore, he could not love India.

It could only be one or the other—but that was wrong.

Earrings could be shiny and sexy.

What if she *hadn't* confused a week of great sex with a week of falling in love? What if they had *both* happened?

That was why she'd turned around her pickup in San Antonio and come back. She couldn't have a weeklong sexual fling and just leave, because the sex hadn't been separate from the love—not the way Aiden did it.

He made love.

India looked at the two little faces that were looking at her. Aiden had made love long before he'd met India. He had known love with Melissa, and these little girls now existed, like some kind of miracle. Was it any wonder India could not take Melissa's place in her bed?

"Would you like to see our mommy?"

India's heart stopped, just for a moment, because the question had been asked as if the woman was waiting in another room, ready to meet her.

"Here, come here." Little hands tugged on her fingers. She followed where they wanted to lead her.

She saw the picture frame on Poppy's dresser. *No, stop, I don't want to know, I don't want to see.*

But the little girls were pointing, happy and proud. "That's Mommy."

India looked at the photo, a casual snapshot that had been enlarged. The double stroller in the center of the photo was dark green. The two chubby babies, strapped into their seats, wore pink. On the left, crouched down by the stroller, was a younger Aiden, more than four years younger, surely, with that carefree smile—or maybe he'd just aged more than four years since the photo was taken.

India picked up the frame to get a closer look. To the right of the stroller, crouching down by her babies, was Melissa.

"Isn't she lovely?" Poppy said.

The word struck India as unusual for a child. Aiden must use it to describe their mother to them.

"She's very lovely," India said.

She was. But as India held the frame and willed her lips to curve pleasantly for the sake of Melissa's daughters, India felt some fear slip away. Melissa was lovely, but she looked like a real person. She was certainly attractive, but she wasn't a flawless woman. Her hair was windblown. Her clothes were unremarkable: denim shorts, a blue top, white Keds on her feet. Melissa looked like someone's very pretty wife, someone too busy with little babies to have the need—or the time—to pose for a photographer in full makeup and elegant clothes.

In India's imagination, Aiden's wife, the mother of Poppy and Olympia, had been an angel, a vision in white, perfection India could never attain, all porcelain wedding bells and gold letters.

I've been scared of her.

But here the real Melissa was, captured in the middle of a day that had probably been just another day. Melissa was just a woman, a real person whom India might have known as a neighbor or a coworker's wife. Her smile was as open as Aiden's. They'd been a couple. Happy in a normal, human way. Happy in all the ways that mattered in life.

They'd been happy in a way India had never known.

"Look what else I have," Poppy said.

India braced herself, wishing she could say *No, not another photo, not another snapshot of a life that is gone*.

Poppy plopped a green plastic alligator's head on the dresser. The cartoonish gator head was almost as big as hers. Its mouth was wide open, its white teeth standing neatly around a pink plastic tongue. It wasn't new. They had a whole batch of new toys under the Christmas tree, but they were showing her this…thing.

"Oh, that's—that's an alligator," India said.

"You do this." Poppy, whose eyes were barely level with the top of her dresser, stood on her toes and reached for one of the white teeth and pressed it down. It clicked into place.

"Okay." India set down the picture frame with one hand as she pressed a tooth down with her other. The girls found this incredibly entertaining. It was a baffling toy. "Why do its teeth go down?"

Olympia crowded against her legs. "It's going to chomp you."

Poppy pushed down another tooth, and both girls squealed. Touching a tooth was apparently hysterical.

India felt old and out of touch. The toys she'd played with had been board games like Candy Land or pretty things like a ballerina Barbie. She put her finger on a white plastic tooth and pushed. Toys today—

The jaws snapped shut.

"Ouch!" She jerked her hand out of the plastic mouth, pure reflex. The girls squealed and jumped and laughed. The bite hadn't actually hurt, but considering how surprised she'd been, India was relieved that she'd only said *ouch*.

"Where is everybody?" Aiden stopped in the door frame.

"She got chomped!"

India must have looked as indignant about that toy as she felt, because as angry as Aiden was with her, he still gave her a quick snort of amusement.

"They invented a toy that's even worse than a jack-in-the-box," she said under her breath.

Poppy dragged the plastic head off the dresser. She sat on the floor with it to reset the contraption, but Aiden was still looking at the dresser where the gator had been.

No—he was looking at India's hand, which was still resting on top of the picture frame.

India let go. Their eyes met again, but she couldn't decipher his feelings any more than she could neatly catalog her own. *She was real, and you loved her. And I'm real.*

Her heart was pounding. *I'm real, too, and you...*

"Dinnertime," he said to everyone. Then, to her, he asked, "Coming, or going?"

"Coming," she said. She sounded kind of breathy.

Aiden let the girls climb into their seats themselves today. He had their plates ready, their carrots cut up into safe bites, their chicken drumsticks wrapped with napkins so the bones wouldn't be too hot for their little hands.

He had the parenting thing down. He didn't need India as a coparent. He hadn't needed Melissa as a coparent, either. When he'd lost her, he hadn't lost a cook or a laundress or anything else that he was perfectly able to do himself.

Aiden had the parental love down, too. Those girls adored him. He adored them. But that was only part of the whole, wasn't it? He should have another kind of love, too. An adult love. A woman, an ally, a friend. Sex.

Their week hadn't been about rebound or revenge sex. They'd both been filling themselves up on a part of life that they'd been missing.

Finally, she had thought from the very first, finally she'd found a man she clicked with. And Aiden? He'd found in India a woman who'd loved him with an adult kind of love. Who'd fallen in love with *him*—not with his parenting skills.

India sat at the table, finishing her Christmas dinner, marveling at the miracle that was the Nord family. Aiden was the source of all the love in this house. It radiated from him, warmed the house, and came back to him tenfold in the love of these two little girls.

And me. I got love from him. I can give it back.

He wanted her to stay for one more week. After that…

There would be an ocean between them. They could text each other. They could do a video call. She needed to remember his words. *How long will it be, before we realize that we're pretending we're still involved, when we aren't?*

Standing in her driveway, packed for San Antonio, she had only been offered one more week—with a warning. If they extended their vacation romance through this week, it would involve his family, he'd said. It would get messy.

She stood and smoothed her hand over Poppy's hair. "Are you done eating? Let me take your plate."

India stood at the sink and looked out the window. The land rolled away in gentle waves as far as the eye could see, so very different from her view in Belgium.

I finally know what I want.

She wanted Aiden and Olympia and Poppy in her life. It would get messy when she had to leave, because she would be leaving a whole family behind, not just a man with whom she'd had a vacation fling.

She'd handled that mess before. Adolphus, Bernardo. One family had welcomed her. One had not. Neither had really mattered. She had left their whole families behind, because she hadn't loved the man who was at the center of it all.

She loved Aiden.

For the first time in her life, she wanted to be part of a family, because it was Aiden's family. She was part of them today. Aiden had said so.

But she would not be part of them one week from now. She must return to Belgium. The US Army had a claim on her that could not be ignored.

Aiden would let her go. He'd already let her go once, hadn't he, with no promises to ever see her again?

She had cried all the way to San Antonio when she'd left the only man she'd ever really wanted. If she accepted his offer of another week, her tears wouldn't stop falling even once she reached Belgium.

"Here you go, Miss Major." Olympia's voice jolted India out of her reverie. That, and the way she pushed her cup and plate up and over the edge to clatter into the sink. Thank goodness they were made of plastic.

Aiden spoke quietly, intimately, into her ear. "Is everything okay?"

No. I'm going to miss you forever. "I'm going to go to Tom and Helen's and close all the windows."

"You don't have to. I planned on doing it."

"I know. You didn't expect me to be here. But since I am, I need… I'll just go do it. Alone."

He was still for a moment, then he took a deep breath. "And then? Are you leaving?" He touched her earring, pulling a strand of hair free from the hoop. "Or have you decided to stay on board?"

"I don't know. I just need to make sure everything is locked up neatly."

Aiden knew India would be gone for at least thirty minutes. She would need ten minutes to walk there, ten to close and lock the windows, then ten to walk back. He shouldn't look for her until more than thirty minutes had passed.

He only lasted twenty.

"Come and put your coats on, girls. We're going to walk Fabio over to his house."

Between sudden bathroom breaks and a hunt for a missing shoe, it took another ten minutes to get out of the house. The delay was fine. They'd probably just run into India as she was coming back over the bridge.

They didn't.

They made it all the way to the house without seeing India. When Aiden walked up the flagstone stairs, he noted that all the windows had been closed already. India had not left the house and started walking toward his place yet because...well, she could be doing anything in the house, really.

She wouldn't have left without discussing it with him first.

What is there to discuss? You never changed the ground rules. The ship is in port. She is free to disembark.

What had she been doing before dinner? Had she put her few toiletries back into the only overnight bag she'd brought in from Tom's truck? While he'd been cooking, she'd let Fabio out. Had she put her bag back in the truck at the same time?

He opened the patio door and let Fabio go bounding in. The girls followed, exclaiming about the still-strong smell of the polyurethane, adding noise and motion to the house—the only noise and motion there was. The house seemed empty.

Aiden's stomach dropped.

"India!"

Too loud. Too desperate. Poppy and Olympia stared at him in sudden silence, their eyes big in their small faces. Fabio dropped his squeaky toy and waited, panting, tongue hanging out of his mouth.

"Why don't you help Fabio decide which toy to bring back to our house? Test them all out, see which one he likes the best." *While I lose my mind, looking for the woman I kept too many secrets from.*

He strode down the hall, barely master of himself, heading straight for the guest room. Their room.

She wasn't there. The bed was as they'd left it, stripped bare. The sheets were in a small pile on the floor where he'd told her to leave them, because he could wash them and make the bed up after she was gone. They'd stolen those extra nine hours of happiness. He hadn't wanted to waste a minute of it on laundry.

They'd made love on those sheets instead.

He'd let their bodies do the communicating, but he should have given her the words. He had never really told her he loved her, not one simple *I love you*. He'd only spun scenarios about how their love was going to hurt them in the long run, how much pain they'd feel when they were apart. *She's not dead, you idiot.*

No, she wasn't. But she wasn't here.

Move out, soldier. Move further, move faster.

She wasn't in the master bedroom or the master bathroom, but Aiden was grimly determined now. If India was gone, he would find her. She loved him. He loved her. There was no way he would let this vacation romance end, not like this. *Surrender is not a Ranger word.*

He'd already texted Helen and Tom yesterday morning, twice, asking for India's number. India had his—he'd seen it on Helen's list in the kitchen—but he had never gotten hers. There'd been no need. They'd been together every minute, day and night. He'd texted Helen and Tom again, asking if India was staying one night or two in San Antonio, and where.

Then she'd shown up on his doorstep, only to find out that he hadn't trusted their love enough to share the best part of his life with her—nor his worst.

Aiden returned to the kitchen, where he could keep one eye on the girls and the incredible mess of dog toys that now lay in the living room floor, and took out his phone. Neither Helen nor Tom had answered him yet from yesterday.

He tried again. Do you know which hotel she was going to on Padre Island?

No answer. He didn't know what time it was in Belgium. He didn't know if Tom and Helen were even in Belgium, frankly. It didn't matter. He and his daughters were about to drive to Padre Island.

His phone buzzed. It was Helen. Are you stalking my friend?

No, he typed impatiently. She invited me to join her, and I was too much of an idiot to say yes. My mistake. I need to fix this.

He and the girls would walk the beaches until they found India. Then he'd go down on one knee in the sand...

If they didn't find her, then he'd be flying to NATO

headquarters as soon as he could get Debra to come and stay with the girls. *Readily will I fight on to complete the mission...*

The mission had changed. He was no longer trying to extend a vacation romance. He was going to tell India that he loved her, full stop. That she was it; that he wanted her in every part of his life. And because she was the one for him, if he had to love her from across an ocean, then that was what he would do.

"Put the dog toys away now. We're leaving in a minute."

He'd swept the house. He only had to make sure the garage was locked, and then he'd go back to his own house and start packing his girls' suitcases one more time. Quickly. Maybe they'd see Tom's truck on the highway to Padre.

Aiden walked into the garage and came to an abrupt halt. There she was, the woman with the gray eyes, the beginning and the end at once. Sudden impact.

This time, he couldn't screw it up.

"India."

She looked up from the phone in her hand, still trying to catch her breath from reading Helen's text.

I think my battalion S-3 is in love with you. He's been asking me how to reach you since yesterday morning. He wants to go to San Antonio and Padre Island and everything. Do you want me to pass on your contact info?

Three words stood out: since yesterday morning.

Before India had come back, before she'd shown up on his doorstep, he'd decided to find her, knowing his girls would be with him. He'd planned on telling her everything. He'd planned on making their vacation romance a real part of his life. Hadn't he?

"You're still here," he said.

"Yes, of course." She sounded all breathy, about a hundred times more Marilyn Monroe than usual.

"You're still here," he repeated as he closed the distance between them in two strides and wrapped her in his arms. His next words were spoken against her lips. "You're still here. There's no *of course* about it. I'm lucky you're here. I wasn't honest with you for a week."

"You never lied to me."

"I should have told you about my children. About Melissa. You walked into the situation blind, and that was inexcusable of me. That day at McDonald's—I was so afraid of losing you—"

"You wanted those three nights."

"I did." But he bowed his head to rest his forehead against hers as if that had been a bad thing, to want as much time with her as he could have.

"I get it. I have six more nights before I fly back to Belgium. I came here to decide where I should spend them. I took one look at that bed and knew I would do anything to spend them with you."

He exhaled, a breath of relief, and leaned back against the wall, pulling her with him.

She smiled gently. "You told me never to regret any hours spent being happy. I want another week of happiness. I understand that you wanted those three nights."

"You understand." But he said it like that was amazing, and then he kissed her, hard and sure, for one moment of happiness. "You're letting me off easy again."

India was still clinging to the phone in her hand. "Not really. I realized that I wanted six more nights with you just now, but I didn't exactly run back across the bridge to tell you that, did I?"

He backed up just enough so that they could look at one another. He looked so grave, but he touched her face so tenderly. "Why didn't you?"

"Six nights means six more days, too. And those days would include Poppy and Olympia."

His hand stilled.

"Aiden, I want six more nights with a generous lover. But how generous are you, really, when you didn't tell me about the very best part of your life?"

"The very best?" He asked that so cautiously, afraid to believe her words were true.

She squeezed him, pressing her hand and the phone into his waist for a little shake. "Those girls are wonderful. You let me leave without telling me what mattered to you. You let me leave without knowing what I was missing. I know I'm the woman who said she didn't date fathers, and I know I said I don't do families, but you said you loved me, anyway. If you loved me, you'd have to share that side of yourself with me. You didn't."

"I should have—"

"So while I've been spending Christmas getting to know Poppy and Olympia and falling in love with them, I've also been growing more and more insecure. I had to admit to myself that you must not really love me. Not the way I was hoping you loved me. I stood in that spare bedroom just a little while ago, and I knew I could extend our vacation romance another six days, but only because I happened to have stumbled into the situation. Not because you told me you had two daughters."

"I'm sorry. That was my mistake. Please believe me, I was going to fix it. I had a plan."

"I know." India glanced at her phone. Helen's text messages were still bright on the screen.

Aiden was so very serious. "I was going to let the girls have their Christmas morning, and then I was going to pile them and their new toys in the truck and drive to Debra's in San Antonio. I was going to leave the girls at my sister's house while I found your bed and breakfast, and then I was going to tell you the truth, that I was one of those fathers you avoided. In my mind, I planned to break it all to you gently, somehow, in some way that wouldn't be too much of a shock, and then I was going to ask if you'd like to meet my daughters. Instead, I opened my front door yesterday, and you were standing there, and… I am so sorry. That was not a good way for you to find out. I never meant to do that to you. I love you."

"I know that, too."

"You know— Did you say you knew I had a plan?"

India felt all the happiness welling up, threatening to make her laugh when she needed to speak. "Helen's text beat you by about two minutes. I was just standing here in the garage reading that *yesterday* you'd been trying to get Helen to tell you where I was in San Antonio. You were going to share your girls with me. You were going to take a chance on this woman from Belgium who swore she wouldn't date a father. I just showed up before you could. You weren't quitting on me."

It was huge, this realization that she was loved. This man loved her enough to share everything precious with her—and to risk having her say *no, thank you*, and walk away. He loved her enough to risk more pain, even though he had survived so much pain in his life already.

He *loved* her. Suddenly, she felt more like crying than laughing.

"Don't cry, India. Everything will be okay."

She threw her arms around him and let his hug soothe her. He felt warm and strong, and she buried her face in his throat, inhaling the scent of his skin.

After a moment, she pressed her lips against that skin. A kiss. A taste.

"Do you realize this is where we met?" she asked.

She felt his smile. "Yes."

"Do you remember the last time we were in this garage together?"

"Like it was the day before yesterday."

She laughed. "So you remember this? In the garage?" She tugged on his belt buckle, bringing them into intimate contact.

"As I recall, our positions were reversed."

She knew he wanted her, which was just what she wanted for the rest of her life. "So, reverse them."

Her back was against the wall in a heartbeat, Aiden leaning over her. "I have to warn you, that last time might have been a bit of a desperate farewell. I'm not going to ever touch you again as a farewell."

"Good. I'm not leaving."

Aiden braced one hand on the wall over her head. He ran his other hand down her body, from shoulder to waist, like he had the right. He looked very satisfied with everything he touched.

Her pulse heated up. "And I'm not going to say *I can't* again."

That brought his gaze right back to her face. His hand stilled, his palm warming the side of her breast through her shirt.

"I love you, Aiden Nord, and I believe you love me. But I said *I can't* because I was a little confused by all the love flying around your house. You and your sister, you and your children. I think you even love Fabio a little bit. And you and your Melissa."

His hand stopped. "India, it's really okay—"

She put two fingers over his lips. "Where I come from, the max amount of love is two. Me, Mom. No pets, even. So when I walked into your house, I thought your life was already overflowing. You didn't need me."

"I need you."

"I need you, too. I need you to help me learn how to handle so much love. I think if I start with you, the rest will come naturally." She lifted her fingertips from his lips and let her hand drift down the front of his shirt. She slipped her hand between them and settled her palm against the denim that couldn't hide the hard heat of him. "It's a lot to handle, but I'm willing to try."

He narrowed his eyes at her, and she bit her lip to keep herself from laughing.

"Are you speaking in double entendre?" he asked.

"It's one of my better languages now."

"I have to use plain English." His hand moved then, the warmth leaving her breast to cup her cheek. "I love you, India Woods. You're it. This is no vacation romance. We can date and court and text and video conference and fly across the Atlantic, and we might as well do all of it, because you're the only woman I'm going to love."

"I love you, too, so you should marry me—*oh*," India said, at the exact same time Aiden said, "So you should marry me—*yes*."

Epilogue

"I'm going to send you a new penny."

Olympia bounced with excitement at India's promise. Aiden dodged a swinging pigtail and looked around his daughter's head to keep an eye on India's face on the video app.

"The army is sending me on a trip to Norway next week. They have their own pennies in that country. I'll get you one, and a penny for Poppy, too."

Aiden tilted the phone down a bit to make sure Poppy was in the frame, too. His daughter smiled at India's image. "Pop-ee-pen."

"Oh, shucks, I couldn't understand that," India said. "Could you take your fingers out of your mouth and say it again, pretty please, so I can hear it?"

Poppy did. "A Poppy penny."

Aiden winked at India. *Very smooth way to get her to take her fingers out of her mouth.*

"Poppy penny," India said with a smile. "That's fun to say. Lots of letter *P*. Daddy can show you where Norway is on the map."

"In a minute." Aiden lifted Olympia off his lap and

stood with the phone in his hand for a little semiadult conversation. "Do you speak Norwegian now?"

"No." India sighed. "But I guess I'll learn."

"You're amazing, baby. You don't even realize that the average person doesn't say, 'Oh, well, going to this foreign country, guess I'm going to pick up another language this week.'"

The satellite connection was nice and smooth this time, so her shoulder shrug was smooth, too—a painfully clear, painfully beautiful reminder of how smoothly she moved in real life.

"You never know which language will come in handy on a trip," she said.

"I'm sure at least one will." Aiden left it at that, but he was certain that she wasn't being assigned to a diplomat's entourage for a Norwegian conference just to pick up a new language. She'd actually be listening to the leaders from one of the countries that spoke a less friendly language than Norwegian.

He admired the hell out of her abilities. He worried like hell about what really went on during these trips. He wished like hell he could personally keep her safe, but she was across an ocean.

For now.

She'd had to fly back to Brussels on New Year's Day. Aiden had made it until the end of February on phone calls and texts and letters, on all the things he'd once said would not sustain a vacation romance—but this was not a vacation romance. This was *it*.

India was it—so at the end of February, he'd flown with the girls to Connecticut, left them with his parents, and flown across the Atlantic to Belgium for four days of bliss.

In April, the army had sent India to Washington, DC,

for an international event of some kind at the Pentagon. Since she'd already crossed Europe and the Atlantic, she'd tacked on a long weekend to fly the remaining 1500 miles from DC to Austin. Aiden had met her at the airport with two girls and three bouquets. *You told me I should marry you. I wondered if you'd like to do that today?*

Tom and Helen had met them at the courthouse, stood as their witnesses, and then taken their little flower girls back to Fabio's house for the night. India had flown back to Belgium forty-eight hours later with Aiden's ring on her finger. Copies of their marriage certificate were sent on their way to their respective commands. As a legally married couple, they could start the process to request joint domicile.

Roughly four out of five military couples were stationed together. With India's unique skill set, they weren't likely to be one of those lucky couples, but it would be much easier to spend time together if they were stationed on the same continent. If Aiden could get an assignment in Germany, he'd be able to see his wife in Belgium much more frequently.

India, however, wanted to live in the States. Her language skills would probably never allow her to be stationed in Texas, but the Pentagon was another matter. If she could be stationed permanently in Washington, DC, they'd be able to fly to see each other at least once a month. They had to wait and see if either option would be approved.

Aiden tried to be a patient man. He wasn't quitting, no matter how long it took for them to live on the same side of an ocean.

"By the way, I never told you who I ran into when I was at the Pentagon last month," India said. "A classmate of yours from West Point. Do you remember Pamela Grant?"

"Not a classmate. She was a firstie when I was a plebe. That means she was a senior when I was a freshman, but I remember her well. She terrorized me."

"Well, she's a lieutenant colonel now, and she told me she'd always thought you were sharper than the average plebe. I thought you'd like to know."

"It's a small world."

"She's back at your alma mater now. She's chairing the Department of Foreign Languages at West Point. She'd brought a dozen cadets to the conference, so they'd get a feel for military terminology between allies."

"Okay." He waited. There was more to this story, he could tell.

"You know how I said the army would never need an officer who speaks Danish to be stationed in Texas?"

"Right." But Aiden put his hand on the kitchen island for balance. For some reason, he thought he might need to keep his balance.

"Yes, I was right, unfortunately. But do you know what the army does need? They need officers with advanced language degrees to teach all the current young Cadet Nords their foreign languages. Cadets are required to learn at least one foreign language. Your Colonel Grant said they could use a professor who knew more than Spanish and French, although I assured her I could go ahead and get certified in those, too."

"India."

The satellite beamed him an image of his new wife biting her lip.

"Baby, are you going to teach at West Point?"

"I have until Friday to let her know. Do you think it would be good?"

"Yes, hell yes."

"Daddy, that's a bad word."

"Sorry, but—sorry." The girls were still in the room, of course, but he'd forgotten because this news was—well, it was making his heart pound. "Baby, we'll be on the same side of the ocean. A flight from New York City to Austin is only three hours."

"More like four, but it's better than fifteen hours. And it's four hundred dollars for a ticket instead of two thousand."

"No customs, no passports. You're going to say yes, aren't you?" He was squeezing the phone so hard in his hand, it was a wonder it didn't crack.

"I met another guy at the Pentagon who knows you, too. You ring-knockers do get around."

"You got a second offer?"

"No, this guy had nothing to do with languages. Rich Moore? He says hello."

"Okay. Nice—but this West Point thing...you'd be so good with the cadets—"

"Rich is working in personnel now at the Pentagon."

Aiden remembered his tough, athletic classmate and laughed. "He's a desk weenie?"

"Hey, I resemble that remark."

"If you're a desk weenie," he said, "I'm a ballerina." She tilted her head and glared at him.

"Okay, sure, you're a desk weenie, baby. You've got me totally fooled."

"Listen, Rich was standing there while I was talking to Colonel Grant about becoming an instructor...and about being married to you, his old discus-throwing buddy..."

"Right. We were on the track team together." He

leaned against the island at that, after glancing at the girls to make sure they weren't doing anything danger- ous. They were only getting into a tug-of-war over a fairy doll, nothing unusual there.

"And he mentioned that the athletics department at West Point has a slot for an operations officer, because there are apparently millions of dollars at stake when it comes to the logistics of all of the academy's inter- collegiate teams. He didn't know if you'd be interested, but when Colonel Grant called me yesterday to offer me the instructor slot, she said Rich was hoping you'd give him a call."

The girls were popping off with every *P*-word they could think of, *Poppy's penny, princess, Pop-tarts, pop- corn*, so oblivious to how much their father's life was about to improve. To how much their lives were about to improve. They were about to be a family of four.

"What do you think?" India asked.

How could she sound unsure?

Yet, she did. She was rushing now, explaining her- self. "I didn't make any commitments for you. You're on the fast track for battalion command right now, and this isn't a traditional step after battalion S-3, but it would have other benefits. West Point is supposed to be a beautiful place to live, up on the Hudson River. I guess you already know that. Would the girls like to live at West Point? The fact that it's a college sounds fun. I mean, there'd be football season and we could take the girls to the games—"

"Yes."

"You might have to travel with sports teams now and then, but I would basically be working Monday through Friday. You know how rare that is in the army. It would make childcare arrangements really easy. I'd be able to be home with the girls on the weekends if you had to travel for varsity games on Saturdays."

"Yes."

"We'd be so close to your parents in Connecticut, less than an hour's drive. The girls wouldn't get to see Debra as often, but they'd get to see their grandparents a ton more. That might be good for them."

Aiden knew that *them* referred to his parents, not his daughters. It would be good for his parents. Maybe, just maybe, they could enjoy their grandchildren instead of blaming themselves for Melissa's death. India knew. She understood.

"Without any of that," Aiden managed to say, feeling like he was choking on the happiness of hope, "I would still say yes. I just want to live with my wife."

"But if you could live with your wife on a beautiful post on the Hudson River, wouldn't that be even better?" India was wiping tears from the corners of her eyes.

"It would be a dream come true. I could reach through this phone and kiss those tears away."

"You need to talk to Rich Moore. He wants to fly you up to West Point to make sure you know what the job would entail. Tom and Helen said they'd watch the girls for you. Right, guys?" She turned around and held the phone a little farther away from herself. Tom and Helen were standing near her. They waved.

"Hey, guys, thanks," Aiden said automatically.

Then he froze. Tom and Helen? Tom and Helen, his neighbors, were in this video chat? "But—wait—"

"We'll live together in just a few months! Isn't it great? I'd love to celebrate with you, but there's this door in between us."

Before India could hold up the phone to show him

his own front door on the video app, Aiden had run past his daughters to rip that door from its hinges.

They lived happily ever after.

* * * * *

COMING SOON!

We really hope you enjoyed reading this book. If you're looking for more romance, be sure to head to the shops when new books are available on

Thursday 15th November

To see which titles are coming soon, please visit
millsandboon.co.uk

MILLS & BOON

to recover, and it was difficult because he hadn't changed at all. Oh, sure, there was a slight maturity in his face but really…it was like it had been eight days rather than eight years since they'd seen each other. Dark, perfect hair, just a little stubble on his chin, and the way his coat fit on his shoulders…as if it had been specifically tailored for his build.

He'd always carried himself with that calm confidence. She'd envied it back then. Still did.

And then he adjusted his garment bag, turned around, and saw her.

His face paled. 'Delly?'

Her throat tightened. Damn. He'd used his old nickname for her, and that made it a hundred times worse. She wasn't Delly. Not anymore.

'You know Adele? Oh my God, that is so weird!' Holly seemed totally unaware of the shock rippling between Adele and Dan.

Dan recovered first, and the color came back in his cheeks as he smiled. The smile didn't quite reach his eyes. 'We knew each other in university. I haven't seen her in eight years.'

Eight years, seven months, and a couple of weeks, if they were going to be exact about it.

'Hi, Dan. It's good to see you.' It wasn't a lie. It was a huge mess, but it was good to see him.

Continue reading
MARRYING A MILLIONAIRE
Donna Alward

Available next month
www.millsandboon.co.uk

MILLS & BOON

Coming next month

BEST MAN FOR THE WEDDING PLANNER
Donna Alward

They were just making their way to the lobby when Holly
gave a squeal and picked up her pace.

'Dan!'

Adele was adjusting her purse strap, but when she finally
looked up, her heart froze and her feet stopped moving.
Holly skipped forward and hugged the man standing in a
tan wool coat with one hand on the handle of his suitcase
and a garment bag over his other arm.

Dan. Just saying his name in her head made her heart
squeeze a little. Daniel Brimicombe. Of all the Dans in
Toronto, he had to be the best man. It was too far-fetched
to be even comical, but here he was, in the flesh, smiling
widely for the bride. The man Adele had once planned to
marry. The one who'd whispered plans in her ear in the
dark.

The man whose heart she'd broken…and in the breaking
of it, broken her own.

Best Man Dan.

Adele Hawthorne, wedding planner extraordinaire,
solver of problems and manager of crises, stood rooted to
the spot with her mouth dropped open and her hands hanging
uselessly at her sides. This was one wrinkle that she hadn't
seen coming.

Adele tried to unscramble the mess that was her brain.
Dan hadn't noticed her yet, thankfully. She was still trying

LET'S TALK
Romance

For exclusive extracts, competitions
and special offers, find us online:

- facebook.com/millsandboon
- @MillsandBoon
- @MillsandBoonUK

Get in touch on 01413 063232

For all the latest titles coming soon, visit
millsandboon.co.uk/nextmonth